Lord of the Runes

Sabrina Jarema

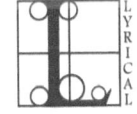

LYRICAL PRESS
Kensington Publishing Corp.
www.kensingtonbooks.com

LYRICAL PRESS BOOKS are published by

Kensington Publishing Corp.
119 West 40th Street
New York, NY 10018

All Kensington titles, imprints, and distributed lines are available at special quantity discounts for bulk purchases for sales promotion, premiums, fund-raising, educational, or institutional use.

Special book excerpts or customized printings can also be created to fit specific needs. For details, write or phone the office of the Kensington Sales Manager: Kensington Publishing Corp., 119 West 40th Street, New York, NY 10018. Attn. Sales Department. Phone: 1-800-221-2647.

Lyrical Press and Lyrical Press logo Reg. U.S. Pat. & TM Off.

First Electronic Edition: October 2016
eISBN-13: 978-1-60183-880-3
eISBN-10: 1-60183-880-8

First Print Edition: October 2016
ISBN-13: 978-1-60183-883-4
ISBN-10: 1-60183-883-2

Printed in the United States of America

Acknowledgments

Writing is a solitary endeavor, but behind each author there are people who provide encouragement, advice, and shoulders to lean on.

I want to thank my agent, Nalini Akolekar, for backing my decision to write stories about the Vikings I've loved so much all my life. Your efforts are helping me live my greatest dream.

Thanks to my editor, Martin Biro, for saying yes to this series, and for being so enthusiastic about it. You gave me the shove I needed to make this book the best it can be.

I cannot express enough appreciation to my critique partners, Karen Fleming, Carol Post, and Dixie Taylor. You lifted me when I fell, honored me with your cherished friendship, and gave me the critiques that made this possible—Skittles and all.

My gratitude also goes to the members of the Tampa Area Romance Authors chapter of the Romance Writers of America. Each meeting is an advanced course in all aspects of writing, and a warm group hug from incredible writers. Tarans rock!

And finally, thanks to my close friend and first reader, Teresa Pierpont, for being with me every step of the way. When I told you I wanted to write a romance novel, you said, "Go for it."

So I did.

Glossary

Arrha—A down payment on the bride price of a woman, made to show good faith during marriage negotiations.

Draugar—Spirits of the dead

Fjells—Mountains.

Fylgjur—Personal guardian spirits in the form of animals. Seeing one indicates death is near, but not always that of the person being guarded.

Handsal—A ceremony sealing the marriage contract. It must be witnessed by at least six men and the agreement is in effect as long as any of them are alive.

Heiman Fylgia—The bride's "accompaniment from home" or dowry. It remains hers as a sort of life insurance policy in case she is widowed or divorced.

Hóvgythiur—A temple priestess.

Knörr—A merchant vessel, partially enclosed with a lower deck for carrying cargo.

Mundr—The bride price paid to the family of the woman, to compensate them for the loss of her labor.

Nithingr—A coward, without honor.

Seax—A long knife, worn horizontally below the belt.

Sjaund—The "Funeral Ale." Seven days after a person died, the heirs gathered at a feast, drank ale, and settled his affairs. After this, the deceased was considered truly gone.

Tafl—An ancient Scandinavian board game played by both men and women. The full name is *Hnefatafl*.

Chapter One

Village of Haardvik
Hardangerfjorden, Hordaland, Norway
Late fall, 850 AD

She stood before him like a flame-haired Valkyrie—strong, proud, a warrior.

Not as she had been in life.

Eirik Ivarson had seen his dead wife in his dreams before, but in them, she was always as he remembered her—gentle and too weak to survive their brutal world. Her soft blue eyes would gaze at him with reproach like she blamed him for her death, sending her to dwell forever with the goddess Frigga. She'd been right.

But this dream was different and as he struggled to cling to it, she spoke.

"Why do you sleep, husband, while your kinsmen die?" Her eyes darkened into a deep brown as though she was sullied by passing so close to the earth. The vision turned as crimson as the blood that had gushed from her and carried her away from their life together. A scream split his sleep apart.

He tore himself awake and reached for his sword before he even opened his eyes. At least he was still dressed, having fallen across his bed well after midnight, passed out before he'd hit the furs. Head spinning with the mead he'd drunk, he staggered to the door of his small chamber.

Another cry cleared his thoughts. He eased open the door and took in the state of his father's main hall. An unfamiliar warrior, an outcast from the looks of him, stood over two cowering serving girls.

Another servant lay in his own pooling blood beside them. The attacker raised his sword and the women shrieked again.

Yelling to divert the man's attention, Eirik bounded across the room. He swung his blade as the invader turned. They clashed, flesh to flesh, iron to iron. Eirik's momentum smashed them into the wall and the outcast's head cracked against it. Dazed, he paused for an instant. It was all Eirik needed.

Using his forearm, he struck the upper edge of the intruder's shield into his face. His nose shattered. Eirik pushed the shield aside and whipped his blade across the man's neck. Blood arced down his body as the attacker fell.

He knelt beside the fallen servant. "What has happened?"

"Outcasts invaded us at dawn." The older girl tried to rise, but her knees buckled. "Even now, they fight outside. This one hacked his way in, though we locked the doors as the mistress bade us."

As he helped her to her feet, the sounds of the battle he'd slept through because of his drunken stupor came to him from beyond the damaged front doors. His blood rose again. But he couldn't just rush outside and join the fighting. He had to know what he faced. "Where's my father? My mother and sister?"

"Jarl Ivar fights. And the thrall, Nuallen, took the mistress and your sister to try to escape to safety."

He gave a quick nod. "May the gods will it so. Find shelter for yourselves." He ran to the entrance before they could answer. Stepping outside, he entered a world of war.

The attackers outnumbered them several to one. His father's warriors engaged them with bravery, but too many of the valiant men lay dead in the yard. Livestock ran free and two of the outbuildings burned. Villagers screamed and tried to hide, but many were already cut down.

While he'd lain insensible from his celebrations, his people had been dying. His family, his everything. He swallowed his shame. This was not the time.

The familiar stench of fear and bodies in their death throes seared his nostrils. He breathed deep of it to fortify himself. Confidence welled up in him. Now he was in the world of warfare he had chosen three years ago, the world he'd left behind when he'd returned here.

He ran through the yard, searching for his father. Three of the attackers fell to his assault as he went. A shield lay on the ground and he grabbed it as a man rushed toward him. Their blades met in a burst of sparks. The other man staggered back under Eirik's superior power, crying out. Most of them had to be outcasts, with little more than the element of surprise on their side. They were no match for him. Eirik hit his opponent's blade, driving him back farther until the invader stumbled and nearly fell. Using the delay, he swept the battleground for an instant with his gaze.

There. His father stood in the midst of the melée. On the ground, the bodies of his warriors surrounded him. They had guarded him to their deaths, but now the jarl struggled alone against two men. They came at him, one from the front and one from the back, toying with him. Eirik's heart swelled with molten rage. He had to get to him. Ivar was sick. Weak.

Eirik struck his opponent's shield again. His sword fragmented. He thrust the blade's jagged end under the shield, into the man's thigh. Hooking his hand under the lower edge of the shield, he yanked it toward himself, pivoting it on the outcast's hand. The upper edge tore into his opponent's throat, dropping him. Eirik leaped over the body, roaring to his father to disengage, to break off. But the noise of battle drowned out his voice.

Weaponless, and using only the shield, he battered his way through the tumult, yelling. The crush of men impeded him and desperation clenched his gut.

The outcast behind Ivar hefted his axe and threw it at the jarl's unprotected back. The blade hit hard and deep. Eirik skidded to a stop. The chaos around him receded into a pinpoint centered on his father.

The jarl stood for a moment, looking around himself as though he wished to remember his land while he was in Valhalla. Then his gaze fell on Eirik and he straightened. He smiled, holding out the ancestral sword, Star Slayer, like an offering to him. Then his eyes rolled back and he drifted down, still clutching the weapon. He lay still.

"Father!" Eirik's voice was high and thin, as it had been when he was a young boy calling for his sire in the night after a terrible dream. But this was no nightmare from which to awaken. Grief, sharp as a dagger, plunged into him and twisted. His breath came hard, his eyes filling.

"Hakon, how much silver do I get for killing a jarl?" The outcast grinned down at Ivar's blood-drenched body.

The silver-haired coward who had distracted Ivar from the front moved off, laughing, stalking other prey.

The clash of blades behind Eirik jarred him from the shock of his father's death. He spun.

One of his father's warriors fought a marauder. While Eirik had stood useless and staring, the man had shielded him from an attack. The warrior dispatched the outcast with a quick strike of his blade to the gut, and turned to Eirik, raising his dripping sword in a salute.

"Jarl." He offered the weapon to Eirik, hilt first. Eirik drew a deep breath at the title, then took it with a nod of thanks. Lifting an axe from his belt, the warrior moved off to intercept another attacker.

Jarl. He was the jarl now. These men were no longer his father's men, but his. So many of them lay around Ivar's body, having given their lives for him. But they had failed. And so had he.

The bastard who had attacked Ivar from behind rushed to the body, put his foot on the jarl's back, and pulled his axe blade free. It came out, covered in bone and flesh. He focused on the fine blade still gripped in the fallen jarl's hand. With a smirk, he slid the axe into his belt and reached down for it.

Pain shot through Eirik, as though he himself had been struck. He surged through the battle, toward his father's body, screaming his rage. He flipped the sword in his hand and threw it, point first, at the whoreson. The marauder raised his shield to deflect it, but the impact knocked him off his feet. He rolled away and came up, pulling the axe from his belt.

Eirik reached his father and pried the sword from his hand, keeping an eye on the outcast. Ivar had no further need of the weapon. Already the Valkyries circled and soon he would feast with Odin. Star Slayer, the sword of their ancestors, the symbol of the jarl and of all they were, was his now.

He tamped down the agony that threatened to release his fury. This adversary was a fighter, and Eirik needed his wits about him to do battle.

His eyes cool and assessing, the coward hefted his axe and threw it. It hit Eirik's raised shield. His father's blood spattered over his face. The metallic smell tightened his muscles. As he lowered the shield, he shook the axe free. The man unsheathed his sword and came at him. Eirik met his blade with his own, the shock of it driving his breath from him. He slammed his shield into the man, knocking him back. He followed with a blow from his sword. The outlaw answered in kind.

Eirik's thirst for revenge gave him strength. He drove his father's killer backwards toward the fjord cliff with blows from his sword and his shield. As they neared the edge, the man glanced back and his eyes opened wide in realization. Eirik threw away his shield and, gripping his sword with both hands, struck the man's shield with the pommel. The damaged wood fractured.

Following through, he swung hard, slicing the man's belly open. The outcast tipped backward, silent, his gaze hard and resigned at his own death. At the instant he went over, he grabbed Eirik by the belt and yanked.

They fell together. Eirik tried to twist around, to dive in head first. But he was tangled with the body when they hit the water.

Cold like a thousand knives stabbed him. The water closed over him and crimson darkness surrounded him. His head swam and his blood slowed in his veins. He fought the cold and the ache of smashing into the fjord, though the man's body had hit the water underneath him, saving him from the full impact. He had to stay awake, couldn't succumb to the cloying call of death tugging him deeper. He fought his way clear of the corpse. They'd fallen in a shallower area near the cliff, so he kicked off from the bottom. Bursting into the light, he took a deep breath and looked up at the rock wall above him. The sounds of battle and the smell of smoke drifted down to him. He swore in frustration.

He needed to get to shore before he passed out or froze. The current carried him farther down the fjord. He stroked toward a small inlet where the shoreline wasn't so steep.

The bottom rose under his feet and he stumbled onto the thin strip of land. Shivers racked his body and he fell to his knees. Lying down, he sprawled on his back, gazing up at the mountain towering above him. The battle was too far away for him to hear it. The taunting quiet of the sunny morning was almost painful.

Who were these invaders? Why had they attacked? He had to get back home, to continue the fight. His father was dead and he was jarl now. They were his people and they needed him.

He'd come home from his journeys when he'd heard his father

was dying, setting aside the pain of his past to assume the mantle of responsibility as the heir. But many of his father's warriors had dispersed to their homesteads for the winter, never dreaming they would be attacked so late in the year. If he hadn't been too drunk to hear the beginning of the battle, he might have saved his father. He'd failed them all.

If only Thor would give him the strength to continue, to rise up and resume the fight for his home and his people. He touched the gold hammer pendant at his throat. But he could only close his eyes, his body stiffening with cold and pain. His head spun with hatred—at his enemies, the fickleness of the gods, and at his own weakness.

Darkness pulled him under and he closed his hand . . . On nothing.

His heart paused. In the waters, when he'd fallen, he had lost his family's ancestral sword.

Cold. He was so cold. It held him in a tight embrace as though he had descended into Hel itself. Had he died and lost the chance for Valhalla because he no longer held a blade?

He opened his eyes. The mountains still rose overhead, but the sun had moved behind them and he lay in shadow. How had he lost an entire day? His clothes were still damp. He needed to find warmth and shelter before the sun set. The late fall night would be frosty and in his condition, he would likely be dead by morning.

What was happening in the village? He couldn't just walk in there and find out. If the outcasts had won, he would be killed, and no one could go get help.

Groaning, he sat up. He ran his hands through his hair and scooped it back behind his shoulders. When he tried to stand, the stiffness in his muscles made him sink back down again. Cursing, he made another attempt. This time he rose and swayed.

He had no weapon, no fire-starter, no food. Nothing.

Forcing his legs to move, he climbed up the steep side of the mountain so he could look down into the village and see what was happening. He knew these woods as the outcasts did not. He could evade them if need be.

The sun had moved farther down in the sky, and the air had grown cooler by the time he reached the narrow ledge. He sat down, still unsteady, and studied the village.

Strange men roamed the streets. No women or children were

about. Two buildings stood smoldering, but the main hall, the granaries, the smith's shop, and the other houses had not been touched. As if the outlaws had planned it that way. This was no complete devastation. It had been calculated to take out the jarl, his warriors, and enough people so they could mount no further defense, yet leave the village itself relatively undamaged.

Eirik's blood ran cold through his heart. They intended to take the village for themselves and overwinter there. Men of their ilk had no homes, and the season of storms and snow was nearly upon them. They needed the shelter, the food, and supplies the place held.

They would be there all winter, along with survivors from the village. But what of his mother and sister? Had they succeeded in escaping? If they were still there, he would have to rescue them first.

Whatever the circumstances, he had to find help. Even if he could get to his other warriors who had dispersed for the winter, there weren't enough men to fight so many outcasts. He needed numbers, fighters who were seasoned, strong, and fearless. Like those he had just traveled the world with, fighting beside.

Looking to the north, he cracked a dry smile. He had access to hundreds of the best warriors in Norway. It would be a long, dangerous journey to get to them. Because of his failures, the gods were challenging him to redeem himself. He would see this through.

Wincing, he rose and climbed down and to the east, around the flat land where Haardvik was. As he moved, he opened himself to the woods, the air, the sounds of everything around him. He'd done it often enough when he was still young and full of belief in the gods, relying on the ways his mother had passed on to him. She'd taught him to be one with the things beyond what he could see and hear and touch. But then he had put all of that behind him, embracing instead the sharp reality of steel and the calm certainty in his own prowess.

Now, weaponless, he would have to depend on what lay within him, even if he had rejected it long ago. The forest closed in around him, the darkness of the twilight covering him. The spirit of the land had never left his heart. It remembered him.

A twig snapped, too near. He pressed himself against a tree. The sound of horses walking through the leaves came to him and he stilled.

"With that white hair, the little bitch won't be hard to find."

The outcasts spoke of his fair-haired sister. His heart sank. They had seen her, knew of her, and were looking for her. His sword hand fisted. They rode past him, making crude comments while he flattened back against the tree trunk. Holding his breath, he waited until they were gone. It went against everything he was to allow them to live, but he had no weapons. Even though he could kill without them, the sounds would bring others and he would be outnumbered. Stealth, not engagement, was his best course now, for they didn't know he had survived and that would gain him an advantage.

A flash in his mind made him pause. So familiar and sweet. He reached for it and the image of the sacred grove crossed his awareness. Of course she would be there, waiting for him. He moved a short way up the mountain to the clearing where his ancestors had worshipped the gods for centuries.

"Silvi?" He kept his voice low.

His younger sister stepped from the trees, leading a horse. Sacks, blankets, and a sword hung from the saddle. The dark hood of her cloak fell back and her white-blond hair blazed like a beacon. "There you are." She dropped the reins and held out her arms.

He strode to her and crushed her against him. "I sensed you in my mind, like we used to do when we were young."

"Mother knew you were still alive." She leaned back to look up at him. "She sent me to find you."

He didn't ask how they held the wisdom they did. Such gifts from the gods were best left unquestioned. "I heard Mother's thrall tried to get you to safety. What happened? Where is she?"

Silvi gently broke his hold on her, stepping away. She could never touch anyone for too long a time. As gentle and sensitive as she was, living in the world was too painful for her. She kept herself apart, from fear of taking on the sorrows of others.

Her gaze darted away from his. "The outcasts caught us and brought us back. By that time, the fighting had stopped or else we might have been killed before they learned that Mother is a rune mistress. She swept into her chamber and put on her regalia, her blue cloak, fur boots and gloves, her glass beads. And of course, she had her rune staff. When they saw her come out, they nearly shat themselves."

He smiled. "They had no way to know they would tangle with a woman of power. Her rank will see her safe. But what of you? You're not initiated." It was well-known what happened on raids, and his breath caught.

She gave him a slight smile, her strange silver gaze sad. "No man looks twice into my eyes, Eirik. Except you. I will be well. The runes have said so."

"The runes." He laughed, short and harsh, anger curling through him. "What good are they? Did they warn you of this? Did they warn me of—"

"They *did* tell us. Of Father's death. Mother saw it weeks ago. Since he was ill with the wasting disease, we thought they were foretelling his death from that. We had prepared ourselves for it. Not for this." Her pale eyes filled and she turned away.

Whether she wanted his touch or not, he wouldn't let her grieve alone. He pulled her against his chest and she leaned back, shaking in her silent sorrow.

"And we no longer have Star Slayer. Father wielded it and it was lost in the battle." One of her tears splashed on his arm.

"I had it," he said. "I took it, still warm from his hand after he died."

"Then you do have it." She whipped around to face him.

The hope in her eyes cut him as no blade ever could. "I lost it. I slew the *nithingr*, the coward who killed Father, but he pulled me over the fjord cliff with him and we both plunged into the water. When I hit, I must have been knocked senseless for a moment. I dropped it. It's gone." He didn't want to look at her, but he did.

Her eyes lost focus for a moment and he held his breath, waiting for what she would say, what the Sight would tell her.

"Then it's beneath the waters, safe from those who would defile it with their touch. Hidden." She looked at him, her gaze clear and sharp once again. "As you must be. No one must know you're alive."

"I know. Were you able to find out anything about them?"

"Their leader, Hakon, plans to stay here for the winter. In the spring, he's going to take revenge on his own family, who he says betrayed him years ago. They live in the *fjells* to the north, where the glaciers are. Then he'll take their wealth and homestead for himself."

He'd been right. That was why they hadn't destroyed the village. "I'll journey to Vargfjell, Rorik's holding in Trøndelag and get his help. In the years I've been fighting and raiding with him, I have come to know him well. As our cousin, he won't let this outrage go unanswered. It's a matter of family and honor. He has great wealth, more than most kings, with four-and-twenty longships, and the men to crew them. Several hundred of the best warriors follow him. When he dropped me off here days ago, he was to head home for the winter. I'll go to Vargfjell, and return here with him to have our revenge. Then, I vow, I'll retrieve Star Slayer from the waters and we'll rebuild our village and our lives."

Her eyes widened. "To get the sword—that's impossible. It's said the fjord bottom follows the mountains down to the depth of a hundred man-lengths. Even the god Njord might not be able to find it, though he rules the sea."

He shook his head. "In the waters below the cliff, there's a shallower ledge. I know it from when I was a boy. I pushed off from it to gain the surface today. If the sword fell with me, there's a chance it rests there still. If it was thrown out farther, it's in the depths and Njord is welcome to it. For it means the gods have chosen to take it back from us."

She bit her lip as she studied him. "Mother has doubted your sanity ever since you dove off the cliff in your youth. She might be right."

He took her hands, his fingers enveloping her small, slender ones, and pressed them. "Don't you see, Silvi? That blade has been passed down to us from the early times, when the gods walked with our ancestors. It's a link with all we are. It gives us the right to bear the rank of jarl. I have to try to get it back, or how can I take my inheritance? I won't accept the title if I don't retrieve it, for without it, I'm not worthy."

Silvi slipped her hands from his. She looked into the growing shadows and her eyes became distant again. He braced himself. Why had he been cursed—no, blessed—with a sister who had the Sight? "When you find the sword again, it won't be for the reason you think. And you'll give it up for the sake of a woman a handful of days later."

How could that be? "It would mean I've given up Haardvik, and that will never happen."

The gelding pricked his ears and lifted his head. Another horse nickered not far off in the woods. If theirs answered, it would disclose their location and he would have to fight, bringing all the outcasts down on them. He would never make it away from the fjord to find help. He locked his gaze with Silvi's and they moved back into the shadows of the trees. He reached for the sword hanging from the saddle, steeling himself for battle.

But Silvi set her hand on his arm and shook her head. She whispered to the horse, cupping her hand over his muzzle. He closed his eyes and chewed, relaxing. Harsh voices threaded through the trees. Eirik tensed, still gripping the hilt.

Three outcasts rode through the sacred grove. They were dirty and unkempt, their weapons bloodstained with the lives of his people. But though his gut screamed to slay them, he could only let them pass.

As they vanished into the woods, he released the sword—his father's personal sword. He raised his brows in question.

She touched the scabbard. "Weeks ago, when Father knew he was dying, he told us to leave the sword for you, not to burn it with him. We'll send him to the afterlife in the flames as is his right, no matter what the outcasts say. We have a fine sword for him so that when he fights tomorrow in Valhalla, he'll be well armed. Even now, he drinks with the gods." She sniffed as her eyes moistened again.

"Drinking and fighting, his two favorite things." They shared a slight smile, then he took Silvi by the shoulders. "There's no time to waste. The bastards infest the woods and it's only a matter of time before they find us. We have to leave now."

"No, Eirik, I must stay here. They said if any of us leave, they'll kill one villager for every measure of the oil lamps that we're gone. Even knowing this, Mother sent me, and we've likely lost one or two of our people already since I left to find you and get these supplies to you. I can't stay away." Her voice shook.

His stomach tightened as though he'd been punched. How could he leave his beautiful, otherworldly sister here? "You did well, Silvi." He kissed the top of her head, letting none of his turmoil show. And yet, she was right. "Father would have been proud of you and Mother. We cannot allow the welfare of a few to overshadow that of the many."

"Already we have lost over ten warriors and as many villagers."

So great a number? His jaw tightened with rage, but he couldn't falter. "I may not be back until the spring, even if I can get through to Rorik now. Though the sea stays free of ice in the winter, most of his men will have dispersed to their homesteads, as many of ours did.

And he will have beached his longships to repair them in the season of storms. We'll likely have to wait, as will you."

"I know, Eirik, but we won't be idle. Swords are not the only weapons we have, for the mind is also powerful. These men are ignorant and superstitious. They'll fall prey more easily to fear. Mother and I will use that to our advantage."

"Be careful. Fear may be a weapon, but any blade can turn on the one who wields it. Unease makes men dangerous. Let them eat and drink until they are so fat they cannot walk and so drunk they cannot think. It will make their bellies a larger target for our blades when we return to slay them." He drew her into his embrace. "I should just throw you on the horse and take you from here."

"Then they would come after me and discover you. This way, you can travel unimpeded. It's for the best." She pulled back from him. "Besides, Mother had a vision that I would one day be at the great temple in Uppsala." She waved her hand toward the clearing. "Does this look like Uppsala to you?"

He gave her a smile he did not feel as he pulled her hood up over her hair. "No."

"Then I will survive to go there to be one of the *hóvgythiur*, as I've always known I am destined to be. Now go. And may the gods watch over you."

He gritted his teeth. She would never be one of those temple priestesses if he had anything to say about it. "The gods will be too busy watching over you to worry about me. I've fended for myself quite well without their intervention. All I need is my own skill, a good sword, and a fast ship."

Instead of chiding him for such talk, as she always had, she gave him a kiss on the cheek. "I'll watch for the lengthening of the days and imagine that, somewhere in the world, there is still light."

He tightened the girth of the horse's saddle. When he turned back, she was gone, disappearing before he could weaken and take her with him. He slammed his fist into the trunk of a nearby tree and the pain centered him. What manner of man was he to leave his own sister behind? But she knew, as he did, that it was for the good of their people.

With the darkness of the coming night settling around him, he changed into the dry clothing she had brought him, mounted, and rode into the sacred grove. Reining in the horse, he looked at a solitary rune stone that stood at one end, as it would for centuries more. In the center of the carving stood Yggdrasil, the World Tree, and runes traced around it, made by his own hand. He didn't need to read the words he'd chiseled into the stone. They were seared into his mind.

Eirik carved this stone in memory of his wife, Sela, and their son who never drew breath. May Thor consecrate these runes.

Everything. He would leave everything behind. All he knew and loved. It wouldn't be the first time. But he would return, whether the gods willed it or not. And when he had exacted his vengeance, he would carve a rune stone to honor his father, so that he, too, would never be forgotten. For Eirik had failed him, his family, all of them. This day. But come the spring, he would not.

Voices erupted from the south, in the direction of the village. Had Silvi allowed them to see her, to draw them away from him? He fought the impulse to go to her. She made the sacrifice for him, and for their people. If he went after her now to protect her, everything she had done, as well as the deaths of the villagers, would be in vain.

He set his jaw. It would *not* be in vain.

He turned the horse to the east, where tomorrow, the new day would begin.

Chapter Two

Village of Thorsfjell
Lustrafjorden, Sognefjell, Norway

It had been too many days since she'd had the weight of her sword in her hand.

Asa Sigrundsdottir hefted her blade, smiling as she faced her brother, the jarl Magnus. The blizzard had stopped them from training outside, but as always through the freezing months, they pushed back the tables and made room in the hall. It didn't pay to become weak over the winter.

"Don't trust that smile, brother." Magnus's twin, Leif, leaned back on the bench where he watched them. He shifted his dark hair behind his broad shoulders. "It never bodes well."

"And I don't know that?" Magnus circled her and she danced away as though she retreated. Then she pivoted, striking his blade. It spun out of his hand and hit the floor.

They both stared at it. Magnus appeared as shocked as she was, but she straightened as though it had been her intent all along. She rested her sword's tip on the ground in front of her, meeting his blue eyes.

"Now, finally, she's bested you." Leif chuckled as he raised his mug of ale to her. "Though it may make finding her a husband more difficult. Come to think of it, her cooking will make that impossible. Once a suitor tastes it, he'll spit it out and she'll run him through. Like the shieldmaiden who stabbed her husband because he said she was too warlike."

"Ah," she said. "A woman after my own heart."

"No." Magnus picked up his sword and flipped it from hand to hand. "A woman after her *husband's* heart. With her blade."

"*If* I wanted a husband, having you two hulking brothers always challenging any suitors would make that impossible."

Magnus narrowed his eyes. "If they can't survive us, they don't deserve you."

"You mean if they can't survive us, they'll never survive her." Leif took a swig of ale as the other men who sat watching them chuckled. "We're just doing them a favor, weeding out the weak ones. And they're all weak." As always, his eyes twinkled as he teased her.

She smiled at him, love welling up in her. Though both her brothers tried to keep her laughing, Leif was the best at it, for he saw the world through his easy, light nature. Magnus had had the weight of their people on his shoulders ever since he'd inherited the jarlship when they were all still quite young. Few people could tell the brothers apart, but the humor in Leif's eyes always made it easy for those who knew them.

"You're the one who thought it a good idea to teach her to defend herself, Magnus." Leif shrugged. "This is what you get. In any case, with her being a shieldmaiden, it spares the looms, and the men, her temper. And her cooking."

"I never thought she would take to weapons so well." He grimaced.

"Or be better than you." She laughed.

Leif drained his ale. "She's got you there, brother."

"It's the only way she'll get me from now on. I'll be watching for that trick." He raised his sword. "Again, Asa."

Before she could engage him, the great front door opened on a blast of frigid air. Two villagers staggered in, bearing a man wrapped in snow-drenched furs.

"Jarl, his horse came in from over the peak of the mountain, probably from the south, and he was passed out on its back. He's nearly frozen to death, barely alive."

"*Over* the mountain?" Magnus set his sword on a table. "Take him to my chair by the long fire. And get those wet furs off of him. Where's Estrid?"

"I'm here, Magnus. I'll order hot water for his hands and feet, and broth to warm him from the inside." She hurried off to the cooking room, her white-blond hair glowing in the dim firelight.

Asa sighed in relief. Their cousin could take care of him and she wouldn't have to have anything to do with him. She stayed where she was, across the room, but her heart pounded. They were so isolated here. How had he even found this place? A traveler in this weather, a stranger, would have to stay here, perhaps for weeks. They couldn't turn him away.

Two servant girls stripped off his soaked furs and cloak. He leaned back in the chair, barely conscious, his eyes half-closed. His long blond hair hung unwashed down his broad chest, but his clothes were finely made.

No one had built up the fire. He would need heat. She couldn't let her fear hold her back from doing something to help him. The servants were getting fresh furs, taking off his shoes and bringing in the bags that must have been on his horse. Others carried in bowls of warm water to ease the cold from his hands and feet.

As she laid her sword aside, the confidence it gave her fled and her legs grew weak. She stayed on the opposite side of the fire from the stranger and threw several more logs onto it. As sister of the jarl, it should fall to her to take control, seeing to his comfort. But she couldn't bring herself to come too near to any man. They never had visitors here, except the traders her brothers did business with. And she had always remained out of sight of them.

But she was a shieldmaiden, was she not? She'd fought beside her brothers in past summers when they were attacked while traveling to the markets in the south. She could do this.

She glanced at the stranger as she arranged the logs in the fire. His blue eyes were glazed. Yet he watched her and she couldn't look away. The servants set his feet in the buckets of warm water, but he didn't react.

"Sela?" His voice, so deep, was weak. "Have I traveled so far? Too far to ever return?"

"Here's broth." Estrid set the bowl next to him and picked up the horn spoon in it.

At her words, Asa broke free of his gaze. Let Estrid deal with him. Being around men was what she did best.

"No." He took his hand from the water and pushed Estrid away as she tried to feed him. "I don't know you. Any of you. I'll have only her." He looked at Asa. "Sela."

"He isn't thinking well because of the cold." Magnus stood beside her. "He thinks you're someone else."

"Give him time." Her knees melted like the ice in his hair. "He'll accept help when his reason returns."

"That may be some while. Perhaps days. We don't have the time if we're to save him." He put his arm around her shoulders. "Try. See if he'll take the broth from you. We'll be right here. You know that."

Leif stood behind the stranger, his powerful arms crossed, and nodded.

Sighing, she firmed her resolve. Her brothers wouldn't let anything happen to her. Magnus squeezed her shoulders, then let his arm drop.

She moved around the longhearth toward the traveler, ignoring Estrid's smirk. After she took the bowl of broth from her, she sat beside him so he could see her. He frowned, but didn't move. Her hand shook. She had to do this. His life was more important than her foolish fears.

"You need to eat, but you're too cold. Let me help you."

He raised the hand he'd used to push Estrid away. Leif and Magnus moved closer, but he only touched her thick braid where it had fallen forward. "Red, like a flame. How I have missed its softness in the night, my wife."

Magnus raised his brows, but Leif grinned. "Someone else indeed. May he not miss more than just her hair."

She shot Leif a glare and scooped up a small amount of broth. The traveler sipped it. Not meeting his gaze, she fed him until his eyes closed and he slumped forward, exhausted. She stood up and backed away, taking a deep breath.

Servants spread furs next to the fire and helped him lie down. His breathing deepened, steadying as they covered him.

"We've done all we can for now. Thank you, Asa." Magnus kissed her on the forehead. He and Leif crossed to their table and their waiting ale.

Estrid took the bowl and looked down at him. "He's well made. Not that such things matter to you, cousin."

"Such things matter to you too much, Estrid. Leave him be. He won't stay any longer than he needs to and he's already married."

"So? A man may have more than one wife. Though I can see how, being the sister of a jarl, you wouldn't lower yourself to accept that."

"And you would lower yourself to accept anything, as long as you had a man." She walked away and joined her brothers.

Magnus glanced at him. "He's not going anywhere for a time."

"Nor for the rest of the winter, I'd say." Leif shrugged.

"Magnus." The snows might trap the stranger here, but they would trap her as well. The cold forced them all into close quarters, and she wouldn't be able to avoid him.

"What would you have me do, Asa?" His voice was soft but firm. "Turn him back out in the blizzard? I don't know why he was in this area at such a time, unless he was lost, or how he survived this far. But the winter has set in now."

Her cheeks heated. Of course, Magnus was right. He couldn't risk a man's death because of her. Welcoming travelers and providing aid was the one unalterable responsibility they all bore.

She'd always used their isolation as a shield against the outside world, but now, that shield had been breached. This was beyond her control, an invasion into her own realm. Everyone here knew her, the way she was. Her brothers' men, the thralls and servants, the men of the village—she knew them all, had known them all her life. She trusted them.

When she'd gone with her brothers to the markets of Kaupang, Birka, and Hedeby, their warriors had surrounded her, keeping all others from her. She'd traveled, yes, but on her own terms. And with her own sword.

But this man wasn't one of them, just as *he*—her attacker—hadn't been one of them. With a surge of anger, she drove the thought of *him* from her mind, as she always did, as Magnus had said she must.

"I'll talk to him when he regains his mind," Magnus said. "We'll see where that leads us. But if he sickens, you may have to see to him for a time. He might not trust anyone else." He studied her.

Her stomach dropped and she swallowed. "I will. I know my obligations to all who pass this way."

"His care won't involve looms, needles, or cooking pots, so you should do all right." Leif gave her a soft smile. "He thinks you're his wife. He misses her, wherever she is. I think his love will keep you safe."

A chill crept up her back at his words and she glanced to where the man slept. He lay still, his face turned toward the fire. The glow played across his fine, high cheekbones and straight nose. He was no longer so pale. Now that his hair was drying, it had become a lighter, richer gold, but his brows remained a bit darker. His mouth, though, even in sleep, held a touch of grimness, as though he'd seen much of the world and the brutality it held.

As she watched him, a warmth spread through her body from deep within, and the muscles in her thighs relaxed. What was that? She shifted on the bench. It had never happened to her before. Uneasy, she looked away from him.

Magnus watched, as always, concern plain in his eyes. She forced herself to smile.

"I'll be fine. Right now, he poses no danger, and once he's well, I'll return to my work and not have to cross him again."

A serving girl approached the table, two small bags in her hands. "Jarl Magnus?"

"Yes, Birgitta? What is it?"

"We went through his bags to dry his things. We found clothes, a fine sword, and this pouch." She set it on the table. It clinked like coins. "And this." She handed Magnus a small leather sack.

It was of unmarred deerskin. A skilled hand had sewn gemstones and gold charms onto it, and it was closed with a silk cord. Such material must have come from beyond distant Miklagard. Only a man of great wealth could possess such a bag.

He pulled open the drawstring, looked inside, and his eyes widened. "Runes. He carries a magnificent set of runes." He tilted the bag so they could see into it.

They were beautiful, carved of oak, intricate and painted in brilliant colors. Many men carried a crude set and could read them well enough to know what the next battle held for them. But this was no common set. Only a rune master could have runes of such beauty.

"He carried no staff." Asa leaned back, away from them. "They always do that. Even our old rune master carried one until the day he died."

"He might have lost it in the storm." Magnus drew the bag back to him.

"Close it," Leif said. "No one but he must touch them."

"I know." Magnus retied the bag and set it on the table between them.

They all stared at it. This changed everything. It was more imperative than ever that he survive. If they let any harm come to him, it might unleash the anger of the gods against them. Those who read the runes were especially blessed and they held powers no one else could understand. She glanced at the sleeping traveler.

Now, not only his welfare was at stake, but the welfare of them all.

Wrapped in a shawl, Asa stepped into the common room. It was quiet and dark, except for the light from the dying flames in the long-hearth. The servants would never allow it to go out completely, but they were asleep and there was no sense in rousing them. Their day would start soon enough.

Her brothers had sought their own beds some hours before. Many of the warriors who had remained at the village for the winter slept on the benches pushed up against the walls in the hall. She wasn't alone.

She hadn't been able to sleep. Her small chamber had grown so cold, and thoughts of the traveler had continued to roam through her mind. Could he truly be a rune master? What would happen to them if he died?

His survival might depend on her. If she failed, at least the gods would know she'd tried her best. That had to count for something. Asa knelt and put more wood on the low fire.

The flames leapt between them as she studied him, forming a protective wall. If only she could stay here, he on one side, she on the other.

He still lay on his back, his hair spread out over the furs. He shifted, moaning, and threw back the covers. A moist sheen glowed on his face in the firelight. Her stomach lurched. Her fear no longer mattered and she dashed around the fire to him and put a hand on his forehead.

His skin burned. She sat back on her heels, her heart pounding. Ingeborg, the healer, was in her own house and the blizzard still raged outside, so she would have no help. Not until the storm passed, anyway.

Wrapping her shawl tight around her, she took a bucket outside. The cold wind hit her like a sword blow. No wonder he was ill. It could only have been the will of the Norns that he survived, and it made no sense for them to take him now.

She gathered snow and went back inside. She set down the bucket and made her way through the darkness into the cooking room. She searched through the jars and vials on the shelves until she found the one she sought. Yarrow.

She dipped a bowl into a pot of hot water hanging over the cooking fire and tossed in a handful of the dried yarrow. She might not be able to cook, but at least she could do this, for many people had fevers during the winters and an infusion of it was a well-known cure. The brew was bitter, so she found a jar of honey and poured a measure into a soapstone cup. Balancing everything on a wooden tray, she took it back into the common room and set it all down near the traveler.

She moved the bowl nearer to the fire so it would remain warm, and settled herself at his side. His eyes were glazed over with fever, staring at nothing. She dipped a cloth into the snow water and put it on his forehead. He jerked, tossing his head, trying to shake it off, but she persisted.

"Don't make me get one of my brothers to hold you down. They don't like to be awakened in the middle of the night. You'll have to contend with me."

She ran the cold, damp cloth down his strong neck, to beneath his tunic. A lump lay under the material and she lifted his shirt. A solid gold hammer of Thor hung on a thick gold chain over his chest. She pulled back. Wealth, indeed. Whoever he was, he must have a family, people who would miss him. A wife.

It was no matter to her. She wet the cloth again and ran it over his face. He quieted, closing his eyes, though he hadn't seemed to see her. The sleeves of his shirt weren't gathered at the wrists, so she slid the cloth underneath and drew it down his right arm. It was like iron under her hand.

His scent came to her, very male, hinting of leather, horse, and the winds. She washed his left arm, leaning across him to do so. Except for brief hugs from her brothers, she hadn't been this close to a man since—

Fear rose in her throat. This was different. He was different. At least, right now it would be safe to be near him, when he was feverish and weak.

Finished with his arm, she tried to sit back, but a tug on her braid stopped her. She looked down. He held it with his right hand, watching her.

"Always your touch was gentle." His voice was so soft, she almost didn't hear him. "Have I gone where you are, Sela? I've dreamed often of you. Are you truly here?"

What could she say to that? She had to make him let go of her. "I must wash you and make you well. I can't do that with you holding me."

"So long since I have touched you." He raised his free hand and cupped her cheek. She held her breath, her heart racing. She had to keep very still, fight down the panic that would surely come.

His touch was gentle, not like the only other she had known. She closed her eyes, exhaling, dreading the fear, the memories. Though they stirred, they didn't awaken. He ran his hand down her cheek to her neck, the touch like a feather on her skin. No violence, no anger.

She dared to look at him. His eyes were distant again, as though what he saw did not lie in this world. He touched her lips with the tip of his finger. "Can you ever forgive me for what I did?"

She had to answer that. No doubt his wife and he had had a fight at some point. Or he had strayed. He was a man, after all. "Of course I forgive you. Now, let me bathe you and cool you off. Then you must sleep more."

He smiled. His face softened and she could only stare at him. The grim line of his mouth was gone. He was beautiful. Perhaps that wasn't the right word to use for a man, but it was the only word that fit him. Surely, in spite of being married, he had broken hearts from here to the Volga river.

His hand had loosened, allowing her to pull her braid through his grasp. But he tightened his fist around the end of it again. Though she was still tethered to him, at least she could sit back now. She wrung out the cloth and ran it over his forehead again, pushing his hair back. Someone would have to comb it out in the morning. It was so long and thick. What would it feel like?

She touched it and it was as soft as her own. Turning his face into her hand, he nuzzled it, sighing. Her breath came light and swift as she held still. His blue eyes opened again, filled with such longing, it captured her as no hold on her hair could. What would it be like to have a man such as he truly look at her that way, not just in a fever-dream? When he didn't think she was someone else. She'd never considered it, never wanted it.

The scent of yarrow took her gaze from his. The infusion was ready. She'd have to touch him again. Run her hands over him. Her stomach knotted, but it was a different sensation from what she had known in the past. Not a blade of fear cutting through her, but a warm tightening, as though she craved a food she had never tasted.

Taking a deep breath, she reached for the bowl and the cup. She poured some of the infusion into the cup and set it aside to mix with the honey. Dipping the cloth into the hot yarrow-laced water, she allowed it to steep and warm for a few moments. She wouldn't look at him again. Just do what she had to in order to make him well.

She washed his face, wrists and neck, even his ankles, any place his blood ran close to his skin so it could carry the herb inside his body. He kept his eyes closed, but still held on to her braid. Its length was so great, it didn't impede her, so she worked until the water was gone.

She stirred the mixture in the cup with her finger and tasted it. Even with the honey, it was still bitter, but he would have to drink it regardless.

"Lift your head for me now so you can take this." She slid her hand beneath him. He tried, but he was still too weak. He was a large man. She would never be able to make him sit up, so she shifted him until his head rested on her lap.

Tipping the cup to his mouth, she said, "Drink." He sipped until the cup was empty.

"Yarrow." He fell back with a smile. "It will help."

Did he know herbs? If he was a rune master, it was possible. Perhaps he was better already. His skin wasn't as flushed and hot, and he had quieted. She had done all she could for now, so she eased his head off her thighs and pulled the furs back up over him.

The fire burned lower and she set more wood on it. When she tried to rise, he still held her braid.

"I—I need to leave. You must let me go."

He opened his eyes, but didn't focus on her. "No. I let you go once and I never thought to be with you again. I don't know how you're with me now, but you cannot leave me."

He tried to sit up, then collapsed, breathing hard, and clutched her braid to his chest. She brushed back his hair. He needed to rest.

"I'll stay. I'll stay this night with you. Please sleep now." Lying down beside him, she made certain there was space between them. And furs. He kissed her braid, and a fluttering stirred deep within her at the tender gesture. She tried to settle and rest, if not sleep, so she would know if he worsened in the night.

"Will you not lie close to me? Rest your head on my chest, as you always did?" He tugged at her braid.

What would it be like? His arms around her, a gentle embrace . . . What was she thinking? She quieted her quick breath, steadying herself to answer him. "You have a fever and are overly warm. You need to cool. Rest now. I'm not far away."

"You're still angry with me, Sela. Please just stay with me and forgive me." His whisper in the darkness hit her like a sword stroke.

"Forgive me for killing you."

"He said what?"

Magnus glanced back at the sleeping stranger, his blood chilling as he pulled Asa into his chamber to continue their conversation in private. Leif followed.

"He thought I was his wife, Sela. I let him think it, for he needed to rest and it seemed important to him. I gave him yarrow. It calmed him enough for him to go back to sleep. But before he did, he apologized for killing her."

Leif's eyes narrowed. "Could that be why he was making a journey this time of year? To run from his crime? The outcasts in these mountains seek to escape from those who would hunt and kill them. They've given us enough trouble in the past with their stealing. Perhaps he was looking to join them. Their chances of survival aren't good, but they're better if they band together."

"Many people travel in the winter because it can be easier than in the summer. Just not here." Magnus rubbed the bridge of his nose. "You didn't find out his name?"

"How could I ask him, if I meant to be his wife?"

Magnus nodded. Asa was wise to think of that. "We'll have to wait until he regains his mind. But we can't question him about his wife. It might have been an accident or some other issue. I want to watch him, get the measure of him. That will tell us more than his words. No one must know about this, lest it come back to him that we're aware of it. If he's an outcast, then by spring, the word will have spread."

"Is it safe for him to be here?" Asa bit her lip. "Have we let a wolf into the fold?"

"We are scarcely sheep, Asa," Magnus said. "Including you.

We'll be vigilant. It may be only the ravings of a fevered man. We can't count what he said in the night as certain."

"There's still a risk." Leif glanced at Asa and placed his hand on his dagger. "He's just a man alone. No one knows he's here."

"You forget what he might be." Magnus touched the leather bag on his table, set there for safekeeping. "A rune master. The gods follow his kind and know where he is and what we do. We must be very careful. In all ways."

Asa and Leif went back into the common room to start their days, though the sun had not yet risen. It would not do so until late in the morning so far north. But Magnus had to consider his actions before the traveler awoke.

He ran his finger over the gemstones on the rune bag. Why would Asa go near the stranger, even stay alone with him through the night? Granted, she'd said he'd held her braid until his hand had loosened enough so she could slip it free. And she'd needed only to shout and many warriors, including Leif and him, would have been there before she could draw another breath. And, granted, the man had been fevered and delirious. Helpless. But still . . .

In the past six years, she had never allowed a man near her, aside from those she knew in Thorsfjell. And even then, she remained distant from them all. Their cousin, Estrid, called her an ice queen, but then, that was Estrid.

Whoever the man was, he journeyed well. His horse was of excellent stock, and had likely saved his life. His sword was magnificent, of folded iron, engraved with protection runes, the hilt wrapped with gold wire. His clothing was well made of costly fabrics and leathers. Just his hammer of Thor pendant alone would have paid for many male thralls. It could be that he had stolen all this, but it was unlikely. A thief would have sold it all for gold, more easily spent.

Yet, it paid to be wary. He hadn't told Asa, but on their last trip to get winter supplies, Leif and he had heard of a band of outcasts who were infesting Rogaland. They had been seen heading north into Hordaland. Their leader's name was Hakon.

It was a common enough name. And six years had passed without a word about their aunt's former husband. But he could have been gathering other criminals during that time. If he was going to make a move, he might have sent a man in advance to see what the situation was here. No one would dare question someone who claimed to be a rune master. It would be a good cover.

Hakon might be lying low somewhere, waiting to attack them in revenge for having him declared an outcast. He had lost everything, and any man was allowed to kill him. No one could help him, just like the men who infested the *fjells*. Unlike lesser criminals who were outcast for a set length of time and could return to society if they survived, he never could. It was, in essence, a death sentence.

Magnus allowed himself a grim smile. Let him come. He rubbed his stomach as he stared into the darkness. Hakon might think to take revenge for what he, himself, had wrought. But he had no idea what revenge truly was.

Yes, let him come. Then he would learn well enough.

Chapter Three

Warmth. It seemed forever since he'd been warm.

The smell of wood smoke and food, the sound of people's voices, and the feel of footsteps vibrating on the ground beneath him, brought Eirik awake. He was warm and dry, but when he moved, weakness weighed him down.

He opened his eyes. He was in a large common room, nestled in a bed of furs on the floor before the central longhearth. No light came through the few small windows, nor through the smoke hole in the roof. Was it morning or night?

People sat at tables, eating, though which of the two meals of the day it was, he couldn't tell. Where was he? He remembered nothing after the storm hit. Apparently they had helped him. He would, however, reserve any trust until he was certain of the situation.

He tried to sit, but his head swam. He leaned back on his elbows.

"Don't rise or you may be ill."

A beautiful woman knelt down beside him. Her long hair was like snow, white-blond like his sister's. Her large blue eyes held concern, though they darkened when she glanced at his chest.

"I'm Estrid, cousin to the jarl. Stay here. I'll get him." She cast him a glance over her shoulder and her hips swayed as she left.

He watched her with interest. If that was the type of women they had here, maybe he had died and gone to live with the Valkyries. No, he wasn't dead yet, if his reaction to her was any indication.

He glanced around. Fine large weavings hung on the wooden walls of the room. Even the floor was made with planks instead of bare earth. Interlaced patterns coiled around the wooden pillars, carved by a talented hand. Two chairs stood on a dais at one end of the room. This, indeed, was the longhouse of a jarl. A very rich jarl.

A man walked in front of him and he looked up. Dark-haired, he was as tall as Eirik, and every bit as powerful. He would sooner go to Hel itself than meet him while remaining on the floor like a child.

The room spun as he rose, and his legs threatened to give out. But he clenched his jaw, forcing himself to stand. The blond woman stepped forward to take his arm, but he held up his hand, stopping her. He needed no woman to help him. The room slowed as he focused on the man.

"I'm Jarl Magnus Sigrundson. You came here yesterday, nearly dead of the cold, then you fell ill. My sister nursed you through the night and brought down your fever."

"My thanks, then, to her and to you. I'm Eirik of Hordaland."

Magnus's eyes narrowed, then he nodded. "Come and sit. Have some buttermilk. We're at the morning meal. I'm not certain you should try sausages, though the bread might help you regain your strength."

"Anything would be welcome." Steeling himself, he followed Magnus to a table and sat down with a sigh. At least he had made it this far without falling on his face.

Estrid handed him a glass cup and he took it, impressed. Such a thing also spoke of great wealth. But Estrid kept her hand where he would have to touch it with his own, and he took the cup as gently as he could. He didn't need any games, especially with her cousin watching him.

Men and women ate their breakfasts, casting glances his way and talking low. They must not have many visitors here. Wherever here was.

Estrid brought a hunk of oat bread, spread with honey, and placed it before him. He nodded his thanks and took a bite. It was soft and fresh, of very high quality. "I don't remember even getting here, much less how."

"Your horse brought you in." Magnus chewed half a sausage and swallowed. "You were unconscious on his back, but he must have sensed this place and come here."

"Did he survive?"

"He's munching hay in a nice warm stall right now. He didn't suffer any ill effects. As to where we are, we're in the *fjells*, at the end of the Sognefjorden. Where were you headed? It must have been important to risk travel now."

He shook his head at himself. How could he have gone so far off course? "I was trying to reach my cousin in Trøndelag. Because the Sognefjorden doesn't ice over in the winter, I couldn't find a way across. I wanted to go along the shoreline as far as I needed to until I found it frozen, then head back to the northwest, to stay closer to the coast, where it's warmer. But the storm came up." He had to smile. "I must be a better navigator on the seas than I am on the land. I didn't even think to bring my sun crystal with me." Silvi, never having been on a ship, wouldn't have thought to pack it for him.

"Even with it, you wouldn't have been able to see the sun through this blizzard," Magnus said. "The winters start earlier here."

He nodded. "All I could see was snow. I tried to find any kind of shelter, but there was nothing but white surrounding me. Is there a way to get to the lower lands? I need to continue as soon as I can."

Magnus refilled his own mug from a pitcher of ale on the table. "You wouldn't want to risk your horse in these mountains. The sides are steep, the gorges narrow. And there are the glaciers. It would be all too easy for you to slip and fall down the cliffs. Thor must have watched over you on the way in. You could ski out, but it's still treacherous and there's every chance you wouldn't survive. You're welcome to remain here until it's safe to travel."

Should he risk leaving? Even if he did reach Rorik, the ships would be on land now and the storms would keep them from sailing to his village until the early spring.

Perhaps it would be better to overwinter here and leave at the first opportunity. If he got to Rorik in the spring before he left to go raiding, the ships would be ready and provisioned. They could sail immediately to attack the outcasts and win back his home. If he left now and died in the attempt to travel farther north, no one would know about it or about the attack. His people would be left without help, and no one would avenge the death of his father.

"My thanks. I'll take your offer to overwinter with you. I wouldn't be able to leave without my horse, for I'd need him to carry my supplies. That's too much for me to take on skis. Did you find my bags?"

"We did and your things are safe. I have your gold, your sword, and clothes." He set down his eating knife. "And your runes."

His runes? He didn't let his surprise show. His mother must have included them, for people would welcome a rune caster before they would a strange warrior. She was not called wise for no reason. The set could not be replaced and had been consecrated to him. He'd cast them aside years ago when Sela died, but he had been wrong in doing so. They were a connection to his mother and Silvi, perhaps in more ways than one.

"We found no rune staff. Did you lose it in the storm?"

"No, that would be only for a master to carry, and I'm not one. I can answer the four questions of the runes, though. How to carve them, how they should be read, how they should be colored, and how they should be tried. My mother is a rune mistress, and insisted I learn from the time I was young. She said Odin had given an eye to learn their wisdom. The least I could do was to give some time each night to study them with her and my sister."

"That sounds like mothers everywhere."

Eirik looked up at the voice—and had to look again at the man walking to the table. If he didn't know better, he would have thought his fever had returned and was making him see double.

"I'm Leif, Magnus's brother. Welcome to our home."

They were twins and appeared alike at first glance. But Leif's blue eyes held humorous lightness in them and his dark hair was a bit shorter. Magnus's eyes, though the same color, were sharper and more intense. Both were well made and obviously warriors.

"I would like to repay your generosity."

"And insult us," Magnus said. "There's no need. It's the way of our people to aid travelers. We're too isolated to do otherwise."

"Then I would read your runes for you through the winter." He paused. "Unless you have a rune master here already."

"We did once." Leif speared a sausage off his brother's plate with his knife and took a large bite. Magnus shot him a quick glare. "But he died this past summer. Have you traveled much? Do you know any good stories so we don't have to listen to Magnus tell us of his fascinating trading forays to Kaupang again?"

A laugh welled up in him, but he didn't dare relax too much. One brother might be trying to make him lower his guard while the other one studied him. But he could play that game as well. He grinned. "I've been from the isles in the west to the vast southern inland sea that has no tides, and walked the lands of the Moors. I could tell you of monasteries that lie open and waiting to be plundered like unlocked chests of treasure. I've been to places in the East where the sands and the women glitter like gold beneath a burning sun."

"You can stop at the stories of the women," Leif said. He leaned forward and lowered his voice. "Do they truly glitter? All over?"

"I heard that, Leif."

He grimaced and stepped back. A woman walked toward them and it seemed all the blood drained out of Eirik's head. She was tall and elegant, her blue dress beautiful. The richness of her brooches and her necklace of rare glass and amber beads would bring envy to a queen.

But her hair . . . It fell in a braid over her shoulder to her knees and was the same deep red as Sela's. Very rare and beautiful. Her eyes were dark, a rich brown, not pale blue like his wife's had been. There was a quiet strength about her, a still intensity that Sela had lacked. She bore a fluidity to her movements he couldn't quite pinpoint. It tickled the back of his mind. She smiled, but her lips trembled, as though she was uncertain of him, and her eyes didn't quite meet his.

"Our sister, Asa." Magnus held out his hand to her and she took it. "She cared for you through the night. This is Eirik. He was traveling from Hordaland to Trøndelag and became lost in the storm."

He swallowed, searching for his voice. "It would seem I owe you my life, mistress. I hope I wasn't any trouble. I have no memory of the night."

She looked down and her cheeks colored. "No trouble at all. I just happened to know the right herb to use. Eir, the goddess of healing, brought you through, no doubt." Her voice held just the right amount of depth, yet it was feminine and soft.

"No doubt." He glanced down. Her fingers were white where she gripped her brother's hand. As though she sought strength from it.

She regarded Leif. "You promised to finish our game of *tafl* this morning. Remember?"

"What would be the point? You don't have any of your work to do?" His expression was one of hope.

"Of course. But I need better light than this to work in, and the sun won't be up for some time yet."

He sighed and grinned at Magnus and Eirik. "Never play against a woman who's intent on capturing a king. She'll get him every time."

They laughed as she led Leif to another table. The board game was set up there and they sat across from each other.

"She'll kill him." Magnus sighed. "As always. I don't know why he bothers, except that she loves it so and he's the only one who will open himself up for the slaughter."

He glanced at Magnus as he spoke. The jarl's eyes were filled with such love as he watched Asa laugh at something Leif said. Why wasn't she married? She looked to be about twenty, well past the age of fourteen when it was common for women to wed. Perhaps she was a widow. Not that it mattered.

He had no time for a woman until he had his revenge. The heat of his hatred and anger must have been what kept him alive through the storm. He needed to keep that edge to see him through. He'd leave here in the late winter and slay Hakon, or die trying. If he was victorious, he would continue his own life at Haardvik.

"As a guest, you may have one of the small sleeping chambers. If you want to be warmer, you may sleep in here with the others by the fire. Or, if you like, I'll ask one of the serving girls to go to you this night."

He shook his head. "I won't take a woman who has been ordered to come to me. If one wishes to be with me of her own accord, then I'll welcome it later on. But I'll never take one unwilling."

Magnus lifted an eyebrow. "And I would never order one, only ask for volunteers. Even at that, I don't think you'll be alone for long." He nodded to a place behind Eirik. He looked. A group of serving girls stood in a doorway, staring at him and giggling.

The jarl rose. "I must speak with my brother and sister of household matters. Eat and drink as you please, and avail yourself of the sauna. I'll have your things brought to a sleeping room."

He walked over to the table where his brother and sister played *tafl*, and sat down beside Leif. Leaning back against the wall, Eirik watched them.

Asa made a move and Leif followed a moment later. She moved again, grabbed a playing piece, the king, and held it up, smiling at her victory.

Her brother slammed his fist down on the table, scattering the remaining pieces. His voice carried throughout the room. "You planned that five moves ago, and lured me in."

Eirik's muscles tensed. Leif was certainly a warrior and if he lost his temper . . . No matter that he was a stranger here, he would never stand for a woman to be cowed.

Asa only burst out laughing. She leaned forward and spoke softly to Leif. He shook his head. She gave him a pleading look. He folded his arms across his chest and rested back against the wall, gazing up at the ceiling with a long-suffering glare. Then he nodded.

She beamed like a child who had been given a honey-sweet, and Eirik's breath caught. Her beauty swept over him, carrying him away like the Aifur cataracts in the Dnieper river. And it was just as dangerous. He could only watch her, his body tightening. He did not need this.

She began to set up the board for another game, but stopped as Magnus spoke to them both, his words too low for anyone to hear.

Estrid came to them, carrying a pitcher. Magnus waved her away, paying no attention to her. As she turned to leave, her face was dark and sullen, not so pretty any longer. But when she glanced Eirik's way, she brightened and gave him a coy smile and a little wave.

He dropped his head, groaning, and stared into his cup of buttermilk. It was going to be a long winter.

"He's a warrior."

Asa stopped setting up the next game as Magnus spoke. He turned his palm up. "I looked at his sword hand and he has the same calluses we do. Also, his weapon is an Ulfberht. The best. The bones of the bearer's distant ancestor are ground up and put into the molten steel as the sword is made. Only a wealthy man would have one of those blades. Not a rune reader who simply wants to defend himself on his travels."

Asa set the king piece on the center square of the board. The hardness of Eirik's body beneath her hand last night had told her the same thing. He was a fighter, a man who lived by his sword. He had killed, and perhaps not just in battle. She didn't pick up another playing piece, lest Magnus see how her hand shook. It had been all she could do to approach Eirik as he'd sat with her brothers. But she was the jarl's sister and, as such, she'd had to extend her hospitality to him. Now, she'd avoid him as best she could. But Estrid wouldn't avoid him, and if all he saw was her pretty face . . .

"Why were you so rude to Estrid, Magnus? She only wanted to offer you some ale."

"She only wanted to listen in on what I had to say, Asa. She's always doing that. You still see her as she was when you played together as children, not as she is now."

"Perhaps if you included her more often, she wouldn't be so angry all the time."

"She's been angry since her mother left with ours to return to their homeland." Leif set up several game pieces. "And she was a sullen child before that. As her cousins, we took her in, gave her a place with us, but she holds us accountable for her loss."

"It's no secret that Estrid blames you for not letting her go with her mother when she left, Magnus." She sighed. "Maybe you should let her go, now that she's older. She feels like the unwanted member of the family."

"And how much more outcast would she feel among the Irish as the half-breed daughter of one of their captured noblewomen and a hated Viking raider? They wouldn't even recognize her as legitimate, since our mothers married our fathers here with our own ceremony. It would not have been according to their Christian beliefs. I wouldn't have that for either of you. Not seven years ago, and not now." Magnus picked up the king and turned it over in his hand. "You don't begrudge my not sending you with Mother."

"After Father died, she made her choice. She loved her homeland more than she did us. Besides, I have you both."

"And Estrid has us, but that's never been enough for her. And no man will wed her, because of her spitefulness." Leif set down another ivory piece. "Watch her, Asa. There's something not right with her. I've noticed it for a long time, but I don't know how to help her."

Magnus glanced at Eirik. "And we have other things to watch, as well. I've heard of a large band of outcasts to the south. We must be vigilant come spring."

"They would never find us here in the *fjells*." She tried to catch Magnus's eye, but he wouldn't look at her.

"Even though he said it was by accident, Eirik found us. And if he did, others might follow. He's to be treated as an honored guest, but keep your eyes open and your heads clear. Our ancestors chose to live here to keep our wealth and people safe. For many generations, it's been successful. We've had our skirmishes from time to time, and the outcasts here have taken a few sheep, but nothing more serious than that. Still, nothing lasts forever."

At that, her enthusiasm to play another game of *tafl* faded. She released Leif from his promise to have her trounce him again, and her brothers left. Besides, she had work to do. She contributed to the community as much as anyone did, if not more. Magnus always said her work brought in more gold than all of the women's weavings combined.

Pride filled her. At least her family had accepted her talents, encouraged them, in fact. But it was as Magnus had said: Each to his own way. Every person in the village used his own gifts to create, mend, build, weave, and forge items Magnus could take to the markets. He sold or traded them for the commodities that helped them survive here.

This daydreaming wasn't getting her anywhere. It must be light enough now.

She stood and almost collided with Eirik, who was behind her as she turned. It was the first time he had stood before her, and he was so tall and powerful. Jumping away by instinct, she put her hand to her throat and faced him. She didn't need to see calluses on his palm to know what he was. Even in his weakened state, he carried himself as a warrior. The straightness of his shoulders, the arrogant angle of his jaw, the confidence he exuded, all spoke to her.

He held out his hand. "I didn't mean to startle you. I only wanted to thank you again for helping me last night. I'd like to repay you, if I can, though I know the jarl said I wouldn't need to."

"Repay me?" Her thoughts lay scattered about her like snowdrifts. They blew further away as she looked up into his blue eyes. They were as deep as the fjords themselves.

"I'd like to do a reading for you. I'll cast the runes for everyone, of course. But I could do a more extensive one for you. The past, the future, whatever events swirl around you even now."

Just how much would he be able to see? She suppressed a shudder. She could never take that chance. "That's not necessary. Last night, you didn't want to accept help from anyone else but me. I must have reminded you of someone. A woman named Sela."

His face paled. Was he about to fall ill again? He took a deep breath, and his gaze slid from hers. Did he feel guilt? "I must have seen your hair and thought you were my wife. Yours is a very similar color to hers."

Her heart shouldn't have tripped as it did when he mentioned his wife. She slipped past him, giving herself plenty of space so she wouldn't be trapped between him and the wall. Strength poured from him, surrounding her, even though he hadn't moved.

"I thank you for your offer, but there's no need. I know what happened in the past. And I'll keep my dreams of the future for the time being, for they may be all I have of it."

She walked away, her head down. She would never have her runes read. Magnus had said she should never again allow the past to enter her mind. She was never to speak of it, remember it, or it might conquer her. As to her future, it had been ruined long ago. And she would keep the present for herself.

It was the safest place to be.

So beautiful.

Eirik was so beautiful, shining golden and powerful like the sun. His glory entered her, bursting into her, filling her with light even in this cold darkness.

Estrid lowered her head, her hair veiling her view of the bed-chamber around her. The night had held her for far too long, just as it imprisoned the sun in the winter. Coldness. Darkness. Stillness.

But not where *he* walked. Not in the warmth of his voice. And not in his eyes as he'd looked at her.

Long ago, the heart, her mother's heart, which had held her within it, cracked and died, spilling her forth into the world, alone. The sea had swallowed her hope, the winds and the tides carrying Mother far away forever. Then the other promises were broken. The hair of flame, luring him in like a moth to the light. Then the screams, the blood, the betrayal like a knife blade to the soul, and she was left alone again.

Now the gods had seen her sorrow and sent Eirik to her. She would turn her face into his radiance, drink him in. Finally, after so long a time, she would be filled.

She would never be alone again.

The chamber was tiny, but it served him well. It was scarcely large enough for a bed and a chest for his things, but most long-houses didn't even have separate rooms. Privacy was a rare luxury and Eirik welcomed it.

A couple of the serving girls had made their interest known. He had turned them away with a smile. Another time, perhaps. He still hadn't quite regained his strength and he had other things to do this night. A good evening meal, time in the sauna, and a bracing cold rinse after-ward had restored him. Now, he was ready to seek answers.

A single lamp lit the room, shining on his sword where it leaned against the wall beside the bed. It wasn't his family's ancestral sword. That rested in the fjord. This had been his father's personal weapon, made by a swordsmith so legendary, no one knew if he'd even existed. Why Ivar hadn't used it in the battle against the outcasts instead of the more valuable blade, he might never know.

Still, having it there allowed him to feel nearer to Ivar, just as the runes brought his mother and sister closer in his mind. He held the gem-encrusted bag in his hand. Silvi had stitched the stones and gold charms on it for him. He ran his hand over them, his eyes closed. Remembering.

He had cast them aside in his grief three years ago—the runes and his family. Would the runes speak to him now? Take him back as his family had? He'd promised to read them for Magnus and his people, but what if they wouldn't open to him any longer?

He'd never completed his training as his mother had wanted. To do that, he would have had to become a priest, studying for years. He'd wanted to follow in his father's footsteps instead, learning the ways of a warrior, sailing the vast trade routes, seeing the world. He'd done so.

It hadn't been for glory and adventure, as he'd dreamed of when he was a youth. He'd traveled to escape his pain and anger. Perhaps it was better not to know what the gods had planned. Still, he needed to arm himself as best he could, for now and in the months to come. A wise warrior sought the weapons at hand.

He hadn't mentioned the outcasts to Magnus. It would be well to keep those playing pieces to his side of the board for now. Nothing would happen until the spring. He had time to decide whether they could be allies, for at that point, he would have an idea of who these people were and if he could trust them. Until then, he dared not reveal any of his vulnerabilities to them.

He needed answers. From the time he was a boy, the runic knowledge had always come from a place deep within him, perhaps passed along to him from his mother's blood before his birth. Though he had never told her so, she'd known. He'd never delved far down, not wanting to look too deep within himself, but now he might have to.

Bowing his head, he cleared his mind. A familiar sphere of light grew from within him, surrounding his thoughts, pushing aside any shadows. There was no room for the forces that dwelled in the dark places. There could only be the radiance of the Aesir, and of the All-father who had first sought this wisdom.

He spilled the runes into his hand. Dropping them onto the blanket where he sat, he studied the ones that had fallen faceup and what they would tell him.

Like a river whose dam had broken, their power coursed through his body. He closed his eyes as the forces pummeled his thoughts. The ancient symbols spiraled around him until they caught him up in their whirlwind and he could no longer hold on to reality. Trusting, he let go. They carried him into another place.

He stood on a mountain peak. Overhead, a storm roiled in a blood-red sky. A sword sky, a wolf sky.

Five points of light, like stars, whirled down out of the clouds. They slowed and formed the cross of Thor in front of him, the casting pattern he'd used most often. They burned molten and golden. He reached out and touched the first one at the bottom of the cross, the position of the forces surrounding him now.

The rune of Jera sparked under his hand. A time of waiting. It was the beginning of an end to one cycle and the start of a new one. He must wait. He could not push a river, only stand on the shore for this time.

The next rune, in the position of obstacles, burned so hot as it appeared, it seared him. Kenaz. It held the power of the forge to transform him into a new form. He must have the strength to withstand the forces pounding against him.

Lightning struck, almost at his feet, but he stood firm. A rune, thrown by the bolt, flashed into the uppermost position, that of favorable forces. He smiled. Tyr, the rune of the warrior. He'd fight, rise through his own efforts, but his prowess would bring him victory. It also indicated a man in love, a thing from his past. Why would it come now? The runes were timeless. The past, present and future could all be as one to them. As a mortal man, the difference lay within him.

The storm eased. No wind, no sound, nothing moved. The star to the right of the others, in the position of the near future, slid down and vanished. It left a glittering frozen trail behind it. Isa. Like ice, the present was immovable. But as an iceberg lies mostly below water, so were things hidden from his view. Dangerous things.

He brushed his hand over the star at the center of the cross, between the other runes. Ing grew from the light, showing a new stage of life. A completion of beginnings and the realization of a dream.

He stepped back to study the cross. This was what he sought. It all made sense, except the Tyr, indication of love. He couldn't afford such infatuation again. In this, he *would* defy the gods.

The ground beneath him shook and opened up. He leaped back as tendrils grew out of the earth and arced into the sky. Leaves unfurled from it and it widened into a massive tree trunk. The branches swept up the rune casting, carrying the symbols into the heavens.

He stared up and his legs almost buckled. Yggdrasil, the World Tree.

Stepping forward, he put his hand on the trunk. It was warm, pulsing with life. Oval pieces of the bark peeled away and he caught them in his hands as they fell. They became his set of runes, the ones he still had in another reality.

His mother had carved his and Silvi's sets from the same branch of the sacred oak in the grove at home. Would the runes still have a connection because of it?

He closed his hands over them, bringing them to his chest. Bending his head, he called, envisioning his thoughts winding through the darkness, over the fjords and valleys. Southward toward home.

Warmth opened out within him. And love. Silvi. Had she heard him through their runes? When they were young, they played such games. Now it was no longer a game.

Joy touched him and he smiled. With a thought, he cast the rune Gyfu into the leaves of the World Tree, willing it to show her that he'd accepted the gift of love she had sent.

Yggdrasil faded and once again, he knelt on the bed. The runes he had dropped lay before him, each turned faceup, different from before. How was that possible? A chill stiffened his spine. The gods walked in this time, bringing all possibilities to bear, with powers that could crush the weak.

He was not weak.

Perhaps Odin had guided him here to this place. For what purpose? For allies? Tyr still shone in his mind, the warrior's force, harnessed by courage, bringing about destiny. He would need Tyr's strength to help him in the months to come.

But it also brought love. That, however, was a weakness. Anything that weakened him, no matter how pleasant, must be cast aside. And yet he had rejected love, even of his family, after Sela died, and what had it gained him? Lost years, and a lost legacy. His family had forgiven him, and it would appear the power of the runes had, as well.

If only he could forgive himself.

Chapter Four

A sa studied the carving in the corner of the weaving room where she worked each winter. This dragon's head was the largest she'd ever done, standing as tall as she did. It could go on the bow of only a jarl's or king's longship.

Few carvers made dragon heads for longships. Most made serpents and flat spirals. But the dragon had always spoken to her, so she made one each year.

Each spring, Magnus took her dragon to Kaupang to sell. Before Magnus could even tie the ship to the dock, men swarmed on board, fighting over it.

This piece was her finest and would go to the great market at Hedeby in Denmark. It would fetch far more there than at the smaller places. Her reputation had grown with her talent so that now other jarls asked for her work, and it was said even the Danish king himself had expressed interest in one of her dragons.

She smiled, running her hand over the scales at the back of the head. Its mouth was open in an eternal snarl and the eyes were large and so well wrought, they seemed to follow her as she walked around it. Interlaced creatures ran down the front of the throat, but the sides of the neck were smooth.

She wanted to carve the runes of protection there, for that was what made her dragons so unique and valuable. But their old rune master had died, and she had no one now to guide her. A small deviation in the symbols could spell disaster. They varied each year, depending on what the master had seen, so she couldn't just repeat the same ones. And each must be colored a certain way.

Of course, there was one among them now who said he understood the runes. But how could she bear being near him while he guided her?

In the days since Eirik had come, she'd had nothing to do with him. Even though she hadn't looked at him, she'd felt his eyes on her. The thought of being close to him brought strange feelings to her, like melting inside, a weakness in her legs. It must be fear. He might have killed his wife, and she'd seen enough violence from men like that.

Who could say if he would show her the correct runes? How could she know if he possessed such a talent or not? It was said that a rune master had written the wrong staves over the bed of an ill woman and she'd nearly died. When a more competent master had seen them, he'd rewritten them and she'd recovered.

She couldn't take that chance. Not only could she not risk her reputation, but she wouldn't endanger other lives. The men who sailed those ships made long, treacherous voyages, and they needed all the good fortune they could have. They believed her dragons brought them that luck and protection, and she couldn't fail them.

Using a piece of dried sharkskin, she smoothed the edge of a tooth. She'd already used an iron file to shape it. Now she only needed to sand it further so it would hold the paint she'd finish it with.

"Magnificent."

She jumped, her hand to her throat, nearly knocking over the carving. Eirik steadied it and rested his hand on the top of the head as he smiled.

"It seems I have a talent for startling you."

"I was lost in the carving and didn't hear you." She tried to calm herself. They were alone in the weaving room, but the door to the common room was only a few steps away. And she always had her carving tools on the table beside her.

"A ship's prow piece." He studied it, frowning a bit. "I've never seen another like it. And you did this?"

She swallowed and nodded. "One winter, when I was a girl, my father tired of my running about through the rooms, bored. He gave me a small knife and a piece of wood, and showed me how to make toys for myself. He often carved on long sea voyages, as many men do. In time, I became better at it than he was. He would take my work to the markets and it sold quite well. Eventually, I tried to make these prow heads."

She hid a smile behind her hand. "The first ones weren't very good, I'm afraid. But at least they provided good fuel for our winter fires. Eventually, I became more skilled, and Magnus risked taking one to the market. After that, I've done one each year and they help bring in much gold."

"I can see why. Any shipbuilder would be honored to set this on the bow."

His voice was low as he ran his hand over the dragon. His fingers were long and sensitive. They caressed the wood and she grew breathless as she watched them.

"This is maple?"

"Yes." She tore her gaze away from his hands. "It's the only wood hard enough to take the detail I'll be adding soon."

He regarded her, his eyes narrowing a bit. "It is unusual for a woman to do such work."

"Unusual, perhaps. But not unknown. Magnus believes we all must give of our talents for the good of the village. The dragon is just as beautiful no matter who carves it."

He nodded as he walked around it again, his arms crossed. Perhaps he disapproved. But he didn't have to worry about how to feed the village in the long winter and how Magnus would keep his warriors. Men stayed with the jarl who had the most to offer—food, drink, gold. To keep them satisfied took a great deal of wealth, and her dragons brought them that.

It was also why she would never marry, even if she could bring herself to do so. How could she take this source of revenue from her people? Even with as many artisans, smiths, weavers, and farmers as lived here, her work made the difference between mere subsistence and living in comfort and safety. Her bride price, no matter how high it was, wouldn't make up for it.

"Your father seemed a fine man," he said. "But your brother is jarl now. What happened?"

It had been seven years, so she should be able to speak of it. Still, the words stuck in her throat and a familiar ache started in her chest. "He was killed while returning from a trading trip in the East. He and Leif and his men were portaging the ship past the Aifur rapids in the Dnieper river."

"I know of them. It's unusual for our people to travel there. Generally the Swedes do so, while we head to the isles in the west and also south to Francia."

"Long ago, he'd heard from a trader in Birka of the riches to be had. He'd made one successful trip years earlier and thought to repeat it, but he wasn't so lucky."

"I've been attacked there myself. The robbers hide, waiting for travelers to pass, knowing they are vulnerable then, with their ships out of the water."

She nodded. "That's what I've learned since. Leif survived to carry the tale back to us, thank the gods. He could have been lost as well, and we never would have known what happened to any of them. Father died fighting, with a sword in his hand, so we had some comfort in that." It had been the only comfort. Magnus had been so young to take over, just ten-and-nine winters. But he had risen to the task and they had prospered.

Eirik continued to study the carving. "The sides of the neck are bare. What will you do there?"

She looked away from him. If she were to put the runes there, could she ask him to help her? Work with him? Trust him? She could almost see the symbols writhing in the wood—a part of it, and her, forever. And his hand would guide hers, holding and touching it. His essence would join with hers on the dragon and would remain that way as long as it roamed the seas.

Her stomach dropped. She stroked the carving over its left eye with her thumb. "I haven't yet decided what to put there."

His voice was low as he regarded her work. "Perhaps you need only listen to it and it will tell you. Dragons are that way. They know what they want and they take it. It's best to give in to their wishes."

"So I've heard." She gave him a hard glance. But he only met her eyes with his and they sparkled, as Leif's did when he teased her.

With a slight smile, he inclined his head to her and left. Sitting on her bench, she took a long, calming breath. She would need to wait now to work, for her hands shook with her heartbeat.

Estrid walked into the room. "Have you seen Eirik? Birgitta said she saw him come in here."

"He was here, but he left."

"Ah." She nodded.

"What do you mean by that?"

"Nothing." She gave Asa a sideways glance.

Asa crossed her arms and waited. Her cousin wouldn't be able to resist a verbal jab, and sometimes they had their uses. Estrid had ways of finding out things no one else knew.

"It's just that he looks at you—Oh, it doesn't matter." She picked up one of the knives Asa used to carve with and watched the light play on the blade.

Asa held her hands together so Estrid wouldn't see them tremble. "And just how does he look at me?"

Estrid shrugged. "With lust in his eyes. But then, he's a man. They all look at women that way. You know what they want. Eirik has already tried to seduce some of the girls here. I've heard from them that he's insatiable. He's very forceful, they say, though so many of them like that in a lover." A sly grin slid across her lips. "I just thought to warn you, Asa. We wouldn't want that part of him to be frozen if he chose to take you. What a waste that would be." She set down the knife. "It is as I've always said, that all you have to do is look at a man and talk to him, and he'll want to have you. I wouldn't encourage Eirik any longer if I were you. You know what will happen."

Asa forced a smile, never letting Estrid see how her words affected her. Fisting her shaking hands, she hid them in her skirt.

Estrid left as the other women came in to begin their day of weaving and ribbon making. Asa didn't return their greetings.

Eirik had only appeared to be teasing her, but now she couldn't be certain. What did she know of the ways of men? She'd made a horrible mistake once, long ago, and nothing had been the same after that. What if she misjudged again and Estrid was right? She needed to stay away from him, and not speak to him any longer, no matter what help he might give her. The price could be too high.

She couldn't work on the dragon that morning. Being so close to Eirik had unsettled her and she wouldn't be able to concentrate. It'd be better not to risk a slip of the hand with the knife and the destruction of the carving.

She covered it with a large woven cloth as Eirik's words skittered across her mind. *They know what they want and they take it. It's best to give in to their wishes.*

How had he meant it? As lighthearted teasing such as her brothers would give her? Or was it a warning, as *he* had threatened so long ago?

The casting made sense. Eirik closed his eyes and let the meaning of the runes flow through his mind, sensing what they wanted him to know.

Each evening, sitting in a corner of the common room, he had read for several people. The sessions left him drained but exultant, for he hadn't lost touch with the runes. True, they had burst into his mind when he'd cast them for himself, but that was one thing. He couldn't be certain they would respond to the queries of others.

But they did. Magnus sat across from him, his arms folded over his wide chest, waiting. Eirik tried not to smile. The runes were very clear, yet still left a great deal unanswered. Perhaps it would be interesting to do a deeper casting for the jarl one day.

"The influences moving around you now are those that will lead to new attitudes. The rune in this position is Ehwaz, and combined with Birkano, as it is, it means traveling to a family occasion, most likely a wedding. Do you have any relatives a distance away?"

Magnus shook his head. "Not that we would visit easily. Our mother and Estrid's mother are across the seas in their homeland of Leinster in Ireland, but we have no contact with them. And if they've remarried, we wouldn't know."

He'd have to ask about this after the casting. "In the position of obstacles, you have Berkano, the rune of life, birth, and the home. In this place, it shows a vulnerability in the home, a darkness that must be cleared."

Magnus said nothing, but his eyes narrowed.

"In the position of that which is favorable, Gyfu appears. It indicates a gift, but mostly a union or partnership. Have you been thinking of this? A marriage? A venture with another trader?"

"No. We're so isolated here, it would be difficult. And I haven't had the time to search for an advantageous marriage."

He glanced up at the jarl. "This rune carries the meaning of love. And the gift can be from a man to a woman, even in the form of a child."

Magnus snorted. "I'm most careful in my pursuits. I'll not have any baseborn child in my family. As for love, the skalds can speak poems about such things. I have no use for it. When I marry, it will be for my own advantage and the allies I can make through it."

Very wise, as he knew all too well. Eirik inclined his head and touched the next rune. "Here we have Othala reversed." He hesitated. "May I speak freely?"

"Of course. What would be the point otherwise?"

"Indeed. In the position of the short term, you will refuse to see a situation clearly. It will cause pain to another."

Magnus paled for a moment. Then his eyes hardened and his lips pressed into a thin line. He stared at the rune, then gathered himself and took a deep breath. "Can that be in the past?"

Eirik shook his head. "Sometimes the past, present, and the future can be as one. But this is a very specific position. It will happen soon, perhaps even now."

"What will be the outcome?"

"In the long term, we have Kenaz. It speaks of renewed clarity, so in spite of Othala reversed, you'll resolve the situation through strength. It also tells of a new relationship." He hesitated.

"And?"

"With Birkano, it repeats the aspect of a child."

Magnus shook his head with a slight smile. "Then I must be even more careful than usual. All this talk of marriage, love, and children is making me nervous."

The jarl didn't look as though he would be nervous about much of anything. He was too controlled and certain of his place in life. He'd lean back, cross his arms, and weigh all his options. But perhaps, because of his certainty in his own views, he would be too slow to take action and it would end up hurting someone.

Eirik held his hand up. "These weddings and children might not even be yours. They might be of someone in your family. You said you don't see your mother any longer?" It might help him to recognize the undercurrents in this place if he knew more of their past.

"No. I know Asa told you of our father. How he died while on a trading journey. He had stolen my mother and her sister in his wilder raiding days, from a holding near Waterford in Ireland. They were noblewomen and he thought to hold them for ransom, as is customary. But he fell in love with my mother, Ailis, and when the money came, it became her dowry and they married. Her sister, Cliona, he gave to his finest warrior, Togur. They had Estrid, and Ailis bore my brother and me, then Asa.

"But after my father died, my mother said she wished to return to Ireland. She missed its green mountains and the beauty of it. And her family. Togur had died some years before of a pain in his chest, and Cliona had remarried. But she divorced her second husband and left with Ailis. I took them back myself, to be certain they would be welcomed, and they were. I haven't returned since."

"And yet, they left their children behind." It was difficult for Eirik to understand.

"They wanted to take Asa and Estrid with them, but I forbade it."

"To separate mothers and daughters must have been painful."

"It was. But it was their choice to leave. They loved their land more than they loved us. I couldn't risk the two girls being ostracized and rejected because they were the half-breed daughters of Norse raiders. The priests there would have called them illegitimate, for they would not have recognized our marriage rites. They were just becoming of marriageable age, and would have no prospects there. I couldn't have that. For either of them. As the jarl and the ranking male of the house, it was my decision."

After the jarl had thanked him and left, Eirik took a sip of ale and regarded the casting.

It had been Magnus's decision, but had it been wise? And yet, Asa and Estrid had grown up in a jarl's house with all the comfort and privilege they could wish for. Who knew if women who would leave their children behind would take care of them at all in a strange land? What were the repercussions for Asa and Estrid? However, that responsibility lay with the mothers for abandoning them, not with Magnus for trying to protect them.

A new respect grew in Eirik, for this was a man who was able to make the hard decisions. Perhaps Magnus was someone he could form an alliance with. The runes spoke of a new partnership, and that could go in many ways.

Magnus said Asa and Estrid would have no marriage prospects in Ireland, and yet neither of them was married now. Had they been widowed? Why did Asa seem so afraid of him? Magnus had asked if the pain Eirik saw in the runes was in the past. Had Asa been abused? He'd seen such women before, how nervous they were, and how afraid they were to speak to men. She was much the same as they.

A slow anger built in him, his fists tightening. The winter would give him further wisdom, as would the runes. And when they spoke, he would listen.

"Asa, why don't you make a loaf of your bread? We'll need ballast for the ships come spring." The voice of the bearlike, red-bearded warrior boomed through the longhouse. He stood with his legs braced, hands on his hips, taunting Asa as she ate her morning bread and honey at one of the tables in the common room.

Eirik looked at Leif. He took a swallow of his ale and ignored the insult. They'd moved the tables aside to make a place for the men to train, even though there wasn't much room. Still, when the land lay covered in waist-deep snow, it was better than nothing.

"Why are you and Magnus allowing that?" Eirik slammed his cup down. He might be a guest, but he would never allow a woman to be misused. The men had been disparaging Asa's cooking and lack of domestic talents for some time now. But she paid them no heed.

Leif took another swig and grinned at a serving girl who walked past. Magnus stood in the middle of the room, taking several practice swings with his sword, his back turned to them.

"No, the loaf would be for the anchor," another warrior said. "We need her rolls for the ballast." They all laughed, nudging each other.

"What in the Hel?" Eirik had had enough. He rose, but Leif reached across the table and grabbed his arm.

"Just watch."

He sank back down with a scowl.

Asa took a last bite of bread, and stood. She stepped out from behind the table and the men all moved back. Her arms crossed, she regarded the huge red-haired warrior. "Arne, you were the loudest, as always. I'll start with you."

Their hoots trailing behind her, she strode to her small chamber and slammed the door shut.

"I don't understand," Eirik said. "Now they've hurt her. For you and Magnus to tease her is one thing, but the others should respect her more than that."

Leif emptied his cup. "Oh, they do respect her. They'd better. Just watch."

They all kept their eyes on the closed door. Even Magnus glanced at it as he loosened up.

Eirik's blood boiled. Was this why she was so quiet and nervous? A beautiful young woman like her, being harassed by a group of hardened warriors, would have to live in fear. It made no sense for her brothers to tolerate it. And now she was hiding.

The door to her room opened. He dragged in a shocked breath as she stepped out. She wore a tunic and leggings, similar to what a man would wear, only the tunic was longer, to mid-thigh. She'd put her hair back in a braid for, being an unmarried woman, she often wore it loose. An empty sheath hung at her side.

And she carried a sword. *A sword?* He looked at Leif, his brows raised.

"Just watch."

She stalked Arne. The others cleared the floor, and even Magnus leaned against the wall, though he kept a close eye on them. Asa faced Arne, her feet braced apart, rolling her shoulders. He grinned and motioned her to come at him.

She tilted her head to one side, as though considering. Then in a move so fast Eirik would have missed it had he blinked, she spun and struck. Arne barely brought his sword up in time and knocked hers aside. She pivoted in a counterstrike and the clash reverberated throughout the room.

Arne was solid and massive, but Asa was fast and agile, like the fine horses of the eastern deserts compared to the huge warhorses of the west. She was just as beautiful. Sleek and fiery, her hair was like a flame, her sword like the lightning. She spun and wove, almost dancing around the larger warrior as he turned, until she hit him in the hip with the flat of her blade.

"Better you eat less of anyone's bread, Arne," she said. "Or we'll be using *you* for ballast this spring." All the men laughed, even Magnus. Arne laughed the loudest.

"That's one for Asa, as usual," another man said.

"Sounded more like two good blows she gave Arne." Leif raised his mug to her.

Magnus pushed off from the wall and nodded at Arne. "That will do for now." As Arne left the floor, chuckling, Magnus faced Asa, his sword raised.

"Just pretend Magnus is a loom, Asa," Leif said. "As big and immovable as he is, that shouldn't be too difficult." He leaned over to Eirik. "She hates looms. Nearly destroyed one of ours the only time she tried to weave something. Her sword marks are still in the wood of the frame."

Magnus bore down, his sword arcing toward her. Eirik nearly shouted, but if he distracted her—

Asa met his blade and deflected it. She wouldn't be as strong as he was, but she could use his own momentum to turn aside his attack.

He brought his blade up and around, and she spun out of the way. As she passed, she smacked the flat of her sword into his back.

He yelled, and came after her, but she stood her ground, unflinching. "I have first strike, Magnus. It stops at that."

He stared at her and the room grew quiet. Then he smiled and bowed. "I concede. This time."

"You mean, you concede *again*." She gave him a sweet smile.

The men hooted with appreciation, then broke up into pairs to train. Asa and Magnus discussed her movements, why she did as she had done, and what he wanted her to try next. They moved together, slowly, going over each turn of the blade. He repositioned her hand on the hilt and she nodded, loosening her thumb and first fingers, gripping it harder with her fourth and little fingers. Magnus told her this would allow the sword to flow more with her movements and let her use its momentum for more force. She'd grip it completely only at the instant of impact when she pulled the weapon back in a slicing motion. Eirik listened, fascinated. He'd never heard of this technique before.

They sheathed their swords and Magnus drew her into his embrace, saying something in her ear.

Eirik watched as she accepted the compliments and more teasing from the other warriors. It was obvious it was only the jests all comrades give each other. She stood tall among them, confidence pouring from her, as though she was one of them.

Speechless, he looked at Leif, who grinned. "Don't you know a shieldmaiden when you see one, rune caster?" He rose and went into the cooking room, no doubt in pursuit of the serving girl he'd smiled at.

A shieldmaiden? Asa? He'd fought beside them before. In fact, Rorik had six of them among his warriors, one of them his sister. But they were all tall, elegant, bold, strong.

Everything Asa was when she held that sword. She always sat with the warriors during meals, seldom with the other women. He'd assumed it was because her brothers were there as well, but what if that wasn't the reason? What if she fought alongside them in battle? If she was as lacking in household skills as it seemed, she might have very little in common with the women of the village.

It was difficult to believe that two brothers who loved her as much as they appeared to would allow her to endanger herself this way. And why had she learned weapons to begin with?

"Rune master?"

His head still whirling with what he had seen, it took him a moment to realize Estrid had taken Leif's place at the table across from him.

"I'm not a master. Only a rune reader."

"Oh, but I think you could be a master of anything you desire." She leaned forward, smiling at him. "Or anyone."

Her eyes held a strangeness, a wildness. Just a hint, but it raised the hairs on his neck. "Did you want something, mistress?"

"Oh yes. But I'll settle for a reading, if you'd like." She let her icy-blond hair spill forward over her breasts.

She was very beautiful. Yet her beauty left him cold, like looking at frost-lit night. Pretty to see for a short time, but something much warmer lay elsewhere. He looked again at Asa as she laughed with the men, her hand on the hilt of her sheathed sword. The tunic and pants outlined her slender body, and her long legs seemed to stretch like the fjords through the mountains. Her bare arms were toned and strong and it was obvious she had trained for years. Such speed and accuracy. She would have to make up for her lack of male strength and power.

Estrid slid into his view, blocking his sight of Asa. "So, will you read my runes now, Eirik?"

She was being very familiar, using his name like that. It wasn't proper and he needed to prevent any problems with Magnus. She was fast becoming a problem.

"I'll give you a reading this evening when I do the others. You can be first." If there were others waiting for their readings, he would have an excuse to cut it short.

She smiled. "First. I like that. I'll be waiting."

As she slid from the seat, he leaned over so he could see Asa. Estrid stopped, blocking his view again. Her eyes flashed, just for a moment, then she smoothed her expression.

"I wouldn't bother with Asa, if I were you. You'd get more than you bargained for. She won't have anything to do with men below her own rank. She won't even talk to them."

If he could draw out the information, it might help him understand the puzzle that was Asa. And a little flirting never hurt anyone.

He gave her his best smile. "I don't know. She's spoken to me. And she was quite nice."

"Of course. She's done that before. She's so sweet. She lures men in, then spurns them, telling Magnus they've insulted her. Then he takes revenge. When she doesn't want someone around, it's what she does. And she doesn't like strangers. Oh, she'll laugh and pretend she's a man. But when it comes to outsiders, it can be dangerous for them. Don't make the mistake of having anything to do with her. It will end badly for you, as it has for others. Magnus thought to teach her to defend herself from men, but it's the men who need protection from *her*."

She smiled and ran her fingers over his hand. "I'll see you tonight, rune caster."

He didn't watch her leave. Asa walked toward him, on her way back to her room. As she approached, she kept her eyes averted. When she drew near, she did glance his way, and fear glimmered in her eyes. Then she lifted her chin and swept past him, her strides long and graceful.

Could Estrid be right? It seemed as though Asa had a shield around her at all times, and she lowered it only for her brothers and when she wielded her sword.

Strong men surrounded her all the time. Why would Magnus think she needed to learn how to defend herself?

His sword arm tightened. He could use a practice session himself, but it might not be wise to reveal his abilities just yet. Let them continue to think he was just a rune caster who needed to protect himself on his journeys.

Any man could have a weapon, but not all were trained fighters. And even fewer were true *vikingr*, as he was. He grimaced and took another drink of ale. He *had* been a *vikingr*. Then, for a few moments, a jarl. Now he was neither. He had lost everything in one morning. His inheritance lay at the bottom of a fjord and his heart had remained back in his village. It was as the runes had said. He hung suspended, like Odin had from the Tree of Knowledge.

He only needed to withstand the uncertainty and pain of his losses in order to come out, like Odin, wiser in the end.

Chapter Five

Asa changed into her dress and put away her tunic and pants in the chest. She hadn't wanted to train with Eirik sitting and watching in the common room, but she couldn't let her brothers' men tease her for too long and get away with it. She'd fought too hard for their respect. Few knew of her talent with a blade. The men did, for Magnus had trained her for years along with them, and she had fought beside them on the seas. But in the region beyond this village, it wasn't common knowledge. She wanted to keep it that way.

True, shieldmaidens were not unknown, but they were rare. The Danes had many of them in their armies, and the historians and skalds told stories of them and their viciousness.

She smiled as she put on her amber and glass necklace. She wasn't trying for viciousness, or glory for that matter. But Magnus had been right in thinking it would help her regain a little of her confidence to know she could handle a situation. As she had not been able to before.

She sat down on her bed. Although learning to fight had given her confidence, she still had her moments, especially with outsiders. And Eirik was an outsider. But he also might be the only one who could help her with the dragon. For the past several nights, she'd dreamt of the carving. It had come alive, screaming its demands, unable to rest in its true form until it carried the runes on its neck. In the dreams, she'd touched the wood and it had been warm under her hand. When she'd brushed her fingers over the blank area, another hand had covered hers. It was strong and large, and power coursed through it. The ancient symbols sparked from the touch between them. They settled on the wood, burning into it, then blazed into colors. The dragon had cried out one last time, then melted into its position, becoming still once again.

She'd had the same dream several times, but she never saw whose hand guided hers. She didn't need to see. In the dream, his scent enveloped her, his strength embracing her. The deep knowledge that he was a warrior carried into the vision as the dragon accepted Eirik and allowed his essence to join with its own. And with hers.

Did the dragon speak to her, or did the runes? One way or another, she had to find a way to ask Eirik to help her. It had to be done or she couldn't continue the carving. The image sang in her mind, how the scales would wrap around the runes, and how the interlaced creatures on its front would slide beneath them. She had to carve them together, all of it intertwined as one.

How could she approach him? Perhaps when he sat with Leif. The two of them had become friends, playing *tafl*, drinking together, and talking into the night.

She left her chamber. Leif had gone into the cooking room to find either the serving girl he favored, or a bite to eat. She smiled. Or both.

He was there, sitting at a table with a girl under each arm. He grinned when she stood in front of him, hands on her hips. The girls giggled and slid away. He frowned at her.

"Come to spoil all my fun again?"

"They do have work to do, Leif." She sat and nodded her thanks as Birgitta set a mug of ale in front of her.

"Would you like me to leave your evening meal in your work area this night, as usual, mistress?" She poured Leif more ale.

"That would be fine. My thanks." She sipped at the brew. No one could make it like their ale-woman. It was more food than drink, rich and dark.

"So, Asa, why have you invaded this dreaded domain? They're still trying to scrub the soot off the walls from your last baking attempt."

One of the women laughed. "That's not true. We finally washed it all off just last week."

Asa winced, but joined in the laughter. Once, her lack of such skills had bothered her. But she had found her own way. It would never be that of other women, buried in kitchens and bearing child after child. Not for her the bedchamber, but the open oceans. Not for her the glow of a cook-fire, but the flash of a sword blade. It was enough.

"I need to ask you a favor."

"Oh?" He raised his brows.

"You've been spending time with the rune caster of late."

"What of it?" He took a long drink.

"You know that in the past, I've carved runes on my dragon's heads. Our old master always guided me, but he's gone now. This dragon calls to me in my dreams. It wants them also, but I don't know the proper symbols. If I carve them incorrectly, it could bring disaster."

"So ask Eirik to help you. His readings have been impressive. More than even the old master's, may he forgive me for saying so."

"Could you mention it to him? You know it'll be difficult for me to approach him."

He put his hand on hers where it lay on the table between them. "It's your carving. You need to speak to him of it. If you can't even do that, how will you have the courage to work with him? Just pretend he's a bit of sewing you have to attend to. Very nonthreatening." He considered. "Maybe not. You don't want to hack him to pieces, just talk to him."

She shot him a glare. "You're an evil, evil man, Leif."

Several of the women called out in agreement and he grinned, giving them a wink.

She hit his arm. "You're not taking this seriously. You never do."

"That's Magnus's duty. I had the good sense to let him slide on by me first, out of the womb. He has all the responsibility." He patted a girl on the rear as she passed. She giggled and scooted away. "And I don't." He faced Asa then, and sobered. "But the runes are never a laughing matter and neither are these dreams you're having. They both speak to you, the dragon and the runes. Listen to them. Follow where they lead. And it would seem they lead to Eirik. Perhaps there's a reason for that."

He finished his ale as he rose, and set the mug back on the table. With a small bow to the women, he left. He was right. She needed to speak to the rune caster herself. Only she could tell him what she had in mind, what protections she wanted. He would seek the right runes and then guide her, as the old master had done. That was all.

But his hand wouldn't be cold and wrinkled. His arm wouldn't be weak, his voice brittle with age. His scent would be that of the wind and leather, not herbs and cobwebs.

Perhaps the spirit of the dragon tested her to see if she was worthy to bring its essence into the world.

She dealt with strong, powerful men all the time. Her brothers. Their warriors. What threat could Eirik be? She had faced far worse than he, a guest in her brother's hall. She was the strong one, and if the dragon wanted to test her worth, she would not fail. She was a shield-maiden. And that would have to be enough to make her worthy.

A good, hot sauna was just what she needed. Asa stretched her neck to the side to loosen the muscles as she walked through the darkness toward the bathhouse. She had spent the day sanding and detailing the parts of the dragon she had already carved, but the sides of the neck remained empty, untouched. Waiting for the runes.

She'd eaten her evening meal as she'd worked, as she often did, so she hadn't seen if Eirik was in the common room. She would have to face him eventually. The sooner she did so, the sooner she could finish it.

Now, she only wanted to relax in the heat of the sauna. The others were gathering for the evening activities of board games, drinking, and telling stories. Eirik should be giving rune readings. The bathhouse would be empty.

She pushed open the door and stepped inside. A pile of men's clothing and a fur cloak lay on the bench of the outer room. Her heart sank. She would have to wait. She started to leave, but the knife lying on the top of the pile caught her eye. It was Eirik's knife. He always wore it, as most men did, to eat with and to have at hand in case he needed to defend himself. Even women wore them. Usually. But she was without hers this night since she'd only intended to bathe and return to the longhouse.

The other women conjectured about what Eirik looked like under his thick shirt, tunic, and cloak. Whether his body was that of a rune caster who never worked at physical labor, or that of a warrior, as many whispered about. Of course, if he was as successful with the women as Estrid had insinuated, then they should know. That, however, didn't seem to be the case.

Magnus had wondered if Eirik was actually a fighter but hid that fact from them for some reason. If she could just glimpse him, she might be able to tell.

To see a man, unclothed . . . Heat rose into her cheeks. If she could do this, it might be a matter of their safety. That was her responsibility, the same as any other warrior. Maidenly modesty played no part in this.

She crossed to the door of the bathing room and cracked it open. At first, the steam from the moist, heated stones blocked her view. But her opening the door created a slight draft and some of the mist lifted upward toward the smoke hole in the roof.

Eirik stretched out on one of the benches, leaning against the wall, his head tilted back on his strong neck. His eyes were closed and his blond hair streamed down his back, gleaming in the thin light of the fire. The golden radiance played on his glistening skin as he reached up to comb his hair back with his fingers.

She caught her breath. His arms were defined, like river rocks in a swift-running stream. His stomach was flat, his thighs strong, and scars crossed the slabs of muscle in his chest. An old, deep scar ran along one heavy shoulder, and he bore several others on his forearms.

He was perfect. This was not a man who sat all his life in the shadows, pondering the meanings of ancient symbols. His was a warrior's body, with all the marks of war. As he leaned forward to toss more water on the hot stones, she looked closer. He had no scars on his sculpted back. He would never retreat from a fight, but face his adversaries without fear, with much skill. Most of his scars were light and small, except for the one on his shoulder. That should have killed a lesser man, or rendered that arm useless.

But he had healed, and from the condition of the other scars, he had gone on to fight again after that. Who was he? No doubt, he had a great deal of talent with the runes. And with a weapon. Did he follow the wisdom of Odin, or the strength of Thor?

He rose and picked up a bucket of cold water. He poured it over himself, as was customary to rinse away the sweat brought on by the steam. The water cascaded over his naked body, running along his strong arms and down his chest and stomach. It sluiced down his hips and his hard thighs. With the firelight reflecting on the water, his body glistened as though covered in molten gold.

Her head swam. He was like one of the gods who dwelled in Asgard, come to earth. Primal. Powerful. So beautiful, she trembled, her legs weak. Was this fear, as she had thought before when she looked at him? Or something else? Something she had never known?

The women often spoke of desire. She'd listened, but such things weren't for her. That part of her had been destroyed before it'd had a chance to blossom. She'd always looked at men only for their potential as allies or as rivals in warfare. She'd been interested in their skill with weapons, not with kisses. How they held their swords was more important than what their embraces would be like.

Her breath came shallow and her skin heated as though she sat in the sauna herself. With him.

She drew back, away from the door. This couldn't be. She wanted nothing to do with him. He was too male. Too dangerous. And it was not the type of danger she'd faced when the pirates had attacked their ship in the Baltic when they were sailing to Birka last year. Then, all her years of training had come into play and she'd slain two of them while Magnus and Leif had dispatched the rest.

No, this was very different. Far more threatening to everything she was. Shaking, she eased the door closed, needing to put distance between them. She would bathe later, once Eirik was in the longhouse.

Her trembling made her hand slip and the door banged against the frame. Her heart faltered. He must have heard it. She ran to the entrance. If she could get out fast, he might never know who had been there. But just as she reached the door, he grabbed her from behind and spun her around. He caught her wrists in his hands and pressed them to either side of her head against the wall. Trapping her.

"Thought to do a little spying?" He grinned, his eyes alight with laughter.

His body leaned against hers, caging her in.

She tried to find her voice as she turned her arms to twist free. "I only wanted to bathe. I'll come back later, when you're done." The night closed in, but she fought the darkness. She couldn't weaken, couldn't panic. Fear was the mind-slayer.

His hands tightened as he chuckled. "Perhaps you need to pay a small fee to leave here. A tiny kiss."

She shook her head, closing her eyes. She couldn't look, couldn't see.

Brown eyes, hard and cold, froze in her memory, and she stilled. Rough hands held her captive. The scent of the smoke and the heat of the steam rolled through her. The pulse of blood in her head grew louder and louder, until crimson covered everything. Everywhere. Pouring over her as she screamed and screamed . . .

Time. Just. Stopped.

Asa's eyes went blank. One moment, he'd thought only to tease her a bit, maybe try a playful, fleeting kiss as payment for her curiosity, and the next she turned white, staring into nothingness. He'd seen that look before, on men who had seen too much blood, too much death on the battlefields. Their minds had retreated into themselves. Some never came back.

"Asa?" He let go of her wrists and cupped her face in his hands. "Asa, it's all right. Tell me where you are."

She cried out and sank to the floor, crouching there, her hands on her throat. He grabbed his fur cloak, threw it around himself, and fastened it at his right shoulder. He knelt in front of her, not touching her. Should he get Magnus? He didn't want to leave her like this, as though she didn't even see this world any longer. He wouldn't leave her alone to face whatever shadows haunted her.

Sometimes, when Silvi couldn't come out of her visions, she seemed to see another world, like Asa did now. But Asa wasn't having a vision. Was she reliving the past, seeing something so horrible it still held her in its grip?

"Asa, what do you see? What do you fear?"

She curled even further into herself and her eyes filled. "Magnus. Oh gods, Magnus. Why did you do this?"

He drew back, his jaw tightening. Had her brother done something to her? When Magnus had heard what the runes told him, he'd seemed to regret something in his past. And yet, they seemed so close. Still, sometimes it could be that way, even with an abuser.

"He's dead, isn't he? Magnus is dead and it's because of me."

Relief flooded into him, his muscles unknotting. If Magnus had been injured in the past, as close as they were, it would have horrified her. "Asa, Magnus is fine. He's alive. He waits for you in the longhouse. You have to come back now, so you can join him there."

She nodded, tears slipping down her face. He reached out to wipe them away, but she pulled back and focused on him for the first time. She glanced at his bare right arm. He had only his cloak on, and it was designed to fasten on that side, leaving his sword arm unencumbered for fighting. She would be able to see that he was naked.

He pulled it around him and held out his hand to her. "Let me help you up."

She didn't take his hand. Rising, she wrapped her cloak around herself. "I'm sorry to have disturbed you. I'll leave and you can finish."

"I'm finished now." He stepped back to give her room. The last thing he wanted was to make her feel threatened. "Just give me a moment to dress and you can have the sauna."

Gathering herself with a visible effort, she raised the barrier between them again, becoming distant, as always. "I'll wait outside."

When she was gone, he ran a drying cloth through his damp hair and down his body and pulled on his clothes. What could have carved itself so deeply into her mind that the wounds still bled like this?

He strode outside. It was doubtful she had waited around, and had most likely fled back into the house. A short distance off, she stood staring into the trees. His heart lightened.

He approached her, taking care to make noise so she would know he was there. She didn't need another scare. He made his voice pleasant as he reached her side. "Aren't you afraid the trolls will come and steal you away in the night? They do that, you know. They take the most beautiful women to their caves and make them cook for them for all eternity. But then, from what I've heard, if they did that to you, they'd send you back once they tasted your cooking. So I doubt you have much to fear."

She ducked her head and he winced at his tactlessness. He had hurt her feelings. But then she looked up at him and, just for an instant, she smiled.

His mind stopped working. Her smile was a gift, so beautiful and rare, he stood witless, his thoughts slain by its power over him. As he stared into her eyes he was lost; every weapon he held shattered in his hands. He had no shield against this, nor blade, nor ship to escape in.

He didn't want to escape. This had been coming. He'd known it since he first saw her. Now it struck him like one of Thor's bolts, tearing him open, naked and exposed in the storm raging in his soul.

She covered her mouth with her hand, as though she regretted the smile, and looked away, back into the night. "The spirits in the woods have never harmed me. Perhaps it's because I don't fear them.

I've found that what I see in the day poses a far greater threat than anything I can imagine in the dark."

He needed to touch her, to know that this was real. But when he lifted his hand, she shied away from him. What could have made her this way? If he asked, it might drive her back into the horror lurking in her mind. He wouldn't risk reopening that wound.

"Forgive me," he said. "I've been too forward. Is there someone else you favor? I don't want to step where I'm not welcome."

She shook her head. "Where would I find a man who would want me for my strength? For who I must be? They want me because I'm the sister of a jarl. To bear children, to run a household, for the dowry I bring. I'm not meant for that. I've chosen to be a shieldmaiden instead."

"I've sailed with several of them, and they love as does any other woman. Even they sometimes marry."

"If a man is brave enough."

"I think it would be well worth the risk." If he didn't part from her now, he wouldn't be able to resist her. "It's cold out here. You still need your bath."

"Yes, and you still need to read the runes. Estrid has been bragging all day that you chose to read for her first."

Only so he could get rid of her the soonest. "So I did."

"Besides, you're the one standing out here in the snow, with wet hair."

He laughed. "Sometime I'll tell you of the days I've spent on the North Sea, with waves washing over the sides of the longship. The water froze our hair solid. I think I can survive this threat."

The corners of her mouth tilted up. "You got what you deserved if you sailed in the cold time of year. I've been on the North Sea, but in the summer. We sailed one year to Hedeby in the land of the Danes and had to skirt it into the Kattegat. We were in one of our *knörrs*, our merchant ships, so we just lumbered along. Still, it was wonderful to be out there on the seas. I loved it. But to be in a sleek, powerful longship, slicing through the waters . . ." She fell silent, looking up at the stars.

If Thor had come and brained him with his hammer, he wouldn't have been more shield-struck. A woman of her strength and beauty, wielding a sword and loving the sea? He needed to find his wits wherever he'd left them and go inside before he did something he shouldn't.

"As you said, we both have other things we need to do."

She nodded. "Good night, then."

He watched her go to the sauna and close the door. By the gods, he needed to take care. They all knew him as a rune caster, and while that position would be honored and respected, it was not the same rank as the daughter and sister of a jarl. She could not marry below her station. Magnus would never allow it.

He walked back to the longhouse. Marry? What was he thinking? He didn't have time for this, or for her. He couldn't tip his hand just yet. He might be equal to them in rank, but right now that didn't matter. He had nothing and would continue to have nothing until he regained what was his by right and by birth. If he was victorious, then perhaps . . . If he wasn't, then he would be dead, for nothing short of that would stop him.

Estrid already waited for him at the table where he had read the runes for others on previous nights. He nodded to her and went into his small chamber to get them. When he returned, Leif sat nearby, leaning on the wall with a mug of ale. Eirik didn't need privacy to do a casting, but why would Leif be so interested in Estrid's?

She focused on him, smiling, her eyes dancing. "I've been waiting to see what you'll say to me."

Leif raised an eyebrow, taking another sip of ale. Eirik gave her a quick smile, then closed his eyes to concentrate. The bag in his hands grew warm. He never knew if it was just from his own body heat, or if there was something more to it, but it always heralded a powerful reading.

Still, when he tried to envision the light surrounding him, shadows lingered nearby. They crept up the walls, and hovered over them all. This was not good.

He reached into the bag and stilled his hand over the wood pieces. Energy built on the palm of his hand and he felt for the rune that lay closest to that place. He placed it on the table, not looking at it, and repeated the process. When he completed the pattern, he set the bag aside and turned over any of the pieces that lay face down.

He kept his expression closed, letting no emotion show. His heart faltered. This was a dark, negative casting. What could such a beautiful young woman have within her that would warrant this? He studied the staves, considering what he would say. He could not lie. Each rune had several meanings, and it was part of the innate talent of the caster to know the right choice. He would have to pick the most positive meanings, yet still impart some warning about the influences around her.

He straightened and glanced at her. "The rune in the position of what is happening around you now is Eihwaz." It often indicated death and setting a goal that was unattainable, but he couldn't say that. "It shows an apparent blockage that may be to the good. You should foresee the circumstances of your actions before you do anything. Keep your mind open to change."

Tapping the next rune, he said, "Naudhiz indicates what stands in the way of what you want." Shadows resulting in weakness, misguided action leading to ruin, obsession. No, he couldn't say any of that either. "You should use the shadows that sometimes surround all of us as teachers. It warns of a delay that could inflame passions. You must be patient."

At least the next rune was positive, but joined with the following symbol, it meant she would draw failure to her. He took a deep breath and smiled. "In favor is Dagaz, a very good rune. You have a great change coming in your life, as different as possible from what you know now. But to attain it, you may have to leap into the void."

"The void?" She frowned. "What do you mean?"

"Only that sometimes we must simply trust, without knowing what the outcome will be. We take a leap of faith."

Then Mannaz, reversed. A stranger, and a blockage inside of oneself that one refuses to see. He picked up the carved piece. "This shows an individual who may block some of your plans, but it's only short term. You must look within to release yourself from this. With Naudhiz, it can mean you need to lie low for a time. Again, the runes speak of patience.

"With the last rune, in the place of the long view, you have Elhaz reversed, which shows this to be a time of vulnerability and an offer which should be refused. A time to take care." Also it showed self-deception.

He sat back. "You need to wait out this time and be patient and careful. A great change is coming for you, but it may seem blocked for a time. Just lie low and understand what is within you before you act, and you will succeed in your dreams."

She beamed at him. "And leap into the void."

"In a manner of speaking. But it's more important to use caution and patience first. Remember that."

"I will."

Birgitta waited for her turn, so Estrid had to leave. She ran her hand over his shoulder as she passed him and he suppressed a shudder. As he gathered the runes to put them back in the bag, they were still warm, though they had lain on the table in the cold room for a time.

Leif rose also, draining the rest of his ale. He sauntered away and sat down next to several giggling young women. But he had listened with even more interest than Estrid had. Why? Did Leif feel the same darkness around her that he did?

Before he closed his eyes to start the next casting, he glanced up. The shadows filling the room had fled with her, leaving only the glow of the firelight around them.

He'd picked her first.

First, first, first, first.

Estrid danced through her room, hugging herself. And he said such beautiful things to her, about inflamed passions, transformations, and a great leap into the unknown. But she needed to be careful. They both needed to be careful and wait, to be patient, as he'd said. The others couldn't know, of course. He couldn't speak of how he felt about her in the open, so he spoke in the riddles of the runes. She alone understood. He had seen their love written there. The great leap would be when he took her with him in the spring. And she needed to trust in him. Oh yes. It would be leaping into the unknown, but they would be together then.

She sat down on her bed. He'd warned her that someone would block the way. She'd have to watch for it. No one could stand between them. The others had left her behind and she would never allow it again. Not when she would have his beauty, his strength, and his power all to herself as they roamed the world.

Lying back, she ran her hands over her body, and cupped her breasts, as he would. He'd be so strong, so masterful. He would take what he wanted and she would belong to him. He would revel in her curves, in her woman-shape. Softness, sweetness, gentleness. Not like—

She clenched her fists over her heart. What if Asa was the one who stole him away? Jarl's daughter. Jarl's sister. Weapon-bearer. The high-born. But she was too cold, like an ice queen. What man would want her? Still, one man had, and Asa had taken him, then cast him aside just to spite Estrid.

But now, *she* would be the one doing the taking. And if Asa stood in her way? The runes had said it would be only for a short time and that she must look within herself to put an end to it.

She ran her hands over her body again and closed her eyes. His smile shone down on her like the sun, heating her skin.

Soon. She would start soon.

Chapter Six

Sorrow wrapped around Asa, as heavy as her cloak as she walked through the village. She and their healer woman, Ingeborg, hadn't been able to save old Alv from the fever raging through the household on the outer edge of Thorsfjell. Only the healer and she had entered there, and they were taking a risk doing so. It fell to Ingeborg to help them, and Asa couldn't let the elderly woman work alone. So, against Magnus's wishes, she'd done all she could, though it was in vain. Alv had died, but his younger wife, Hetha, still lived.

They needed more than herbs to save her. In the past, their rune master carved the staves that brought healing to them. But he was dead. She drew a deep, cold breath as she glanced up at the longhouse. Several men stood outside, talking.

The days had become a bit warmer since the blizzard ended. The men had decided to go hunting that day to put fresh meat on the tables. Eirik had mentioned he'd like to go as well, so Magnus had outfitted him with a fine bow and arrows. They were obviously back now, and time was short for Hetha.

Leif had said she needed to speak to Eirik about helping her carve the runes on her dragon, and she'd been putting it off. But this was far more important and she couldn't hesitate any longer.

She'd had a difficult time keeping her eyes from Eirik as he'd prepared to leave that morning. He'd stood in the common room, his sword at his side, the bow in his hand. Power, so primal and male, had rolled off of him as he'd spoken with the other men. Estrid had given him a cup of mead to warm him, and the serving girls had clustered around the doorway to the cooking room, watching him. They were so fresh-faced and innocent. They still had their dreams of husbands and homes of their own to keep them smiling. No doubt, those dreams included Eirik.

All he'd known of her was her swordplay, her lack of feminine skills, and her panic when he'd touched her in the sauna. What had she been thinking when she'd peeked at him? Yes, it was obvious he was a warrior. But what was she going to do with that knowledge— tell Magnus she'd seen Eirik's beautiful, powerful, scarred body naked? *And, oh yes, by the way, brother, he does look like a warrior?*

She winced. And then she'd had one of her recurring memories. She should have been over that years ago. Magnus had ordered the old sauna torn down and a new one put up in its place. Nothing had been the same. Except the scent of the steam and the wood and the sensation of being held, trapped against a man's hard body.

Eirik had moved so fast, he'd caught her off guard. At the feeling of his hands around her wrists, everything had crashed in around her, even though it wasn't the same situation as the one so long ago. But she couldn't stop it.

He must think her mad. Maybe she was. The past had changed her, made her weaker, yet harder. At times, it was all she could do to keep the darkness from engulfing her forever. Only her love for her brothers, and theirs for her, kept her grounded. It was all she would ever have, but it was enough.

Their fates were set. Perhaps hers was to die on the battlefield instead of in childbed. That suited her. Their belief that such things were unalterable made their people the fighters they were, unafraid of any death. Indeed, who would want to die, old and infirm, in bed? It was their greatest horror. For each of them, it would be as the Norns willed.

Something had passed between Eirik and her, though, a shining, enticing link forged in that instant afterward when he had been a steady light for her, a strength she could lean on. That link would have to be broken when he left. He'd made no secret of it that he had been on his way to Trøndelag when he'd become lost in the blizzard. What was so important that he would risk his life for it?

She could never allow that tenuous link between them to grow into anything more. For one link would lead to another, until they formed a chain that would soon wrap itself around her heart.

Asa stepped through the front door to the common room along with a swirl of snow. As she removed her cloak, she glanced at Eirik, her lip between her teeth. Then she raised her head as though preparing for battle and walked toward him. He tilted his head and watched her, keeping his gaze locked on hers. A shadow touched her eyes as she stopped before him. What could she still fear?

"Asa. Will you have some ale? It will warm you."

"No. Thank you." She swallowed and cleared her throat. "You know the runes, how to cast them, how to read them. But do you know the healing runes and how to carve them?"

"Yes. My mother is a healer of some renown. She taught me so I could use their power in my travels."

She sank down on the bench on the opposite side of the table. "There's a fever in a house at the edge of the village. We've already lost the old man who lived there, but his wife still lives. We have tried everything we know, but nothing has worked. Can you carve the proper runes for her? We would forever be in your debt."

"It is I who am obliged to you for letting me overwinter with you. And in such things, there is no debt to me. The power does not come from me, but from the gods. Do you have any small pieces of wood that I could carve them on?"

"Of course." She rose and led him to the weaving room, where her dragon head stood, covered with a cloth. "What do you need?"

She knelt at a pile of wood and he joined her. On a low shelf nearby, stood dozens of small carvings. She'd created all manner of animals, ships, dolls, boxes, utensils, and other trinkets. The bowls, spoons, and cups showed her talent. They were intricate, so beautiful, it near took his breath away.

She followed his gaze. "I do those through the year to give to the children of the village at Jul time. We also sell them at the markets in the summer. It keeps me busy."

"No wonder your work is so sought after. They're magnificent."

She blushed and the color only enhanced her beauty. "I enjoy the work and it brings much joy to the children and much gold to the coffers."

A woman of such strength—she wielded a sword against pirates on the seas—yet of such imagination and delicacy as to make these things of beauty. He almost reached out to touch her as she sorted through the wood, but kept his hand where it was.

"Will these do? They're oak and should hold your carvings well enough." She poured several small, round wood pieces into his hands, and for a moment, she so filled his senses, he had to remember why he needed them.

"They'll be fine." They stood, and for the first time in his life he was tongue-tied with a woman. She stared up at him. He avoided her gaze and looked instead at her worktable. "I'll need to borrow one of your carving tools, if I could. Just the knife should be fine. I'll make two cuts for each line, meeting in the center. It will be simple. Not like chiseling stone for rune markers."

"Have you made many rune stones?" She handed him her carving knife. "Our old rune master was too weak to carve them, so we never had any for memorials for our dead."

"Not even for your father?" Shock spread through him. So far-traveling a man as he had been should be remembered. Word-fame was everything to the Norse people.

"No." Her voice caught and she cleared her throat. "We have nothing to mark his life except our memories of him." She removed the woven fabric from the dragon's head. She hadn't worked on much more of it and the sides of the neck were still blank. Biting her lip, she ran her hand along its curves. Her movements were soft, caressing, her touch light, and he couldn't take his eyes off her fingers. What else could she do with those talented hands?

He stifled a groan. "I'll take these out to one of the tables and begin my work."

"Wait." She didn't look at him, but her hand stilled. "There's something I need to ask you as a rune caster. A favor."

He raised an eyebrow and waited.

She drew a deep breath, as though gathering her courage. "Our master knew the right symbols to carve on my dragons. Every year, he studied the signs, and the gods showed him the ones to use for that year. But he died last summer and I don't know what to do. I could make scales here on the neck. In fact, I tried designing them. You can see the charcoal marks I made. It didn't work. I've even dreamed of it, but my dreams didn't show me the right runes. Only that they must be here. The dragon has told me so."

She looked up at him and spoke in a headlong, breathless voice, as though she tried to say it all before she lost her nerve. "I can't use the runes I have in the past. They might not be the right ones. Or I might not carve them correctly. I know that each of the lines must be done in a certain direction. And I'm unable to channel the power like a rune master can. I'm afraid of making a mistake that would bring disaster down on us. And then there are the colors I should use."

Why would she be hesitant to ask him such a thing? He put a finger on her lips, silencing her. "I'd be honored to help you."

She didn't pull back, allowing him to keep his finger there as she lowered her gaze. He moved his hand until he brushed her jawline, then he drew back, tightening his will. "I'll do a reading for it. But I must wait until after Alv has been released to the afterlife, for he is still here and I don't know what effect that will have on the runes. Once the *sjaund* is over, I can do a casting and we can begin working on it. You'll need to design the runes so they fit the space after I show you the proper ones. By the time that's done, we should be ready to start carving."

Her shoulders relaxing, she nodded. "My thanks. It's so important to all of us."

Before he did something even more foolish than allowing his thoughts to run rampant, he left and sat down at one of the tables in the common room. He turned the wood pieces over in his hands to get the feel for them, to understand exactly which runes they called for. But the healing symbols he needed didn't form in his thoughts. Instead, runic lines tumbled through his mind, chiseled into stone to tell their tale through the ages. The branches of the World Tree, Yggdrasil, wound through them as they circled it.

Why wouldn't they speak to him as he wanted them to? He needed only simple pieces to slip beneath the woman's pillow and direct the healing powers to her. Afterward, he would burn them and release their magic as a tiny sacrifice to the gods as thanks. Runes were only carved into stone to last as a memorial.

The idea hit him like a sword stroke. They were speaking to him, but they were telling him what *they* wanted him to do, what he needed to do to discharge his debt. He bowed his head, hiding his smile. It was perfect.

The certainty of it spread through him. This would be his masterwork, a tribute to a fine man who had raised his sons and his daughter to be filled with honor and selflessness.

He looked up as Leif and several other men came in, boasting of the deer they'd brought down that day. The men had been successful in their hunt and they would all eat well for it. He'd hunt also in the days to come, but it wouldn't be for meat. It would be for something far more lasting than that. It would ease, not the body, but the heart and the soul of a family. For all time.

"We may have a problem." Magnus eyed Eirik as he sat at a table, carving small pieces of wood. Leif had just sat down to quench his thirst with a mug of beer after the hunt, and Magnus had joined him.

"And that's any different from usual?" Leif took a large swallow.

Magnus kept his voice low. "This might be serious."

"Let me know when you find out if it is or not. I wouldn't want to waste my time getting upset unless it's necessary. That's your re-sponsibility, and you do it so well." He grinned into his beer before he took another swig.

"Leif." He loved his brother, but there were times . . .

Leif set down his mug. "What is it?"

"I came in a few minutes ago and I could see into the weaving room. Eirik and Asa were together."

"You're right. That could bring down the entire house." Leif's voice was wry and he shrugged. "She did want me to speak to him about helping her with the runes. Maybe she finally found the courage to approach him about it."

Magnus shot him a glare. "He had his finger on her lips. And she didn't pull away. She allowed it."

Leif raised his brows. "That just might bring the house down. From shock."

"I don't like it. He doesn't have the rank, or the wealth."

"Do we know that for certain?" Leif glanced behind him at Eirik. "All we know is the little bit he volunteered when he first came here. It's not much to go on. I've been spending time with him, talking, drinking, playing *tafl*. He's very good at it, by the by. He should play with Asa." He winced. "Forget I said that. Anyhow, I've found him to be well educated, far-traveled, and easy to get along with. He does have a streak of something dark running in him, though. But then, don't we all? That's why the world fears us. He would make a good raider, if he isn't one already."

Magnus drummed his fingers on the table. Leif might be light of heart, but he was a keen observer of people. While it seemed nothing penetrated his mind too deeply, he was always watching, assessing. His humor was the way he handled the world, but he knew how it worked. Magnus always listened to him, to see what lay beneath the jests. And even those sometimes annoying statements could strike right to the heart of the matter.

He closed his fists. "We can't let him get too close to her. There's no knowing what further damage that would do."

"There's always a risk where love is concerned."

Magnus grimaced. "Love. This is our sister we're talking about. Not some starry-eyed girl. She can't go off with a low-ranked rune caster who wanders from land to land with nothing to offer her but the road they walk on."

"She was a starry-eyed girl once. But that was torn from her." He faced Magnus and leaned forward, his hands around the mug on the table between them. "Eirik was touching her, and not only did she not try to gut him, though she had a lot of sharp instruments nearby, but she didn't stop him either. What if he, whoever he is, is the only man who can awaken her? Shall we deny her this chance? Maybe it will come to nothing. And if he hurts her in any way, we can always slay him. But should we discount him out of hand until we find out more about him?" He drank down his beer and wiped his mouth. Then he chuckled.

"Perhaps he's actually a misplaced jarl who's wealthy and power-ful. Isn't that how the story should go?"

"Should I have any idea what you're talking about?" Magnus sighed in exasperation.

"Gods, I hope not. That would be disturbing."

"And then there's the tiny detail about his having killed his wife. By his own admission."

"When he was fevered. Listen, Magnus, I'm not saying let them go for a romp in Asa's bed. Not yet, anyhow. But I think we need to watch and wait. It's going to be a long winter and you never know what's going to happen." He nodded to a table across the room. "And Estrid has her sights set on him as well. This might be interesting, and the gods know there's not much else to do during the winter but stare at each other."

Estrid sat at a table with several other women. They were all sewing, but her work lay in her lap, forgotten. She had her chin on her hand and her eyes on Eirik.

"She likely sees him as a way out of here," Magnus said. "Maybe we should encourage a relationship between them. When he leaves in the late winter, she would go with him and Asa would remain here. We would win twice."

"What has Eirik done that you would saddle him with such a burden?" Leif frowned into his empty mug as though it offended him. "I wouldn't do so to my worst enemy. Then again, maybe I would. She'd kill him and save me the trouble."

"You have no enemies, Leif."

"True. Everyone loves me. I'll have to get some enemies then, so I can foist Estrid on them." He cocked his head to one side. "Just how *do* you go about making enemies, Magnus?"

"Leif." Sometimes his brother made him want to pound his head on the table. Of course, he could always pound Leif's head on the table. Much better.

Leif rose, holding his mug. "Don't condemn Eirik to that fate. I rather enjoy his company. Something dark lies within him, as I said. I wouldn't want to get on the wrong side of it. I would, however, want to fight at his side, if it came to it. Now, all this depressing talk is thirsty work. I think that pretty little serving girl is in the brewing room. I'll just have to persuade her to, oh, fill my mug." He winked and left.

Magnus sighed. What should have been a quiet winter had started off in a bad way. A fever was raging just outside of the village. The band of outcasts was robbing farmsteads, and the blizzard had brought a stranger to live among them. Perhaps he shouldn't have been so quick to offer Eirik shelter. But what choice did he have? It was the way of their people that they would take in any traveler, especially during the brutal winter in the *fjells*.

And what if the rune caster truly was the one for Asa? He had long ago accepted that he could never force her to marry, no matter how politically advantageous it might be. His own guilt about what had happened to her froze him when it came to decisions about her. If his father had lived, she never would have been hurt. But Magnus had failed her.

He shook his head. What was past was past. Now, everything might have changed. What if he didn't need to persuade her to marry? What if she wanted to wed a man of her own choosing? He had political connections enough. He'd always thought that being with a man would make her miserable, frightened, and angry. Not to mention it might be dangerous for the man, her talent for weapons. What if he kept her from the one man she could love? Might that not be just as destructive to her?

Though the runes had warned him that, through his inaction, he'd cause harm to someone he loved, he'd back off and watch throughout the winter. He'd keep a very close eye on the situation between Eirik and Asa. He wouldn't interfere. For now. Asa was a woman grown, not a young girl. And she was a shieldmaiden. She could handle herself, for he and Leif had given her that.

All he wanted was a peaceful winter to think about where he would trade in the spring. There was always the East, where his father had traveled. Where the sun was warm, the women exotic, and the silver lay in piles on the tables of the merchants. He smiled to himself. Eirik had mentioned that the women glittered like gold—

"Magnus."

He looked up, blinking that particular vision from his mind. Asa stood in front of him, pain in her eyes. "What's wrong, Asa?"

"We've lost Alv. He died from the fever and now Hetha is ill."

He closed his eyes.

So much for his brief moment of dreaming.

The pillar of smoke from the pyre rose heavy and thick over the trees. Eirik tilted his head back to watch it flow into the low clouds. It elevated Alv to the other worlds where he would dwell. It was a fitting ceremony for him, and his ancestors would be pleased.

Asa stood with her brothers. She had dressed as befitted the sister of a jarl, with a fine wool gown, hemmed with colorful ribbons and fastened at the shoulders with two gold brooches. Her cloak was of white fur, closed with another intricate gold brooch. A string of amber and rock crystal, hung with silver charms and coins, dangled between the brooches on her gown. Her hair hung free, showing her unmarried state, and it shone like a sunset over the western sea. Falling snow settled on it, diamonds nestled in fire.

She stood, quiet and reserved, as they all did. Her eyes shone a bit too bright, as though she was on the verge of tears. But she would never show her grief. No one would.

As the flames died down, the people walked away toward the long-house. Eirik stayed behind, listening to the crackling of the pyre. He had not been able to attend the funeral for his father, and he needed to remember to keep himself from becoming too complacent. The fire of revenge must continue to burn in him, strong and bloody. The thought of his mother's and sister's suffering was ever in his mind, fanning the blaze.

They'd eat the deer the men had hunted the previous day, but the feast for the dead wouldn't take place for another week. It involved a great deal of drinking and marked the true end of life. He had never drunk to his father's life. After he returned home and regained his birthright, he would remedy that. He'd host a *sjaund* unlike his people had ever witnessed.

First, he had to honor another man. He went into the warm stables. His horse nickered to him and he entered the stall and stroked his thick neck. The gelding nuzzled at him, looking for the carrot he often brought.

"I don't have anything right now." He chuckled as the horse nipped his cloak. He was hardly lacking for food, for there was a large pile of hay in the corner. "But I'll get something for you at the feast this day." He ruffled his mane, stepped back out of the stall, and walked to the back where the stableboys often sat. They had a small brazier there and the heat from it, combined with that of the horses, cows, sheep, and other livestock, made the stable warmer than the longhouse was.

"Sjurd?"

The young brown-haired man rose with an easy smile and came over to him. "Yes, rune caster." He glanced back at the others, then said in a low voice, "I found a place that may have what you're looking for. And there's a small storage shed out behind the stables where you can work without anyone knowing."

Eirik smiled. He'd spoken with Sjurd many times about his horse, and he was a good man. He'd taken him into his confidence about his plans, for he would need help to implement them. He'd also promised him a gold coin for his silence.

"Then tomorrow we can go?"

"Yes, rune caster. As soon as I've finished my chores. It'll be daylight by then."

"Excellent. I'll be here."

He walked to the longhouse. The snow fell harder and he bent his head against it, so he didn't see Estrid until he almost ran into her. He'd wanted to avoid her. She'd watched him in the past days, when he was playing *tafl* with Leif, or just speaking with the other men in the common room. Her attention on him appeared to sharpen after he'd read her runes, though he couldn't remember saying anything encouraging.

"You didn't come back right away, so I wanted to be certain you hadn't become lost in the falling snow." She gazed up at him, moistening her lips.

Coldness lay in her blue eyes, like a layer of ice over the water of a still lake. Her beauty left him untouched, sending a chill into his heart. It was obvious she wanted to find him here by himself. The snow wasn't falling so hard he couldn't see the longhouse a short distance away. And if he could see it, anyone there could see them, as well.

He needed to get her back to the others, but he couldn't be impolite. "Then we'll both head back there now. We wouldn't want to be late to the meal."

She smiled and tried to take his arm. But he tucked her hand back under her cloak and pulled it around her.

"It's too cold out here. Stay warm inside your cloak. You wouldn't want to catch the fever."

"That's thoughtful of you." She walked close beside him, leaning against him when she could. "The ground is slippery and you're so solid and strong."

He kept himself from rolling his eyes and was careful to disengage himself from her by opening the door so she could enter before him. Once they were inside, he nodded to her and squeezed himself onto a bench at an occupied table so she couldn't sit next to him.

He'd had women chase after him before, but he could always leave in a ship and sail on to their next stop. Although there was that girl in Gotland . . .

That was long in the past. And he might be stuck here for the winter, but he was hardly defenseless. If it came to it, he would have to let Estrid down gently. Unease curled through his mind. Was this his gut warning him? It had saved his life more than once. But that was on the battlefield. What harm could a young, pampered woman do to him?

He thanked the serving girl who set a platter of venison in front of him, and speared a slice with his knife. That night, he'd think on the runes for Asa's dragon. Then, he would help her draw and carve them. They'd be very close then, his hand on hers, whispering the right words, showing her just how to carve them. Perhaps if Estrid saw that, it would dissuade her from her pursuit. That way, he wouldn't have to let her down. Her pride should keep her away.

He didn't want to give Asa the wrong idea, though. And yet, she didn't seem to harbor any fantasies where life was concerned. She saw clearly.

The image of Asa's warm brown eyes melted the lingering ice around his heart.

"Have any of the men from the village been up this way?"

Eirik studied the footprints. The snow had stopped during the night, so these could have been made any time since then. But he didn't like how close they were to the holding.

Sjurd knelt beside him and touched the prints. "No, not since the fall when we gathered the animals from the slopes for the winter. The animals we don't slaughter for meat stay in the barns until the grass returns. There would be no reason for anyone to be up here now. Except for us."

Eirik smiled as Sjurd stood. "And I doubt anyone else would be here looking for a stone for carving. You were right. These are fine."

A cliff on the side of the mountain was exposed and part of it had come down. Several large, flat stones lay on the ground. He could use any of them. He loosened his sword in its sheath. The outcasts weren't often bold enough to come this close to a jarl's house, but if they were desperate enough for food, they might risk it.

He and Sjurd walked through the stones until one caught his eye. It was half his height, about as wide as his arm was long, and flat on one side. Perfect. Perhaps the gods were smiling on him for doing this and had guided him to this place.

That, and Sjurd. He was proving very helpful and resourceful, and perhaps he knew of tools he could use. Many farms had hammers and chisels for other purposes. If he asked Asa for some of her tools, she'd have to know why. And most of her tools were iron. The metal would clash with the power of the runes. Though it was softer, a copper chisel would be best.

He needed to figure out a way to get the stone down the slope and into the small storage shed. Once it was there, he'd work on it whenever he could, in secret. Magnus had a sled. If he could use it, and his own horse, it just might work. Between Sjurd and him, they could lever it up onto the sled.

The hair on the back of his neck rose. Keeping his head still, he scanned the area around them. Nothing moved, but they were being watched.

"I have an idea of how to get this stone down to the holding," he said. "Let's head back." He didn't want to alarm Sjurd. The young man likely hadn't had a chance to fight much yet, living as he did with merchants. Eirik could hold his own, especially against outcasts, but if he had to protect Sjurd also, it could get dangerous.

Once they returned to the village, Eirik studied the slopes behind them. Perhaps the outcasts often came this close and it was nothing out of the ordinary. He would let Magnus know. But what could he tell him about why he'd been up there? The runes. He'd never lie about any aspect of them, but he could say it had to do with them. No one would question him further, having too much respect for his art. His mother had been right in thinking his talent would be to his advantage.

Still, he'd watch for the outcasts. He turned his back to the slopes and walked toward the longhouse. They'd dispersed Alv's essence into the afterlife. The magic in this place could flow unhindered now. He had runes to search for this night, runes powerful enough to protect a dragon.

Chapter Seven

"These are the symbols I envisioned for your carving."
Eirik handed Asa a piece of wood with three staves drawn in charcoal on it. She settled on her bench beside the dragon and studied them.

"I know this one. I've used it several times before."

"That's Elhaz. It's a strong protection rune."

He sat down beside her and his clean scent washed over her. In the past few days, she hadn't seen him much. She'd wondered if he'd forgotten about her request. Or that perhaps he hadn't wanted to do it and had been avoiding her.

Now he sat beside her, his warmth sinking into her, his nearness opening an awareness in her body. This might not be such a good idea after all. But she had to finish the carving. Too many people depended on it to bring gold to the village, and she couldn't let Magnus down just because she found Eirik's presence disturbing. And enticing.

The dragon wanted the runes. Her dreams hadn't subsided, so she would have to ignore the weakness in her legs that Eirik caused. His wild, male scent. His deep, rich voice . . .

"See?" He took her hand and placed his against it, palm to palm. His hand dwarfed hers. Then he spread his fingers wide, taking hers with them. "Elhaz looks like a hand splayed out for protection. That's how you can remember it. The other runes are Thurisaz and Eihwaz, also powerful shielding runes. Alone, they have their own meanings." He moved his fingers and curled them down between hers. "But together, they become something more, no longer separate, but joined into one, their destinies intertwined."

He let their hands slide apart and her stomach tightened at the feel of his skin against hers.

"My vision showed me that these are the symbols your dragon desires."

She gave him a quick glance at the last word. His eyes were deepest blue, but they held a touch of humor, as though he knew that what he said would make her blush. It did. And she melted a little more.

Gathering herself, she studied the runes and the dragon's neck. They would fit. It seemed as though he had chosen them to flow with the lines of the scales and the interlaced patterns that would frame them. Or, perhaps, the dragon had chosen them. She would have to match them on both sides, measuring and drawing them the same way.

"Does it matter how I draw them initially with the coal?" She ran her finger over the neck where the first rune would be. "I might have to start over several times to fit them just so."

"It's the carving that brings the true power. And the painting of them with the proper colors. Still, I'll watch how you draw them to be certain they're correct. There's still some power involved."

She nodded and picked up a piece of charred wood she'd collected from the longhearth. Concentrating on the area, she brought the image of the rune into her mind, matching it to the shading in the wood. Often, the grain itself showed her the way to carve, its colors shading the pattern.

Eirik placed his hand on her shoulder and, even through the layers of clothing, his touch made her skin tingle. He whispered soft words, as if speaking to a lover in the night. They were ancient words, their rhythm that of the skalds of long ago. Though she couldn't hear what he said, the sounds wove through her. The dragon's eye seemed to shift, gazing back at them.

She drew a sharp breath. It was there. Thurisaz. The shape of the rune already displayed itself in the grain. She traced it with the blackened wood.

"Do you see it?" She darkened the symbol again as the feeling grew more certain.

"Yes." His voice was low, right beside her, but she concentrated on the image beneath her hand. "The dragon already knows. The stave lies in its heart and it only waited for your touch to set it free."

"And your knowledge to open the way." She moved to the area below it. The power of creation that flowed in her broke loose, like a chunk of ice breaking away from a glacier into a raging sea. It always flowed when she carved, but it was usually gentle, like a stream. This was different. It cascaded through her, cold and pure, and she drank it in.

His hand tightened on her shoulder and she leaned into it. Elhaz. Her strokes were sure and sweeping this time. She followed what had grown into the wood centuries ago. The ancient maple had developed from the time it was a seed, just so, for this moment. She never glanced back at the symbols he had drawn for her. She knew them already. They burned in her as though dragon fire had scorched them into her soul.

"Yes, that's right. Now—"

"Eihwaz." She allowed the rune to curve, just a bit, to match the lower turn of the neck. It might not be correct, for the lines should always be straight. But it felt right and Eirik didn't stop her. She started drawing lines above and below the runes, as was often done, but then she hesitated.

"What is the dragon telling you, Asa?" He caressed her shoulder and leaned closer, his breath moving her hair. "What should you do now to finish the design? Listen."

She closed her eyes, absorbing the magic emanating from him. The answer came from deep within her, with a power that could have come only from the spirit of the dragon—or the runes themselves. Why would they speak to her when they had him to channel their power? And yet, she would not ignore their wisdom. "There should be no lines to separate the runes from the scales. They should all flow together."

"Yes."

Drawing in the scales, she tapered them to join with the staves into one pattern, forever sealing them with the essence of the dragon. She added to the interlaced animals and vines on the front of the neck to merge with the rest of the design.

When she leaned back to study her work, Eirik's hand dropped away. The energy running through her receded. She took a deep breath. What had happened? She'd never before rendered a design with such precision, not without having to try several times before getting it right. This was the most intricate drawing she'd done and yet it had flowed without effort or flaw.

Working with the old master had never been like this. Before, the power hadn't flowed through her, the images of the runes hadn't burned in her mind. His touch hadn't weakened yet strengthened her, like Eirik's had.

"Something happened just now." He brushed back a lock of her hair.

She didn't pull away. His eyes were so deep, so beautiful with the knowledge and power he carried. His was the way of the night. The ancient magic he'd touched her with was alien to her. She was a warrior and her world was one of steel and the light of day. For her, there would be no soft words whispered in the night. In more ways than one.

A gasp came from the door and she broke his gaze, looking toward it. But no one was there. It had likely been one of the women who'd seen them and didn't want to interrupt.

She shook her head to clear it and to deny what he'd said. "Just some dragon magic, I think, or the spirit of the tree. It happens sometimes when I carve. It must happen to you when you cast the runes."

He watched her as she rose and moved over to the other side. "I think there are talents and abilities in you that you haven't allowed yourself to experience. Hidden things."

She dropped the piece of coal and picked it up with a shaking hand. Her stomach knotted. "I don't know what you mean." Just how much could he feel? When the power had flowed through them both, had he seen the shadows that lay within her? The runes were strong. And dangerous. She would have to be careful and guard against their power, and his.

He stayed until she finished replicating the image on the other side, but he didn't say anything more, or touch her again. He looked at it when she finished and nodded at her. After he left, she stared at the design. The runes were correct, the scales perfectly drawn, the interlacing beautiful and complex. It was an exact replica of the other side.

And yet, without his touch, without his strength flowing through her, they were only black lines drawn on dry, dead wood.

"The rune caster. I saw you in here with him yesterday."

Asa chipped away a small piece of wood and didn't look at Estrid. "Oh?" The sound she'd heard at the door must have been her cousin then. No matter. They'd done nothing wrong.

"His touch holds much magic, does it not?" Estrid sighed.

The knife almost slipped as her heart sank, but she caught the movement before it did any damage. "I wouldn't know, Estrid. That's your area of expertise."

Her cousin's eyes narrowed, but she only smiled. "He's the experienced one. He's already visited me and half the girls here."

Asa's fingers tightened around the handle as her heart jumped. Just then, the outer door slammed open and loud voices rang through the longhouse. Taking her carving knife with her, Asa brushed past Estrid and went into the common room. A farmer stood in the midst of several men, shouting about his livestock.

Magnus strode into the group, Leif following. "Calm down. Tell me what happened," Magnus said.

"Jarl, those outcasts came and took three of my sheep and two young pigs. I slaughtered almost all I had in the fall and these were the ones I kept back to breed in the spring. They came in the day, bold as you like, and threatened me if I tried to stop them. Now I have little left."

Magnus nodded. "You and your family won't go hungry. I swear it to you. Leif, send for the warriors who went to their own homes for the winter. We can't let this stand. The outcasts are becoming bolder and more dangerous. We'll slay them before this goes any further."

"It'll take some time to travel to so many homesteads."

"Then we'd best begin now. No one is to go alone. Several men will travel together and return here as soon as possible."

Leif gathered the men, assigning them into groups.

Magnus took Asa aside. "Eirik told me the day after the funeral that he'd seen fresh footprints in the meadows above here. None of our people would be up there this time of year." He looked around the hall. "Come to think of it, where is he?"

"I haven't seen him much lately, except yesterday when he helped me with the runes for the dragon."

Magnus frowned. "I don't like that. The outcasts have never been this bold before. Since he arrived, they've change tactics. He's been gone a great deal these past few days. Suddenly they begin taking more livestock, and in the light of day."

Asa glanced toward the door to the weaving room. Eirik couldn't be involved. Not a man with such magic in his soul. She would know. Or would she? She'd been wrong years ago about another man. And with what Estrid had insinuated, she could be wrong again.

"He appears to be a man of honor, Magnus. Surely the runes wouldn't speak to one who is a common thief."

"How do we know that? The outcasts have nothing to lose. They can never return to society, for they have committed the unspeakable. Rape. Slaying a kinsman. Or a wife. I've often wondered at the wisdom of turning such men loose in the countryside, where they become desperate."

He set his hand on her arm. "I want you to be careful, Asa. None of the women are to go outside the village until we track down these men."

"The *fjells* are vast. How can you find them all?"

"Perhaps we won't need to. If we kill several of them, it will send a message and they'll back off. If someone is instigating this, he'll find out we're not just isolated farmers and merchants here. He'll have no doubt that we can fight for what is ours, both on the seas and in the mountains." He gripped the hilt of his seax. "Whoever he might be."

Asa stepped out of her room dressed in her long leather tunic and leggings, her sword at her side. Over the past few days, Magnus's warriors had trickled in from their homes in answer to his call. They ate and slept wherever they could, on the tables, benches, and even the floor. Fights had broken out over mugs of ale and who would sleep closest to the longhearth.

It hadn't been easy. These were hard men. They knew only fighting and drinking and—well, the serving girls nearly found out what else they knew. Magnus had forbidden any of the men from taking an unwilling girl, but still, there had been several near rapes.

She did what she could to protect the girls. None of the men dared touch her, or disrespect her rank and her abilities. She kept her seax on her at all times, the long knife's sheath hanging below her belt. At night, her sword stood close at hand near her bed. Other women and children who lived in the hall had gone to stay at homes in the village. It was safer that way.

So she was relieved on the morning Magnus declared they would begin searching for the outcasts. The hunt would help vent some of the tensions. That night, they would hold the *sjaund*, the funeral ale for Alv, and the men could drink themselves into a stupor. Then, perhaps, there would be a night of peace.

She winced. Or it might be worse. If only she could just shut herself in her room until morning. But she needed to be there along with her brothers to honor Alv. Only after they had drunk the ale would Alv's life truly be over.

Several other men had arrived during the night, and her heart sank at the sound of a loud voice. Hjellmar. He'd never been able to tolerate her being a shieldmaiden. To him, women had one purpose, perhaps two.

He stood across the room, bristling with weapons, his unkempt hair hanging down his back. Hjellmar was nothing but a brawler, uncaring of anything else. Magnus kept him on because he was a good warrior in battle, but he hadn't invited him into the longhouse to stay for any length of time. Until now.

Magnus would see to it that she wasn't near him for very long. She would search in a different group with one of her brothers. Once she told them she intended to go.

Eirik stood near the hearth talking to Leif. He was dressed for battle in an expensive leather tunic. It was no doubt his own, covered by metal links sewn onto it. His fine sword hung at his side and he'd braided back the front of his long hair. He was magnificent.

All men knew something of fighting. Even a rune caster would know how to defend himself in his travels. And yet, his golden skin had shown the scars of warfare and he was hardened and strong. His arms were sculpted, his body as sleek as any blade.

"Asa? What are you doing?" Magnus, thankfully, interrupted that path of thinking.

She faced him as the room quieted. "Since I have my sword, I thought it would be obvious."

"You are not going out there with us." He spoke low, but his powerful voice carried.

"I am what you made me. A shieldmaiden. This is what I do, the same as any of you."

"Not the same." He crossed his arms.

"The same." She met his angry gaze. "Would you deny me my word-fame? You trained me to fight."

"To defend yourself."

"So I am. Along with this village and its people. Would you do any less?"

"I do this so that you and the others may live long lives."

"And die old and wrinkled and toothless in my bed. I fear that as much as any of you, Magnus." She softened her voice. "I'll always do as you ask, for you're my brother and my jarl. The Norns decree the moment we each will die, no matter where we are. If it is my time, then I'll pass to the next life whether I'm here or in battle. Don't deny me my chance to sit with Freya in her hall at Folkvang while you drink and fight in Valhalla. She takes half the warriors as well for her hall after each battle, so we may be together there even after we die. I don't want her to ask me where my sword is and why I died alone while others fought."

He regarded her for several moments, his jaw clenched. Then he gave her one short nod. "You stay with Leif or me at all times. And you do as we say."

"Thank you." She wouldn't show him any sign of sisterly affection now in front of the men, but he knew how she felt. She picked up her own shield from a table at the center of the room and tested its weight.

"You should obey your brother and listen to his wisdom." Hjellmar stood behind her and her muscles tensed. "A woman doesn't understand these things. The only time they understand anything at all is when they're on their backs. Even then, it doesn't matter what they think."

One or two of the men chuckled, but most stayed silent. Her chest tightened and the blood pounded in her ears. There was only one thing he would understand. She chose an axe from the table and pivoted, slamming the shield into him and throwing him off balance. Hooking the beard of the axe behind his leg, she yanked him off his feet. He fell backward, flailing. She dropped the axe and had the tip of her sword at his throat before he hit the ground.

The room darkened around her until she saw only him. He lay frozen, his hands up, eyes wide. Her neck throbbed with her heartbeat and his fast breathing filled her head.

"What were you saying about being on one's back, Hjellmar? I'm guessing you're thinking very, very clearly now, aren't you?" She gripped her sword hilt harder in spite of the gold wire wrapped around it. The discomfort anchored her. "I am the sister of your jarl. You will respect me, if not in your thoughts, then in your words."

He nodded, but still she couldn't move. The darkness closed in, the welcome darkness, where no one would ever see her pain, her shame.

"Asa, I think you've made your point. Don't put it in his throat." Leif's words penetrated the shadows surrounding her. "He's an idiot, yes. But we need numbers here."

The humor that was always in his voice broke through her anger and she stepped back. Hjellmar rose, eyeing her, his face red. He backed away from her and looked at the other men.

"Wait until she stands at your back in battle and her woman's arm isn't strong enough to stop an enemy's death blow. Then we'll see how welcome she is to fight with us." He grabbed his cloak and strode out of the longhouse. She almost went after him.

Leif stopped her, smiling, and nudged her shoulder. "Do you still have some of that stew you tried to make last month? I think some of it's still stuck to the bottom of the pot. We could dip our arrows in it and set them aflame to fire at the outcasts."

Her heart lightened at his familiar teasing.

"Or," the warrior Arne said, "we could have her make some more and leave it for them to steal. They would be too busy with the shits and we wouldn't have to fight them."

Several of the men chuckled and she had to smile.

"What? And deprive you of your bloodletting?" She sheathed her sword. "Besides, our shipwrights used it to seal the bottom of the boats when they ran out of tar and animal hair, remember?" The men shouted their appreciation of the banter. "Leif, I can always see if there's any left on the walls of the cooking room that the women couldn't pry off. I can coat some arrows with it and fire them at you to see if it works."

The men roared and she laughed with them, her hand relaxing on the grip of her shield. They, at least, accepted her. It hadn't been easy, but she'd proven herself to them more than once.

Eirik smiled with the others, but he looked only at her, his blue eyes glittering with humor. She avoided his gaze and walked over to Magnus.

"I see Eirik is coming with us."

"Yes. He offered. I accepted. I think it's better to have him with us, where we know what he's doing. And we can use the help. We don't know how many outcasts there are or what we'll face. He'll be with you and me. Leif will take the second group and Arne will lead the third. That will allow us to spread out but still have the strength to engage whatever force we meet."

He turned to the men. "We'll head out. The days are short, so we won't have much time to search before dark. Tomorrow, we'll be better organized and can leave at first light."

"If any of us survive the drinking tonight," Arne said. "It is our solemn duty to honor Alv in fine style. This is, after all, his *sjaund.*"

The men cheered and struck their swords on their shields.

"Then we head out now, so that we may return all the sooner and begin." Leif raised his sword above his head and they all followed suit, shouting.

Once she got outside, she stuck her shield upright in the snow and knelt to tie on her skis. They would use them to travel faster and farther while they searched the woods. If necessary, they could fight with them on, but they could cut the laces in a moment. She carried an extra set of the walrus-hide strips for such a situation.

Eirik skied over to her. "You need to watch out for Hjellmar."

She picked up her shield and stood. "He's never been silent on how he feels about shieldmaidens. He can disagree with women fighting, but he can't disrespect me, if only because I'm the sister of his jarl."

"I know. But you embarrassed him in front of these men. He won't forget it."

She checked her sword, loosening it in its sheath. "Good. I won't have to remind him again."

He slid closer and spoke low. "You've made an enemy this day."

She smiled. "Then I'll have to tell Leif how I did it. He said he asked Magnus how to make an enemy, but he didn't say why he wanted one."

He shook his head. "I'll watch your back, then, if you won't. And Magnus will be there."

She touched his arm. "Eirik, don't take my levity as complacency. This is an old war between Hjellmar and me. It goes back to the time when Magnus first started my training six years ago. Hjellmar thought to dissuade me with his words, but it just made me more determined. I learned quickly that I had to protect myself against men like him."

"I'd say you learned your lessons well, judging from what I saw in there." His smile was warm. "You're very quick. That can triumph over brawn any day. He's just too foolish to see it."

Heat crept into her cheeks. She wasn't accustomed to praise about her abilities. "We'd best join the others. The sun is low. There will be shadows enough, even now."

They skied over to Magnus's group. He nodded at them. "Eirik, show us where you saw the tracks the day of the funeral. It's as good a place to start as any. They may have returned there since."

Eirik led the way out of the village, into the woods. Asa stayed beside Magnus, while several of his warriors flanked them. The rest spread out behind them and to their sides.

He stopped near a cliff that had partially collapsed. There was nothing except piles of large, flat stones where they had sheared off in the landslide. Some of the ground had been disturbed and it appeared as though a couple of the stones had been shifted.

"Strange," Magnus said. "Why would they want these rocks? They're too big to carry any distance, especially in these mountains."

Eirik had skied a short distance away. He motioned to them. "There aren't any tracks here, but something has gone through this brush. It's dried out and breaks easily." He pointed to broken branches.

Magnus examined them. "It might have been an animal. But it's all we have to go on and it's as good a direction as any."

Asa's heart sped up. She'd fought before, but those had been quick skirmishes against pirates on their ships. There'd been plenty of time to prepare once they'd seen the sails on the horizon. Their merchant vessels were no match for the speed of the sleek longships the pirates favored. No other ship on the seas was faster anywhere in the world. In the slower ships, her brothers and their men had had no choice but to stand and fight. Neither had she. She'd held her own, her brothers backing her.

This was different. They couldn't know, from one moment to the next, when the outcasts might attack them, nor where, nor how. They might be a few leaderless men, or there might be an army of them, well led and well armed.

She glanced around at the men. Their eyes were bright, many of them smiling. They lived for this. Tonight, some might drink in Odin's hall in Asgard, and others in Magnus's longhouse. To them, it made little difference.

They skied through the area, finding nothing, until the shadows made it too dangerous to continue. Magnus called a halt. "We'd best head back while we have a bit of light. We're not too far from Thors-fjell."

"Wait." Eirik lifted his hand. Voices filtered through the trees to the north.

He shifted closer to Asa, and Magnus moved to her other side. They all unsheathed their swords, the archers arming their bows. She hefted her blade, the familiar weight steadying her.

Light laughter drifted to them and she looked at Magnus. He rolled his eyes as they all relaxed and sheathed their swords. A group of men came through the trees toward them.

"Leif," Magnus said, "why don't you just announce to everyone in the *fjells* that you're here? We could have ambushed you and had you killed already."

"Do you think so?" Leif nodded behind Magnus as he skied up to him.

Five of the men assigned to Leif moved out from the trees to the south, grinning.

Leif clapped him on the shoulder. "Now who would have ambushed who?"

Magnus shot him a disgusted look. "Well, at least you haven't forgotten everything I taught you."

"*You* taught me?"

"All right," Asa said. "You can argue about your male pride over a mug of ale this night. Right now, it's getting dark and we need to return. And with the way the sky looks, we may have a storm tonight. Leif, did you see anything?"

"A few signs of old fires, but that was all. With the intermittent snowfall, and possibly another blizzard, it's going to be difficult to find any trace of them until they make a move."

Magnus took a deep breath. "And that's what I'm concerned about. With as bold as they've become, what *will* their next move be?"

Chapter Eight

The hearth fire in the center of the common room provided the only light. Shadows leapt up the walls behind all those gathered for the funeral ale. Magnus stood in front of the two ornate chairs on the dais at the front of the room. He didn't often use them, preferring to sit among his people, but for high occasions, they were a symbol of his title.

Asa spoke with Alv's wife. The widow had recovered from her fever, perhaps thanks to Eirik's runes, and stood with a little girl before her. Magnus smiled to himself. Asa was so beautiful, dressed in her finery. Even as she bent to talk to the little girl, she held herself as befitted her rank, with pride and strength. It was said that only the tallest and most elegant of women became shieldmaidens. In Asa's case, that was true.

He glanced at the rune caster. Eirik stood in the shadows, but he didn't watch the ceremony. He watched Asa. All that day, Eirik had remained at her side, as though he had a right to guard her. That remained to be seen.

Magnus looked at his people. "We are here to acknowledge Alv. By now, he is with the gods. And as we drink the sacred ale, we mark the final line between life and death."

They raised their horns and then drank without stopping. The ceremonial vessels, once filled, could not be set down until they were emptied.

He wiped his mouth and walked down to Asa and the young widow.

"The real drinking is about to start. It might be wise to take all the children elsewhere for the night."

"Yes, Jarl Magnus." The woman took her daughter's hand and joined the others who were leaving.

Asa sighed. "I hope the men remember there's plenty of food as well."

"I doubt it," he said. "But we can always hope. We'll need them at least standing on their skis tomorrow morning, if the weather allows, when we go searching again."

She gave a short laugh. "We can always hope, indeed."

He sat down and watched her as she showed the last of the women and children out. She would be a natural mother, if only she could accept it. If only a man could see beyond the past that had shaped her, and love her for who she was.

Beautiful. Strong. Proud. Damaged. Somewhere, there must be a man who would love her despite that, and who could heal her as well.

Magnus studied Eirik as he stood talking to several of the men. Come tomorrow, he would likely disappear. Again. It was becoming a habit for him to go elsewhere in the day, and sometimes at night until late. If he were meeting with the outcasts, he wouldn't be so obvious as to do so now. Whoever he was, he wasn't a fool.

He could have Eirik watched, but Eirik would likely know it. No, the truth would come out when they found and fought the outcasts. Then he would see what the rune caster was truly made of. Perhaps Eirik would be a valuable ally. Or maybe, as Asa had feared, Magnus had let a wolf come among them. If so, he would protect what was his.

After all, he had hunted wolves before.

As it was, the hungover men were able to sleep it off. The blizzard Asa had predicted hit hard during the night. Eirik smiled as he wove his way through the common room. The warriors, and many of the women, had stayed up playing drinking games and telling wild stories until hours after midnight. Now they lay, passed out, all over the tops of tables, benches, the floor, and each other. Several of them still clutched their empty cups.

He had done his fair share of drinking, as well. But he had spent the past three years raiding and traveling with his cousin, Rorik. That had taught him to hold his ale and mead with the best of them.

Blizzard or no blizzard, he had work to do. He huddled inside his cloak and fought through the blowing snow toward the small shed out behind the stables. The wind almost ripped the door out of his hands, but he slipped into the building and shut it tight behind him. In the darkness, by feel alone, he took out his metal fire-starter and struck it with a hard stone. A spark jumped into the small brazier in the center of the room. With the small flame, he lit the other brazier and then several oil lamps. In so tiny a room, they would warm it well enough for his purposes.

He positioned one of the lamps hanging overhead so it shone on the large flat stone propped against a barrel. Working in near darkness was proving difficult. He'd had to keep the door closed, not so much because of the cold, but to keep anyone from hearing him.

This was some of his finest work. The World Tree, Yggdrasil, stood in the center of the stone, as it stood in the axis of all Nine Worlds. Its roots curled down and around the bottom. He'd begun to carve one of the swans that swam in the spring of Mimir that gushed from beneath the tree. On its branches, he'd drawn the image of an eagle. He would carve it next.

Sjurd had found him a hammer and copper chisel. He needed to get in a full day's work, for once the storm subsided, they'd resume the search for the outcasts.

It was important that he go with them. Outcasts had taken his own village, killed his people, and forced him into exile. He wouldn't allow this to happen to Thorsfjell and to Asa. The outcasts would grow in numbers until they become strong enough to attack, as they had in Hordaland.

Even if Magnus could fight them off, many of these people would die. Eirik had been too late and too weak to stop them at home, but that wouldn't be the case here. It was one of the reasons he'd remained relatively sober last night. Magnus and Leif had done the same. They couldn't risk letting down their guard, even for such a ceremony.

The eagle took shape beneath the point of the chisel. This was simple work. But soon, Asa would carve the runes on the dragon, and he'd call upon the ancient powers to guide her. She wouldn't be able to work on it during the days, though, for she would go with the warriors again on their search. He hesitated.

Rorik had six shieldmaidens fighting with him, so Eirik was accustomed to the idea of women in battle. One of them was Rorik's sister, his cousin. Still, the idea of Asa fighting chilled him.

He should maintain his own distance. But ever since he had helped Asa with the runes, that had been impossible. Something had happened between them when he'd placed his hand on her shoulder and spoken the words to bring the power. The lines of the drawings had wrapped around them, holding them together with their magic. They'd work together on the runes at night when everyone else was asleep. Alone.

If she were his, he could just lock her away and never let her pick up a sword again. But how could he deprive her of her right to protect her people? She blossomed when she held her blade. She stood taller and with more pride, as though she could take on the world. It gave her strength, bringing light to the shadows that haunted her dark eyes. He could never douse that light.

Besides, a woman didn't need to fight to be in danger. Even now, Silvi and their mother were fighting for their people in their own way. He closed his eyes as the pain flickered in his heart. Also, simply by giving birth, women risked more than any man ever did. He knew all too well just how much.

A warrior had his weapons, his skill, and his strength to guard him. A woman had nothing but her own body when she brought a child into this world. No shield, no battle-luck, no one else standing at her back to block a death blow from an enemy. Yet, she would risk her life over and over, with joy, to become a mother.

Eirik shook his head. To think Hjellmar had scoffed at the strength of a woman.

And what of Asa's reaction to Hjellmar's taunting? She'd struck with such control, dropping him to the floor so fast, no one could have moved to stop her if she had chosen to slay him. Her hand holding her sword had turned white with the strength of her grip. Her eyes had been dark and distant, as though she saw something only in her mind. Or in her past?

Many warriors entered another mind-place when they fought. Perhaps she did, as well. She'd come out of it easily enough when Leif spoke to her.

Eirik continued chipping at the stone. He'd stay close to her when they went back out, as would Magnus. The jarl still didn't quite trust him. He'd sensed it from the start. Eirik didn't blame him. He was unknown to them. Soon he would prove himself to the brothers, and especially to Asa. His skill in battle would help them trust him, as would this memorial stone.

The rest of the winter still lay ahead. Perhaps he could use this time to consider an alliance, to build their trust in one another, and to gather the power he would need. The magic of the runes had already spoken to Asa and him, binding them both together. She had to have heard it in her soul.

And in the nights to come, he would make certain she understood what it said.

With dried shark's skin, Asa sanded the piece of interlacing on the front of the dragon. But it was already as smooth as she could make it and she tossed the skin on the table. She was ready to carve the runes, and yet she procrastinated. Every time she looked at the symbols, drawn in coal along the neck, the memory of when and how they were made crashed into her.

The other women in the room chatted as they wove on the great looms, speaking of women's things. Usually their talk didn't bother her. But lately, it had been distracting. Perhaps it was because they were all trapped inside. The blizzard that had struck a week ago hadn't let up. The snow was so deep and the cold so harsh, it was difficult to go outside. The men were testy, the children bored, and the women short-tempered because they had to put up with all of them.

At least the midwinter celebration of Jul, the longest night of the year, was only a few days away. The men would brave the cold to go hunting tomorrow. It would give them all a reprieve from each other and put a fine feast on the tables.

She picked up a small horse carving she had just finished. The children of the village would have their gifts on Jul night. Then their mothers would settle them by the hearth and they'd listen to tales told far into the night.

She sighed. The next time she saw Eirik, she'd speak to him about helping her carve the runes. There was no more reason to delay. But she had seen little of him of late. He was gone almost all day, coming in only for the late meal. Where would he go?

His touch holds much magic, does it not? Her stomach flipped at the memory of Estrid's words. How could she have known about the feelings he created unless she had been with him? Was that where he was spending his days? With her? Or with any of the other women

who followed him with their eyes? Most of the people here were related in some way and they looked to outsiders for marriages. Often
people had to wait for the yearly Thing meeting in the summer to
find potential spouses.

Much of their interest was also because of Eirik himself. His clothes
were very high quality, and the hammer of Thor pendant he wore would
cost many years' income for most men. His strength, his comeliness,
and his rare smile spoke to all the women near him. He carried himself
like a warrior. With his fineness and easy pride, he could have been a
king's son.

She set down the horse with the other trinkets. It was no matter to
her. She only needed him to bring the power into the runes. Let the
other women have him as long as he helped her with the carving.

Once the snow stopped, they'd search for the outcasts during the
short days. Estrid and the others would just have to wait for him to
finish helping her each evening. The nights were long enough this
time of year for all of them.

He was at the evening meal, sitting with Leif and several other
men. When they finished eating, she crossed to the table.

"Rune caster, I need to speak to you, if you have the time."

"Of course." He stood with a grin as the others nudged each other
and chuckled. She shot Leif a halfhearted glare for instigating it, then
walked with Eirik to the door of the weaving room.

"I'm ready to begin carving the runes. I know the days will be full
when we resume the search, but if you could spare a little time from
your nightly activities, I would appreciate it." She couldn't keep the
sharpness from her voice. He gave her a questioning glance, but she
remained silent.

He went to the dragon's head and circled it. She stayed by the doorway. The only light came from the fire and lamps in the common
room. The thin glow played over his long hair and the planes of his
face.

He touched the dragon on the side of the neck. The symbols
seemed to writhe under his hand in the flickering light. Nodding, he
raised his eyes to hers and awareness spread through her body, tightening her muscles. He held her gaze captive and she couldn't look
away from him.

He smiled. "I think we're ready. Tomorrow night, I'll meet you
here after the meal. We'll begin at the top with Thurisaz. With as

quickly as you work, it shouldn't take long for each one." He hesitated. "You must have felt the power of the runes when we drew them the other day."

She had sensed something, but what? "I'm not certain. I always feel some kind of energy when I carve. It comes from within me."

"I think they speak to you. Have you ever considered carving them? You could learn, and with your skill, you—"

"No." She backed out of the doorway. "I don't have the mind for such things. I'll see you tomorrow night." With her heart racing, she left, and went back to her room. Settling on the bed, she folded her legs up to her chest and wrapped her arms around them. She rested her chin on her knees, closing her eyes.

If she ever allowed the runes to reach what lay within her, they would tear open the wounds once again and allow the world to see them. The piercing touch of the runes, the intimate touch of a man. They were the same. She could never risk either of them.

She opened her eyes and gazed into the darkness. She would have to allow it, just this once, to give the dragon what it demanded. Magnus would sell it to the Danish king at Hedeby and she would never have to see it, or Eirik, again.

Then, there would be no more dragons.

Asa studied the carving. It was only wood, wood she had shaped herself. Its eyes seemed to gaze back at her, but that was nonsense. If it were not for her, it would never have existed at all. She was the one with the power. It could hold no sway over her unless she allowed it. The runes were only lines she would create with her knife.

She waited for Eirik to arrive. He'd been enjoying a mug of beer after the evening meal with some of the other men when she'd walked through the common room. He must have seen her, and yet she was still waiting. She ran her hand over the black lines of the symbols, but they remained asleep under her touch. They didn't writhe as they'd done when Eirik had brushed his fingers over them. That must have been the firelight playing tricks on her eyes.

Several oil lamps lit her workspace. She'd built up the small central hearth so Eirik and she would have their heat and light. And so they would drive back the shadows.

"I'm sorry I'm late." He walked into the room. "Leif was telling one of his stories and I had to hear how it ended."

"Don't believe any of them." She shifted closer to the carving so there would be room on the bench. Perhaps she should have found another bench for him so he wouldn't be close, but it was too late.

He sat down beside her. "Oh, I don't. I've told a few of those tales myself."

"Perhaps, then, you can tell them at Jul. We always listen to stories of the gods and the other worlds on that night. It seems fitting since it's the longest of the year and all the worlds draw closer then."

"I might be able to think of something." He leaned forward to study the dragon. Much closer to her.

She held herself still. They would be working together for the next few nights. She'd done this before with the old master, so it shouldn't bother her, but he had been old enough to be her great-grandfather. It wasn't the same with Eirik beside her.

His scent came to her, mixed with that of newly carved wood and the smoke from the fire. The weather was finally calm outside and the smoke didn't draw up through the hole in the peak of the roof very well, leaving the room hazy. Already, the world seemed further away, as though they had left Midgard and entered some other realm where the ancient powers walked. He carried the essence of such magic with him and she breathed it in.

She needed to steady herself. He was so male and so obviously a warrior. That must be what she was feeling. No different from any other woman, and that should have given her comfort. But it didn't.

"Now, for Thurisaz, we want to start with the upper diagonal and carve it down and to the right." His voice was deep and right beside her.

She picked up her knife. "I would think you begin with the vertical line."

"I know. But they were created in realms other than ours, so they don't yield to our ways."

"Carving downward is more difficult than up." She set the edge of the knife to the wood, holding it at an angle. She would carve each line into a V.

He set his hand on hers. His touch was so light, it wasn't even a caress on her skin, but it hit her deep, like one of Thor's bolts coming too close.

"As the thorn protects the rose," he said beside her ear, "so Thurisaz protects all who wield it. May it lend its strength to any vessel that bears it."

He sat at her back. His arm came around her and he kept his hand over hers. The heat from his body seeped into her, his voice wrapping around her like a soft cloak. His other hand rested near her hip. She'd braided back her hair to keep it out of the way, and the bare skin of her neck tingled. She wore three layers of clothing and still the power from him penetrated her.

Keeping her hand steady, she finished the first cut. His hand dropped away, but as it did, his fingers drifted over her skin.

"Perfect. Now for the other angle."

She swallowed. This was too close, too dangerous, too . . . everything. Biting her lip, she applied the blade to the wood, angled in the opposite direction. Once again, he leaned forward. This time, his chest rested against her back. He touched his fingertips to her wrist and she drew in a sharp breath as her thighs weakened.

He murmured soft words she couldn't understand, the sound of them floating through her mind. The room fell away, but the dragon sharpened into hard focus. As she completed the incision, the wood loosened. She made the two small cuts at the ends and the piece dropped off.

As it did, the darkness within her lightened, just a touch, as though she had cut away a heavy, dark part of herself. What magic did he have? What words did he speak that had such power?

"Beautiful. Now, the next cut—"

"Is the vertical line, downward." The line she'd drawn before pulsated in the dim light.

"How did you know that? Did you do this rune with the old master?"

"No. I just saw it. In the image." She sat back even though it brought her into closer contact with him. He didn't move, but pressed his hand against her hip.

"It's only the runes speaking. Their gift to you. We need to continue. We can't leave this undone." He pushed his cloak back and rolled up his sleeves.

It *was* getting a bit warm in the room. Drawing in a deep, steadying breath, she set the knife to the black vertical line. He placed his arm alongside hers and cupped her hand with his larger one. The light sprinkling of hair on his muscular forearm shimmered in the golden light of the fire. His wrist was thick with strength, his hand well formed, his fingers long, sensitive.

"Asa. The cut." Humor laced his voice.

Her cheeks heated. She must have built the fire too well. She made the long cut downward. At least it was strong and sure, not revealing the quaking inside her.

"Let the sensation flow through you, Asa. Don't try to fight it." He spoke close to her, his breath ruffling her hair. "The magic you feel between us is older than we are, older than time itself. It is meant to be. Everything that happens, everything you experience, is fated by the gods."

His voice was as powerful and deep as a sword stroke, and it plunged into the heart of her. She made the other score for the line, and the knife seemed to move of its own accord. Two more cuts, and the center of the line fell out. Without waiting for him to tell her, she carved the other diagonal downward from right to left.

"Yes." He caressed her hand, not moving back from her. "That's perfect."

She moved her hand from beneath his. He traced the lines in the wood with his finger, whispering. His eyes closed. The cuts were still rough and she'd smooth and shape them in the days to come, but the rune itself was completed.

She couldn't move until he did, trapped between him and the dragon as he spoke his magic. How could she do this, night after night, until the other five were finished? She must. Just this one last time.

He stopped speaking. The room came into focus, the magic broken, and she shifted to the side.

"Eirik."

He leaned back, and she glanced at him. His eyes were a darker blue, the pupils large. Blinking, he smiled at her. "I think we depleted all the power for the night. It turned out very well."

"Yes." She looked at the dragon. "It fits beautifully. I think he's pleased. Will we carve the next one tomorrow night? The night after that is Jul, so we won't work then."

"I'll meet you here again after the second meal." He stood.

She did as well, so he wouldn't loom over her. "Thank you. I think it will come out very well in the end."

A smile touched his eyes as he inclined his head. "I hope so."

After he left, she placed the cloth over the dragon. The room was still hazy with smoke, and for a time it hadn't seemed to exist. Now, everything was back to normal as though nothing magical had happened at all. But it had.

Shaking her head, she left for her own bed. The feelings that had washed over her were, no doubt, caused from her own fancies and dreams. His nearness. Her fears.

His touch, though, had been anything but frightening. And that was the strangest thing of all.

Eirik skied through the trees, ahead of the other men. This hunt should clear his head of the evening before, when he'd brought the old power into Asa's carving. Perhaps.

The magic still swirled through his mind, holding him in its grip. Was it Asa?

The soft skin of her arm against his. The fragrance of her hair. The power coursing through them both, combining the symbols and the wood.

What had he told Asa? To allow the sensation to flow through her. Had he spoken only of the power he'd called, or had he referred to the growing emotion between them? She would deny it, but not forever. Now, with the forest surrounding him, he opened himself to the natural forces there.

The connection to all things sharpened his senses. Life rested in the winter lands, but underneath it, energies still streamed, and they rose up into him. The cold faded away. In spite of how long he'd been skiing through the rough forest, energy hummed in his body.

Magnus glided on his skis a short distance off, to Eirik's left. He'd rarely let Eirik out of his sight as they hunted apart from the others, the better to find the elk they sought. Eirik smiled to himself. That matter of trust again.

Something was wrong in the forest around them. Something dark. He poled to a stop, listening, sensing. The hair on the back of his neck rose and he scanned the shadows between the trees. A shape moved just ahead.

Eirik stuck his poles in the snow and shrugged his bow off his shoulder. He took an arrow from his quiver and set it in the string. The man might be another hunter, but no. He'd stopped and had Magnus in his sights. He had to be an outcast. Eirik's shot would be difficult, for the man stood sideways to him and hadn't seen him yet. Eirik froze, watching.

The man raised his bow toward the jarl, and drew back. In an instant, Eirik steadied, aimed, and let his arrow fly. It struck the man in the great vein in the side of his neck. He fell in an arc of blood. As he collapsed, he released his arrow and it sliced through the air at Magnus, but it pierced the ground at the jarl's feet.

Magnus spun on Eirik. His eyes narrowed as he took in the spent bow and he moved toward him, unsheathing his sword. "By the gods."

Eirik gripped his own sword, but didn't draw it. "Hold, Jarl. That's not my arrow. You gave them to me yourself, so you should know. It came from him."

He pointed toward the fallen man. Magnus glanced at the body, then went back and picked up the arrow in the snow. He skied to the dead man and took an arrow from his quiver, comparing them. Then he examined the arrow in the outcast's neck. Throwing the arrows to the ground, he shook his head.

"I owe you an apology." He sheathed his sword and came toward him.

"I would have thought the same under similar circumstances, Jarl." He grinned. "And I wouldn't be that bad a shot, even dying."

"Judging from the skill it took to hit him as you did, you might be right." He offered his hand and they grasped wrists. "I owe you my life."

"And I owe you mine from the blizzard."

"That was Asa's doing. Besides, you might have been Odin. He has a habit of traveling disguised as a man to see who will offer him their hospitality. We dared not refuse."

"I'm not that old, and I'm not missing an eye."

"Thank the gods for that, or you might not have made that shot."

Eirik looked at the body. "What about him? Was he alone or are there more here?"

Other men came through the trees, and Eirik tensed, but they were Magnus's warriors and hunters. At Magnus's command, they spread out to act as guards and to search for more of the outcasts. At least now, they had numbers.

"Should we bury him in the snow, Jarl?" One of the men shoved the body with his spear. "Or leave him as a warning?"

"Leave him," Magnus said, his voice hard. "Let them find him. And if they don't, the wolves need something to eat."

"It might escalate things between you and the outcasts, Jarl."

Eirik slung his bow on his back. "They might want to take revenge for this."

"Good. Then it will bring them out in the open instead of skulking like rats. We'll be ready. I've gathered all of the people that I can into Thorsfjell."

One of the men approached them. "Jarl, we found fresh spoor from elk in the ravine over the hill."

Magnus nodded. "We've already had one successful hunt. Let us go have another." But as the man left, the jarl didn't follow him. He studied Eirik for a moment and Eirik met his regard. "In spite of what you say, I do owe you my life, rune caster. That's a heavy burden to bear, but one I do gladly for such a man as I think you are."

"Eirik. To my friends, I am just Eirik." He held out his hand again.

"And to mine, I am Magnus." He grasped his wrist, warrior to warrior.

As Eirik skied through the woods, he smiled. He had wondered how to win Magnus's confidence, and the gods had provided. Perhaps this was the spark that would ignite that trust. And maybe, just maybe, they would join forces to rid both their lands of this plague.

If he could trust them as well.

Chapter Nine

"You're quite the hero now." A mug of ale in his hand, Leif sat down across from Eirik in the common room. "I do have to thank you for saving my brother. If you hadn't, I would be jarl now, and we couldn't have that." He winced and took a deep drink. "Of course, Asa could always take over. It does happen. And she's already a warrior."

Eirik chuckled. "A woman may act as a son, having the same rights and inheritance. But only if she's not married, a crime has been perpetrated against her family, or there are no male heirs. I don't think that last one applies here."

"No." Leif sighed. "Magnus and I look too much alike for me to claim illegitimacy. I already tried that once and no one believed me. Gods curse my luck."

"That, and the fact that you both were born at the same time." He smiled into his cup.

"That doesn't prove anything." Leif lowered his voice. "I heard about this woman once, who swived two men at the same time. She gave birth to twins and it was said that one looked like one man and the other babe looked like the other."

"Leif. Tales again?"

Asa walked up to their table, hands on her hips. Her lips twitched as though she tried not to smile.

"I swear it, Asa." Leif held his hands up. "I heard it from—"

"Never mind that." She looked at Eirik. "Do you want to work on the next rune tonight? Or do you wish to enjoy the celebration? It's not every day that Magnus's life is saved and that we have three elk roasting for the Jul feast tomorrow. Thanks to your fine bow work on both counts."

"I only shot one of the elk." Eirik stood.

Leif snorted. "And one outcast. A good catch for any day."

Eirik clapped him on the shoulder, laughing. He followed Asa into the weaving room and closed the door against the noise. She'd already lit the lamps and the small central hearth. The fire burned low and the room held a chill. He hid a smile. Perhaps she didn't want him to roll up his sleeves again so his arm wouldn't rest directly against hers. She was going to be disappointed.

He slipped off his cloak and laid it on a bench. She wouldn't look at him as she lifted the cloth off the carving. With the light lower than it had been last night, the shadows rose deeper. But darkness wouldn't stop the ancient power from gathering around them when he called it.

"Perhaps you would prefer to stay out there with the others. They're all hailing you for what you did for Magnus today." She sat down on the bench.

"We'll be celebrating Jul for the next twelve nights." He settled beside her and rolled up his sleeves. "I would rather be here with you anyhow."

She glanced at his arms and blushed. Shifting so she faced the dragon, she said, "Then we should begin."

He allowed himself a brief smile. "Yes. The next rune is Elhaz. It's the major rune of protection and anchors the other two. It will bring a spiritual guardian to the ship. You'll begin by carving the vertical line straight down first."

She nodded and he set his hand on hers. She began the cut. Her hand was so long and slender, yet she wielded the knife as she wielded her sword, with great accuracy and skill.

As he closed his eyes, the rune formed in his mind. He placed his hand over it, matching its shape with his fingers. Its power heated his skin and the warmth spread up his arm, and down into his heart. The energy flowed along his veins then, filling him with the power.

The room had grown hazy, the smoke from the fire curling around them. Asa sat before him, still carving the first line. He bent his head and breathed her in. Her essence, like her scent, entered him. It swirled with the magic he had called, mingling together within him, as one.

He just touched her hair with his cheek. "By the power of Elhaz,

I protect you. By the strength of my sword, I guard you. And by the force that courses within me, I hold you, safe, always."

The first piece of wood fell away. She didn't move, their arms still together as they touched the dragon. He wrapped his other arm around her, very soft, very easy.

"Now for the next line. Carve the left side upward."

She shuddered, but placed the blade to the wood. As she made the cut, he reached deep within himself and called the ancient magic again. The words came to him as Lifa, his mother, had taught him so long ago. Even he didn't know what they meant or where they'd come from, though she'd told him they were from the language the gods themselves spoke.

Power crept into the room. It stole in, surrounding them like a fog on the seas, and he uttered the words louder. The energies climbed. He tightened his arm around her, pulling her closer to his chest.

She hesitated, but he touched his mouth to her ear. "Don't stop. The power guides you now. Feel it. Hear it. Let it flow through you into your hand, and back through your body. Become one with it, and with the rune. Its magic shields us from anything of the world in this time and place. There is only us now."

The second piece slid away from the rune. He said nothing as Asa made the correct cut upward along the other side. He ran his fingers along her wrist and the back of her hand as she carved. A small log split apart, hissing, and in the dim light, the dragon appeared to shift under their touch.

As the final piece of wood came away, completing the rune, a surge of power hit him. Asa lowered her head, moaning, and he caught her closer to his chest. She dropped the knife and placed her hand over the rune, fingers spread along the grooves. He put his hand over hers, matching it as the energies rushed through them.

Touching the side of her neck with his lips, he tasted her. Like wildflowers and rare spices. She tilted her head to one side and her hair slid away, baring her skin. He kissed her there, then moved down to the curve of her shoulder.

She caught her breath, as though she tried to awaken from a dream. He kissed her hair, running his hand over her flat stomach. Her hand clenched over the rune as he enfolded it in his much larger one. Bringing it to her shoulder, he kissed it and she looked back at him. Her eyes were large and luminous, dark with the power churning there.

"Asa." He couldn't keep the deep thrum of desire from his voice.

She blinked and her eyes became blank, touched with fear, like they had in the sauna. The link between them snapped.

He turned her to him and, cupping her face in his hands, brushed her forehead with his mouth. "Asa, come back to me. The rune protects you, as I protect you. That which you fear has no power in this place. The dragon wears Elhaz now and will stand guard over you."

She focused on him, her eyes becoming sharp once again. As though she had just surfaced from the depths of a vast fjord, she took a deep breath and lowered her eyes. Clearing her throat, she shifted away from him and took her hand from his. He allowed it, his hand slipping from her waist.

"Eirik. I—I thank you. For your help." She stood, swaying a bit, and brushed at the wood chips on her skirt. "I don't know if we should work on this anymore until Jul is finished. There may not be time with all the festivities and, with the darkness this time of year, it might be dangerous to call any more magic."

Rising, he said, "As you wish. We can continue anytime. I'll be here for you."

She wouldn't look at him as she nodded. But when she skirted around him, he took her arm with so light a touch, she could have continued on had she wished to. She stopped. "Asa, I would never let anything dark touch you. Remember that."

"I will." She spun and opened the door to the weaving room.

He picked up his cloak and followed her. Leaning against the frame, he watched as she took her cloak from the wall peg and rushed outside, her head down. Several people glanced between them as the door slammed, but he ignored them.

Hjellmar sidled up to him. "Looks like the ice queen has melted and in her place stands a true woman. Who would have known?"

Eirik pushed himself from the door frame and spoke low. "Say anything like that again, Hjellmar, and *you'll* know what it is to be frozen. In the ground." He swirled his cloak over his shoulders and pushed past Hjellmar toward the front door.

As he stepped outside, the night was clear and cold. But there was no moon and Asa had vanished into the darkness. With the tracks of all the people who had gathered there for the evening, he would never be able to find hers.

The last of the magic vanished from his mind. He stood looking at the stars. For each person, his mother had said, there was one other. She'd tried to tell him Sela was not the one for him, but he hadn't listened. There were other voices speaking to him now, older, deeper, wiser.

When the ancient magic had entered them, he'd touched Asa's soul. The power of Elhaz had protected her, but when the magic drained away, her fears had rushed back in. Instead of welcoming the closeness they'd shared, she'd feared it. And him. She had thrust both of them away and run. Why? It seemed she'd remembered her past once again and it had come between them.

In that moment, the dreams left her eyes.

Arms wrapped around him from behind and he smiled. Perhaps in the clarity of the night, Asa had realized he meant her no harm. He turned with a smile.

"I saw you come out here." Estrid gazed up at him with her beautiful, cold blue eyes. "Don't bother following Asa. She toyed with you, letting you do as you wished, and left you wanting more, did she not? She's done this before, as I warned you. Perhaps she suspects our love. She never could let me have any man without trying to take him from me. They all want her. She'll come between you and the others, and they'll drive you out in disgrace because of her lies. We must keep our love secret, but I know places we can go to be alone."

Our love? What was she talking about? He took her by the arms and stood her away from him. "Estrid, there is no love between us. I don't know why you think this, but it isn't so."

For an instant, something ugly flashed across her face, but she smoothed her mouth into a smile. "She's cast her spell on you, too, then. Like she did to him, and now he's gone from me. This time, I won't give up so easily. I was too young before to fight for what I want, but not now. Just wait, beloved. I won't let her destroy you, as well."

How had this happened? She was not right in her mind and he needed to tell Magnus. Shock sped through him so hard he didn't have time to react as she stood on her toes and kissed his mouth. Then she ran back into the longhouse and he let her go.

Something was very wrong here. His touch frightened Asa so

much, she retreated into her own thoughts to escape the terror. Estrid was unwell in her mind and blamed Asa for something in their past. He didn't believe anything Estrid told him about Asa, but could there be a connection? There was only one way to find out.

Magnus. But would the jarl's newfound trust extend to exposing the shadows that lay within his family?

Estrid was losing him. He had wanted her. He had. She'd known it since they first saw each other. He had picked her first. He'd wanted her to be warm. Now Asa was coming between her and the man she loved. Again.

Estrid watched the others in the common room as they laughed and played games. The light from the long fire shone on them all, and dozens of oil lamps illuminated everything. And again, she stood on the outside, looking in.

In the shadows, as always.

The darkness closed in on her, oozing down the walls, along the floor, rising up into her body. She closed her eyes, but it kept coming, replacing the blood in her veins with blackness. No one stood against the darkness for her. No one drew his sword and tore it away from her. Everyone laughed and talked, sitting in the light like they were safe. But they all cast shadows, as well. They just faced the light so they wouldn't see them. What was she to do when there was no light? When everything was shadow and darkness?

Even if it meant defeat, she could fight. The warriors believed their fates were already decided. So they fought with all the bravery and valor they had, each time embracing whatever the gods had in store for them.

She could do no less. Even if she failed, like those who went raiding she would fight for Eirik and shield him against the darkness. He was so bright and beautiful, it hurt her eyes to look at him. She would show him she didn't need to be a shieldmaiden to win him.

She needed an ally. Someone who would understand how she felt being shunned and humiliated. Being alone. A man who wouldn't succumb to Asa's false allure.

He sat there, alone, at a side bench, angry, resentful, filled with hate for the jarl's highborn sister who had embarrassed him in front of all the other men. Just what she needed. Estrid filled a mug with ale and went to him. He raised his brows in question as she sat down beside him and handed him the ale. Then he smiled at her, sweeping his gaze along her body. She pressed closer to him in invitation as he took a drink.

Yes. He would be perfect.

Asa gathered up the wooden toys she had carved for the children for Jul and put them in a large cloth bag. She'd bear the rest of the evening as well as she could. Eirik had been at the feast, of course, and she'd sat as far as possible from him. She hadn't even been able to bring herself to look at him, for she would see him as he was last night. His hair had gleamed in the firelight, his eyes deep and luminous with the power coursing through him. And with the desire twining between them.

It was all she had thought about all day, and each time, her heart would shred a bit more.

When she'd gone outside last night with just her cloak, she'd realized how cold it was and had started back to the longhouse. Eirik had stood in front of it. In Estrid's embrace. They'd talked, standing close together. Then he'd held her by the arms and looked down into her eyes. Estrid had kissed him and left.

For once, her cousin hadn't lied. He had turned to Estrid right after being with Asa. But what could she expect? While they'd carved the rune together, it all had been so magical and beautiful. Though his touch was strong, he took such great care with her. His mouth was so gentle on her skin. So believable.

But then, when she'd completed the rune, her past had rushed over her again, as though a spell had been broken. It had engulfed her in the terror and blood.

She shuddered and put a little toy sword into the bag. The memory hadn't lasted but an instant this time, and hadn't been as overwhelming. Perhaps, after all these years, she was getting better. But he had seen her like that again and had turned to someone else in the next moment. Just as Estrid had warned her so many times.

"Are the toys for the children ready?"

She looked up at Magnus standing in the doorway. "Yes. Odin brought many nice things for them this Jul."

"That's good." He chuckled. "There's hay and carrots all over the common room from where they put them in their shoes. It would seem Sleipnir ate well last night."

"They'll want to hear the story again, as they do every Jul."

"Well, Eirik is said to be a good storyteller. Perhaps he'll do the honors this year and spare you." He took the bag from her. "He wanted to speak to me today, but I had too much to do to oversee all the festivities. I had to put him off."

"I thought Estrid worked on the festivals." She walked with him to the door.

"She does. But she disappeared this morning and was gone for so long a time, I was concerned that things wouldn't get done. You were busy finishing up the last of the toys and Leif is useless in such matters. Several of the women did most of the work. I just agreed with them when they came to me with ideas. I know better than to do otherwise."

Giving him a light punch on the arm in reproof, she went with him out into the common room. She looked around at the gathered crowd. Eirik sat with Leif, listening to another tall tale, no doubt.

She managed to walk to the head of the room without glancing at Eirik. Magnus had stopped to speak to him, but she kept her back turned until her brother joined her on the dais. It wasn't unusual for Eirik to disappear for a good part of the day, but where had Estrid been? Had they been together? Again?

It didn't matter. If he was that fickle, Estrid could have him. She would have nothing to do with him. She didn't need any more pain where her scarred heart was concerned.

"Now, I want to know who left this hay and these carrots all over the floor last night." Magnus set the bag down at his feet and put his hands on his hips. He looked at the children, who had gathered by the longhearth. "I think I see the culprits. Suppose you tell me why you would make such a mess."

They laughed and one of the boys said, "We didn't do it, Jarl. Father Odin's horse, Sleipnir, did it."

Magnus raised his brows. "Bergen, are you telling me there was a horse in the hall last night?"

They giggled. "He's a magical horse, Jarl. So it's all right," Bergen said. "And we want to hear his story."

"We want our presents." A younger boy frowned.

"And so you shall have both, all in good time." Magnus nodded to Eirik.

He got up from the table and walked over to the children. Sitting down on a bench near them, he smiled at them and they settled at his feet.

Leif sighed. "I don't suppose we're going to hear about the glittering women in the East."

"You men can have your fantasy women," Birgitta said. "We have the rune caster to look at and he's real."

Everyone laughed, including Eirik. "That tale is for another night, Leif. And not when there are children around."

The chuckling subsided. "Now," he said, "who knows who Odin is?"

"He's the Allfather." Several children spoke together.

"He's known as that sometimes. But the true Allfather existed even before Odin did. He is unseen and has lived forever. He also bears eleven other names, like Spear Shaker and Ruler of Weather. He began the creation of all things. Odin is one of the most powerful of the gods. He's an Aesir, which means he lives in Asgard, and has a spear named Gungnir that always finds its mark when he throws it. He watches over the worlds on a throne called Hlidskjalf. His ravens, Hugin and Munin, fly from there every day and then come back and tell him what is happening in the Nine Worlds.

"Best of all, he has a horse named Sleipnir, who came from Loki, and who is the finest horse in the world. Sleipnir has eight legs and travels over all the Nine Worlds with great speed. He has runes carved on his teeth and Odin rides him in the Wild Hunt on nights like this."

"How did he come from Loki?" A little girl chewed her fingernail.

Eirik glanced at Magnus, who shrugged and grinned. He gave Asa a pleading look, but she just crossed her arms. He'd get no help from her. It was obvious he had plenty of knowledge about such things.

He cleared his throat. "Loki had to stop a man from winning a bet against the gods. The man needed his own stallion, Svadilfari, to help him. So Loki, who could change his shape, became a mare and lured him away and the man lost the bet." He hesitated. "And Sleipnir appeared by magic after that."

"Oh." The older ones nodded.

"Each year, on the longest night, like tonight, Odin rides Sleipnir across the lands in the Wild Hunt. It is the darkest time of all, a time of beginnings and endings, but it's also the time of the greatest hope. The god Freyr rides his great boar over the world, bringing light and love back to us. After this night, the days become longer and longer until the sun is in the sky almost all day.

"But Sleipnir gets hungry on his journey, so all the children put hay and carrots into their shoes and set them by the hearth. He eats it all as he goes. In thanks, Odin leaves gifts for them." He glanced up at Magnus on the dais. "I think the jarl has the presents he left for you."

The children laughed and shouted as they ran up to Magnus. He handed each child a toy—swords and ships for the boys, dolls and animals for the girls.

Asa gazed around the room at all the parents who watched their children with such pride. The laughter of children, the wisdom that came with childbirth, the sense of belonging with a husband, none of that was for her. Or so she had always thought.

She looked at Eirik as he showed a little boy how to hold his toy sword. He caught her eye and came toward her, smiling. Lowering her gaze, she turned away. There was nothing for her here.

Before she could escape, he took her hand in his. "Aren't you going to stay for some of the Jul cake?"

"No. I spent the day finishing the toys and I'm tired. I've worked so much on the dragon lately, I got behind on the gifts." She gave her hand a light tug to free herself.

He tightened his grip. "Asa, last night—"

"Will never happen again." She looked down. "Just tell me how to carve the lines and I'll do it myself. I don't care about powers or magic."

"What's wrong? Why are you being so cold?" He brought her hand closer to him.

"Why does it matter? You have plenty to keep you warm. Now let me go. I don't want to cause a scene."

He did release her and she went back to her room. She was likely walking away from the only man who could ever touch her. But she wouldn't be one of the many women in his life, even if she had to be alone. She entered her room. It was tiny, but it was hers and no one would bother her there. She shut the door against the shouts and laughter of those celebrating the rebirth of the light. It all just gave her an aching head.

The closer they came to spring, the closer they came to the time when he would leave forever.

And she'd never have to worry about his touch again.

Village of Haardvik

"We don't know how he died, Hakon. There were no marks on his body. He just lay on the side of the road he was guarding." The outcast twisted his hat in his hands. "At first we thought he'd fallen asleep on duty. But he was dead."

Silvi glanced at Lifa. Her mother's face never changed, and neither did that of Nuallen, the thrall who stood behind her. His auburn hair glinted in the firelight, his eyes hard with resentment. It was part of their plan.

Last year, when Rorik and Eirik had raided Northumbria, Rorik had wounded Nuallen as he'd defended his land. Eirik had admired his prowess and strength, so they'd taken him as a slave for Lifa. He nearly died as they crossed the sea and Rorik wanted to throw him overboard so he didn't waste their provisions. But the sun turned black above them, though it was day. The stars came out. And Eirik told them it was a sign that the gods wanted him to live.

When he'd felt the iron collar of slavery around his neck, Nuallen had tried to kill himself, tearing his wounds open with his own hands. But Lifa stopped him, and told him of the sun and that he could not cross the will of the gods. He might, one day, earn his freedom, according to their laws. It had taken him a long time to heal, but as he did, they could see that, with his powerful body and sharp mind, he was, indeed, a warrior. In return for saving his life, he swore himself to Lifa and tried to get them to safety during the raid. Silvi and Lifa had other ideas, though, and he was forced to accept that. He still stood guard over them both, and laid plans with them to do what they could to thwart Hakon and his men.

He had lived up to his word. He'd told Lifa he could kill without leaving a mark on the body of the outcast, and it was true. Now they would put the first part of their plans into motion.

Lifa stepped to the center of the room and all the men shifted, eyeing her with trepidation. Lifa, Nuallen, and she had managed to walk a fine line between fear and uncertainty. But now they'd cross that line, and hoped it worked.

She wore the blue robes of her office, hemmed with gemstones, and carried her rune staff. Drawing herself up to her full height, she said, "It is the longest night, Hakon. The Wild Hunt rides tonight. When your man heard the rustling of the tops of the trees, he should have stayed in the center of the road and fallen facedown. He would have taken no harm other than the cold paws of the black hounds running over him. If he had been so brave as to join with them, he would have shared in the spoils they collected from the dead. But his fate was that of all *nithingr* who fear their own death, and so Odin took him." She looked up at the roof that trembled in the storm building outside, and raised her staff.

"Above us is a sword sky, a wolf sky. Do you not hear it? The thundering of Sleipnir's hooves? The shrieking of Odin's hounds with fire flashing from their eyes? Odin gathers the dead, and so it will go on until the spring when the Hunt will end. You've left no food out for the ancestors. You left no wheat in the fields for Odin's horse. You would not allow us out to do these things, and Odin knows this. He's taken one of your men as payment. And so it will continue until he's appeased."

The men all grumbled, watching what Hakon would do. Lifa lowered her staff and set its end hard on the ground in front of her. Lightning flashed through the room and the men cringed. She did not move.

"And how do I appease the gods, rune mistress?" Hakon acted contrite, but he had to bow to his men's unease and their respect for her status.

They were a rough lot, ignorant and volatile. It wouldn't take much to cause a rift between them and Hakon, and that was something Silvi and her mother might be able to use in the future.

Silvi's hair raised, crackling. She stood beside Lifa. "Listen now to Odin's answer."

Lightning smashed into the ground outside the longhouse. It blinded them for a moment and the men fell to the ground in terror. She met her mother's gaze and Lifa nodded. She'd felt it before it happened as well.

Hakon dropped to his knees beside the high seat. He looked up, his eyes wide. "Odin, tell me what we must do to please you."

"He doesn't hear you, Hakon," Lifa said. "For the winds sweep away your words, like the dried-leaf whisperings they are. He'll speak only to me, through the runes."

"Tell him I will make any sacrifice. Cows, horses, slaves. Whatever he wants of me."

Silvi glanced at Nuallen, but he never flinched. He watched Lifa with cold eyes. He was as much a warrior as any of their own men. He would not fear death.

Lifa only smiled. "Anything you offer him would be of this village and is not yours to give. Odin will not accept it. It belongs to those whom the gods decreed would live here always. With each piece of food you eat, each cup of ale you drink, you make another debt."

He rose from his knees. "We won Haardvik with our swords, the same as any raid."

"You won it, not in lawful battle, but with treachery." She looked into the shadows, her eyes unfocused. "Long ago, a star landed in this place. My husband's ancestors saw it fall, found it, and took it as a sign that they should remain here. They forged the star into a sword and this land into a home. To have the right to sit in that seat, you must wield that blade, which the gods gave to us long ago. But it is lost now, so you cannot rule here."

He sneered. "Perhaps they took it back to tell you that you no longer have the right to this place."

She struck the ground with her staff. "They protected it, assuring that you could not soil it with your touch."

His face reddened. "You listen to me, woman—"

"No, you listen well to me, outcast." She stepped up to him and pointed at the group of his men. They grumbled and stared at Hakon, no doubt troubled by his lack of respect for her magic. "One by one, they will pay the price for your cowardice. One by one Odin will take them, until the debt you have incurred is paid. And one by one, you'll travel the path to Hel. For you will never earn the right to sit as heroes in Valhalla, though you cling to your swords as a baby clings to its mother's teat." She snapped her fingers at Nuallen. "Attend me, thrall."

The men backed away from her as she swept out of the room. Silvi and Nuallen followed her into the rear chamber she shared with her mother. Nuallen shut the door and stood guard in front of it.

Silvi said, "That was impressive. The lightning struck at just the right time. A fine coincidence."

"Don't be so certain it was mere coincidence, Silvi." Lifa leaned her staff against the wall. "It is the longest night. The gods do walk the earth now. I can't help but feel they see what has happened here and will aid us. They promised us we would always be here. But we need to help ourselves as well."

She regarded Nuallen with a wry look. "I'm sorry for snapping my fingers at you and calling you 'thrall,' but you've become most sullen." She smiled as his lips quirked. "And how goes your campaign to convince them to accept you into their ranks?"

"It's slow, but progressing, mistress. They don't quite trust me yet, but they speak more freely around me now. By spring, I should have them believing my resentment toward you runs deep. When I disappear, they'll think I've run away."

Her voice softened. "Thank you for what you did, Nuallen. I think it is we who will owe you the debt when all this is over."

"And when it is over, Mistress, I shall ask your son, the jarl, for payment." He lowered his green eyes.

"I would not expect otherwise. For now, we must continue our efforts until he returns. We should hold off on any more deaths until they relax their guard. But then—"

"I will be ready." He raised his head, the iron collar around his powerful neck dark against his skin.

Silvi poured them cups of mead and handed them out. "To the Wild Hunt, then. May it be even more successful in the coming months."

She sipped. How much longer could they hold out? The outcasts had abused many of the women in the village. Hakon had forced their men into back-breaking labor and kept their warriors chained and half-starved. Their stores would be depleted before winter ended and before they could harvest the early crops.

Perhaps that didn't matter to Hakon and his men. They wouldn't be here once the snows melted, so it wouldn't matter to them if the people starved after they left. As long as they had enough for themselves.

And if there wasn't enough? Silvi's blood ran cold. The outcasts might just kill off the villagers to ensure the food wouldn't run out too soon. Her hand shook as she set down her cup.

Odin might have to "hunt" more often and sooner than they had planned. If her mother and she could make Hakon's men even more afraid than they already were, they might rebel against him, or leave here altogether to save themselves. A divided force was always weaker.

Eirik knew he needed to return as soon as possible. But where was he? He was safe, for the runes had shown her so, not long after he'd left. It was important that he be at Vargfjell before their cousin left on his raiding journeys.

However, what was important to their family might not be of interest to the gods. Then again, the gods had made a promise to them long ago with the fallen star, and so Odin must help Haardvik.

Lightning struck close by again, as if in answer. The longhouse shook.

She needed to seek her own answers with the runes and within her heart. Find and touch Eirik's life force from time to time through them, as she had done before. This was the right time of year to call on the ancient wisdoms.

During the twelve nights of Jul, when the doorway between the worlds was open, she would have to step through and see what lay beyond.

Chapter Ten

Eirik tied the bone skates to his shoes and grinned as Birgitta slipped on the ice. Of course she just happened to fall close enough to Sjurd so he could catch her before her rear hit the frozen surface of the lake. She gave the stable hand a pretty smile and wobbled off.

Everyone from Thorsfell was out for the day. The weather was fine and they were still celebrating the twelve nights of Jul. Even he was taking a rest from his work on the rune stone.

He wanted a chance to speak to Asa. Ever since the night they'd last carved the runes in the dragon, she had avoided him. She'd done so when he'd first arrived in the village, but then she'd thawed somewhat. Or, in the case of their work together, she'd thawed quite a bit.

But after that, she'd been distant and he wanted to know why. If only he had found her right away after she'd fled outside that night. But Estrid had stopped him.

He drew a quick breath. Could that be it? Had Asa seen Estrid holding him? He would have seemed heartless at best, having been with her, then embracing Estrid right afterward.

Nodding to himself, he rose. He needed to make this right with Asa. Even if this misunderstanding meant nothing in the future, it would impede their work together now. She had already asked him to just tell her the right way to carve the last rune, but there was so much more to it than making cuts in a piece of wood.

He skated out onto the lake. Clusters of people laughed and fell and showed off their prowess. In the past, he'd skated as a means to travel, of course. It was often the quickest way to cross a fjord in the winter. But he'd seldom simply enjoyed himself as the villagers were doing.

Even Magnus's warriors were out for the day, though they were armed. What many of the large men lacked in grace, they made up for in sheer determination to skate the fastest and hardest. The skates were difficult to turn and stop, so there were several collisions, sending the victims flying across the ice. They ended up in laughing heaps on the snowy shore and he took care to avoid them.

Asa, though, skated with such grace, he could only watch her, admiration growing in him. She turned and spun in tight spirals, then stopped short, to head off in another direction. Her body had the strength of a warrior, with the lightness and agility of a woman. But their skates wouldn't allow such moves, so how could she maneuver like that?

Perhaps he'd ask her. Then he'd speak further with her and make certain she knew the truth about her cousin. He still hadn't spoken to Magnus about Estrid, but he would try to this day.

She sped off toward another part of the lake, away from the others, and he followed. He couldn't turn like she did, but he could skate fast and he glided over the smooth ice, matching her speed.

So beautiful and graceful, she appeared to fly, her cloak and her hair streaming out behind her. They rounded a curve in the shoreline, cutting them off from the others' sight, and he closed in.

Her foot slipped out from under her. She lost control and went down hard on the ice. It gave way beneath her and she plunged in, disappearing as though she'd never been there. If he hadn't seen it happen, he would never have suspected it.

Shouting for help, he sped up. She had to come back to the surface. He had to see her head, her hand, anything. But there was no sign of her. He approached the spot and slid to his knees. The ice held.

The water in the hole was still, small bits of ice floating in it. Crawling flat, he grimaced as the surface of the lake crackled beneath his weight. Thin lines spread out from beneath him like spider webs. He glanced behind him. No one had heard him. Even if they had, no one could come in time.

He reached the edge of the hole and looked in. "Asa?" Nothing moved. His heart pounded as he lay on his side and plunged his arm into the freezing water.

"*Asa.*" He felt around as far as he could, but found nothing. He would have to go in after her, though he would likely die as well. Still, if there was a chance . . .

Something touched his hand. He pushed himself farther over the edge and it cracked, but he reached in just a bit more.

He hit her arm and grabbed it, hard. The wrench almost pulled him in, but he hauled back, scrabbling on the slick surface as it shifted beneath him. A large crack appeared beside him, but he kept pulling.

Asa's upper body broke the surface, but she was limp, her eyes closed. He grasped her arm with both hands and heaved. She almost came onto the ice, but it shattered, sending her back in and he nearly went in on top of her. He backed up toward the shore, where the ice was thickest, still keeping hold on her arm while pulling her head out of the water again. He wouldn't lose his grip, or her.

Waterlogged and heavy, her clothing had likely kept her from gaining the surface to begin with. He tore the pin from her cloak, freeing her from the weight. It sank beside her. Ripping the bronze brooches from her woolen dress, he tore it away until she was clad only in her thin linen shift.

He gave another heave and drew her onto the ice. In the past, on his voyages, he'd seen warriors pulled from the waves, saved from the goddess Ran, who collected those who had drowned. They had water in their lungs that had to be expelled, and he'd seen it done.

He turned her over onto her stomach and pushed hard on her back. At first, nothing happened. He tried again. "Ran, you live in the sea, not the lakes. You won't have this woman."

Over and over, he pushed on her back until, finally, she coughed and water rushed out of her mouth. He kept pumping until she was coughing and breathing on her own.

She was still unconscious and had turned blue, her skin as cold as death. He took off his own cloak and wrapped her in it so that only her head showed. The frigid air hit him and he gasped, but it would be so much worse for her. When he'd fallen into the fjord during the battle at Haardvik, the coldness of the water had nearly killed him, but it hadn't been full winter yet. Now it was. He had to get her to warmth immediately.

He slid her along the ice until they got to a more secure place. Balancing on his blades, he picked her up and pushed off. She was breathing but wasn't moving, and her skin was gray. He moved more slowly with her weight. Their skates weren't designed for a quick acceleration, but he clutched her closer to him and pushed with all his strength.

As he rounded the curve of the shoreline, he looked toward the crowd, far across the lake. They hadn't seen him yet, but he didn't head toward them. It would be shorter to the longhouse if he just kept going straight. He made it to the bank and climbed up, glancing back. The others must have seen him then, for they had started toward him, but he set Asa down, tore his skates off, and picked her up. He was stopping for no one.

He ran along the path to the village and rushed her into the longhouse. The fire burned low in the central hearth and he laid her beside it, where they'd placed him when he'd first come there during the blizzard.

Throwing more wood on the fire, he built up the blaze until it roared. Then he unrolled Asa from his cloak. She still breathed, though she hadn't woken yet. The servants had laid blankets near the fire to warm so when they all returned, they could wrap up in them. He grabbed several and knelt down beside her.

"You won't be happy with me, I think." He tore open her shift and slipped it off her. "But I have a feeling you saw plenty of me in the sauna. You have to awaken to be even angrier at me than you already are."

He'd dreamed of what she would look like beneath her heavy winter clothing. Now, all that mattered was that she was warm. And alive. He wrapped her in two blankets and placed her on another one. Her hair was sodden, so he pulled it out from under her and blotted it with another smaller blanket, then left it wrapped beside her.

She still wore her shoes and skates. He untied them from one foot and laid them aside, but when he took off the other skate, it didn't look right, so he examined it. It had broken. The bone had split along the length of it and the lower part, the blade, remained attached but might have shifted under her. At the speed she'd been going, she couldn't have controlled her movement, and when she fell, her impact against the normally safe ice must have shattered it beneath her.

The bone blades were sharper than usual, as though she had carved edges in them. Was this how she was able to turn like she had? But had it also weakened the skates? There was time to think on that later. He set them aside and went back to her. Her skin was a better color now and his shoulders unknotted in relief.

The front door burst open and Magnus strode in. Leif followed him, as did many of the villagers. He looked at Asa's wet shift on the floor and narrowed his eyes.

"What in the name of the gods happened?" He knelt beside Asa and Leif followed suit.

"She fell through the ice." Eirik also dropped to one knee. "I was skating behind her and saw her fall. When I got there, I couldn't see her. I reached down and was able to find her in the water. I pulled her out."

Magnus spoke to the crowd that had gathered inside the door. "She's alive. Everybody out except Birgitta."

The villagers filed out, some craning to try to see Asa, but the brothers remained kneeling in front of her, blocking the view. When they had all left, Birgitta closed the door and hurried past them, promising to bring broth from the stew they were to have that night.

Magnus touched his sister's cheek, then regarded Eirik. "Do you want to tell me why her shift is lying on the floor?"

Eirik met his gaze. "I had to strip most of her clothes to get her out of the water. They weighed her down and she couldn't get back up to the surface. Her cloak and dress were of thick wool. They were like anchors. With them off, I was able to pull her out. I wrapped her in my cloak and brought her here as fast as I could. Her shift was wet. I couldn't let her stay in that while she was wrapped in blankets. You would have done the same thing."

"Yes, but I'm her brother." Magnus's voice was curt.

"And that makes it better to see her naked?" Leif pulled the blanket over her shoulders. "You know Eirik did the right thing. He saved her life and that's all that matters. We can never repay that."

"No, we can't." Magnus sighed. "And I thank you. If you hadn't been there, I don't want to think of what would have happened. Why were you following her to begin with?"

"I wanted to speak with her. That's all. We had a misunderstanding. I only wanted to straighten it out. We still need to work together on the runes for the dragon. There can be no animosity between us for the magic to work."

"As long as that's all there is to it."

It wasn't, but Magnus didn't need to know that. Yet.

"I have to show you something." Eirik stood and they followed. He picked up the skate and handed it to Magnus. "It's broken there, along the length on the underside. She lost her balance just before she fell. But she is such a skilled skater, that's hard to believe. I think this is why."

"I've rarely known her to fall, even when she was a child." Magnus studied it, turning it over in his hand. "Look here." He held it out for them to see. "This appears to be where a knife blade was driven into the bone and twisted, causing a split."

Leif took it. "It wouldn't have been noticeable when Asa put them on. Who checks their skates that closely each time?"

"She's the only one who uses these?" Eirik took back the skate and examined it. There were marks at one end of the fracture. In his quick glance at it earlier, he had missed them.

"Yes. She keeps them in her room. See how she's altered these? The edge lets her turn more sharply."

"Eirik?"

At the sound of Asa's soft voice, they all knelt beside her again.

"I'm here." Eirik brushed back her damp hair. Magnus cleared his throat, but Eirik ignored him. "How do you feel?"

She opened her eyes and looked at all of them. "Cold. So cold. My foot gave way and I couldn't stop. I went under, like I had rocks in my clothing. And I couldn't swim upward. I could see the surface. It was just out of reach. But then I heard Eirik calling me. And there was a light. I had to reach for it, so I did, one last time. I don't remember anything after that."

"I took hold of your arm and pulled you out. Thank the gods you tried once more, or I wouldn't have been able to find you." He pulled up the blankets so they covered her to her chin. "Your wet clothes were pulling you under. I'm afraid I had to tear off your three bronze brooches and they were lost in the lake. I'm sorry."

"That's all right. I have others." She closed her eyes with a slight smile. "Now, if it had been my gold brooches, that would be another matter altogether."

"I'd buy you a dozen more." He stroked her face for a moment longer, then moved away. He'd best back away before her brothers pulled their seaxes on him.

"Asa, Birgitta is bringing you some hot broth," Magnus said. "It will help warm you from the inside. You need to drink it."

"Yes, Magnus." She seemed to slip back off to sleep, but the color was coming back into her face. Leif covered her with another blanket that had been warming by the fire.

Birgitta carried in a bowl of steaming broth, and Magnus roused her. He helped her sit up and the blanket slipped, baring her shoulders. Clutching the woven fabric to herself, she glanced at the wet shift lying on the floor near her. Her eyes widened. She looked up at Eirik as her cheeks colored.

He inclined his head to her and, after grabbing another cloak, left the longhouse. She would be in good hands between her servant and her brothers, so let them have their time with her. Soon, he would have his.

A group of villagers still lingered outside, but he didn't speak to them. He walked to the small shed where he carved the rune stone, and shut the door against the world. Sitting down in front of the stone, he leaned forward, his elbows on his knees, and stared at the World Tree he'd engraved on it.

How close he had come to losing her. Echoes of the loss of his wife raced through him and he shuddered. Asa had filled his heart, little by little, when it had been empty of everything else. Sela, his son, Haardvik, his father, the sword of his family. So much loss had led him to her, and now it had nearly happened again.

He sat back and set his jaw. The gods had given him a gift. Now he needed to grasp it with both hands. He'd been so focused on what he needed to do to get his people and home back that he'd thought to leave her behind and perhaps return to court her another time when everything was settled. But how could he know that would ever happen? In this uncertain, brutal world, that day might never come. In the meantime, their lives would slip away.

Her destiny was becoming intertwined with his. Her family had saved his life and now he had saved both Magnus's and Asa's lives. That created a bond between them that would not break. Then there was the power that coursed between them when they worked on the runes together. And the rightness that filled him when he was near her. Perhaps the gods were trying to tell him what he needed to do.

And when the gods whispered in one's ear, it was always wise to listen.

* * *

"Do you think Eirik could have tried to harm her?" Magnus picked up the skate again from the table in his sleeping chamber. The damage was intentional.

Leif grimaced. "Whoever did this wasn't very skilled. Eirik doesn't strike me as being this careless. And why would he want to harm her? It's obvious he's drawn to her."

"But she doesn't return his attentions, the same as any other man who has wanted her. I've seen her ignore him, especially since the last time they spent the evening carving the runes on her dragon. He might resent that."

"I don't see it, Magnus. He said he wanted to speak with her about some misunderstanding between them. That would have been after the damage was done to the skate."

"Perhaps he was covering his tracks. He might have wanted to see what happened to her. I'm not saying he wanted to kill her. He may have wanted to frighten her in retribution and it went too far."

"Someone wanted to frighten her." Leif crossed his arms. "But not Eirik. He saved your life, by the gods. And now he's saved Asa's." He winced. "I hope I'm not next. The third time tells the tale."

Magnus sighed. "I don't see it either. But then who would do this? It would have to be one of our own people, and that's very disturbing."

Someone knocked on the door frame. "Magnus, can I speak with you?"

He glanced at Leif and set the skate on the table. "Of course, Eirik. Come in."

"There's something we need to discuss," he said as he closed the door behind him. "It involves your cousin Estrid."

"What of her?" Leif sat in one of the chairs at the table, as did Magnus.

Eirik joined them. "I don't want to offend any member of your family. I'm a guest here and I appreciate all you've done for me. But I fear Estrid has imagined some type of relationship between us and it may have gotten out of hand. I don't want any misunderstandings."

"She's just lovesick over you," Magnus said, "like half the women here."

Eirik frowned. "Not half."

"You're right." Leif grinned. "More than half."

"Leif." Magnus shot him a glare. "We're very isolated here, Eirik. There isn't much of a chance for our young folk to meet others. You're bound to cause interest among the women. And Estrid. She's very needy. She lost her father when she was young, and her mother remarried too soon, then ignored her. The man she married committed a heinous crime. I tried to kill him for it, but I was wounded and he escaped. Then, not long after that, her mother and ours returned to their homeland."

He leaned back in his chair. "All of this has made her temperamental and sharp. She fears being left behind again and she clings to men so much that it is off-putting. None of them will marry her, no matter how much I increase her dowry."

"It's more than just that she makes it clear she wants me. She imagines I love her as well, though I swear I have done nothing to make her think so."

"All you have to do is smile at her," Leif said. "She'll jump at that. In some ways, I'm thankful Magnus and I are so closely related to her. We're off limits. Then again, we *are* related to her." He winced.

"I can handle myself." Eirik took a deep breath, as though he wasn't certain of the road he was about to travel. "She said some things about Asa that, in light of what has happened, have me concerned."

"What sort of things?" Magnus narrowed his eyes and his blood stilled at the grimness in Eirik's voice.

"That Asa has never let her have anyone and that she's cast her spell over me. She said she won't give up and won't let Asa destroy me, as well. That sounds like something more than a lovesick woman."

"When did she say this?"

"The night before Jul. I tried to speak with you after that, but with all the festivities, I didn't get the chance. I didn't think it was urgent. Now, I'm giving that another thought."

Magnus looked at Leif. "I can't believe it of Estrid. She and Asa played together as children. We'll keep an eye out for anything or anyone that comes near Asa. And we won't tell her about it. I don't want her to be afraid or concerned."

"Don't you think it's better to let her know so she can guard herself?" Eirik's voice was sharp. "You can't be with her day and night. By keeping this from her, you leave her defenseless. I've seen her with a blade. She's a shieldmaiden, by the gods, yet you treat her like spun glass."

"How we treat our sister is none of your concern." Magnus fisted his hands on the table between them. "I may call you friend, rune caster, but you overstep yourself in this. I am still jarl here, and yet you speak to me as an equal."

Eirik's eyes grew sharp and hard. "In our concern for Asa, we are equal. Perhaps one day, my right to protect her will outweigh yours."

Leif had been sitting back, one ankle crossed over the other, listening. But at Eirik's words, he went very still. "Watch your dreams, rune caster. Her bride price is such that only a jarl could afford it. And a very wealthy one at that. Anyone who is worthy of her would have to pass through us first. So far, none have. Don't forget it."

Eirik smiled at both of them as he rose, but it didn't touch his eyes. "Forget it? I'm counting on it. I'll stand by your decision not to tell her. For now. But know that I'm also watching out for her. And, if the gods are kind, I always will."

After Eirik left, Magnus sat back. "What do you make of that?"

"He wasn't worried about the bride price. I told you when he first came here that he's a lost jarl, trying to find his destiny."

"Be serious for once in your life. This thing with Estrid is disturbing. She's always been a problem, but she's never shown signs of being dangerous." He raked his hand through his hair. "I'd be inclined to just stay back and watch, but when Eirik read my runes, he said that through my inaction I would cause harm to someone I love."

"And that's why I don't bother with all the gods and signs and portents. They just muck up everything." Leif stretched. "Do what you think is right, as always, Magnus. We'll only have to make certain the seas are smooth around us and we can sail until the late winter, when he leaves. Then all will be back to normal and we can get on with our lives."

Magnus stared down at the damaged skate. Yes, that was Leif's outlook on the world. His ships always sailed on calm oceans and a fair wind always blew in the direction they were headed. But what about the shoals one didn't see and the storms that lay hidden over the edge of the world until they bore down on one? With this threat against Asa, along with the menace of the outcasts, when the storm did hit, they might need help guiding the ship to safety.

With Eirik's intelligence, quick thinking, and clear vision, what if he proved not to be the storm, but the best navigator through it?

"You've already trounced me three times in a row, Asa. As usual." Leif swept his hand over the *tafl* board where the slaughtered remains of his king's army lay strewn. "I'm not letting myself get killed a fourth time."

"Just one more game?" Asa picked up the king and bobbed it in front of her brother. "You and Magnus haven't let me do anything all day except sit around and drink hot broth. I feel fine."

"It's only been one day since you fell in the lake. We want to be certain you don't tire yourself. Tomorrow you can go back to carving." He grabbed the game piece out of her hand and laid it down sideways on the board. "See? The king's dead. Or sleeping. So either everyone has to mourn or they have to go to bed. I'm for sleeping, myself. And you should be, as well."

"I'm not tired. All I've done all day is rest."

He rose and came around the table and ruffled her hair. "I didn't, so I'm tired. Sleep well, Asa."

She let out a sharp breath in frustration. Magnus and Leif hadn't let her out of their sights all day. They'd insisted she stay by the fire, wrapped in warm blankets. And up to her neck in boredom.

A log on the fire cracked, sending sparks up toward the ceiling. The heat felt so good. She thought she'd never be warm again, even after Eirik had pulled her out of the water. The wind and the freedom had been so exhilarating as she'd sped across the ice yesterday. Then, in an instant, freezing darkness had burst around her and she couldn't breathe, couldn't swim, couldn't scream for help. But she could hear. A voice, so deep and strong, called to her. At first, she'd thought it was one of the gods beckoning her, and she'd seen a light above her, like that of Asgard.

Eirik. She'd reached for him, but the darkness had pulled her under, in the water and in her mind, and she remembered nothing after that.

How long would it be until she stopped reliving it? She already had enough of the past crawling through her thoughts until, at times, it pushed out everything else. Perhaps, in time, it would fade. After all, she'd been through worse.

"Asa?"

The same voice, Eirik's voice, made her stomach wrench. She looked up at him and strengthened her resolve. He had saved her life and she hadn't even thanked him yet.

He sat down where Leif had been. "I heard you asking Leif for another game. Would you like to play someone different for a change? I heard no one else will take you on."

His eyes, so blue and clear, pierced something inside of her. She didn't need any more wounds. She lowered her gaze. "I don't know. I'm more tired than I thought."

"No, you're not." He picked up the king and stood it in the center of the board. "See? The king has awakened."

She glanced at him. His eyes held a sharp twinkle in them. Not a look of lust, like Estrid always told her, but of teasing, the way her brothers taunted her. She could never resist them. And she couldn't resist him.

"Very well. I'll play you one game."

"I always took a board with me on long voyages," he said as they set up the pieces. "It helped pass the time. And I'll warn you, I went on many long voyages."

She only smiled as she put her final pieces in place on the squares. Preferring to be the attacker, she would try to keep the king from reaching the safety of the edge of the board.

He moved his pieces out from the king, keeping him surrounded and protected. She advanced toward him. The farther away from the center he got, the more he had to spread his defenses out.

Asa swept around behind him with a wave of attackers in a few moves, taking down the defenders. She seized the monarch.

Eirik studied the carnage on the board. She sat back and waited for his reaction. Most men couldn't accept defeat at her hand. How would he take it?

He only pushed his hair back over his shoulder. "Ah, you've captured me, as I always thought you would. Have mercy on me and give me another chance?"

The slow, wicked smile he gave her drove straight into her like a knife strike. His eyes crinkled a bit at the edges and the dimple in his cheek drew her gaze. Warmth pooled between her thighs. He wasn't talking about the game.

He likely used this smile on his other conquests. She took a fortifying breath. It *had* been nice to play someone different.

"Just one more. To give you a chance at redemption." She bit her lip. Why had she put it that way? She didn't need him trying to redeem himself. She just needed him to leave her alone.

The second game traversed the entire board, with her chasing his king in all directions before he overran her warriors and gained the safe edge. She'd lost.

He grinned. "I knew if I tried long enough, I could crash through your defenses."

She inclined her head in acknowledgment. "And so you have. I should not like to meet up with you in warfare. You play an excellent game of strategy. But now, I need to go to bed. I have quite a bit of work to do tomorrow to make up for lost time."

She started to rise, but he put his hand on hers. "Please stay a moment. We need to talk."

"If it's about yesterday, I want to thank you for saving my life. I'll always remember it." She tried to pull her hand away, but he held firm.

"It's not that, Asa. Please sit. Just for a moment." When she hesitated, he surrounded her hand in his and caressed her palm. "Please."

Pressing her lips together, she sank back down. She didn't want to hear what he had to say, didn't want it to make a difference in what she would feel for him. The pain would still be there.

"I know you're hurting."

She frowned at him. "What do you mean? I was almost frozen, but I wasn't injured."

"That's not what I mean." He looked at their joined hands. "What you saw on the night before Jul, with Estrid and me, wasn't what you thought."

"I don't know what you're talking about."

"Asa, I can put things together. While we carved the second rune, you and I shared something very rare and powerful. But it wasn't just the ancient powers that coursed through us that night. It was something more. Something between us as a man and a woman."

She drew a breath to deny it, but she let it out, leaving the words unspoken.

"After that, when you left, I followed you outside to speak to you, so I know you were there. But Estrid stopped me and you saw us talking."

"I saw you embracing." She drew back, though he didn't let go of her hand. "That's your choice. It has nothing to do with me."

"You saw her embracing *me*. I didn't return it." He paused as though searching for the right words. "She misunderstood my feelings for her. I have none. I told her so and I fear she became upset. I didn't want to hurt her, but I had to tell her the truth."

That sounded like Estrid. She was so desperate for a man to love her that she often overreacted to any small kindness. She'd even thrown herself at *him*, the snake who'd been her stepfather. Granted, it had been before he'd turned on them all. Asa shuddered, blocking the memory as always.

Did she dare believe Eirik? And even if she did, why should that matter? But it did matter. The weight of anger and hurt that had lain within her these past few days lifted.

He picked up the hand he was still holding and brought it to his lips, kissing her palm. She stared, her bones all but melting under his gaze.

"They do this in Francia. They say it is pleasing to women."

His smile was infectious and she ducked her head as she gave in to it. This pressing of the lips to her hand was nice. Kissing was known in their culture, and the women of the village seemed to approve, judging by their talk in the weaving room. She wouldn't know.

"Very sweet, as I thought it would be." He kissed the back of her hand and let go, the tips of his fingers brushing along her skin. "It's late and you should rest. I enjoyed playing our games and I hope we can do so again soon. Sleep well."

His eyes held that sparkle again. She could become accustomed to their light and to the warmth it stirred in her. He rose and walked to his sleeping chamber. His stride was so free and easy, that of a man who knew his way in the world and took hold of it.

She sat up and struggled to shake off his spell. That had to be what it was. He was a rune caster. Who knew what powers he held? They had swirled around her as they'd carved the runes, and look how she had fallen under his influence then. And now.

Even if he hadn't been with Estrid, that still didn't mean he would want Asa. He'd seen her fear, her panic at his touch. Why would he wish to be with someone like her when he could have any woman? In the past, she'd seen couples together, embracing, kissing. Loving. For other women, that was natural. But not for her. He needed a beautiful, affectionate, undamaged woman who could give him what he wanted. What every man wanted.

She stared into the fire. And it couldn't be her.

Chapter Eleven

"My husband is dead, Jarl Magnus."

Asa dropped her carving knife and ran to the door of the weaving room. Rakel, a woman who lived on a farmstead nearby, knelt at Magnus's feet as he sat in his chair upon the dais in the hall. He reached down and drew her up. Several of the women of the household came to support her. She collapsed in their arms, crying. "The outcasts came and took everything. All our livestock and our food. My husband tried to stop them and they cut him down."

Magnus stood. "Arne, gather the men. We'll pursue them while the tracks are fresh. This time, we'll find them."

Asa rushed into her room and stripped off her gown. The men been hunting the outcasts every day for the past week, but all the traces of them they found were old. Now, with no falling snow to cover their tracks, the criminals would be easy to follow.

The warriors had all gathered in front of the longhouse. Asa set her shield on her back and tied on her skis. Her mind was clear, focused, and she needed to remain that way. Magnus skied over to her.

"Either Leif, Eirik, or I will be beside you at all times. Don't lose sight of us, no matter what happens."

Eirik? That was interesting. She smiled. "Ah yes, so I can better protect you all, brother?" She spoke loud enough that the men heard her. They struck their shields in appreciation, laughing.

"I mean it, Asa." He spoke low. "They have bows, which means they can kill us from afar. We may have to make a shield wall in an instant and you have to be near us. Don't get separated."

She sobered. "I won't. I know what I'm about, Magnus. After all, I had the best instructors."

"Flatterer." He raised his voice to his men. "We'll fan out in our assigned groups. Everyone will move toward the farmstead. Stay sharp. We can be certain we'll have to mount a defense first. Then we'll draw them in."

Eirik had stayed to the side. He poled his way to her and his face was grim. They hadn't spoken much since the night they'd played *tafl*, but he'd been gone from the longhouse so often, she'd only seen him late at night. He ate, then went to bed. In the mornings, by the time she rose, he'd already vanished for the day again. He'd gone with the warriors a few times, but not always.

"If your brothers or I tell you to do something, don't even think. Just do it." He checked his sword, loosening it in its sheath.

She looked at him. "I *have* done this before."

"On the seas. This is different. We can expect an ambush, whereas when you fought, you could see them coming."

"I know." A tiny flicker of trepidation spread out within her. She ignored it. It would be as it would be.

Not knowing if the outcasts were nearby, the warriors kept silent as they left the village, reining in their usual banter. Gliding on skis through the surrounding woods, Magnus and Eirik stayed to either side of Asa. Leif was with his own warriors a short way off. They traveled in groups, staying within hearing range in case the outcasts attacked one of them. Then the others could come to assist.

The farmstead was in ruins. The outcasts had smashed all the furnishings, broken the dishes, and killed or taken all the livestock.

Magnus cursed as he leaned on his ski poles. "There was no reason for them to do this unless it was in retribution for Eirik's killing one of them to protect me."

"Or to draw us into a confrontation," Eirik said. "To raise the stakes."

"Why?" Asa glided closer to them. "They can't want to take us on in direct conflict. We're too powerful."

"We don't know how many of them there are." Magnus watched as his men checked the buildings. "For all we know, they might outnumber us."

"If it comes to a war with them," Eirik said, "do you have any allies farther west, near the coast?"

"My closest neighbor in the next valley is my greatest rival in trading, and we keep apart. He killed the old jarl who ruled there, and took over the village. I have many other contacts for trade. But not for warfare. We're so isolated, we've never worried about it before. We're equipped to defend our merchant vessels, but you only need so many men per ship for that. This is something very different."

Eirik nodded. He looked deep in thought, his gaze on the trees beyond the clearing.

"I've found their tracks." One of Magnus's men poled over to them, and pointed. "They've headed north."

"Then, we follow." Magnus signaled the groups to start off.

They hadn't skied far when Eirik slowed. "Wait."

Everyone in their group stopped. He held his hand up, his eyes unfocused. Magnus looked at Asa, but she shrugged.

"They're ahead of us. Coming this way." Without waiting for the others, Eirik slashed the ties on his skis and pulled his shield from his back.

Magnus watched him for a moment, then nodded. "Prepare for battle."

She cut her own skis free and slipped her shield into position. If Magnus trusted Eirik, so did she. Perhaps the gods had given him, a rune caster, other ways of sensing. Their warriors couldn't take the chance and not heed him.

They moved, silent and wary, through the trees. Warning the other groups would give away their own position. All they could do was move forward and hope they engaged the outcasts first.

An arrow struck Arne's shield. Shouting, they all raised their own. Asa lifted hers and an arrow hit it at chest level.

Magnus leaped to stand at her back, and Eirik moved to her side. Magnus yelled for the men to circle. They all came together, their shields to the outside. Those in the center held theirs high while the men on the outside knelt and held theirs in front of them at different levels. Magnus hauled her behind him, into the middle. She lifted her shield flat overhead, blocking the top space.

Arrows impacted the shields from all directions. Several of them penetrated the shield wall, hitting men. One man fell. None of the other wounds appeared to be life threatening.

Leif's yell echoed through the woods and Asa smiled, waiting. At the sound of battle, those with bows readied them.

Magnus nodded. "Shields down."

The men on the outside lowered their shields. Those behind them let their own arrows fly, aiming for the outcasts who were running from Leif's men.

Eirik stood with Asa and four of their men, his sword raised. "Good tactic. Concentrate their attention on one group. Attack from behind with another."

Several of the outcasts ran toward them. They met, shield to shield. Asa couldn't withstand the full impact of a line of men, so she hung back. As the men battered each other with their shields, she turned hers edge first and struck through the openings. The metal rim shattered a shield and she followed through with a sword cut. Ducking a spear thrust from overhead, she slammed the iron boss in the center of her shield into the arm of an outcast. He tried to sweep her shield aside with his own, leaving himself open. She slew him, then looked for another opponent.

Eirik fought not far from her. He was unstoppable, never hesitating, his blade like an arc of light. The bodies of the men he had killed lay in a bloody pile around him. He stepped over them to take on another man.

Magnus dispatched his own adversary and turned toward her. His eyes went wide. Air whistled behind her and she spun and ducked, wedging her shield against her entire arm and shoulder for more strength. An axe smashed into it, shattering it. The impact stunned her. Pain speared up her arm, into her shoulder. She dropped the remains of her shield. Eirik yelled her name from behind, but she didn't take her eyes off the large man grinning at her. He hefted his axe again and came at her.

She grabbed her cloak and swept it in front of her as she leaped aside. Her shoulder blazed when she flipped the material over the man's arm as he tried to strike her. It tangled in his axe and she yanked. He didn't let go of the handle. The unexpected tactic threw him off balance, right toward her. Aided by his momentum, she drove her sword blade into his stomach. He fell, screaming. She tugged the blade back out of his body and sliced his throat, silencing him.

Her arm burned as she stood staring down at him, his blood pooling at her feet. Her own blood raced, her breath coming hard and fast. Her muscles tightened with strength and elation. Eirik and Magnus reached her side together. Her brother grabbed her.

"Are you all right? Your arm—"

"Is fine."

"Fall back to safety," Eirik said. "Get your breath. We all do it. There's no dishonor in that."

"I know. I'm fine. Let me just get another shield."

"No need," Leif said as he walked up to them. "We've won." He pointed with his sword. "A few still fight, though most of them are dead, and we're chasing the rest of them. Some may get away, but not many."

She closed her eyes, light-headed as the battle receded and realization hit her. That had been too close. She'd often used deflection for her defense, but she'd had no time to angle her shield. They weren't made to take that kind of impact straight on. At least her hand had continued to work well enough so she could grab her cloak.

"Was there any sign of a leader?" Eirik shrugged his shield over his back.

"No. They were quite a mismatched lot," Leif said. "No leader, no plans or strategy that we could see. They were fighting to survive, while we fight to win."

"Any idea of how many we lost?" Magnus shook the blood off his sword.

"No. We'll have to wait until the men who are chasing them return for a final tally. Not many, I think."

"Any number is too much," Magnus said. "Gather our men, strip the bodies of the outcasts, and dump them in the ground somewhere. They don't deserve a pyre that will send them to the gods."

Leif nodded and strode away, calling out orders. Asa knelt and wiped her blade on the clothes of the man she had killed. Blood had flecked her arms and spattered her clothing during the fight. If she was as filthy as Magnus and Eirik . . .

Wincing, she glanced up at Eirik.

"You fought well today." His eyes were filled with admiration.

She shrugged and stood, sheathing her sword, but Magnus frowned.

"No, you didn't. You didn't stay near us as I told you to. Then your shield broke." Magnus pulled her to him, embracing her hard. "We could have lost you."

"No, Magnus. It was not the will of the gods." He smelled of sweat and leather and the metallic tang of blood. She likely did as well. She leaned back in his strong arms and met his angry gaze. "We can't know where the tides of battle will sweep us. I couldn't look for you and fight my opponents at the same time."

"Listen to me, Asa."

"Leave me be, Magnus." She stepped away from him. Weariness sapped her strength and her legs threatened to give out. Now that the fighting was over, all the battle-strength left her. She just wanted to get clean and go to sleep. She would ache tomorrow, but she couldn't show it. Magnus needed only a small excuse to forbid her to fight. She wasn't going to give him one.

Her brother turned his attention to Eirik. "How did you know they were ahead of us in the woods?"

"It was a feeling in my gut. Many warriors get it, if they've fought enough. It's more a matter of experience than anything else."

Magnus smiled. "Do rune casters have to fight that often?"

"In some parts of the world I've been to, they do."

Asa studied him. She'd had glimpses of him during the skirmish. Eirik hadn't fought like a man who had to defend himself from time to time. He'd fought like no one she'd ever seen before, even her brothers, with no regard for himself. None of the outcasts could have seen him deal them their death strokes, he'd moved so fast. He'd never used his shield to protect himself. It was part of his attack as he'd slammed it into the faces and bodies of those who faced him, and pressed it against their sword arms to render them defenseless while he slew them.

Magnus's warriors knew those tactics, but Eirik had used them with such efficiency and skill, he must have learned at a very high level. Blood spattered him, but none of it was his. Even her brothers and she had cuts and scrapes.

No one else showed the weariness that weighed her down. She stood taller and straightened her shoulders. And winced when the right one twinged. At least it wasn't the arm she used the most. Sometimes it worked to her advantage to use her sword in her left hand. It threw her opponents off.

Asa looked out over the battleground. Magnus and Leif spoke with several of their men who had returned from the woods. Eirik was with them. Their faces were grim, their bodies tense. The game had changed now. The outcasts no longer made quick strikes to take some livestock, which could be replaced. Both sides had shed blood. Now it was a matter of revenge and honor and the need to protect an entire people.

Now, it was a fight to the death.

*   *   *

The dreams came.

Asa dreaded the nights following the skirmish. She stayed awake later and later so she'd be too tired to dream. But nothing stopped them.

She'd considered carving the final rune herself. She had already drawn it on the dragon's neck. If she could just tap into the power she'd felt when she'd made the symbols on the right side, she might be able to do it herself. Then she wouldn't have to risk Eirik's touch again.

It didn't matter that he hadn't been with Estrid, or any of the other women. She couldn't be what he'd want her to be. It was better not to allow things to go further than they already had. If he helped her again, with what lay between them, it was inevitable they would become even closer this time. And that could not be. It would open her too wide to the memories Magnus said she must bury within her. But it made no difference how long she stared at the rune drawn in charcoal on the dragon. The magic eluded her.

And still the dreams came.

The dragon cried out and lashed its tail closer and closer to her, anger dripping from it like blood. Its massive wings blocked out the scarlet sun. Runes glowed golden in the air she breathed and their essence roared into her, filling her with the knowledge of what they were. She woke, sweating and gasping, exhausted. She'd asked their healer, Ingeborg, for herbs to help her sleep, and she'd taken even more than she should have.

And still the dreams came.

Eirik stood beside the dragon, his hand on its gleaming scales. When he stepped away from it, runic symbols burned where he'd touched it. He walked to her and she raised her head in defiance. She reached for her sword, but it was not at her side. She was defenseless.

He lifted his hand to her face, the hand that had the power to burn runes into a dragon's scales. She flinched. Would his magic sear into her as well? He cupped her cheek. His touch was soft, yet strong. Possessive. Bringing his fingers up beneath her hair, he held her for his kiss. Just as their lips brushed, she woke.

She lay in the darkness of her room, her skin hot. A longing she couldn't name thrummed through her. What would it be like to have a man look at her with admiration? Not for her sword skills, but for her as a woman? A man like Eirik?

Turning onto her side, she closed her eyes. This was all he could ever be to her—a fantasy in the night, a flicker of another life where her past was different, where she was still free and happy. Where Magnus hadn't almost died because of the allure of her beauty. Where her girlish innocence hadn't been shattered in one bloody moment. Where her honor hadn't hung in shameful tatters ever after.

Her throat swelled as a tear slipped from the corner of her eye. She buried her face in the pillow. Only in a fantasy world could she love a fine, strong man, as any woman could. A world where she could be worthy of him, standing beside him as his equal in all things. A world that didn't exist.

She dried her eyes on the blanket. She had to work with him. The dragon demanded it, wanted its due, needed to drink the magic Eirik had. It would accept no other.

This was madness. She sat up, clutching the blanket to her throat. Eirik was only a man, the dragon only a carving. All these dreams lay in her mind, or perhaps the gods tried to speak to her through them. Whatever they were, maybe if she gave in, she could find peace. Not in the day, when she must see him, and speak with him, and long for him. But perhaps at night when she could forget the past in her sleep.

"I'll do this," she said aloud. "I'll ask for help in carving the final rune. You'll have what you want, then leave me be."

But did she speak to the dragon, or to Eirik?

The World Tree was finished.

Eirik stretched and set down his chisel. All the roots, leaves, and branches flowed in intricate curves around the center of the stone. Some of the branches found their way to the outside edge, wrapping around the back. He'd never done it that way before, but it seemed right.

He smiled. Perhaps Asa's carving was influencing him. And that wasn't the only effect she had on him. He hadn't spent as much time on this rune stone as he should. It was too tempting to seek her out in the longhouse and find some excuse to be with her. Frustration had driven him to go on patrol with Magnus's men. He'd needed the exercise to tire him so he could sleep at night. Knowing she was so near, in her own sleeping room, kept him awake, tense with desire.

In the brief moments he'd glimpsed her during the skirmish, he'd seen that she was a thinking fighter. She would have to be, to stand against men far larger than herself. Her speed and strategy gave her an advantage. She also used the size and strength of those she fought beside to augment her own tactics, and the result had been impressive.

One could learn all that in training. But to put it to use in battle, while slipping on spilled blood amid the screams of the dying, showed a clarity and focus of mind he'd rarely witnessed. Even in himself.

Standing, he arched his back until it cracked. He needed to chisel the runes that would run around the outside of the design, and then he could present it to Thorsfjell in thanks for all they'd done for him. He'd first thought to make it a farewell gift. Now, all that had changed.

He left the storage shed and walked around the side of the stables. The sounds of animals complaining came from within. Magnus had ordered all his people into the village for protection, and they'd brought their livestock with them.

It made for crowded, noisy living, but it was necessary. Until the threat was over, Magnus wouldn't risk any more of his people. If the criminals couldn't find any animals to take for food, they would have no choice but to either leave the area or come nearer to the village, exposing themselves. Magnus would be ready.

Eirik checked the street before he left the side of the stable. So far, no one had caught on to what he was doing, and he wanted to keep it that way. From time to time, through the past weeks, Magnus had expressed his curiosity about where Eirik went during the afternoons. He had managed to come up with excuses, but he was running out of them. It was fortunate that he was nearly finished with the carving.

He drew back. Estrid walked down the road, her hood over her head.

Backing into the shadows, he waited to see where Estrid was going. He usually didn't avoid women, but something about Estrid made the hairs rise on his skin. She walked to a house farther down the empty road and, after looking around, slipped inside. Many of Magnus's warriors who usually lived elsewhere, including Hjellmar, were staying in the house while they hunted the outcasts. Perhaps if she was seeing the disagreeable warrior, it would take her aim off of him.

He made his way to the longhouse. Serving girls passed bowls of stew and mugs of ale around the tables, and he sat down with Arne and several other men. The stew was flavorful, filled with mutton, carrots, parsnips, onions, and peas, and seasoned with dill, wild garlic, and costly imported pepper. Magnus spared no expense to feed his warriors well, but that was the secret to keeping them. Good food and drink and lots of it. Eirik's cousin Rorik had always told him that, and it would appear he was right. The men ate without talking, intent on their meal. He'd had enough of being alone all day, so after he finished, he looked at the other tables to see where a good conversation might be found. Hjellmar was nowhere to be seen, and neither was Estrid. *Good.*

The men at the table where Leif was sitting burst into laughter. As usual. Eirik picked up his mug, intending to join them and hear the newest tall tale Leif was telling, but a hand on his arm stopped him. His skin tightened. Estrid.

But it was Asa. It was rare that she sought him out and, relaxing, he smiled.

She didn't return it. "I need to speak with you. Come with me."

He followed her into the weaving room. She went to the covered carving and stood behind it, as though it would shield her from him. When the time came, nothing, not even a dragon, would keep him from her.

"The final rune needs to be cut," she said. "And I must ask for your help."

His heart became lighter. "Of course. I'll meet you here later, when all the others have gone to sleep."

"Later? I thought we could do this now."

When they would not be quite alone because of the crowd in the next room. "Later. I have a reason for that."

She studied him, suspicion in her dark eyes. "Why?"

"Come here then and find out." He gave her a shadow of a smile and left. Let her wonder. This night would tell him many things, on many levels. Would she meet with him?

He sat down at Leif's table and enjoyed the tales that grew taller as the evening wore on. He told a few, himself. And when the others had sought either their beds, the benches attached to the walls, or the floor, to pass out on, he went into the weaving room to wait.

Asa hadn't remained in the common room after the meal, so perhaps she wouldn't come at all. He drew the cloth off of the dragon's head and set it aside. Then he lit several lamps and built up the fire in the small central hearth. When he straightened to return to the carving, Asa stood in the doorway, biting her lip. It made her mouth even more red and inviting, but she couldn't know that.

He smiled. "Come and sit on your bench." He carried a chair over and set it on the left side, where they would carve the rune.

She frowned as she sat. "You were behind me before, so you could hold your hand over mine and call the power through it. Why is this different?"

He settled himself in the chair and leaned back. "Because this time you're going to call the power and carve the rune yourself. That's why I wanted to do this without the noise from the other room. So you could concentrate."

She stared at him. "I don't know anything about this, Eirik. The magic answers to you, not me."

"The power of the dragon answers to you. And how do you know you can't understand the runes? They speak. You have only to listen."

"I carved the others on the right side, but you said the magic was already there." She paused, her eyes downcast. "Something did happen. I felt strange and I saw the rune in my mind." She raised her eyes to his. "After that, I tried to carve this one the same way. Nothing happened."

"Didn't want to ask me?" He held up a hand as she started to speak. "I know this is new to you. In many ways. You couldn't call the power of this rune because you didn't know its meaning. But I'm going to tell you. Then you'll understand it and that will make the difference. It's only when you have the knowledge, that it becomes clear."

He touched the symbol. "This is Eihwaz. It holds the ability to harness the power of life and death. It represents the yew tree, which is poisonous, yet is the longest-lived tree we know and is always green. Even after it dies, its daughters will often grow inside its trunk, giving it immortality."

Taking her hand, he placed it on the sketch. She looked up and he met her questioning gaze. "Eihwaz is yours. It is death and life, in the same way you are a warrior who takes life and you're also a woman who has the gift to give it. It is the yew tree, and you are a wood carver. You create new things out of wood that is dead, giving it a renewed purpose. Within you lie both these attributes. They join in you to make you what you are, as they join within Eihwaz."

He withdrew his hand when she turned back to the carving. "I've had dreams," she said, "of you and the dragon and the runes. I knew they wouldn't leave me alone, wouldn't let me sleep, until I did this. But to do it alone . . ."

"Never alone." He brushed her cheek with the tips of his fingers. "I'll be here. I'll speak the words. I want you to open yourself to the energy, the magic. Feel it. See it. Then carve the rune."

Nodding, she picked up her knife. Its blade glinted like a flame in the soft firelight as she held it beside the wood. He sat back, reaching out to all the forces that gathered near the dragon. The energy around them built, tingling along his skin.

After drawing a deep breath, she touched the knife to the drawing of the rune. He hid a secret smile as she drew the blade down the upper diagonal to the right.

He whispered the ancient words so she could hear him. "Poison flows beneath, yet does not daunt the spirit. Its beauty outlasts even the coldest winter, finding rebirth in a new chance at life."

Her knife almost slipped as she set it to the top of the vertical stroke. She took another breath, gripped the handle tighter, and steadied herself. Her cut was smooth and straight.

What could have unnerved her? Was it the words he spoke? She was carving the rune correctly. He could not have done better himself. Her eyes were distant, even as she made her cuts, as though she saw into other places. Truly, the power had entered her, spoken to her, guided her hand.

The runes accepted her, even as they had accepted him so long ago.

She was forged from the same metal as he. They were both warriors. She was as strong and splendid as any shieldmaiden he had ever known. And yet, she would understand the magic he heard in the night, along with the power it brought to those willing to grasp it. She could hold it with him, and together . . .

Together they could make strong, proud sons and beautiful, fierce daughters. She'd fight at his side in the day, while at night, they'd build new lives together and a future that would span the ages.

He looked at Eihwaz as she began the final diagonal cut, down and to the right so that it met the vertical spine. It was, indeed, her rune. Now, if only she would accept it—and him. That would likely take some time, for there was still something hidden behind her eyes that spoke of fear and shadows, when she looked at him,

She lowered the knife but didn't speak. The magic still gripped her as it swirled around them.

"Asa." He placed his hand on her chin and turned her face to him. Her eyes were soft, the pupils large. It was as though she had to look through other places to see him, other places where he had walked. "Asa, come back to me." He caressed her cheek with his thumb, then combed his fingers under her hair to hold her, and touched her mouth with his. Drawing back, he watched her.

She focused on him, once again in this world. He enveloped her in his arms, kissing her again, a true kiss this time. Setting her hands on his thighs, she leaned closer to him. Her lips were sweet and warm. It was all he could do to keep from opening her mouth to his, to stop himself from taking the softness of her breast in his hand. She was still untried, still new to this.

Gritting his teeth, he pulled back, almost groaning with desire. She put her finger to her lips. He almost hauled her back to him at the seductive gesture. But he fought down the impulse. This needed to be right.

"Asa." His voice was thick. "You must have felt the power of the runes flowing through you."

Her hand dropped away from her mouth. "Yes."

"I think you have abilities, like mine. To read them, carve them, know them. Would you be willing to learn? I could teach you, as my mother taught me."

"I don't know. I never felt this way with our old master."

He smiled. "Gods, I hope not. Asa, it's not just the runes. It's us as well. I think the gods sent me here, made me lose my way in the blizzard, so we could meet. I've helped others carve runes before. Believe me, it's never been like this for me either. There's something more between us. I have to believe it's destiny."

She looked away from him, her hands clenched together. "I can't, Eirik. I can't be what you want."

"And what do I want?" He brushed back her hair.

She lowered her eyes. "What all men do. I let you kiss me to see what it was like, just once in my life. But that's all it can be. I'm sorry. It wouldn't be fair to you any other way."

"Why don't you let me decide what's fair to me? Asa, whatever lies in your past is something we can overcome. Together. But I need to know what it is."

"No." She shifted away from him, her eyes wide. "Magnus said I can't speak of it, can't even let it enter my mind. When you first touched me, I thought of it and it frightened me. Now, when I'm with you, the fear has faded. But it still waits within me. You even said it yourself when you spoke the ancient words. My rune is Eihwaz and with it, poison lies beneath."

That's why she'd trembled. He took her hand. "I also said that it doesn't daunt the spirit. You're too strong to allow something that no longer exists to control you. If there's anything that lies in your past, you need to speak of it, whether it's to me or not. Don't let the poison fester inside you."

"No." She rose as her eyes filled, and he let her go. "I must never speak of it to anyone. Thank you for this night, for the rune and the kiss. I'll always remember it." She bent down and kissed him, soft, light, then whirled and left.

He half stood, to go after her. But she was like a fleeing doe and his pursuit would make her run faster and farther. He let out a labored breath. This would take patience, and the gods knew he wasn't accustomed to that. Sela had accepted his suit without much comment, just a small nod. The women he'd sported with had been more than willing at a simple smile from him.

This was far different. It was everything. He didn't need the runes to tell him she was his other half. He'd scoffed at such things when his mother had spoken of it, but he'd been wrong. And it had cost Sela her life.

He rose, setting his hand on the top of the dragon's head. The power they had called still waited there, entwining Asa and him together like the lines on the interlaced pattern that curved beside the runes. Stroking downward, he ran his hand over the scales and traced the symbols.

He let his hand drop.

A noise interrupted his thoughts and he spun, looking toward the doorway. "Asa?" But it was empty. It must have been sounds coming from the people sleeping in the common room. He needed to sleep, as well. Tomorrow, he would begin chiseling the runes into the stone, then the story would be told, and never forgotten.

He made certain the small hearth fire was safe for the night, then doused the oil lamps around the workspace. As he lifted the last one, the light moved on the dragon's eye and it appeared to shift back toward him. How had Asa managed to achieve that much realism?

He lifted the lamp next to the eye, but it was the same as it ever was. Shaking his head, he covered it with the cloth. Then he put out the flame in the lamp, leaving the dragon in darkness.

He was supposed to keep *her* warm, not Asa.

Estrid peered out of the door of her sleeping chamber. Eirik made his way between the inert bodies on the floor in the common room. He went to his own room and shut the door. She leaned against the wall, hugging herself.

Asa had fallen in the lake. It shouldn't have happened that way, for she was just supposed to appear clumsy and unattractive. Instead, she'd gone into the icy water. If she hadn't called Eirik to her with her magic, she would have died. And then Estrid would have comforted him.

Yes. He would have turned to her because he had loved her before Asa lured him away with her beauty. But he had wrapped Asa in blankets, kept her warm and alive. And then Asa had cajoled him into the weaving room with her and she had wound her evil around him with the dragon's power. Not even his runes could prevent it.

He had just been in the room with her again, and even after she'd left, the dragon had held him in its grip, not allowing him to leave.

She'd gone to the door to watch him. He'd traced the runes, trying to free himself with their power that he commanded. He had caressed them as he should have caressed her, touching them in the same way he should have run his hand over her body. Finally, the runes had broken through the magic and he was free. Her own body had heated at the thought of what he could do with her, and she'd moaned. He'd heard her then and she'd left, not wanting the magic to harm her, as well. Then she wouldn't be able to help him, for she would also be caught in its web.

There was only one way to stop a spell. Only one way to free him and make him love her again. Only one way to go with him when he left here, and be with him forever. She clenched her fist until the nails cut into her palm.

The dragon had to die.

Chapter Twelve

Asa walked to the weaving room as Leif and many of the other warriors prepared to go back out for the day to patrol the area around Thorsfjell. There had been no signs of the outcasts since the skirmish. Rather than let them relax as time went on, the quiet made the men more alert. Unless the criminals moved from the area altogether, they would soon be back, foraging for food and supplies. Magnus had ordered all the farmsteads evacuated and stripped of anything that might be useful. It would either drive them away, or bring them here.

She stifled a yawn. Carving the final rune should have stopped the dreams, but she'd had so much trouble sleeping, she couldn't be certain. The vision she'd had while working on the dragon last night still wove through her mind. Everything else had faded away from her as she'd carved. Everything except the dragon. And Eirik.

A massive yew tree had spread out before her, its roots under her feet, its branches arching over her. Eirik had stood near the trunk. He'd pointed to the bark, and little by little, Eihwaz had appeared there, burning into the living tree. It'd formed in the way she should carve it, so she'd followed its pattern.

Ancient words had flowed around her while she'd worked and she'd breathed them in like the exotic perfume her father had once brought her mother from Miklagard. In the vision, Eirik had walked to her and bent his head and kissed her. It had drawn her through the mists, back into reality. Then he'd kissed her again.

She entered the weaving room and the women at the looms greeted her. Sitting down at her bench, she arranged her tools for the day. When he'd held her, she'd felt no fear of him. Was it the magic of the night, or could it happen again? And yet, it was a simple kiss, and he'd been gentle, not as men were when they—

As she set her hand on the cloth covering the dragon, she shuddered. One kiss would not tell the tale, and he would want so much more than that. If not now, then eventually. All men did.

She slid the cloth off the carving. Something was wrong, but for a moment, she didn't understand what it was. Then it hit her and she cried out.

Someone had gouged the left eye of the dragon. The knife was still embedded in the wood. It was as though the blade had been plunged into her heart. She jumped to her feet, knocking over the bench.

"What is it, Asa?" The other women came over from the looms and when they saw the damage, they gasped in shock. One ran from the room, calling for the jarl.

Magnus and several other men rushed into the room. "Asa, what's happened?" He caught her in his arms.

"The dragon, it's ruined." Her eyes filled. "Why would someone do this? It was so beautiful. I won't have time to make another one before the spring. We won't have the gold we need for the year."

Her stomach hurt. All those months of work, gone. It was her main contribution to the village to help buy their supplies and food. Now others would have to work harder to make up for it. She could carve smaller pieces, but all of them together wouldn't bring what the dragon would have. This one was her best yet. Even King Horik had shown interest in her work for his fine ships. Now she would have nothing to show him when they went to Hedeby.

Magnus bent to study it, his eyes hard. He placed his fingers to either side of the blade and slid it out of the wood. It came out without any further damage. "Is this one of your carving knives?"

She dried her eyes on the back of her hand. "No. I don't recognize it."

"Then that's good. Perhaps someone will know who it belongs to."

Their dragon was gone. *Their?* Somehow, she had begun thinking of it as both hers and Eirik's. Working with him on it had been so beautiful and magical, but now that was ruined forever.

Tears welled up again in her eyes and Magnus embraced her, holding her head to his wide chest. Those who gathered in the room murmured soothing words to her. Their encouragement heartened her and she dashed her tears again. She had to get herself under control. *Think.*

"Come sit with me." Magnus set the bench upright and urged her down next to him. "There are piles of wood dust on the floor here from your sanding. Is there anything you can mix with it to make a paste that you can put into the eye? Then when it's dried and hard, you can carve it anew."

"I don't know." Her mind was in a fog, shock still spreading through her. Why would this happen? It not only hurt her, it hurt everyone.

"Asa?"

She turned back to Magnus. "Perhaps if I mixed the wood dust with some stag antler glue, and filled the damage, it would harden, as you said. But it would never be right."

"You're going to paint this, aren't you?" At her nod, he said, "Then the repair will be covered and no one will ever know. It will be as beautiful as ever, just like you."

She forced herself to smile at him. He smoothed her hair, then took the knife and left, yelling for Arne. The people spoke comforting words to her before they, too, left to go about their day, but she barely heard them.

Just like you. Six years ago, Magnus had tried to fix the damage done to her. She'd buried it deep, painted it over with bright colors and pretty gilding. No one knew. But she did. The scars lay under the pretty coating of her smile and the glinting edge of her weapon-skill, threatening to crack the exterior and reveal the shame within. The rips and tears would never heal, and never let her love.

Her sword-skill was not born of any desire to win word-fame and find glory in the skald's tales, or even to dwell one day with Freya in Folkvang. It was born of soul-shrinking hatred, anger, and the need for revenge. The wound within her had spread, like decay, until it was all she was. She could repair the dragon's eye, and paint over the damage. But who could say the ocean wouldn't permeate the paint and rot the interior? No one would notice it because it was covered. But one day, it would fall apart and the rot would be revealed, because beneath the surface beauty, it was damaged.

Just like her.

The front door slammed and heavy footsteps came toward the weaving room. She sighed. What was this? Hedeby, the crossroads of Scandinavia?

All she wanted to do was sand and polish the rune she'd carved last night. Her nerves wouldn't allow her to try to repair the eye yet, though Magnus had ordered glue brought to her earlier that afternoon.

"By the gods."

She looked up at Eirik. His face was stormy and he radiated anger as he touched the damaged eye. "Oh, Asa." His tight voice shook. "I heard the stable hands talking. I had to come and see it for myself."

"I found the damage this morning when I uncovered it. The knife was still in it." Her voice hitched and he looked at her, his expression dark.

"Do you have the knife?"

"No. Magnus took it. We didn't recognize it."

"I stayed in here for a short time after you left last night, but it was just to make certain everything was well with the rune you'd carved. I prepared the fire for the night and covered the dragon, as I've seen you do. I doused the lamps, and went to bed. Everyone was asleep that I saw."

"I can repair it, I think. I have to try, at least."

"Of course. I have no doubt that you will." He sat on the bench beside her. "Now, if you carve in stone, as I do, that's another matter. One wrong move and the stone could crumble, and there's no repairing that. Wood is a bit more forgiving."

"I hope so. I've repaired breaks before, but never anything like this." She pressed her hand to the back of the dragon's neck. "It's as though someone cut into me, like I was violated."

He put his arms around her from behind and drew her back to his chest. His warm breath played in her hair and his strong arms rested around the front of her shoulders. "If there is ever anything I can do to help you, please know that I am here."

She should move away from him, both for her own sake and because anyone might come in on them. But she didn't. Safe. She was safe now, from anyone who would harm her. All her doubts fell away, about whether or not she could repair the dragon and about what she was coming to feel for Eirik. He haunted her thoughts. She always looked for him in the common room to see if he was there during the two meals of the day. His strength and confidence drew her to him. Though they should have repelled her, they made her feel safe when she was near him.

That truth tore open the wounds within her. She leaned forward and he freed her. "I was going to carve the other rune today, but I don't think I can. It's as though something evil has touched it."

"Perhaps. But the symbols that are on it now will help dispel that. Let the magic work, Asa." Turning her to face him, he cupped her cheek with one hand. "Give it time and all things will be as they should be."

She nodded. Did he speak only of the magic, or of what lay between them? The depth of his voice seeped into her, moving something deep within. He gave her a gentle kiss, then stood. "If you think you need help with the rune on the other side, you have but to ask."

After he left, she studied the dragon's eye. Perhaps it wasn't quite as hopeless as she had first thought. She smiled, and certainty filled her. She'd made it, so she *could* repair it, and it would be beautiful and whole once again, worthy of a king's longship. And perhaps, she could become worthy of a man like Eirik. Did his magic let her see this? Could it help her heal, as well?

Only when she'd completed the carving and the painting would she be able to tell if she'd been successful. If she was careful and worked with great skill, there was no reason to think it wouldn't hold up forever, even in the roughest seas. But by the time she finished it, spring would have come to the coastal lands and Eirik would be leaving.

Someone had attacked her through the dragon, and because of that, they'd threatened Thorsfjell. The need to defend herself, the urge to fight for those she cared about, and the determination to never surrender and accept defeat—these were things she could understand. If she thought of it as she thought of warfare, she would be in her own world. And there, few could stand against her.

She picked up a piece of shark's skin and sanded Eihwaz. As the dragon healed, so would she. They both had been dealt a harsh blow, a terrible wound, but they would heal each other. The magic she'd felt before welled up inside her and she allowed it. A strength she hadn't felt for a long time grew in her, shoring up her mind and her heart. She could do this.

She would become like the dragon.

The rune stone was almost finished. It needed a few small touches, then people would read Jarl Sigrund's story for ages after this.

Eirik chipped at a rune, defining its edge. He should have already completed the stone, but he'd been distracted by what had happened to the dragon carving four weeks ago. For a few days after that, he hadn't been able to concentrate so, rather than make a mistake, he'd taken out his anger by going on patrol and training with the other men.

Asa had attacked the carving with new purpose, reshaping the eye until it was as it had been before. She'd begun painting it first, as though to cover the memory of what someone had done to it. Then she'd painted the rest of the dragon in browns, black, and green. She'd asked him about the proper colors for the runes and he'd advised her, but other than that, he'd left her alone with her work.

She seemed driven to work on it, almost defiant. Magnus posted men night and day to watch for any signs of trouble both in the village and in the longhouse, but nothing more had happened. She'd continued her work without incident and now she had almost completed it.

They would both finish their work, the dragon and the rune stone, at the same time. The winter was coming to an end. It would continue here in the *fjells* for some weeks or months yet, but near the coast, the warmth from the southern currents would soon carry spring with them. The storms would lessen and the ships would take to the sea again. And Rorik would leave to go raiding.

He needed to get to Trøndelag before that. He'd have to leave soon, even before the snows ended here. At times he'd used the runes to reach out to his sister. But was the warm assurance in his mind real? Or was it his own wishful imagination? His mother and sister were strong, but were they strong enough to withstand a winter with those bastards who had taken Haardvik?

He had to speak with Magnus and tell him of the possible threat to him from those outcasts. They'd said they would head this way in the spring to reap revenge on someone in this part of Norway. They might stumble across this place, as he had.

Or had he? He still couldn't give up the thought that the gods had brought him here for a reason. Was it because of Asa? Or was it something else altogether? An alliance between Magnus and him would benefit both of them, and, of course, there was a very pleasant way to cement that alliance.

He stretched and left the building. He hadn't eaten since the morning, and though they ate only two meals each day, it was midday and he could use some ale to tide him over.

He'd just sat down with Leif in the common room with a full mug when the front door burst open and Birgitta and Sjurd ran in. They were out of breath, their eyes wide.

"Outcasts," Sjurd said between breaths. "Up on the ridge. We saw them coming this way."

Magnus strode over to them. Leif and all the men gathered around and Eirik stood with them to listen. His blood raced and many of the warriors grinned. All of them were anticipating a good fight after waiting so long. Asa came to the door of the weaving room, a painting brush in her hand. She glanced at him and he gave her a slight smile.

"Slow down and tell me what you saw," Magnus said. "Where were you?"

Sjurd swallowed and blew out a deep breath. "We were in the woods near the stream, Jarl Magnus." He looked at Birgitta and she lowered her head and blushed. "Just talking. A flash of light caught my eye above, on the mountain ridge. I saw a line of men moving this way. I think the sun must have hit a sword blade or the metal part of a shield. I saw other flashes in the trees around them, so there may have been even more of them. I saw one of them on a large black horse. He was just sitting there, above them, watching."

Magnus set his hand on Sjurd's shoulder. "You did well." He looked at the other men around him. "Prepare for battle. Birgitta, spread the word for all the women and children to come here to the longhouse for protection. We can't guard the entire village, but we can shield this building. Leif, have the men meet in the road. We'll circle the innermost buildings. Let them come in. We can use the walls to our advantage.

"Arne, call in the patrols, but have them stay back, out of sight. When we engage the outcasts, they can attack them from behind. It will leave us shorthanded at first, but in the long run, it will be to our advantage as long as we can hold our line."

Eirik went to his small room and changed into his leather tunic. It was sewn with metal rings over it for protection and was padded underneath. He picked up his father's sword and ran his hand over the protection runes he had engraved there. It wasn't the Star Slayer, but it had always served his father well, and now it was his. He slid it into its sheath and belted it around his hips along with his seax.

Gripping his pendant of Mjölnir, Thor's hammer, he said a brief prayer to Thor. He didn't ask for a good outcome, for that was already fated. He only hoped to fight true and that those beside him would be blessed with hard hearts and firm hands.

Including Asa. She would be there in the battle, and for the first time, fear touched him. Not for himself, but that the future would be denied them. Whether she knew it or not, she was his. Now he had something else to live for—besides saving his people and Haardvik—and if he planned it right, he would have both.

But first, they had a battle to win.

"You'll stay here at the longhouse and guard it, Asa." Magnus crossed his arms over his chest as though he anticipated an argument. "I'll leave my best men here with you, including Arne. Keep it surrounded and slay anyone who breaks through our lines."

She nodded. While she would have wanted to be at the front with her brothers, it would be difficult to withstand the initial impact of battle between the forces of men. She was better off engaging individual outcasts with her stealth and cunning. Of course, if the outcasts broke through the lines, then it would be a melée. But until then, she'd guard the women and children in the building.

Magnus embraced her, cupping her head to his chest. "Take care. I leave my best warriors with you. Leif or I will try to return here as soon as we can to back you up. I imagine that Erik will be heading here as soon as he can, as well."

She looked up at him and he gave her a smile. "As long as all of you celebrate our victory tonight, I'll be happy."

He chuckled, releasing her. "Arne, watch out for her."

"I will, Jarl. Fight true and may the gods favor you this day." The large man struck his sword hilt with his hand.

"To you the same." Without glancing back, Magnus strode toward the edge of the village where the rest of the warriors waited.

Asa lifted her shield high against her shoulder. It was made for her, as all shields were made to the heights of their bearers. Because of that, it was smaller than most, but then, she presented a smaller target.

Arne stepped beside her. "I'll be at your back all day. As will the rest of my men."

She put her hand on his arm. "I'm sorry you won't be in on the first engagement, Arne. That must be a disappointment."

He hefted his battle-axe. "What we do here is just as important. We guard the future of Thorsfjell. There can be no greater honor."

Shouts broke from the northern outskirts of the village and she held her breath, listening. Arne nodded to his men. They fanned out around the area of the longhouse, watching, ready. The battle was joined to the northeast, as would be expected, since that was where the outcasts always came from.

Asa's blood chilled. *As would be expected . . .*

"Arne, come with me." She ran around the side of the building, but stopped short of rounding the corner to the back. Holding up a hand to stop him behind her, she peered around the wall. At least three dozen men stalked toward the longhouse. They carried few swords, for those were the weapons of the wealthy. But they had axes, spears, and bows and those were lethal enough.

She drew back. "Get your men. They've come over the mountain itself. Those my brothers fight may only be a distraction. Send a man to warn them, but they may not be able to help us until they've defeated the other group."

Grim-faced, Arne withdrew while she remained and watched. The outcasts' movements were slow and wary, but they aimed right for the vulnerable longhouse. There was no time to wait for her brothers. Her warriors would have to take them on.

The ragged group split up, each heading for the two ends of the building. That would weaken them, but it would also divide her force. She backed away, then ran to the front where Arne gathered their men.

"They've split up, so we have to, as well. They have mostly spears and axes. We'll meet them as closely as possible to make it difficult for them to use their bows. Once we engage them head on, we should have the upper hand."

"Use a shield wall to advance," Arne said to the men. "Try to drive them back together at the rear of the house and we'll close from both sides, trapping them in the middle. They may not realize what we're doing until they're caught."

"Use the wall of the house to your advantage until the last possible moment." Asa unsheathed her sword. "First as protection, then try to herd them toward it to prevent them from escaping. Their backs will be against the wall and we'll finish them off."

All the men murmured their agreement. As the group split, Arne came with her.

"No, my friend." She gave him a gentle push toward the other group, though he was more than twice her weight. "You need to lead those who go to the far side, as I'll lead the others."

He shook his head. "I swore to your brother I'd watch over you and I intend to do just that. My men know what they're about. My place is at your side."

They had no time to argue. She gave him a hard look before moving toward the back of the house, he and half of his men behind her. Signaling them to do the same, she flattened herself against the wall and listened. Her pounding heart made it difficult, but when the creak of the outcasts' leather clothing and soft jingling of their weapons told her they were very close to the corner, she nodded. She steeled herself with a deep, fortifying breath. This was it.

They brought their shields up. Arne dragged her behind them as they broke from behind the corner. The outcasts were a few man-lengths away and didn't have the time to fire their arrows. They met in an explosion of steel as spears and shields collided.

Asa lifted her shield above her head to avoid a spear an outcast thrust at her from over the wall of men. She crouched and whipped her sword underneath her shield, cutting the wielder's thighs open. He fell screaming. She dispatched him, slicing across his stomach with a backstroke.

She glanced to the other end of the house. Their men drove the outcasts back toward them, as they had planned. Arne must have seen it as well. He yelled. Half of his men backed away, then ran forward, slamming their shields into the enemy. Many of the criminals fell and died beneath their swords. But those who kept their feet were forced back little by little.

Asa moved to the outer flank. She didn't have the weight or strength to join the wall of men, but she could bring down any who thought to circle around and attack from behind. A large man broke from the right side, coming at her with his axe. Bracing her shield with her shoulder, she deflected his first hit with it, while ducking her head. As he over rotated, she struck his side. He wore thick leather padding, keeping her blade from penetrating all the way. She still cut him and he cried out.

He brought his axe back around and overhead. She lifted her

shield up just in time. The impact shattered the wood, though the leather covering held it together somewhat. The axe turned. The momentum drove splintered wood through her leather sleeve and into her arm.

The wood fell apart, dangling from the leather. She dropped what was left of it. He grinned at her, death in his eyes. She held his glare and the world faded so that only the two of them existed.

Holding her sword with both hands, she brought it in front of her. He still had his shield and his axe. She centered herself, balancing so she could move in any direction in an instant. Blood flowed from her arm. She kept her hands raised so that it wouldn't drip onto the hilt, making it slippery. The wood imbedded in her arm moved with the leather sleeve it had pierced, agonizing and distracting. But she focused on him. If she watched his chest, his eyes, she would see when he shifted.

There. He charged her, swinging his axe straight for her head. She ducked and spun behind him, moving in the same direction. Crouching, she brought her sword around and slashed the back of his calf. He roared in pain and rage and came at her, swinging.

He just missed her legs as she leaped aside. Big and clumsy, he couldn't recover from his strikes fast enough and she pierced him in the back with her sword. He should have fallen, but he pivoted with her blade still impaling him, ripping it out of her hands, and charged her again. Weaponless, she arched away from his stroke. His blood streamed onto the ground, making it slippery. When would he die?

A movement to the left caught her eye. Arne ran toward her, his face dark. She shifted to her right and the outcast followed her, lifting his axe. He hefted it back to throw it and she had no defense. She wouldn't be able to dodge it.

He stopped, a look of shock on his face. He dropped his weapon, then fell after it. He lay still, Arne's axe in the back of his head.

Arne never broke his stride, but kept running toward her. An outcast behind him raised his bow and took aim.

She yelled at Arne, pointing. It was too late. He turned, bringing his shield up, but the arrow hit him in the chest. He stood for a moment, staring down at it, then dropped to his knees and stayed there.

Asa ran to him, but he waved her off with a grimace. "You know better. Get your sword back. Fight on. And take this." He held out his shield. "I won't need it."

Swallowing back her tears, she took the shield. It was far heavier than the one she'd been accustomed to, but she'd have to use it in spite of her wounds. She ran to the fallen outcast. Setting her foot against his back, she yanked her sword out, then glanced one last time at Arne. Still kneeling on his heels, he nodded to her with an encouraging smile. The sounds of battle called to her, louder than ever now. She would avenge Arne no matter what it took.

Her anger drove her. Wading into the fighting, she slashed her way through the enemy. The world turned crimson. One of Magnus's men fell in front of her. An outcast lifted his spear to slay him before he could rise, but she slashed his legs out from under him with her blade, killing him. The fallen warrior shot to his feet, thanking her. She raised her sword in acknowledgment and moved on. Bathed in the stench of blood and fear rising around her, she searched through the tumult until she found the man who had shot Arne. His bow was on his back and he fought with a sword.

With a shout, she surged toward him, her blood on fire. Her arm blazed, but she ignored it. The man she sought wounded his opponent. She struck the side of his neck with her blade, almost decapitating him before he could deliver the death blow.

That done, she searched for another outcast to slay. The sound of the battle changed. More men poured around the corner of the long-house, Magnus, Leif, and Eirik at the front. They surrounded those already fighting, taking out the enemy as they moved in. She smashed her shield into the side of another outcast, knocking him down. One of Magnus's warriors finished him off.

Someone took her arm from behind and she spun, bringing her sword down over her opposite shoulder. Eirik ducked and grabbed her wrist at the midpoint of her swing.

"Odin's blood, Asa. Watch yourself." He kept tight hold of her wrist, searching her eyes.

Breathing hard, she forced herself to calm. Eirik. It was Eirik. And she had almost killed him. The crimson battle-haze faded into horror, and her strength drained away.

"Eirik." She swallowed. "Never do that again. I didn't know who you were."

He held her for a moment longer, then let her go. He looked at the blood from her arm that spattered down her side. "You're wounded. You should have withdrawn. The men who patrolled the area are coming in now and will reinforce us. Let's get you out of this crush."

She scooped her hair back from her face and it was sticky. "I couldn't leave. I'm all right. Arne—"

Three of the outcasts broke from the fighting and came at them. Eirik hauled her behind him. She pivoted so that she was back to back with him as the men circled them. Her energy surged once again. The men struck. She blocked a sword with her blade and used her shield edge to hit the man's arm as the blade passed. His grip on the sword loosened. She struck it from his grasp, smashing his hand with the metal edge of her shield. He tried to come at her with his own shield. She let it past her defense and took a hit to the front of her shoulder, but she moved with it, lessening the impact. Hooking her shield around his, she yanked him toward her, straight into her blade. She didn't watch him fall, but spun to see where Eirik was.

Her fight had drawn her several steps away from him. Eirik fought one of the men, while the other eased behind him. The second man lifted his sword, aiming at Eirik's back. Asa lunged just as he struck. She reached out with her shield, blocking the hit. She didn't have enough leverage to stop the blow, and her arm and shield hit Eirik's back. But the shield deflected the impact, though it drove the splinters of wood deeper into her arm.

She gasped in agony and swung her sword hard in reaction. It sliced the outcast's shoulder, but he didn't give up. He smashed his shield into her, driving her back and leaped forward to attack Eirik again.

Eirik glanced at her out of the corner of his eye as she stumbled. He drove his shield against his opponent's sword arm, trapping it, and disemboweled him. Pivoting, he faced the third man, who skidded to a stop. He backed away, eyes wide, no longer able to strike Eirik in the back. Eirik approached him in an almost negligent way, his shield down, sword at his side.

"Come now. You were so willing to kill me when my back was turned. Where's all that bravery now when we can look at each other as you die?"

The outcast broke and ran. Eirik shook his head and drew his knife from his belt. He flipped it at the man and it hit him in the back. He fell, screaming. Eirik dispatched him, then turned to her.

"Are you all right?" He strode to her and took her arm. "You've hurt yourself worse."

"It's nothing. Ingeborg will see to it when this is over."

She stood with him, looking down at the bodies. Most of the fighting had subsided. Only a few pockets of conflict still lingered, though it was obvious it was borne of the outcasts' desperation and not of any hope of their victory.

Then her head cleared. "Oh gods. Arne. He was hit after he saved my life."

Chapter Thirteen

Arne still knelt where Asa had left him. Blood covered his chest, spilling down the front of his body and pooling beneath him. He smiled as she dropped beside him. Eirik crouched down next to him and put his hand on his shoulder to steady him.

"Let me find Ingeborg," Asa said. "She can help you."

"No." Arne held her unwounded arm. "Even that good lady can't do anything for me now."

He gasped and Eirik helped him to lie down.

She blinked away her tears. It wouldn't do for him to see her cry. She was a shieldmaiden, by the gods. She wouldn't weep like some fragile foreign woman.

Covering her tears with a smile, she took his hand. "You can't give up, Arne. Who would tease me about my cooking?"

He chuckled, then coughed. "You'll have plenty of people to chide you about that, Asa. Just promise me that when you marry Eirik, you won't cook for him. We can't slay good warriors like that."

She glanced at Eirik. The edges of his mouth curled up just a bit as he watched her. Her cheeks heated as she looked down at the dying warrior.

"Arne, I don't know what you mean."

He squeezed her hand with surprising strength. "Don't waste my time like this. I don't have it to spare." He grimaced. "Grasp life with both hands, Asa, and take from it what you want. I've been kneeling here, watching the battle, feeling my life drain away. It can all change in an instant, and you wonder why you did not do so many things. When this started, I was looking forward to celebrating our victory in our longhouse with our people. Now I'll drink to it in Valhalla with the gods. I am content." His grip weakened and his hand fell away from her arm.

She nodded. "Here. Take this." She placed her bloodied sword hilt on his palm and closed his fingers around it.

He smiled. "Now I'm ready."

Magnus and Leif rushed to them, many of their men following. The twins knelt beside him, grim, stoic, while the others stood in a circle around them.

"He saved my life, Magnus." She held Arne's hand closed so he wouldn't lose his grip on the sword.

"Of course I did." His voice was weak. "I always obey my jarl."

"I thank you, Arne." Magnus placed his hand on the warrior's shoulder. "For all you have done over the years. Your word-fame will spread and we'll never let you be forgotten."

"That's all any warrior can ask." He closed his eyes. A smile spread over his face. "Ah, there they are. The Valkyries. They circle overhead, calling for me. Never let it be said I kept beautiful women waiting."

He sighed, and then lay still. Magnus bowed his head, his hand fisting over Arne's shoulder. Leif set his hand on the fallen warrior's sword arm for a moment, then rose.

Magnus also stood. "We have wounded to tend to and pyres to build. This night, we'll feast to celebrate our victory, as those who have fallen would have wanted."

The men murmured their agreement and dispersed. But Asa remained where she was. Arne had always been there, a friend to her and her brothers. Life wouldn't be the same without him. Her heart tore and tears filled her eyes. She didn't want any of the men to see her cry, so she lowered her head, blinking hard to press the moisture away. Her tears fell onto Arne's blood, mixing with it and sinking into the ground they had fought so hard to protect.

"Asa." Magnus took her uninjured arm and lifted her to her feet.

"No, Magnus. Leave me alone."

"Asa, look at me."

She did. His eyes were moist as well. "It's all right to mourn, Asa. We all do. Now go get your arm tended to. We have to clean up here."

"I'll take her." Eirik put his arm around her. "Come with me. I see

Ingeborg is setting up at the corner of the longhouse with the other women."

She nodded and walked with him. If only her arm were as numb as her emotions. Exhaustion swept over her and she stumbled. Eirik murmured a curse and swung her up in his arms.

"Eirik, put me down. I don't want anyone to see me like this."

"I think they have other things to think about," he said. "Besides, there are a number of wounded men who need help."

"But you're not carrying them."

"For one thing, they're too heavy." His voice held a hint of humor. "Second, they likely would try to kill me if I did it for the same reason as I do it for you."

"And why is that?"

He set her down on her feet without answering. They'd reached the area where Ingeborg was looking after the wounded. She tended a man, Aksel, who had a wound in his abdomen.

"Eat this so I can know where the sword wound is." The healer handed him a dried leek.

"It's disgusting," he said. "It looks like a shriveled—"

"Never mind that." Her voice was firm as she cleaned his wound. "Just eat it. If the blade perforated your stomach, I'll be able to smell it."

Aksel grimaced, but did as the healer said.

Ingeborg finished cleaning the wound, though it still bled. Looking inside it, she shook her head. Then she bent close to the gash, smelling it.

"Well, woman?" He tried to sit up, but she shoved him back down with no sympathy.

"It would seem the blade went in at an angle. I'll check this again in a short time, but I don't smell the leek yet. The gods may have smiled on you this time."

She upended a wineskin over the wound and he shot up, cursing as the liquid burned him. She called one of the women over.

"Keep an eye on this. Sniff the wound often and let me know if you smell anything other than his own bad attitude."

She stepped over to Asa. "Let me see this." Using her knife, she cut the leather sleeve, but didn't pull it away. "Kept fighting, did you? Stubborn."

"You have other wounds to see to that are worse than this," Asa said. "I'll go sit on the benches they've brought out and wait."

"The women have knowledge of healing." She poked at the wounds and Asa sucked in a hard breath. "I've done what I can for the worst of them so far, and the other women are seeing to the lesser injuries. Now sit down while I undo the damage you've inflicted on yourself."

Eirik chuckled. "Let's go sit here."

He helped her toward the benches set up near the wall of the long-house. She shook off his hand and walked by herself. When she sat down, she breathed a sigh of relief. Leaning back, she rested her head against the wall and closed her eyes.

They had won. The threat from the outcasts was over. But where there should have been elation, there was only numb sorrow. They were victorious, yes, but at such a great price. Where was the glory? The rejoicing they spoke about in the old tales?

Opening her eyes, she watched as the men piled the bodies of the outcasts into a large mound. They placed their own slain in neat rows, each with his weapon in his hands. She had grown up with all of them. Known them, trusted them, and now she would mourn them.

Her arm throbbed. If only she could just curl up and sleep, and when she woke, it would be months from now. She would be healed and all the pain, of both mind and body, would be gone. But that could not be. No matter how much time passed, she would never forget, just as she would never forget those who had fallen. Everyone in Thorsfjell owed them that much.

As she watched the men working, a movement on the side of the mountain above them caught her eye. A horse stood in the shadows of the trees. It was black and blended into the gloom. She narrowed her gaze, focusing. There was a rider on it, also wearing black. They were both so still, they seemed part of the mountain itself.

"Eirik." She glanced at him. He sat, as she had, with his eyes closed, leaning back against the wall. At the sound of her voice, he cracked open one eye. She tilted her head toward the slope. "Look just beyond that clearing, up the ridge about halfway. Do you see the man and horse up there?"

He didn't move his head, shifting his gaze through slit eyes. "Yes. You have good vision. Sjurd mentioned that, didn't he? That he saw someone with the outcasts?"

"Yes." As she watched, the rider turned and disappeared into the woods. "Even if we could saddle a horse in time, we wouldn't be able to catch him. And we're too tired to try."

"No matter. We'll let Magnus know, but if this man is their leader, he's done a bad job of it. And now, with all his men either dead or captured, he can't do much harm for a long time."

He rose to his feet, groaning. He had several scratches and cuts, and one deep gash to his upper arm. Bruises were beginning to darken on his other arm, and his tunic was torn where the metal rings had stopped a sword cut.

"I see your brothers. Ingeborg is coming, so I'll leave you to her tender ministrations."

"Coward." She shot him a glare. "You just don't want her tending to your injuries."

"So true." He chuckled and walked toward Magnus and Leif.

Ingeborg sat down and set to work on her arm. She eased what was left of the leather sleeve over the wood splinters, removing some of them at the same time. Then she used tweezers to pull the rest out, starting the bleeding anew. Most of them were small, but several were as long as her fingers.

"I don't dare stitch these closed." The healer studied her arm as she washed away the blood. "There still might be some pieces of wood inside and they have to work their way out. If you'd only stopped fighting, these wouldn't have gone so deep."

"I had to avenge Arne. I couldn't let it go. Surely you understand."

The older woman sighed. "I do. You'll have scars, but you should heal well enough. Now brace yourself. I have to pour wine on it, then I'll put honey and herbs on it and wrap it well."

Asa set her jaw. She would not be the one to cry out.

Fire hit her arm and she yanked in a breath. But she swallowed her yell, squeezing her tearing eyes shut, every muscle tense and shaking. The searing pain raced up her arm and into her shoulder. She shuddered, gulping in air, willing herself to silence. Her stomach lurched, but she would not scream. Or throw up.

"That's the worst of it. Unless it festers." Ingeborg spread soothing honey over her arm and sprinkled a heavy layer of herbs over that. She wrapped cloth bandages over it all and tied it off. "I'll look at it again tomorrow."

"But no more wine." Asa tried to find a smile, but failed. "We have to import it from the Rhineland and it's too expensive. I'll make the sacrifice and go without it from now on."

"Not unless it festers, as I said." She stood and gathered her supplies.

"I'll make a sacrifice to Eir. Anything she wants."

"The goddess of healing is always helpful." She gave Asa a rare smile and left.

Now that no one was near, she bowed her head, letting a few tears escape. It wouldn't stop the pain, but it helped her heart. She had to get through the funerals later and the celebrations tonight. Then she could be alone to mourn in the way she needed to for those they had lost.

"So the ice queen weeps. Or is she just melting from the heat of battle?"

She snapped her head up. Hjellmar stood before her, Estrid beside him. She was spotless, dressed in her usual finery and had, no doubt, huddled in the longhouse with the other women. Asa just looked at them, too drained to bother with a reply.

"And those scars all over her arm won't make the men want her any more than they do now." Estrid started to put her hand over Hjellmar's arm, then glanced down at the blood spattering him and curled her lip. "Of course, she's so alluring now, covered in dirt and who knows what else. The men will surely be racing to have her in their beds looking like that."

"None of them will want a woman with the scars of battle marring her. Maybe now, she'll see that war is for men and she doesn't have the strength or the skill to play with us."

Several warriors had stopped to listen. Eirik walked through the men and approached Hjellmar. The smaller man tensed and his eyes widened. Estrid stepped away from him, but Eirik never glanced at her.

He stood toe to toe with Hjellmar, though he towered over him. "You once said Asa wouldn't have the strength to stand back-to-back with any of us. But you were wrong. Today, she and I fought off three of the outcasts, and she used her shield to block a sword strike to my back that would have killed me. It injured her further, but she made the sacrifice to save my life and will bear the scars from it that you both revile her for. We fought as one."

"And she saved me." Another man stepped forward. "When I fell before an enemy, she slew him and saved my life."

"She knocked down another, and made it easier for me to finish him." A dark-haired man inclined his head to her.

One by one, Magnus's warriors came forward, telling of how she had fought, of her skill and speed, of how she had figured out where the outcasts were truly going to attack. If it had not been for her, they said, those in the longhouse would have been lost, the warriors caught from behind. The day might have turned out very different.

Her eyes watered and her throat closed with gratitude and love for all of them. But this time, she let the tears fall for all to see.

"Arne gave his life for her." Magnus crossed his arms as everyone turned to him. He gazed at her alone, his eyes warm. "And that is the highest praise of all. She set her bloodied sword in his hand and held it there even as he died. And so he has gained Valhalla."

The men cheered her. It was muted and low, for they were wounded and exhausted, but it was no less heartfelt. Hjellmar's face turned red, but he said nothing.

Magnus looked at them. "The pyres are being built even now. We will honor our dead, and feast to them as they fly to Valhalla. The outcasts we have caught will be sacrificed to Odin to thank him for our victory. Their blood will flow into the ground, nourishing the life that will soon grow from it with the spring. In seven days, we'll hold the *sjaund*, but this night, we'll see our warriors to the next life with much joy for their good fortune."

The men drifted away to see to the preparations and to continue cleaning up after the battle. Hjellmar cast her a sour look, then stalked away. Estrid started to follow him, but stopped.

"They wouldn't be so quick to praise you if they knew what you truly are, Asa. Those scars just make it harder for you to use your beauty to lure them to their destruction."

"Enough, Estrid." Did she think her words could do any further harm to her than what had already happened that day? The dance with death that all warriors experienced tended to change things. It had changed her. "The words you've said over the years always devastated me, but now they're little more than the buzzing of gnats. Go make your own happiness, Estrid. If you can. Arne told me to take what I would from my life, for all too soon, it can end. We travel different roads now, you and I. I am what I am and you are what you are. And you can blame no one for that but yourself."

Estrid pressed her lips together. She ran after Hjellmar, who didn't wait for her. Asa sighed and rested back against the wall. Let them have each other. It was likely all they would ever have.

She'd had no idea how Magnus's men felt about her. Their respect had rung in their voices, and their admiration had shone in their eyes as they'd spoken of her exploits in the fight. She was so much richer than she had ever dreamed, yet she hadn't seen it. Her fears had driven her apart from them, but if she could weather the storms of battle, then she could stand with any of them with pride. And they would stand with her.

Eirik spoke with her brothers and several of the men. Even dirtied and bloodied from war, he shone, the tallest and most powerful of them all. She smiled. Well, perhaps he was equal to Magnus and Leif. Did she dare take Arne's advice and grasp this chance with both hands? Could she be what he wanted? Years ago, when she'd first gone to battle, she hadn't been certain she could do it. But Magnus had said she would never know what she was made of until she experienced it.

She'd always taken for granted that her past would rise again to haunt her if she tried to trust again, so she had never given any man a chance. But, as in battle, how would she know unless she tried? If she could trust Eirik enough to stand with him in war, shouldn't she be able to trust him with the most vulnerable part of her? The part no shield or sword or battle-skill could protect?

Could she trust him with her heart?

The feast was subdued, for they were exhausted, in body and in mind. The people of Thorsfjell had lifted many cups of ale, wine, and mead in appreciation to the gods for their victory. Now, while they were all together, Eirik wanted to give them his own gift of thanks.

He left the celebration and headed for the shed where the rune stone waited. Earlier, Sjurd had helped him lever it up onto a small cart, and they'd pull it into the road in front of the longhouse. He would rather have erected it first, but he wasn't certain where Magnus would want it. So he'd present it on the cart, and tomorrow they could place it in its permanent place.

He smiled to himself as he walked. Asa had been so overwhelmed at the feast when they'd all lifted a cup to her. Even the women had chimed in, for the outcasts would have raped and killed them and their children if they'd been able to attack the longhouse as they'd planned. It was only Asa's realization of what they might try that had thwarted them.

She'd been so beautiful, dressed in her finest blue gown, her necklace of amber and precious stones glinting in the light of the longhearth fire. Because of her bandaged arm, Magnus and Leif hadn't let her do anything for herself, having the servants bring her food and drink. She'd snapped at them about having them feed her by hand as well, but then she'd laughed along with everyone else. And he'd fallen in love with her a little bit more.

He couldn't deny it any longer. She was beautiful, intelligent, and strong—all the things he needed in a wife. Before he met her, he'd thought that could be enough. But it wouldn't be. Not after knowing love with Sela. This was so much more, for Sela and he had never been a match for each other. Asa and he were as two halves of the same whole.

The love he'd felt for Sela seemed as weak and faded as she had been. He'd remember her with fondness and respect, though guilt for her death would always ride with him. But the feelings he had for Asa were as powerful and fiery as she was.

He had to persuade Magnus to allow him to marry her. Then he would have to win her, and of the two, the latter would be far more difficult.

He nodded to Sjurd, who waited for him by the shed. Together, they pulled the cart with the covered heavy stone down to the front of the longhouse. The young man waited while Eirik went into the building. The feast had ended and the evening's games and music were about to begin. He walked over to Magnus, who sat at a table with Leif, Asa, and several other warriors. The jarl preferred to join his people rather than sit above them on the dais. He would have to remember that when he took Haardvik back and regained his title.

He waited at the end of the table until they all looked at him. "Magnus, I did something to thank you and your people for all they have done for me. May I speak to them?"

Magnus glanced at Leif and Asa. "Of course." He called for everyone's attention and they quieted.

Eirik stepped away from the table so everyone could better see him. "At the beginning of the winter, you took me in and saved my life. Since then, I have tried to thank you in any way I could by reading your runes and standing with you in battle. But these things are fleeting and will not survive the test of time."

Several people shouted out denials, but he held up his hand. "I want my thanks to outlast my stay here. The spring comes to the coast and soon I must leave to continue my journey to Trøndelag. My gift to you waits outside."

The people looked at each other and murmured questions, but they all rose. Magnus, Leif, and Asa followed him out first, then the others poured from the longhouse.

He walked to the cart and waited until everyone had gathered around it. "I have learned that the former jarl, Sigrund, never had a memorial erected to him. It's not fitting that such a great man as Sigrund should be forgotten in ages to come. And so, I made this in remembrance of a man of wisdom, far-seeing, and honor."

He drew off the cloth covering the stone and everyone leaned in to see it, those in the back asking what it was. Yggdrasil filled the center of the carving and around the outside of the design, runes circled it, telling the tale of the jarl. The work was precise, detailed, and beautiful, his finest stone.

The people exclaimed at its beauty. Asa and her brothers came forward to lay their hands on it, running their fingers over the leaves and branches, tracing the symbols along the border. Questions came from the villagers and warriors in the back of the crowd.

"What does it say?"

"I can't read it over the people in front of me."

"You can't read at all."

"Say what's written on it aloud."

Magnus held up his hand and all the people quieted. "Rune carver?"

Eirik didn't need to read it, for he knew the words. He looked, instead, at all the people as he spoke. "It says, 'Eirik carved these runes for Magnus, Leif, and Asa in honor of their father, Sigrund. He went to the East in search of gold. On the way back from Miklagard, he died in the Aifur with his sword in his hand. May Thor consecrate these runes."

"By the gods. It's perfect." Magnus strode to him and held out his hand. They clasped wrists, then Leif followed suit. Asa went to him, her eyes down, a slight smile on her lips.

"I thank you, Eirik. This means more to us than you can ever know." She gave him a quick hug as a blush stained her cheeks. He held her a moment longer, then let her go.

"I never had a chance to carve one for my own father who was lost in battle," he said. "I was too late to save him. But I would see yours honored."

"Tomorrow, we'll erect this in our sacred grove." Magnus gazed down at it. "And we'll remember our father and drink to him. We held his *sjaund* long ago, but this will please him in Valhalla."

The villagers came forward, a few at a time, and stared at it in awe, touching it, some crying. The warriors clapped him on the back and thanked him.

Magnus stood beside him and when the crowd had thinned, he shook his head. "So this is where you've been the past months."

"Yes. Sjurd found me a place to work in a storage shed behind the barn so I could carve undetected. We found the stone up on the ridge, where we first saw signs of the outcasts."

"I'd always wondered why you would go up there. And when you spent so much time gone, I thought perhaps . . ." He hesitated.

"That I was looking to join them?" He half smiled. He'd been right in thinking that they hadn't trusted him.

"It was only that you were a stranger here."

"I know. I might have thought the same thing if our positions were reversed."

Magnus gripped his shoulder. "We have much to thank you for. We'll miss your wisdom and your good sword arm. Anything you need for your journey to your cousin, you have but to ask. Let us know when you want to leave. If the ice has broken up in our branch of the fjord by then, I'll arrange for one of my ships to take you to Trøndelag. It will be a much shorter and safer trip for you that way instead of over land. We have a road to the valley where our ships are beached for the winter. They're not as fast as most longships since we use them for cargo, but they'll do."

Eirik grinned. "My thanks. I welcome your help." A weight slid off his shoulders. It would cut his traveling time into a fraction of what it would have been. He'd have to leave his horse behind, but he would have no need of it before he returned home. He could send for it later, and that wouldn't be all he'd want from here.

While Magnus was feeling indebted to him, there were other things he needed to speak with him about. He should strike while the iron was hot, but he'd wait a few days until they had recovered from the battle.

However, this didn't involve only Magnus's feelings. Asa would have something to say about it all, as well. He could chisel the World Tree into stone itself, but could he chip away the wall she had built up around herself?

So much blood.

Estrid stood alone in the stained snow of the clearing, breathing in the metallic scent as the others left. They'd sacrificed the captive outlaws to Odin in thanks for their victory, but also as punishment for attacking the village. Their bodies would remain here until the gods came for them and took them into Helheim. And now the people all went to erect the rune stone for the old jarl, the one who had taken her mother and her mother's sister away from their native land and forced them into marriage, ruining their lives.

She looked at the carnage around her. The gods loved blood. Asa had sacrificed her own flesh in the fight to protect Thorsfjell and look how everyone admired her. Eirik had walked at her side from the death ceremony, even though she would be scarred and ugly now. Her power was too strong for him to resist her.

It wasn't the dragon after all. Asa still worked on it, painting it to hide the hideous eye, as she would hide the damage to her arm with fine clothes. It wouldn't be enough at this point to attack the dragon.

Estrid knelt on the wet ground where the snow had melted from the hot blood of the sacrificed men. She would have to take the next step, and very soon. If she didn't hurry, Eirik would depart without her, and the only man who walked in other worlds as she did would be gone. She had to break Asa's spell before that. Now it was obvious that the evil lay, not in the dragon, but in Asa. The dragon was just her idol she worshipped every day. She even ate beside it.

She touched a puddle of blood and smeared it on her right forearm. Where Asa's blood had flowed from her wounds. But that wasn't good enough. She needed to gain the gods' favor to be successful, and didn't that require a sacrifice?

The seax lay on the tree stump where Magnus had killed the outcasts. She picked it up and the blood on the blade shone in the weak sunlight. So bright, so beautiful. Like the rubies the old jarl had brought back from the East one year.

Coldness fingered through her heart. A wounded arm was one thing, an easy thing, but a hand injury was quite another. It was much more important. She would show everyone how brave she was, how much she was willing to honor the gods. How she would give of herself to break the spell and save Eirik and Thorsfjell from Asa's magic.

Then they would honor her. They would cheer for her. And Eirik would see how worthy she was, and then comfort and heal her.

The knife flashed down, releasing the blood and pain for the gods. She raised her arm and poured out her sacrifice onto the ground. It flowed from her hand like a stream of rubies.

Pretty rubies falling down.

"Jarl Magnus, your cousin has been hurt." Birgitta came into his sleeping chamber, out of breath. "She's with the healer now."

Magnus glanced at Leif as they stood. They had just returned from having the rune stone Eirik had carved for their father erected in the sacred grove. Now they'd been discussing the trade routes for the spring, but that would have to wait. They walked into the common room where Estrid sat whimpering at a table. Ingeborg probed her bloodied hand while people gathered to watch and find out what had happened. They cleared the way for Leif and him.

"How did you do that?" Magnus studied the wound. It seemed to be a thin slice through her hand, like a knife wound.

"I was walking in the woods and fell. My hand hit something under the snow, but when I felt the pain, I didn't stop to see what it was. I ran here." She moaned as Ingeborg cleaned it.

Eirik sat a few tables over playing *tafl* with another man and Estrid glanced at him, then dabbed at her eyes with a cloth. "Oh gods, it hurts." Her voice rose into a wail.

"The healer will make it better," Magnus said. She was under good care. No one had committed a crime against her and she hadn't been attacked. There was nothing for him to do. The others in the room lost interest in the unexciting accident and drifted away. Estrid shrieked as Ingeborg poured wine on her hand, but no one paid attention. Accidents happened all the time and people had their chores to see to.

Magnus and Leif went back into the private chamber to finish making their trading plans.

A short time later, Ingeborg cracked open the door and leaned in. "Jarl, may I speak with you?"

"Of course. Come in." He stood as she entered the room.

"I have a concern that I thought I should bring to your attention, Jarl. In private." She shook her head as Leif rose and offered her his seat. "Estrid's wound and her story don't match."

He glanced at Leif, who raised his brows. "In what way?"

"She said she put her hands out to stop her fall. If that were true, then the wound would have been larger on her palm than on the back. But that's not the way it appears. The entrance to the wound is on the back of her hand. It's longer than the opening on the palm, as though something tapered went through it. Like a knife blade. There's no way for an object to make a smaller hole going in than going out."

"Perhaps the object she fell on moved."

"Perhaps. But it was wider near her fingers than on the other end of the cut. I've seen enough seax wounds to recognize them. There was skin on the inside of the cut on the back of the hand and the skin on the palm showed signs of having opened outward. She was stabbed on the back of the hand, Jarl Magnus. Unless she bent her wrist when she fell so she hit the ground with the back of her hand, it couldn't have happened the way she said."

His heart sank. This was no simple accident, then. But what was it? An attack she was trying to hide? From whom? Hjellmar? Sometimes women who had been mistreated protected their abusers. Was she one of them? He nodded, sinking back down in his chair. "Thank you Ingeborg. I'll look into it."

The healer inclined her head to him, then to Leif. After she was gone, he sat back and glanced at Leif.

"I need to see if Hjellmar has been mistreating Estrid. Someone did this to her and when I find out who it is, he'll be outcast. As insufferable as she is, she's our cousin and we must defend her."

"I agree." Leif crossed to the door and put his hand on the latch. "But I wonder how you'll defend her from herself."

His head grew light as he rose. "What are you talking about?" Instead of leaving, Leif pushed the door shut the rest of the way. "She's always been jealous of Asa. Asa gets hurt in battle and everyone praises and admires her. This might be Estrid's way of getting some of that attention for herself. And some of Eirik's attention as well."

"You're as mad as you imply she is. She wouldn't stab herself. And Asa's admired, not because she was injured, but because it happened in battle. It was a sign of her bravery."

Leif shrugged. "Maybe Estrid doesn't see it that way. Eirik is leaving soon. She might be getting desperate to go with him. Watch her. And take care about blaming Hjellmar for this. He's a sword balancing in a breeze. It won't take much to tip him over and hurt his pride. With as much as he's resented Asa, I wouldn't put it past him to take it out on her."

"Then he needs to leave here. Go back to his homestead. The only reason so many of the warriors are here is because of the situation with the outcasts. Now that it's resolved, they can go back to their lives until we sail for the markets. It will get him away from here and away from Asa."

"And if Estrid is fond of him, he'll be yet another one who leaves her behind, as her father did when he died, her mother did when she went back to Ireland, and her stepfather did when he was outcast. We've always suspected that's why she's the way she is to begin with. She'll likely blame Asa again, as she did before, which will make everything even better." Leif shook his head. "This is why I'm glad you were born first, brother. I'll back you any way I can, of course, but what you do is your decision. I'm just glad I don't have to make it."

He left, and Magnus stared at the closed door. He couldn't make any accusations without some level of proof. Asking Estrid about what truly happened would do no good if she was determined to protect someone. No woman would just stab herself like that.

Not unless she was mad. Everything had been quiet in the past few weeks as far as any mischief was concerned, but he'd continued having his men patrol both inside and outside the longhouse. He would keep them on, at least until everyone left for the trading season. Then those left here could settle into their usual summer routine and all would be as it had always been. And yet . . .

Heaviness had lain for some time in the pit of his stomach, as though a storm built up pressure there, growing darker and more violent. He'd thought worrying about the trouble with the outlaws had caused it, but that was over now and yet the feeling remained. It churned on the horizon of his thoughts. Already he could smell the tempest coming toward him.

What would happen when it finally broke?

Chapter Fourteen

In just a few days, the men would take the dragon's head down to the ships.

Asa touched up the paint on one of the scales. It had to be perfect. Magnus would ask an unprecedented price for this. Word would spread and the king would hear of it. To show off his wealth, he'd have to have it for one of his ships and she'd gain even more word-fame for her talents.

So why couldn't she feel better about it? She should be rejoicing, but instead, the thought of seeing it for the last time seemed to tear her open inside.

Or was it something else? In the weeks since the battle with the outcasts, the snows had lessened. Magnus had sent a man to the main fjord to see if the way to the ocean was clear of ice. Word had returned that it was.

Eirik would leave very soon. They'd spent many evenings playing *tafl*, telling stories with the others. At night, she still dreamed of Eirik. He'd said nothing of what, if anything, he felt for her. Perhaps that was for the best. He would leave and she might never see him again. No doubt he wouldn't want to hurt her by starting a relationship he couldn't continue.

It was the right thing for him to do, but her heart didn't care. And yet, the way she'd caught him looking at her from time to time made her long for him in the darkness of her room. Then, old fears reared up within her and she shrank away from those desires. She still harbored the shadows that would send him away from her. And if he was not going to remain with her, there was no reason to risk reopening old wounds. They wouldn't be as easy to heal as the lacerations on her arm had been.

The scent of the stew Birgitta had left for her made her stomach rumble. Everyone else must have eaten already, but she'd been busy working. Often, one of the serving girls brought her a meal so she didn't have to stop, and today it was mutton with some of the winter store of dried vegetables.

She studied the dragon as she put a small bite of the stew into her mouth. Sweetness burst over her tongue and she spit it back into the bowl. Sweetness in a stew? It wasn't honey. That was the only thing she knew of that could taste that way.

She dug in the bowl with her horn spoon and brought out a piece of mushroom. It wasn't unusual to have dried mushrooms in a stew. But it wasn't soft and cooked like the other dried vegetables. It was hard, like it hadn't been in there long. And it didn't look like the mushrooms they would use.

Fear shot through her and she ran out of the longhouse to the well. A bucket of water sat on the low wall and she set the bowl aside and scooped up water with the ladle. She rinsed her mouth out, spitting out every trace of the stew that she could. Her heart raced. Perhaps it was nothing. Perhaps the stew hadn't cooked long enough and the mushrooms, dried all winter, hadn't softened the way they should.

But they wouldn't be sweet. She rinsed again and again until the taste was gone.

"Did you eat some of your own cooking again, Asa?"

She looked up as Leif walked toward her, grinning. But when he saw her, he sobered and broke into a run. "What's wrong? You look pale."

"The stew is strange. Did you eat any of it?"

He picked up the bowl. "Yes, we all did. What did you taste?"

"Something sweet." She took the bowl and picked out the piece of mushroom with her spoon. "Was any of this in your stew?"

"No, there was nothing like that. Just the usual vegetables." His face turned white as he stared at her.

Birgitta walked past them and he said, "Get Ingeborg and hurry. I think Asa's been poisoned."

"What?" Asa sank down on the low wall as Birgitta ran toward the healer's house. "Why?"

"I don't know. But it's not good that your bowl held something that wasn't in the communal pot."

Eirik came out from the longhouse and Leif motioned him over.

"I think someone has tried to poison Asa with mushrooms. In your travels, have you ever seen this?"

"Gods." He took the spoon with the mushroom on it and smelled it. He frowned, his jaw tight. "What did you taste and did you swallow any of it?"

"It was sweet, like honey, but not very nice." A tremor passed over her body as her chest muscles tightened. Was it fear, or something worse? "I spat it out as soon as I tasted it. Then I came out here and rinsed out my mouth until I couldn't taste it any longer."

"Good, but we need Ingeborg."

As he spoke, the healer and Birgitta ran toward them. The older woman was breathing hard, but she kept up the pace until she got there.

"What did she eat?" She took the spoon.

"Death Cap." Eirik's hands fisted and Asa gasped as ice spread through her veins. "I recognize the smell, very unpleasant, but sweet. It was in Asa's stew, and no one else's."

"Birgitta, get my brother," Leif said, and the girl rushed into the longhouse. He looked at Ingeborg. "What can you do for this?"

"Do you have milk thistle?" Eirik regarded Asa and there was something in his expression she had never seen in him before—fear.

"Yes, we use it for digestive problems and women's issues. But I have no experience with this," Ingeborg said.

"I've seen it used in the East to purge poisons. Make a tea of it with honey. Make as much as you can, and Asa will have to keep drinking it."

As she hurried to her house, Magnus came out with Birgitta. "Asa's been poisoned?" He grabbed her up and pulled her to him in a hard embrace.

"Someone tried," Leif said. "But she spat it out and rinsed her mouth, so maybe she didn't swallow any of it. Ingeborg is fixing her a remedy just in case."

"It was a Death Cap mushroom." Eirik took a deep breath. "Someone put it into her bowl."

Magnus whirled on Birgitta. "Who gave her that bowl of stew?"

Her face screwed up as she began to cry, and she crumbled to her knees. "I did, Jarl Magnus, but I swear I didn't know anything was wrong with it. We always set aside some of the evening meal for the mistress in case she doesn't want to stop working. We put it on the table in the cooking room and whoever has the time will take it in to her." She hid her face in her skirts, weeping harder. "I didn't know. I swear it. We all love her. We'd never hurt her."

"I know, Birgitta." Magnus helped her up and she stood, trembling and sobbing. "I know you wouldn't harm her. Was anyone in the cooking room who shouldn't have been?"

"No, Jarl." She sniffed, but tears still fell down her cheeks. "It was only the women. We were all so busy serving, though, going in and out, that anyone might have slipped in there without us noticing."

"It's all right, Birgitta. It's not your fault." Asa stood and hugged her. She wasn't too steady herself, though. Someone had tried to kill her. Her legs gave out. She would have fallen, but Eirik caught her and held her to his side.

"I feel weak. Is that one of the effects?"

"No, and you won't feel them, if any, for a half a day. Then it would be stomach cramps and vomiting. But you rinsed your mouth out and you'll drink the infusion Ingeborg is making. I've seen it work before."

"You seem to know a lot about this," Magnus said. His voice was light.

Eirik just gave him a half smile. "I know enough not to use the older mushroom if I want to poison someone. Its sweet taste and unpleasant odor will give it away, as it did now. The young mushroom has almost no taste at all and is easily hidden in food. Whoever did this didn't realize that."

Magnus clapped his hand on Eirik's shoulder. "I wasn't implying that you were involved."

Eirik nodded. "I've brought milk thistle back from my journeys for my mother, who is a healer of sorts, so I know of its properties. In the East, where I've traveled, poison is much more prevalent as a tool to kill. It's always wise to know about these things as a defense against assassination when you're somewhere you aren't exactly welcome."

Magnus studied him, then took a deep breath. "And I thank you for that knowledge. It might save Asa's life. Once again, we are indebted to you."

"I'm not keeping a tally." He held Asa closer to him.

"We should go to the healer's house," Leif said. "It will be more private there and the less anyone else knows, the better."

Magnus agreed and they walked toward the small building. Birgitta followed, still sniffling.

Asa leaned against Eirik. His strength poured into her. Even with all that had happened, his comfort wrapped around her like his arm, and the fear faded a bit. Yes, someone had tried to kill her. But she'd faced death in battle and hadn't flinched, so she would meet this head-on as well.

Then, she'd known who the enemy was. Eirik had said that in the Eastern lands, they used poison to kill. That was the way of cowards. Anyone who couldn't look an enemy in the eye had no honor. None of Magnus's warriors would do this, not only because they respected her and her brother was their jarl, but they wouldn't use such a craven, underhanded method. The gods wouldn't favor them, then.

They entered Ingeborg's house. The comforting scent of herbs and potions filled the air. Drying plants hung from the rafters, and shelves and tables were filled with jars. The healer was stirring a liquid in a pot over the fire.

Magnus pointed Asa to a bench. "You're not to eat anything except what comes out of the communal pot and use only bowls and spoons from the same stacks as everyone else. Use your own knife to eat with and keep it with you at all times. Until we figure this out, one of us should be with you always."

"And drive me mad," she said, her voice sharp. "Gods, Magnus, you act as though I'm a helpless child. I don't know what any of you could have done to protect me from this. I'll take care about what I eat, but you don't have to shadow me. I'll stay armed. If this happened to any of you, would you want the rest of us around you day and night?"

"Odin's eye, no." Leif crossed his arms over his chest.

"But it didn't happen to us," Eirik said.

"Oh, and now I need three big strong men to guard me?"

"Yes." They all said it at the same time.

She sighed. They were determined, and there was nothing worse than a determined warrior, not to mention three of them. And since when had Eirik been included in their little group? He'd sidled right in there among them as though he intended to stay. But they all knew that wasn't the case. Even now, men were loading the carts to bring their trade goods down to the ships. And Eirik would be going with them.

Ingeborg gave her a mug of steaming liquid and she sipped at it. It was sweet with honey and warmed her, steadying her nerves. She stared out of the open door as the men made their plans to guard her.

Her dragon would also be packed and taken away, eventually to guide a longship to the ends of the world. And with it would go all her memories of the nights spent with Eirik, carving the runes. The magic, the beauty, and the closeness she'd never thought to feel with any man would be gone as well. Together, they had spun something special and sublime.

But in Thorsfjell, once something they'd created left, it never returned.

"So are you my guard for the night?" Asa would know Eirik's footsteps anywhere. She didn't have to look to see who approached her in the darkness. She stood outside the longhouse, studying the sky. The night was cold, but no wind blew. Spring in the *fjells* would not be far off, maybe only a matter of weeks, though it had come too soon to the coast.

He chuckled as he stopped at her side. "I just wanted to see if you've felt any effects of the mushroom."

She shot him a glare at his obvious excuse. "The time I should have felt ill has passed, so I must be safe enough." She looked back up at the night sky. "Sjurd said he saw a flicker of the northern lights a short time ago. I wanted to see if they'll play in the sky tonight. We don't see them often this far south."

"There." He pointed at a ribbon of luminescence and she held her breath as more of them writhed overhead.

"The fires that surround the lands and seas on the edges of the world burn bright tonight," she said. "They reflect in the sky."

"There are people in the East who say they've known for centuries that the earth is round." He put his arm across her shoulders.

She turned to him and he trapped her in the circle of his embrace. "That's ridiculous. Then why don't we all slide off? And why don't the seas drain away into the roots of Yggdrasil?"

He looked down at her, his eyes alight with mischief. "Perhaps the gods cause us to stick to the ground. And who's to say the seas don't drain away and are replenished again? I've sailed in places where the tides run so fast, not even the swiftest longship can escape them."

She studied him. Was he serious, or was he teasing? But his eyes darkened and he strengthened his grasp on her, bringing his hand up under her hair to hold her still. She should be afraid of him.

He lowered his head and kissed her. Any shadows of fear she'd harbored vanished in a burst of light within her mind. As though a small sun was born within her, she grew warm and her thighs weakened. But it wasn't from fear. This was something very different, and she allowed it to spread out within her.

Lifting his head, he searched her eyes. She opened herself to him so he could see what she felt for him. He needed to know, to take with him the truth of her love. She never thought it would happen, that she could love a man. But he had made all the difference, and when he left, he would take that love with him.

He let go of her hair and combed his fingers through it. "Asa, I think you know how I feel for you. You've captured me with your beauty and strength. What we've experienced together, the magic of the rune carving, fighting side by side, and the talks we've had throughout the winter, are things I've never had with other women. And I doubt you've had them with other men. There's a power that flows through us. You felt it when we carved the runes, but I've felt it all along, from the first moment I saw you."

Kissing her again, he sought her tongue with his. He tasted of mead, sweet and heady. Then he enveloped her in his cloak, shielding her from the night and the world. She looked up at him as he stroked her face with his long fingers. "I love you, Asa. I mean to speak with your brother about us. He needs to know, and I intend to offer for you."

Her heart swelled. When she was young, she'd dreamt of this, that a strong, beautiful warrior would whisper his love for her and take her away to marry her. But that was before.

She tried to step back, but he wouldn't allow it. He tightened his arms around her. To kiss him beneath the northern lights was one thing. But to marry him was quite another. He'd want to take her, as would be his right. If anyone could banish her fears, he could. But if not, it would be a nightmare. For both of them.

"He won't allow anyone to court me but a jarl or a king's son. It was my father's wish." It was the only excuse she could think of. She could never tell him the truth, because of the wound it would reopen in her and the revulsion she might see in his eyes.

He smiled. "I don't think that will be a problem, Asa."

"My—my bride price is too high. A fortune." She lowered her eyes. She had to dissuade him somehow, without revealing her past.

"That's not a problem either." He set his finger under her chin and tilted her head up so she would have to look at him. "I have been raiding these past three years, and I have great wealth. He can name any price and you would be worth it."

She still managed to slide her gaze to the side and avoid his. Why didn't he understand? A movement near the longhouse caught her attention and she gasped. "Let me go. It's Magnus. He's seen us."

"Good. Then I can speak to him."

She pushed at his chest and he released her. "I can't do this to either of us, Eirik. I'm sorry." Clutching her cloak around her, she ran toward her brother.

"Asa? What did he do to you?" Magnus reached out to her, but she darted away from him and into the longhouse. She hurried into her room and shut the door, breathing hard, her heart pounding. Cursing, she dropped onto the bed.

The only man she could ever love, who could love her as well, and she had to reject him because of her own foolish fears. His kiss had been wonderful. But there was more to marriage than kisses. Magnus had seen them together and he hadn't looked happy. There was no telling what he would do now. She pounded her fist on the bed.

She could face swords, warriors, poison, even death itself, and come out whole. But one simple kiss might have just shattered her entire world.

"We need to talk." Magnus didn't move. He stood with his arms crossed, a scowl on his face.

"My thoughts exactly." Eirik walked toward him.

"In my room. We can have some measure of privacy there." Magnus headed inside the longhouse and Eirik followed him. Leif sat at a table with several other men, mugs of ale before them. But Magnus just shook his head as he and Eirik walked past, and Leif didn't join them.

This was it. To press his suit, Eirik would have to reveal who he was and take the chance. He had come to know them all quite well over the winter. He could trust them. They had, after all, fought together and won respect for each other as one warrior for another.

When Eirik had seated himself at the table, Magnus opened a chest standing near the bed. "Mead?"

"Please."

He brought out two goblets made of glass with silver chasing, which was very rare and expensive. Was Magnus trying to intimidate him? He smiled as he watched him pour. It would take more than that, and when Magnus handed him a glass, Eirik didn't take note of the beautiful cup.

They drank. Then Magnus set down his glass.

"I've felt this growing between you and Asa all winter. Too many nights spent together carving runes and playing *tafl*, I suppose."

"That, and other things, yes." He took another drink of mead. "I want to marry her." There it was. A direct strike to his defenses.

"I see. You know our father destined her for a jarl, or even the son of a king. He aimed high for her, and so will I."

Eirik didn't reply, meeting his hard gaze.

"You can't expect me to even entertain this request without knowing who you really are. We haven't learned any more about your past than we did the first few days after you arrived. You're no simple rune caster."

Eirik chuckled. "Are there any simple rune casters? My mother would not think so. She's a renowned rune mistress herself."

"Ah, we know that about your mother, at least. That's a start." He leaned forward. "Why were you traveling? The truth. Who are you?"

Eirik drew a pattern in a drop of mead splashed on the table. Othala, the rune of property. It not only would give him strength for their negotiations, but it would help him speak of the inheritance he had lost. The time had come.

"As I told you, I was raiding with my cousin for the past three years. I got word that my father was dying, so I returned home late last fall. Two days afterward, outcasts attacked my village, Haardvik, on the northern shore of the Hardangerfjorden. We didn't think anyone would strike so late in the season. It turned out the outcasts wanted a place to overwinter, so they were careful not to destroy the buildings and supplies. They left enough people to serve them, and imprisoned the warriors.

"My father was killed in front of me. I slew the bastard who threw his axe at him from behind. But when I did so, he pulled me over the cliff and into the fjord.

"Everyone thought I had died. But I made it to shore only to find that my village was lost. My sister met me in the woods, but she and my mother are trapped there and I don't know what's become of them. I formed a plan to travel to my cousin in Trøndelag to get his help. I raided with him. He has four-and-twenty longships outfitted for battle, and the warriors to crew them."

"Who is this cousin?" Magnus toyed with his glass, but he gave Eirik an assessing look.

"He's Rorik of Vargfjell. It's a large holding near Lade and he's renowned for his raiding tactics and fine ships."

"I've heard of him. They say he's as wild as the North Sea in the winter."

Eirik laughed. "That's true. I traveled with him to the great southern inland sea and also to the farthest desert kingdoms in the East. There are few places he hasn't seen. With his help, I'll seek revenge on those bastards and win back my home. When I fell into the fjord, I lost the sword of my ancestors, which my father wielded in battle. I must retrieve it before I can take my rightful heritage."

"Why is that?"

"It was made from a fallen star the gods sent to us. As long as my family has the sword, we have their blessings upon us and the right to rule our people. Even if the blade is pitted and stained from having been in the fjord and can do nothing but hang on the wall of the longhouse, it's still a symbol of who we are. It's been passed down through the generations to my father, Jarl Ivar Arvidson."

"I see. And you're his eldest son?"

"His only son. I have a younger sister."

He winced. "You're a jarl, then. Thor's hammer . . . Leif was right. Damn him."

"About what?"

"Never mind. I see now why you're not bothered by the fact that Asa is meant for a high-ranked marriage."

"I won't accept my title, though, until I get the sword back."

"Surely your people would accept you as jarl without the sword in your hand."

"They would. But I won't. It would mean the gods have turned from me. And I don't want Asa to know about it until I tell her myself. I won't ask to marry her until I regain Haardvik. But I would still have an agreement with you about it."

"You're right. You won't marry her until you're a jarl. That I can guarantee. We can discuss the bride price and the dowry. However, the formal arrangement will have to wait until we have witnesses on both sides for the *handsal*. The agreement can't be formalized until then."

"Agreed. There's one other thing I have to speak to you about. My sister told me the leader of the outcasts mentioned that after the winter, he'll head north, into this area, and wreak revenge on people here for something that happened in the past. If they come here, you may have just as much trouble as the other outcasts gave you, if not more. I fought these men. They're far more formidable and skilled than the ones we faced a few weeks ago."

Magnus sat up, frowning. "I heard of a group of outcasts who came up from the south last year, perhaps from Jaeren, and were in Hordaland. No one knows for certain where they were before that."

"They're at my village now. My sister, Silvi, said that their leader, Hakon—"

"Hakon?" He half rose. "Is that the leader's name? Did you see him? A man with silver hair? He was young, but it changed early."

"Silvi said that was his name. I did see a man in front of my father who goaded him so that the one behind him could throw his axe into his back. He seemed young, but he had silver hair, as you've said. Why? Who is he to you?"

Magnus sank back down and poured more mead in his glass. He drank it and grimaced, baring his teeth. "It must be him. Estrid's stepfather was a man named Hakon. He was younger than her mother, Cliona. He turned the women's heads when he first came here. After he married, he became abusive toward Cliona and she divorced him, as was her right. I'm not certain to this day if he abused Estrid or not, but after Cliona left with my mother to return to Ireland, he must have filled Estrid's head with all manner of nonsense. She was the cousin of a jarl and he wanted that prestige and connection. If he couldn't have it with Cliona, he would have it with Estrid. She became attracted to him. With Estrid, it doesn't take much, as you've seen.

"But then he committed a heinous crime and I tried to execute him for it. He wounded me and escaped. I had him declared an outcast at the Thing that summer, and we haven't heard from him since. I thought he must have died.

"This Hakon who attacked your village must be the same man."

"It's a common enough name," Eirik said as Magnus poured him more mead. "If it is him, then he intends to come here and take revenge on you for having him outcast."

"And that's not all he'll do. I know him. He won't want to leave any trace behind him. Before he leaves your village, he'll kill everyone there."

Eirik fought down the fear rising into his throat. Every once in a while, throughout the winter, he'd felt a touch in his mind, so gentle and sweet. Silvi. Letting him know she was well. He would have gone mad if he hadn't felt that brush against his thoughts. If anything had happened to them, he would know. Wouldn't he?

"Then it's imperative I leave as soon as possible."

"And it's imperative I come with you with as many men as I can bring on such short notice. I have a score to settle with Hakon and if it's the same man, I will see him dead. I missed my chance six years ago. I won't miss again."

Six years ago? That was when something terrible had happened to Asa. Were the two events connected?

"I'll welcome your help, Magnus. If we join in an alliance, we'll present a much stronger force and we'll both gain, now and in the future." He half smiled. "And there's one way to lock in that agreement."

"By joining our bloodlines. I agree. But there's something I have to ask you first. On the night you came here, you were delirious from the cold. As Asa took care of you, I think you must have thought she was your wife."

He stilled. "Their hair is a similar color."

"Yes. You asked her to forgive you. For killing her."

His skin grew cold as pain filled him. "I said that. No wonder she acted so afraid of me at first." He looked at Magnus. "My wife died in childbirth. That's why I left home and went raiding with Rorik, to get away from the memories. They haunt me still. Sela was very small and slight. Not made to bear children. My mother tried to warn me, but I was in love and wouldn't listen.

"At first, I kept Sela from conceiving, but she became so distraught that I gave in to her pleas. She conceived, but died giving birth to my son. I knew better, but wouldn't admit it. I blamed the runes, the gods, everything else. It wasn't until I traveled the world and became a true man that I accepted the blame myself. I still bear the guilt. That must have been what I meant." He held his head in his hands. "Gods, what you all must have thought of me."

Magnus laughed. "I admit, we were watching you rather closely after that. But once I had your measure, I couldn't see that you would have done such a thing purposely. Perhaps by accident, but you were too honorable to have killed a woman, much less your wife."

Eirik picked up his glass and tilted it, watching the mead swirl. "I loved Sela, but it was the love of a young, infatuated boy." He raised his eyes to Magnus. "However, the love I bear for your sister is that of a man, and I swear I will make her the best of husbands."

"Only if you're a jarl. And only if you have the gold equivalent to the value of three hundred milk cows for her *mundr*."

His stomach dropped. A king's daughter would hardly fetch that much for her bride price. But he wouldn't insult Asa by bargaining. He unclasped the thick gold chain holding his hammer of Thor pendant and set it on the table with a heavy thud.

"I'll use this as the *arrha*, the first part of my payment. This shows my good faith. If I don't win back my title, the marriage is off and you keep this. I'll be dead anyhow, for that's the only thing that will stop me. If I regain my village and earn the title, you'll get your gold from what I have hidden, and this is returned to me."

"Done. Now for her dowry."

"The dragon's head."

"What?"

"The dragon's head I helped her carve the runes on. I want it as her *heiman fylgia*."

Magnus scowled. "That's to be sold to help support the village this year."

"But you have gold laid away, I'm certain, for her dowry."

"Of course."

"Then you'll have use of that now. And soon, you'll have far more than that with my gold."

"True. But a woman's dowry is meant to support her if she's widowed or divorced. What will she have to fall back on if either one is the case? Not that I'd leave her destitute, of course. But only the gods know what our fates are, and I must be certain she's provided for apart from what I'd do for her."

"If I die, she'll have my full measure of wealth. That's no small amount. I won't divorce her, and I'll make certain she'll never have cause to leave me. But to ease your mind, the dragon's head will be stipulated as her dowry, and therefore, it is hers. She'll be able to sell it and keep the money she gets for it."

Magnus tapped his fingers on the table, his eyes narrowed. "I am giving up a great deal. I'm losing a sister."

"And gaining an ally. You'll also gain Rorik as an ally, and he's more powerful and wealthy than most kings. I saw a man on a black horse after the battle with the outcasts here. Who knows who he is? He might cause problems in the future. If so, you'll have backing from both the north and the south. It puts you in an enviable political and tactical position, nonetheless."

Magnus crossed his arms and leaned back. "And I'm losing the income from Asa's carvings."

"That's what the bride price replaces. Any earnings lost because the woman leaves the family. But I'll say this. Every winter, Asa can carve another prow ornament and you can stop at my village to get it on your way to Kaupang and the other markets. You can sell them, as you always have. Agreed?"

"That's very generous."

"That's family. Do we have an agreement?"

"There's only one more problem. Asa may not appreciate this. Even though it's my right to make these decisions, it's never good to do so without the woman's input, and it rarely ends well when they're not consulted. Divorce is too easy to obtain."

"I would never force her to marry me," Eirik said. "I can convince her. It would help, though, if I know what's in her past that makes her afraid. She'll face down the largest warrior in battle, but when I try to get close to her, she runs. I don't understand."

"That is her tale to tell, if she chooses. Not mine. I agree that you do need to understand her past to understand her." He stood and walked to the door, which wasn't shut all the way. A shadow passed outside of it, then disappeared.

Magnus paused before he opened it. "Let me make this clear, Eirik. I don't do this for the gold, or political gain, or for whoever your family is. I do it for Asa. I've wanted to see her married, but no man has measured up to her standards or mine. I've seen how she is with you. You may be the one man she would respond to, who could make her happy. If I didn't feel that way, no amount of gold could force me to agree to this.

"Remember, she's a shieldmaiden and has her pride. But she's also a woman, and I'm not certain which makes her more dangerous. I'll send her in to you. Unarmed."

Eirik laughed. "My thanks for that." When Magnus had gone, he poured another splash of mead and drank it down. If he could get her to agree to this, perhaps he could take her with him when he left. She wasn't safe here. Until they found out who meant her harm, she never would be. The next time she might not be so fortunate. And there would be a next time.

The door opened and Asa came in. Her hair was loose, as though she had prepared for sleep. His fist clenched as the desire hit him to run his hands through the silken mass and kiss her again.

"Magnus said you wished to speak with me. I thought we said all we needed to earlier." Her dark eyes were large and there was a trace of uncertainty in them. She clutched her shawl around her like a shield.

He rose and moved around the table toward a cushioned bench near a small brazier. Holding out his hand to her, he said, "Come and sit with me."

She eyed him, her gaze wary, but she did as he asked, though she kept her hands folded in her lap.

He sank down beside her and took her hand in his. She stared down and shuddered just a bit. Challenging half-mad warriors didn't daunt her, yet this closeness, she feared. Something was very wrong.

"Asa, why aren't you married?" He kept his voice gentle. "You're well past the usual age of fourteen winters. You're beautiful, the daughter and sister of jarls, intelligent, skilled, kind, everything any man could want. This has been a mystery to me since I first arrived. I think we've come to the point where I can ask this, especially with what you have come to mean to me."

She bit her lip. "As a shieldmaiden, I have chosen not the kiss, but the kill. Few men will accept that. I made that choice six years ago and I have never regretted it."

Six years ago. What in the name of the gods had happened? "And if Magnus needed to join his house with that of another for political reasons? What then?"

"I know my duty." She raised her chin, but still didn't look at him. "And I know Magnus would take my welfare into consideration and make a wise choice for me."

Her hand trembled in his as he brought it to his lips. "Asa, Magnus has made a wise choice. Just now."

She stared at him, her eyes wide. Her skin turned pale and he gripped her hand in case she tried to bolt. She shook her head. "I can't, Eirik. Please don't ask it of me. If there were any man I could be with, it would be you. But I can't." She tried to slide away from him, but he wouldn't let her go. Ever.

"Then help me understand and we can fight this together. As we did against the outcasts."

"I've spoken of it to no one." Her voice shook. "Magnus told me long ago that I was never to think of it, or talk about it. If I did, it would come back in my mind and I would relive it all over again."

"Relive what? Asa, Magnus told me this night that this was your tale to tell, not his. He thought it was all right for you to talk to me about it."

"He did?" She looked away. "I don't know. It's lived within me for so long."

"My mother has always said it's better to speak of that which troubles you than to let it live inside you and decay so that you die because of it."

"She said that?" Her lips tightened.

"My sister, Silvi, hopes to become a priestess one day. But to be one, she must gain control of herself. She has much anger and sadness in her and that holds her back. My mother has her talk about it and even cry and scream about it so that its power lessens. It helps her. Asa, I think it can help you, as well." He stroked her hand. "And I want to help you. I want to love you. Let me do both."

Her gaze shot to his and she took in a sharp breath. He placed his free hand around the back of her head and drew her in for his kiss. As she opened to him, he deepened it, willing her to see that he spoke the truth. When they parted, she stared at him, then nodded.

"We will at least see if you still want me after this." When she tried to shift away from him, he tightened his grip on her hand, but didn't pull her closer.

"My aunt, Estrid's mother, remarried after Estrid's father died. A man named H—Hakon."

"I know. Magnus told me of it."

"Then he told you Hakon was outcast?"

"Yes. But not the reason. Only that he committed a terrible crime."

She nodded, her eyes filling. Looking away, she took a deep breath. "Six years ago, when I was fourteen winters, he tried to rape me."

Chapter Fifteen

Asa winced as Eirik's hand clenched around hers. Of course he didn't mean to hurt her, but the twinge of pain was nothing compared to the agony of speaking those words. She'd never said them aloud. Not to anyone, nor even to herself. They tore her open as they left her, and she couldn't stop the sob that followed them.

"By the gods, Asa." Eirik released her hand and enveloped her in his arms. He tucked her head under his chin, pressing her to his chest. "Tell me."

She leaned into him, accepting his embrace. It might be easier to speak of this if she didn't have to look at him. He was like a great shield against the world. She closed her eyes, drawing strength from his touch. Just this one last time. At first, she couldn't make the words come. But he kept stroking her hair until she found the courage to continue.

"I was in the sauna. It was a different one then. Magnus had that one torn down so I wouldn't have to go back in there again. I was dressed, but was just putting my hair up. Hakon came in. I was leery of him. He'd never paid much attention to me before, but there were rumors that he had beaten my aunt, and people whispered that he had done things to Estrid. Back then, I didn't know what they meant.

"I knew what happened between men and women, of course, but my mother had always said it would be because a man loved me." She shook her head. "Hakon didn't love me. He was family of sorts, though, and I thought he'd come in there by mistake, thinking the sauna was empty. But then, he said things. That he'd wanted Cliona because she was the sister-in-law of a jarl. She didn't appreciate him and had divorced him and left. So he'd planned to marry Estrid. Then he realized I was also of marriageable age and that I was the sister of a jarl, instead of a cousin. I would bring him even more power."

She swallowed, unable to stop the tremor that rippled through her. "But, he said, first he wanted to see what I would be like. I didn't understand. So he said he would take me and that we would become lovers. That I would tell everyone I wanted him and had agreed to this, and we would be married. I told him no, I didn't want him as a husband. Only Magnus had the right to choose for me. But Hak—he said I was only a girl and I would do as *he* said or it would not go well for me."

She swallowed. "He grabbed me and pulled me down onto the floor and lifted my skirt. I fought him. I don't think he was expecting it, and I was able to get him off of me. But in the next moment, he was on top of me again, tearing my clothes. I screamed and kept fighting him. Then he held a knife to my throat and told me to be quiet or he would kill me."

The old fear heaved inside of her, like vomit rising into her throat. Every moment replayed in her mind—the pain as his hands gripped her, the weight of him, the smell of his unwashed skin against hers. She raised her hand to her neck, shielding it against the memory.

"Did he . . . Did he take you?" Eirik's voice was hard, his muscles tensed.

She shook her head against his chest. "Magnus heard my scream. He came into the sauna and rushed at Hakon. He drove straight into him and shoved him off of me. Hakon had the knife in his hand and he—" Her throat closed. Sorrow and rage choked her but she fought them down, as she'd done every time the memory smashed into her mind.

"He sliced Magnus. In the stomach." Blood. So much blood everywhere. Every time she was angered, all she could see was red. "Hakon fled and I screamed and screamed, while trying to keep Magnus from bleeding to death. I couldn't move him and I couldn't leave. I was pressing the wound closed with my hands, else his insides might have come out. By the time someone heard, we were both covered in blood and he was almost dead.

"He was unconscious for three days. The wound festered. We kept a sword in his hand the whole time so he would go to Valhalla if he died. He should have died, but Ingeborg was skilled and the gods were kind. After he recovered, he told me never to speak of it again. It would awaken in me, he said, and I needed to forget about it. He swore I would never be so vulnerable again and he taught me to defend myself. I don't think he foresaw how skilled I would be, or that I would choose to become a shieldmaiden. But I had few other choices.

"A woman is expected to marry and have children, but how can I marry? I cannot bear for a man to touch me. Though I have enjoyed being with you, a kiss is very different from what you will want from a wife. From me."

She lifted her head and looked at him. "Don't you see now? I can't be a true wife to you. The thought of being with any man that way fills me with fear."

"It wouldn't be like that between us, Asa. Will I want you? Yes. I want you now. But that doesn't mean I can't control myself. I can go slow for you. I've known of women who have been forced before and yet they have gone on to marry and live happy lives."

"And you believe that I can, especially since he didn't succeed. But it goes deeper than that, Eirik. If that were all that happened, perhaps I would have recovered from it. I know women go through far worse than I did, and many of them aren't blessed with two brothers who love them like mine do.

"Because of me, Magnus nearly died. If it weren't for my beauty luring Hakon to me, Magnus never would have come so close to death and never would have borne the horrible scar that he does now. It was my fault. I still see him bathed in his own blood, lying as one dead in my arms. And I could do nothing to help him. If I hadn't trusted Hakon just for that moment, enough to talk to him instead of running right away, it wouldn't have happened. If I weren't so pretty, he never would have wanted me. If, if, if."

She squeezed her eyes shut and wrenched herself away from him. "If I don't trust and don't let any man near me, then no one will be hurt because of me ever again. Whenever I imagine what it would be like to be with someone, all I feel is Hakon's hands on me, and all I see is blood."

"And so am I supposed to be in danger because of you?" He raised his hand to touch her shoulder, but she ducked away from him.

"That's not it. You're too fine to be saddled with someone like me for a wife. I'm like the dragon I carved, desirable and strong on the outside, but damaged on the inside. You would eventually resent me and we would grow to hate each other. So many women will want you in their beds and you should find one of them. I'm too much of a coward to try."

"Coward?" He took her arms and turned her to him. It wasn't likely he would let her go, so she didn't try to escape. "How can you say that?"

"I just sat there with Magnus gushing blood all over us, my hands inside his body, holding him together. I did nothing but scream and scream until someone finally heard me."

"And what else should you have done, Asa? Any other girl of fourteen would have run from there as soon as she could. If you had, Magnus would have died. You stayed there, even with the danger from Hakon and even with your brother's blood all over you. You were as brave as any warrior, even at so young an age. And because of it, you saved him."

"But if it wasn't for me, it wouldn't have happened in the first place."

His hands tightened on her arms. "No. If it wasn't for Hakon's greed and perfidy, it wouldn't have happened. It was his doing, his fault, not yours. I don't know who's been telling you any different, but they're lying."

Her pulse seemed to stop. Estrid. Estrid had been whispering this in her ear all these years, making her believe she was at fault. Hakon had said he'd marry Estrid and then he changed his mind. As desperate as she was to marry and leave Thorsfjell, could it be that she thought Asa had taken him from her? The resentment might have built up through the years into the hatred she harbored now. Could she be the one?

Eirik released her, but cradled her face between his hands. "When I touch you, Asa, do you feel Hakon? Do you hear his voice, feel his evil, smell his scent?"

She tried to smile. "No. You bathe. And you're nothing like he was."

"I hope not." He gave her a light kiss, but still it seared her mind and her body grew languid. "When I kiss you, do you feel anyone but me? See anyone but me?"

"No." When he was with her, no one else existed. He chased the shadows away. But there must be more to this arrangement. Magnus would never give her to just anyone. How would Eirik come up with the bride price? And they hadn't even consulted her.

Drawing back from him, she narrowed her eyes. "What did you offer Magnus?"

He cleared his throat. "What do you mean?"

"Don't play games with me, Eirik. I'm not some naïve girl. You didn't just walk in here and tell him you want to marry me. Why would he agree to this? He's turned down many others who promised all manner of riches and trade agreements. You're just a rune caster. Aren't you?"

"He put up a good fight. And yes, we did make an agreement to become allies. A large band of outcasts has taken over my village in Hordaland and I was traveling to my cousin's holding in Trøndelag to get his help in fighting them. They may be headed this way, so I warned Magnus of them. We felt it would benefit both of us to join forces."

"And bind that agreement with me." It was expected, but that Magnus would do it without asking her first, was a shock. Hurt welled up in her.

"Asa." Eirik tried to take her hand, but she pulled it away. "Asa, he said no amount of gold or power would persuade him to give you in marriage. He has seen for some time what was happening between you and me. He believes I'm the one man you could accept, who could make you happy. And that's what he wants more than anything."

"So I'm trapped between you both."

"No, not trapped. Never that."

"Yes, I am. I have no choice or this alliance will fall apart, and that could endanger my people. Why would Magnus have a stake in what happens in the village where you live? Why would he need any help to defend Thorsfjell? What difference does it make why these outcasts are coming north? We've always been isolated here and the only one who knows where we are who would be outcast is . . ."

Her stomach twisted and her heart missed several beats. "Hakon."

"Now, Asa . . ." He reached for her, but she stood and whirled on him.

"Hakon has attacked your home and now Magnus wants to meet him there before he can come here and get his revenge on us. That's it, isn't it?" She walked to the table to get away from him. His hammer pendant on its thick chain lay there. The *arrha*, part of her bride price? Pain shot through her. "Neither of you was going to tell me. You've arranged my whole life. Then you were going to set sail for this battle and have me stay here while you fight him. You and my brothers have something else coming if you think you'll leave me out of this fight."

"Asa, we hadn't even discussed that yet." He stood and took a step toward her.

She backed away. "Of course not. *You* haven't discussed it. Notice you've left me out of that little decision. I know Magnus. He thinks I'll lose my mind if I know about this, and he won't tell me. I won't be deprived of my revenge in this. It all started with me. And if I have anything to say about it, it will end with me."

She swept past him to the door. All these years, she had prayed to the gods that Hakon was dead, that he'd died in agony somewhere and would never threaten anyone again. But he was still alive and had gained enough power to attract men to him. Or was it just the promise of power and wealth? Lightning seemed to strike her. *The wealth of Thorsfjell.*

In the common area, Magnus and Leif sat at the table, but the other men had gone. Just the two of them were there, which suited her.

"It's a good thing you made certain I was unarmed, because I'd like to kill you, Magnus." She stopped at the end of the table, her hands on her hips. Eirik walked up beside her, but she ignored him.

"That must have been some marriage proposal, Eirik." Leif lifted his cup to him, then took a drink. "Well done."

"This isn't about that. Although I don't appreciate the way you've decided my life for me without even thinking to ask me. I had to bare my soul and my past to Eirik to try to convince him why I won't be a suitable wife for him. And then I find out that Hakon is still alive and is making plans to come here and attack us. Imagine my delight."

"Asa, I only found out this evening myself." Magnus stood. "We need to take this into my room. I won't air these black sails in an open wind."

That took the wind out of her own sails a bit, but anger still simmered within her. She glared at Magnus as he walked past her, but he made sense. In this, at any rate. The entire village didn't need to know how her brother had betrayed her. It was humiliating that she, a shieldmaiden, would be bartered off like some mindless girl who was good only for bearing children and bringing political power to men.

As soon as they had all stepped into Magnus's room and shut the door, he scowled at her. "It wasn't until Eirik and I spoke this evening that we put things together and I realized Hakon is most likely the leader of a band of outcasts that attacked his village. Up to this point, I knew no more about Eirik than you did."

"Probably less," Leif said. They all looked at him and he shrugged. "They have been spending time together."

"Anyhow, we were discussing an alliance."

Leif winced. "Not smart."

Her temper rose again. "You mean selling me to the highest bidder." She pointed to the pendant on the table. "Is that it? The *arrha*? Or will something else be thrown into the pot? Did you intend to keep this from me, that Hakon is alive and well and coming here to visit us?"

"It isn't something I want known," Magnus said. "I don't want the people to panic. I want to meet him in a place well away from here. I can do that by helping Eirik with as many of my men as I can summon now. We both win."

"You both win. How nice. And if I refuse, what will happen to this alliance of yours?" Magnus and Eirik started to speak, but she continued. "Oh, don't worry. As I told Eirik, I know my duty. That of any woman. It's all we're good for, I suppose. I'll do my part and go through with this marriage if it will help Thorsfjell. I protect it with my body when I fight with my sword. I can give my body for it in marriage as well. But I want something in return. I'm not happy with any of you right now. I can have revenge on all of you, or I can go with you when you leave and spend my need for revenge on Hakon. It's your choice."

"I don't know how I got dragged into this," Leif said behind her as she slammed out of the room.

She had to get control of herself. In the dark quiet of her chamber, she sank onto the bed. But it wasn't so much anger, as fear that had driven her outburst.

Oh gods. She would marry.

Eirik.

She'd told him things no one but her brothers knew, and yet he hadn't turned away from her. Speaking the words should have torn her apart, made everything worse. Instead, as she'd spoken to him, a weight had lifted off of her and onto his broad, strong shoulders. He'd said his sister cried and talked, letting out her anger and fears, and it made her feel better. Would that help her?

Magnus had told her long ago not to talk about it. She hadn't. She'd never even cried over it. At the time, she'd been too numb, too shocked, and too worried about Magnus to be concerned for herself. But then time passed and everything had gone back to normal. Except her. The pain still simmered inside of her, like festering in a wound that had healed over on the outside, but not on the inside. It had been poisoning her all these years.

Who would she have been if she'd overcome this? Would she have still needed to fight, to release the anger the only way she knew how? Or would she have been a noblewoman, lauded for her grace, her wealth, and her beauty? Would she have been married by now, and had her own household and family? How much had Hakon taken from her? How much had she, herself, given up?

How much had she lost?

Grief fountained through her and she couldn't hold it back any longer. Great choking sobs broke loose from deep within her and she curled into a ball, shaking. All that might have been, and yet was not, sped away from her into a past she could only imagine, lost forever. She closed her eyes and let it all burst from her.

Then strong arms gathered her up. Eirik. He'd sat down beside her on the bed and she hadn't even noticed. She tried to push him away. He couldn't see her like this. He was a warrior, like she was. She had to be strong. Had to be . . . But he held her closer and she gave in to his strength, resting her head on his chest.

"Cry, Asa. Let it out. That's what my sister does and it helps her. Just let yourself go. Cry as much as you need. I'm here to catch you, and I always will be."

She cried. For everything she'd lost and for all the things she could not even dream of that Hakon had taken from her. She cried for the innocent young girl who had died inside of her that day. She cried for Magnus, who was so young himself and had nearly given his life for her sake. And she cried for the future, for the love she might never be able to give to a fine man who professed to care for her.

But there, in the darkness, a hope grew in her. She was exhausted and empty, but with that emptiness came a feeling of lightness, as though a great burden had passed from her. She lay in Eirik's arms and he eased them both down onto the bed. He drew her beside him, her head on his chest, and pulled the furs up over them both.

"Sleep, Asa. I'll guard you through the night and we'll face the new day together." He gathered her closer and it was so right to be there in his arms, safe and warm.

Snuggling against him, she smiled. "Already you think you can order me around."

He chuckled. But she did as he asked. Sleep, born of the easing of her pain, drifted around her. And for once, no dragons awaited her.

The dragon had protected Asa again. She'd eaten the mushroom-laced stew and it had seen the danger and warned her. But there was no time to try again.

Estrid moved through the shadows of the night to meet with Hjellmar. Stupid, angry Hjellmar. She'd overheard the marriage arrangements. Eirik was lost to her now. Asa had captured him with her power and he would never be free.

But they'd also said Hakon was in the south, in Hordaland. He had been away from Asa long enough to have shaken off her influences. Now he could love her once again as he had before Asa lured him away. She just needed to get to him, and that's why she needed Hjellmar.

It wouldn't take much to convince him he should come away with her.

Once they got there, she would cast him aside and go with Hakon. Her warning to him about the alliance and their plans to attack him would make him love her. And she'd have revenge against Magnus and Asa when Hakon lay in wait for them and destroyed them.

They could take the wealth of two villages for themselves and leave here and go where no one knew them. Ireland, perhaps, where her mother was.

She would have everything she wanted. Magnus and Asa's deaths and, best of all, freedom from this place. She could find her mother and live in the wealthy holding she'd told Estrid about when she was a child. Her plan was perfect.

Hjellmar was waiting for her in a small house at the end of the road. She'd have to suffer his touch once again, but not for long. She glanced at the wound on her hand where she had given her blood to the gods. When she found Hakon, she'd have much to be thankful for, and Hjellmar would pay for his audacity for touching her.

The gods would receive a far bigger sacrifice this time.

"Asa, I need to speak to you before I leave. Alone."

Asa turned away from the door where she'd been watching the men preparing to leave for the waiting ships. In the three days since she'd learned of the plans for her and Eirik to marry, they'd been so busy helping with packing that they hadn't had much chance to talk together. Eirik was leaving in a short time, along with Leif and several of their warriors.

They'd travel to Trøndelag and then return here with Rorik's fleet and pick up the remainder of the men of Thorsfjell. And her. They didn't dare leave her behind after her threats. She wasn't worried about that. Eirik wanted her to go with him, but Magnus wouldn't allow it. He remained with her, saying he needed to be sure she was safe. They'd certainly come back for him.

Eirik took her hand and led her into her sleeping room. He hadn't come in since the night he'd comforted her. Now it was much too small as he shut the door.

"Asa, while I'm gone, you need to decide whether or not you want me."

Gods, he looked so beautiful in his fine clothes, his long golden hair washed and shining, his magnificent sword at his side. For a moment, she didn't realize what he'd said. But as the words came to her, she blinked.

"I don't understand. You've arranged everything with Magnus. It hasn't been witnessed yet in the *handsal*, but that's merely a formality at this point."

He ran his hand through his hair, brushing it back over his shoulder. "That's just it. Magnus and I *have* arranged it. But I've had a few days to think about it."

Her breath left her. Was he saying he'd changed his mind? Her legs gave out and she sat down hard on the bed. He crossed to her and sank down beside her.

"I don't want to marry you against your will, Asa. I can't. I know you had no choice in this and that's sometimes how it is. I don't want that for you, and neither does Magnus. This has to be your decision as well."

Her heart beat again. He wasn't rejecting her. The lightness blossoming in her at the realization startled her for a moment.

"What of the alliance? Right now we both want revenge against Hakon, but what about afterward? Magnus could use your support in the south as well as in the north, especially with this unknown man in the area. He might have something to do with the man who killed the jarl in the village in the next valley. I can't endanger Thorsfjell by backing out."

His smile was gentle and wry. "Do you think I would risk Thorsfjell myself? I've lived here all these months and have come to care about the people here. You saved my life. The village has become another home to me. I could never abandon it. The alliance will stand, on my end at least. Magnus will have my support. This decision is yours, and yours alone."

Something was missing here. "I don't know how you can offer us this alliance. Who are you to do this?"

He took her in his arms. "When you next see me, you'll know. And I'll know how you've chosen. In a few days' time, Magnus and his men will wait for us on the beach below. I'll bring my cousin and meet them there. If I don't see you with them, waiting for me, then I'll know you don't want me and all our plans to attack Hakon will continue on as before."

Wrapping her hair around his fist, he tilted her head back so she had to look at him. "But if I see you there, you'll be mine from then on. No one, not even your brothers, will keep you from me."

Lowering his head, he kissed her. He ran his hand up her side and cupped her breast, still holding her so she couldn't move away from him.

She didn't want to. She leaned into his hand and returned his kiss. For the first time, she smoothed her hands over his arms and up to his wide shoulders. They were like iron under his clothing. She combed her fingers up under his hair, holding him as he'd captured her, and she gripped the silken strands, determined to never let him go.

He broke the kiss and let his hand slip away from her. He took her wrists and held them. "Think long on this, Asa. For once you're mine, I'll never free you. I don't care what our laws say."

Letting her go, he stood, gave her another small kiss, and left. She stayed where she was, her body humming, her mind blazing. Touching her breast where his hand had been, she smiled. Just now, while he had been with her, Hakon's shadow hadn't come between them. Could she be free of him finally? Could she be the wife Eirik would want her to be? That she wanted to be?

She had to see him again, to tell him she'd already decided. But as she rushed out of her room, Magnus came in through the front doors.

"They've gone. I've sent as much cargo as I can with them this trip so we won't have so much to move later. I sent your dragon along, as well."

Her heart sank. They were both gone, then. Eirik and the dragon. It seemed appropriate. And perhaps it was better this way, for if she saw the carving, it would bring back too many memories and she would only miss him that much more.

She didn't need a few days to think about whether or not she wanted him. During the winter, he'd become not just a part of Thorsfjell, but a part of her. Just as the runes were carved into the dragon, so, too, was Eirik scored into her heart.

When he sailed back up the fjord, she would be waiting for him on the beach. It didn't matter who he was, or what wealth he had. She was his.

She went into the weaving room to clean up her workplace and keep busy. The space where the dragon had been born under her knife looked too empty now. It wasn't the only thing missing. As she worked, she caught herself listening for the sound of Eirik's voice coming from the common room, and for his laughter joining that of the other men's as they told tall stories over ale in the afternoons. There was no going into the meals any longer, hoping to see him there at one of the tables.

It was clear how much he had melded into her life without her noticing it. It had been so natural, so right. And now, he was gone.

Her foolish daydreams weren't getting her work done. She examined her tools, for she would have to sharpen them before she carved again. But when, and where, would that be? Would she ever create another dragon like this last one? Would the people of Eirik's village accept her talents and weapons skills the way her own people had?

Going back to work, she inventoried her wood to see what she might need. It was almost midday when Birgitta came in.

"Mistress, I don't want to bother you, but no one has seen Mistress Estrid all day. And no one can remember seeing her at the evening meal yesterday either."

"That's odd. She rarely misses meals. Have you looked in her room?" She set down a piece of maple. With the betrothal on her mind, and the preparations for Eirik and Leif's departure, she'd forgotten to mention her suspicions about Estrid's guilt to Magnus. But then, she hadn't had much more than a feeling. That feeling grew.

"No one wanted to go in there without her permission.

"You did well, Birgitta. I'll go take a look."

When she entered the tiny room, it was empty. Much of Estrid's clothing, shoes, and jewelry was gone. Certainty grew in her, but she needed more proof.

There might be something in one of the chests that would tell the tale, and give them an idea of where she'd gone. Asa lifted the lids of two of them, but there were only odd pieces of clothing and worn-out items. She opened the third one. It held a length of cloth. She picked up the fabric to check under it and a small leather bag fell out from between the folds.

She opened the drawstring and looked inside. There was powdery residue on the bottom and she sniffed it. A sickly sweet odor hit her and she almost dropped the bag. Death Cap mushroom. She would never forget the taste or smell.

Her suspicions had been right. Sitting down on the floor, she stared at the bag in her hand. Her stomach heaved and she fought down the nausea.

It was Estrid all along. Had she hated her that much? Why? And now she was gone, but where?

She had to tell Magnus. But when she stood, he was there, in the doorway.

"Birgitta told me. Estrid is gone then?"

"Yes." She held up the bag. A strange calm descended on her, as though someone else spoke. "It has dried Death Cap in it. I had a feeling the other night about her, but it was just a question in my mind and I didn't mention it to you. There was no proof. Until now."

He cursed under his breath. "Leif suspected her, also. But I couldn't see it, and because of that, you were in danger. When Eirik read my runes, he told me that my lack of action would harm someone I loved, and so it has. She may have even tampered with your skates when you fell into the pond. If I'd taken action against her to begin with, you never would have been poisoned."

He appeared so stricken, she spoke in a gentle voice. "All of that is in the past, Magnus. We need to worry about the present. Where would she have gone? And with whom?"

He looked at her and they spoke together. "Hjellmar."

Magnus rubbed the bridge of his nose. "They've been seen to-gether for weeks now. He's something of a malcontent, but he's been a good fighter. I never thought he would betray me like this. I'll send a man to check and see if he's on the homestead where he lives, but I'm certain he won't be there."

"If she's gone, then it's her choice," Asa said. "She hasn't been happy here since her mother left."

"It may not be that simple. After I spoke with Eirik about your be-trothal, Leif said he saw her by my door. He didn't think anything of it at the time. She's always drifted around here, listening. He had no way of knowing we were speaking of anything so important." Mag-nus grimaced. "Eirik hit me with his request to marry you like a shield blow to the head almost as soon as we walked into the room. I was stunned, though I couldn't let him see it. I was trying to think of ways to dissuade him, but he kept at me in the same way he fights, pounding away at my defenses without letting up. Every time I thought I struck a blow, he countered it. All I could think of was that I was losing you."

She embraced him. "You could never lose me, Magnus. We'll see each other often enough, I think."

He smoothed back her hair. "Then you've decided to go through with it? He came to me the next morning and said he was going to give you the choice and that your decision wouldn't affect our al-liance. But he berated me about how I handled the situation with Hakon six years ago. Called me an idiot. He said I never should have forbidden you to speak of it, but by the gods, Asa, I was so young when I became jarl. It happened only a year after that. I didn't know. As time went on, we never mentioned it and I thought things were all right with you. I never dreamed of what was happening inside you. The pain and fear and anger you still carried. I'm so sorry."

"We were all very young and we only had each other. Talking about it the other night helped." She firmed her resolve. "What else did you talk about with Eirik that she might have overheard?"

He thought for a moment. "Hakon. I didn't tell Eirik any details about what happened with you, but I did mention the basics. We re-alized Hakon took over Eirik's village and we discussed—" He released her and drove his fist into his hand. "We discussed our plans to attack him before he has a chance to leave Haardvik and come here. Estrid knows that now. She always wanted him. Now she knows where he is and what our plans are. She'll go to him and tell him we're coming, so she can win him back."

She put her hand on his arm. "We're aware of what they're doing, but they don't know that. They'll only know we're coming at some point. Eirik may have ways of getting to his village so they won't see us. We'll have to use stealth to approach them."

"I should send men after Estrid and Hjellmar, but we don't know when they left or what route they took. Now that the snows are melting in the lower lands, there are several ways they could go. I'll send trackers just in case, but I have to keep my warriors here. We need all the men we can bring with us when we leave. Eirik doesn't know about this, but he's aware the time is short. He won't linger in Trøndelag. We'll keep watch on the fjord a few days early in the event he gets here sooner than we thought. If we stay in the lower farmstead there, we can be there when he arrives. We won't beat Estrid and Hjellmar to Haardvik, but we can be close enough behind them that Hakon won't have much time to prepare."

He took her in his arms again. "I wish I could persuade you not to come this time. Now that Estrid is gone, you would be safe here. The fighting will be vicious, unlike anything you've seen so far. Eirik said these are hardened men, not like many of the outcasts we came against here. I fear for you."

She gazed up at him. At the concern in his eyes, she gave him a smile she didn't quite feel. "And don't you think I fear for all of you as well? Although I know now it wasn't my fault that Hakon tried to rape me, he did try. That's what started it all. Because of what happened with me, he was outcast and it drove him to attack Eirik's village. Eirik's father died because of it. This is more my fight than anyone else's, and even if I don't deal Hakon his death blow, by the gods, I swear I will be there to see it struck."

Chapter Sixteen

Vargfjell, Trondheimsfjorden
Trøndelag, Norway

"I thought you said you were Rorik's cousin. Are you certain you parted on good terms?" Leif peered over the bow of the vessel toward the shore of the fjord.

Eirik chuckled. "I'm certain. He just doesn't recognize this ship and won't be expecting me. With all his wealth, he's a bit on the cautious side."

Warriors lined the shore below the sprawling village, all armed. Many had arrows pointed at the two ships as they drew closer to the docks. They'd formed a shield wall and stood ready to fight.

Eirik had breathed a sigh of relief when they'd rounded the curve of the fjord and had seen all of Rorik's ships still there. Some of the vessels were already in the water. But several were still on the beach, though with all the activity near them, it was clear they were ready to be launched.

Magnus had sent another ship with them for protection and they both slowed near the docks. Eirik climbed up on the bow.

He cupped his free hand beside his mouth. "Rorik, is this how you greet one of your mother's family?"

A powerful-looking man with waist-length black hair stepped forward in front of the line of warriors. His deep voice carried well over the water. "I have only two cousins on that side, and one of them is too smart to come here in a strange ship. Since it can't be Silvi, it must be you, Eirik. What in the name of the gods are you doing?"

He laughed. "Can we dock, Rorik? Or do I have to fight my way in?"

Rorik gave a command to his men and they relaxed, sheathing

their swords and lowering their bows. Leif's men rowed closer to the docks, then drew their oars in and let the ships glide the rest of the way. Men threw them lines and they tied the vessels to the pilings.

Eirik leaped off the boat as Rorik strode up to him, grabbing him in a back-pounding embrace. "Why are you here? I always come get you at the start of raiding season." His eyes narrowed. "It's not your father, is it? Did he die over the winter?"

"He's dead, yes, but not from the wasting disease. I have much to tell you. Outcasts raided and took Haardvik two days after I arrived home. They slew my father during the battle. I escaped, but the outcasts don't know I survived. I need your help to retake Haardvik."

Rorik didn't hesitate. "You have it." Then he regarded Leif, who had stood aside as they spoke.

"This is Leif Sigrundson," Eirik said as Leif joined them. "I overwintered at his village in the *fjells*. His brother is jarl there. They'll help us, but I have much to tell you of it."

Rorik offered his hand to Leif. They grasped wrists. "Then you're my ally, as well," Rorik said. "Come up to the longhouse with all your men. You can wash and I'll order a feast. We can talk then."

Rorik's longhouse was large and opulent, its wooden walls carved in interlaced patterns, its floors of fine woods. His wealth was displayed for all to see, and the feast that he'd ordered at a moment's notice would have beggared most men. The wines were imported from the farthest lands, the spices rare and costly, and the meat seasoned with skill. Musicians accompanied their meal and the people filled the hall with laughter. Rorik lived well.

Eirik sat back from the table. He'd eaten his fill, as had Leif and all his men. Between bites, he'd managed to tell Rorik all that had happened since they'd last parted.

"I see the need for haste." Rorik motioned a servant to fill his cup. Again. "I'm almost finished provisioning my ships for their voyages. I'll order it done by the day after tomorrow and we'll set sail then. We'll need extra food and supplies, though. The men who took over your village likely will have eaten and drunk everything during the winter. They wouldn't be concerned with surviving until the spring crops come in. Your people will need food to last them until they recover."

"Magnus said the outcasts would kill everyone in Haardvik to hide their tracks." Eirik held his hand over his cup as a servant tried to refill it a third time. He needed a relatively clear head. Rorik, however, never seemed affected by wine.

"We'll be there before that," Rorik said. "The snows may be melting on the coast, but not as much inland yet. Individuals may travel in the mountains, but to move so large a force of men would be difficult. And if what you say is accurate, they'll have to wait until the passes clear enough in the *fjells*. They won't want to be caught out in the open on the way there. Being permanent outcasts, none of them would have designated safe places. Anyone may kill them at any time, and any place. They'll stay where they are for now.

"But we don't have time to waste. It will take at least four days to get to the Sognefjord if the winds are favorable. And with so large a fleet, we'll have to swing out into the sea to avoid the islands. I'll leave most of my ships waiting at the inlet while we take just a few into the fjord. It's a good thing you brought Leif with you to guide us. There are many inlets there and the fjord splits and narrows farther in. It would be easy to become lost."

Leif grinned. "That's why I came. That, and Eirik has told me of your shieldmaidens who fight alongside you. Did he tell you my sister is one? I have a certain, oh, interest in them. I've always wondered what it would be like to be with one."

Rorik shook his head. "Be careful what you wish for. The gods just may grant it. They sit at that table in the corner." He motioned with his gold cup.

Six women sat together, along with several men. Each of the female warriors was beautiful. They wore clothing similar to what Asa wore when she fought, thigh-length, belted tunics, and leggings. Their arms were bare except for gold arm rings. The seaxes they wore were hilted with gold and silver and gemstones, yet looked serviceable. One of them, a woman with hair as long and black as Rorik's, cast a glance over her shoulder at them. She focused on Leif and narrowed her slanted eyes. He grinned at her. Her gaze slid over the length of his body, before she looked away.

"Who's the woman with the black hair?" Leif glanced at Rorik. "She looks like you."

"She's my sister. I wouldn't tread there if I were you, or—"

"I know." Leif chuckled. "You'd have to kill me."

"No, she would."

Leif raised an eyebrow. "Doesn't she like men?"

"Oh, she likes them just fine. But she won't be with anyone who isn't more skilled than she is." He frowned. "And no one is. If you want to try, best start practicing now."

"Perhaps I won't need to." He looked at Eirik. "Stop staring." He jabbed Eirik hard in the ribs with his elbow. "You're a betrothed man."

"You're the one who's staring." Eirik shot him a glare. "I was just thinking how like them Asa is."

"Of course you were." Leif took another drink of his ale.

"I've fought with them for the past three years. There's nothing I haven't seen."

Rorik's eyes widened. "What's this about your being betrothed?"

"To my sister," Leif said. "The shieldmaiden."

"You left out some details about your stay in Thorsfjell, Eirik."

"I was getting to it." His ribs ached where Leif had slammed his elbow into them. He could have a bit of revenge, himself, for that.

He leaned forward. "Rorik, is she ready for me?"

Rorik frowned. "I don't know who—Oh." He grinned as Eirik tilted his head at Leif and gave him a meaningful look. "Oh, yes, she's been ready and waiting for you for some weeks. I know you meant her for your father, but now, she's all yours."

"Is she as beautiful as I've imagined?" Eirik tried not to smile as Leif turned on the bench to face him, his arms crossed over his chest.

"Only if you've imagined a sleek beauty bending to your will." His voice was low and sensual, with a timbre that brought women all over the known world to their knees. "The scent of her will fill you as you enter her and she'll rock you to sleep at night as you lie in her embrace. She's all curves and dreams and will always be ready for you. As you guide her where you want to take her, she'll respond to the slightest touch of your hand. She's tied up and waiting for your command."

"By the gods." Leif shot to his feet. "I should kill you now, Eirik, if you think to do such things with Asa. You're not even married yet and already you cannot keep from other women. You insult her."

He fought a grin. "Rorik, I'd like to see her now. Such a beauty cannot be kept waiting. Leif, feel free to join us if you want."

"Join you?" He glared at them both as he followed them outside. "I'm going only to see to the poor woman's well-being. Just when I thought I knew a man. Wait, where are we going?"

They walked in single file along a narrow path down to the beach, Rorik leading the way. Leif lagged behind them, grumbling. It was all Eirik could do to keep from bursting into laughter. Rorik's shoulders shook once or twice as he, no doubt, tried to keep from breaking down as well.

They reached the docks, but Rorik continued on through a group of trees near the water's edge. When they cleared them, they came to another beach overlooking a small bay that hadn't been visible when they'd arrived. There, tied to a dock, a magnificent longship waited. It was massive, its lines graceful. With twenty oar ports on each side, it would need a crew of at least forty to fifty men for long voyages. It was under two man-lengths wide, allowing it to slice through the water like a sword blade.

Its mast rose higher than any other. A striped sail was tied up under the lowered long yard that rested on supports set into the deck in front of and behind the mast. The sail would be square, and was designed to lift up the ship so that it skimmed, light and swift, over the surface of the water. The front of its bow was carved with interlaced animals and vines, and rose up like a proud woman.

"It's everything I'd hoped it would be." Eirik walked out onto the dock and jumped in. It was firm and true under his feet. Over a year ago, he'd commissioned Rorik's shipwrights to build it for his father. Now it was his. An unexpected pang hit him. Ivar never knew about it. Eirik had wanted to surprise and thank him for all he had done for him through the years. Rorik was to bring it to Haardvik this spring, but now Eirik would sail it there to avenge his father's death.

When he returned to the dock, Leif was frowning. "So this is what you were talking about? A ship?"

"Of course." Eirik clapped him on the shoulder. "What else would I be speaking of? Honestly, Leif, you need to get your mind out of the cesspit."

"My shipwright outdid himself." Rorik gave Eirik a sour look. "He's never built anything like this for me. Now you'll have the best ship in the family. The only thing it lacks is the prow ornament. I have several, but I thought you should pick it out yourself. We can put it on tomorrow."

"My thanks, but I brought my own." He gazed at the ship, and a longing thrummed through him to see the wind in her sail and feel the sea wrap itself around her. "And if you think I have the better ship, just wait until you see the dragon that will guide her."

"I thought you were exaggerating about Asa's carving skills last night when you told me of her. I see now you weren't." Rorik stood with Eirik as the shipbuilders swarmed over it, making certain everything was perfect for the voyage south. They'd mounted the dragon's head that morning. Now the vessel was complete.

The carving fit as though it had been made for the ship. Perhaps it had been. The gods were influencing this time and nothing would surprise him any longer. The ship had vibrated with power when they'd attached the dragon, but why would that be? Was it the energy in the runes, or just that the ship meant so much to him? It would always remind him of his father, which was how it should be, but now it also symbolized his union with Asa. Her dragon guided the ship of his own design. But it still remained to be seen if she would stand beside him as he sailed it into the world. If she decided against him, he would buy the dragon from Magnus. It would never leave him.

"What have you named her?" Rorik's words snapped him back into reality.

"I'll call her *The Wind of Njord*."

"In honor of the sea god. Very wise. It's a good name." He stood watching his men make their final adjustments to the rigging. "You have the ship of a jarl now, and the title as well."

"Not until I save Haardvik and Star Slayer. I told you that."

Rorik waved his hand, as though sweeping aside his words. "A formality. You know you'll always have my backing, but you'll need to gather more men to you. It's not only to replace those you've lost to these outcasts, but to keep what you have and make your place in the world. Men will follow the jarl who gives them the most food, the best drink, and the greatest chance for riches. That's why I've been so successful. Keep that in mind and you can live like I do."

Eirik smiled. "I'm not certain I'd survive that. For one thing, I've found the only woman I want. You're still looking."

"Looking?" He snorted. "Why would I look for one when I have dozens of them? With so many to choose from, why choose among them at all? Besides, you're not even certain you have Asa."

"I'll know when we come to the meeting place."

"That's not acceptable." He faced Eirik, his silver-blue eyes stern. "You've been raiding with me long enough to know you take what you want. You're being so noble, you'll end up losing her. For as long as you and I have traveled the world, she's the one woman you've truly wanted."

"I've been with plenty of them."

"Been with them, yes. I've been with hundreds." At Eirik's raised brows, Rorik shrugged. "Perhaps not hundreds, but I've had my share. So have you. Yet, I've never heard you speak like this about any woman before. Usually, I'd be inclined to crack you over the head with the flat of my sword and beat some sense into you. But with what you've told me of her, I can understand why you'd want her. In fact, if you don't claim her, I just might."

He glowered at his cousin. "And die trying. If I didn't kill you, she would."

Rorik laughed. "I thought that's how it is. If she's anything like you've said, she's worth fighting for, and worth fighting. Just heave her over your shoulder and the rest will fall into place."

"Wait until you find the one woman you want, Rorik. You'll see it's not so easy as that."

"And that's why I'm not looking." He chuckled. "We leave at first light tomorrow. When you see that sail fill with wind and feel the sea on your face as you stand within your own ship for the first time, you'll forget everything else in the glory of it."

But he wouldn't. For whether or not Asa waited for him on the beach, her dragon would always be a part of his ship, and she would always be a part of him.

Eirik had intended to go to sleep as soon as he entered the guest room where he always stayed when he was here. Leif and his men were comfortable in several of the guest houses and most of them were still drinking with Rorik's men, enjoying his generous hospitality.

Sleep, however, eluded him. An urge tickled the back of his mind. He needed to let Silvi know he was on his way. Throughout the winter, he'd received her gentle sendings. He had touched her mind when he'd first arrived at Thorsfjell to let her know he was well. Could he do it again?

He dug through his pack and brought out the gem-encrusted bag that held his runes. If anything could make a connection between his sister and him, they would. He searched through the set until he found the one he sought. *Ehwaz*, which symbolized the horse and an unbreakable bond. It indicated a journey, though usually by land, but she would understand what it meant.

With the piece on the bed in front of him, he closed his eyes and envisioned a sphere of light encircling him. Stars burst around him, bathing him in their glow. Sitting in the midst of them, he drank in their energy. A light illuminated him from within. He drew confidence and peace from it, finding resolve in the connection he had with the runes themselves. He held his hand over the piece, fixing the symbol in his mind.

The power built between the rune and him until he could no longer hold on to the vision. Then he let it go, flinging it out into the stars surrounding him, willing it to find Silvi.

He opened his eyes. Only the stillness of the room enveloped him. All the energy was gone and he rested his head in his hands, drained. Remaining still, he willed strength back into himself. Little by little, it came. Sighing, he picked up the rune to place it back in the bag. It was warm, even in the coldness of the room.

He had done all he could. Now, if his message found his sister, she and Lifa would recognize that he was on his way with help. And, if he knew them, they would have plans of their own.

The village of Haardvik

Dragons flew close to the surface of the sea, skimming the tops of the dark waves. Behind them, in a blood-red sky, the rune Ehwaz hung like an alien sun, dripping molten gold into the waters, setting them aflame.

A man stood on the back of one of the dragons, coming to her in the time of war with his arrogance and his weapons and his hate. His blood would run into the ground of her homeland, mingling with hers.

Silvi stayed in the dream as long as she could. She wanted to decipher every symbol it held. The vision tore away from her, though, and reality showed through the tattered edges as she woke. But she'd seen enough.

She left her room and eased past Hakon's men, who lay all over the tables and benches in the common room, sleeping off their drunkenness of the previous night. She made her way to her mother's room. Lifa was already awake though it was well before dawn.

"Eirik is on his way back to us." She kept her voice low as she shut the door. "I dreamed of Ehwaz and of dragons on the waters."

Lifa nodded. "Rorik's ships. Eirik sent you the rune so you would know it's a true vision. If he is just leaving Trøndelag, then it could still be many days until he arrives, depending on the currents and the winds. We must act now to summon the warriors who spent the winter at their homesteads so they'll be ready to fight alongside him. Find Nuallen and bring him here. It is time."

Silvi sought him out where he slept in the corner of the cooking room with the other thralls. He woke almost before she touched him, as a warrior would. Without a word, they returned to Lifa's room.

"Eirik is on his way," Lifa said. "We must do as we've planned these past months. We need to make it seem as though you've escaped. Then you can bring back our warriors who did not stay here for the winter."

"It shouldn't be difficult to believe that I've escaped." Nuallen gave her a wry smile. "I've managed to convince them of my resentment toward you, and they've been careless in what they say around me. When the passes are clear, they'll all leave to go north." He looked down. "I'm uneasy with what they've hinted about as far as their plans for us."

"They're going to kill us." Lifa's voice was calm, but it trembled a bit.

"They're going to try." He caught her gaze in his. "I vow that while I breathe, they will not succeed. I'll find your other warriors, and when the jarl returns, I'll join in the fight and we'll be victorious."

"Then you must hurry. It's still some time until dawn. You could leave now and they would never notice it."

"I could," he said. "But with this iron collar on me, I'd just be a runaway thrall. I have nothing to prove otherwise to anyone who might see me and I'm not Norse." He gripped the metal ring around his neck. "I need this off of me so none will question me as I travel, and so your men won't think I've escaped. With it, anyone who finds me can kill me. If I go as a free man, though, I will be safer."

"No one can free you except Eirik. Not even I. And what would keep you from fleeing and not returning at all?" Lifa raised her chin, her eyes hard.

He stepped over to her and she had to look up at him. "If I'm an escaped slave, then that's all I'll ever be, no matter how far I travel. I would die as a slave and I cannot accept that. This collar brought me despair, but it also gave me the determination to live and see it removed one day. By helping you, I'll earn my freedom and I'll have repaid my debt to you for saving my life. Only then will I be truly free."

Silvi studied them both. Something sparked between them, like a metal fire-starter and a stone. Nuallen wore a ring on his neck, yet he came before Lifa with a pride of bearing that spoke of his great strength and quiet confidence. In the year and a half of his slavery, he'd never lost that.

Lifa let out her breath, as though she'd been holding it while she made her decision. "Come with me. Both of you."

Her room had a separate door so that those who wished to keep their consultations with her private could do so. They left the long-house and made their way to the smith's shop. He was up, making a seax blade.

"Mistress. What can I do for you?" He dropped the red-hot metal into a bucket of water, then came over to them.

"Strike off Nuallen's collar. The time has come for us to make our move, as I told you weeks ago."

"Very well." He picked up his hammer. "Come over here, Nuallen, and let's get this business done."

Nuallen knelt at the anvil and put his neck to it, the ring resting on it. He brushed his long auburn hair to the side. The smith set an awl to the seam of the ring with a steady hand and brought down his hammer. The ring broke apart with one blow. Nuallen stood and, closing his eyes, put his hand to his strong neck. Already, he seemed to be taller, more powerful.

Lifa walked to a rack where new swords rested and picked one out. She returned to Nuallen and held it out to him. "Take this. You'll need it."

As he took the sword from her, he put his fingers over hers on the hilt for just a moment, before he moved them so that she could draw her hand away. In the glow of the forge, it appeared that she blushed. Or was that just the color of the firelight? She met Silvi's eyes and looked away. Silvi almost smiled. He and her mother were of the same age. Interesting.

Nuallen sheathed the sword in the scabbard the smith gave him and belted it around his lean hips. "If I have to kill any of them as I leave, it may be difficult to explain."

Silvi smiled. "No, it won't. All winter, we've been feeding them tales of the spirits in these woods and the Wild Hunt. Whenever you've killed any of them and left the body in the woods, they've become even more convinced that these mountains hold *draugar* and trolls. We'll tell them that since winter is over, the wood spirits are awakening and are hungry from their long sleep. The men are half-afraid to walk outside at night to patrol as it is. If more of them die, that will make it worse. They won't guard Haardvik as closely as they would otherwise, which will work to our advantage. Some may even flee. When the number of dead increases sharply, we'll know you've returned. It will make them even easier to manipulate. Hide yourselves and wait for Eirik to come before you make any moves."

Nuallen smiled. "Remind me never to come up against either of you in a battle of strategy."

Lifa cleared her throat. "You remember where all the home-steads are?"

"I remember the directions you've gone over with me all winter, mistress. Now, I should leave before first light."

Lifa took a step toward him, but stopped. "Return to us, Nuallen. We'll need you. Then, I vow that I'll have my son free you."

He closed the distance between them. "I will come back, and not only because I wish to be freed." He lifted his hand as though to touch her arm, but let it drop back to his side. "I have other reasons. I swear I won't fail you."

Gathering his cloak around him, he crossed to the door and was gone into the darkness. When Silvi and her mother left the forge to return to the longhouse, there was no sign of him. It was as if he had never existed.

Silvi paused to look into the shadows of the woods surrounding Haardvik, her senses attuned to the land around her. She couldn't see him, but he was still there, watching to be certain they got back to the longhouse safely.

Would Nuallen keep his word? Whenever the three of them were alone, he'd looked at Lifa with such gentle care. He'd never been anything but respectful to both of them. And yet, when he was with Hakon and his men, he'd cast her and Lifa glares filled with such loathing and resentment that it'd made her skin crawl. He was as good an actor as any storyteller, but which was the real Nuallen?

They would find out soon enough. All their fates lay in his hands, the hands of a proud man whom they had made a slave and who had every reason to hate them.

Chapter Seventeen

Lustrafjorden, near Thorsfjell

Asa sat on a small ridge overlooking the misty fjord. Ever since she was a child, she would sit there, watching the men prepare for their trading journeys in the spring. It was where she'd last seen her father before he'd sailed for the East and his death. Would she ever see Thorsfjell again after this?

The men moving below her caught her eye. The ships were ready to sail. Though they weren't sleek warships, they would hold all of Magnus's men and a large amount of supplies. More boxes and sacks sat on the beach, waiting to be loaded onto Rorik's ships.

Asa, Magnus, and their men had arrived at the beach two days early, staying in a nearby farmstead, but so far there was no sign of Leif and Eirik. She'd spent the days watching the waters, remembering everything about the winter. And she missed Eirik all the more.

A dark shape appeared in the mists on the waters and she stood, straining to see it. It came out of the gray haze, a large longship gliding around the curve in the fjord. It was splendid, like nothing she had seen before, even at the great markets. Fog covered the water, making it seem as though the ship floated on the clouds.

At first, the mists swallowed all the color on the ship. But as it came closer, it broke free of the haze. Shields of all hues lined its side above the oar ports and its sail was striped red and white. Another appeared behind it, also beautiful, though not as long as the first. And flanking them were the two *knörrs* Magnus had sent to Trøndelag.

"Magnus, ships." As she called to him, he looked up at her from where he stood on the beach. She pointed. "It's Leif and Eirik."

The men gathered on the shore to watch them approach. Though the sails were unfurled, because of the still morning air, oars dipped into the water. Their bows cut the waters like knives, their ornaments rising above the waves. As they drew closer, she focused hard to see who stood on their decks.

A man hung on to the dragon on the front of the largest ship, his arm wrapped around it. His blond hair flowed around his wide shoulders and he was dressed in a deep blue tunic and dark trousers. She smiled, her heart melting. Eirik. He rode the ship like he was a part of it, born of the sea itself.

Leif stood on the bow of the second ship with a black-haired man who was at least as tall as he was. That must be Rorik.

They raised the oars and glided onto the beach. She ran down to meet Eirik, but as she got closer to the ship, she looked at the dragon's head. It was hers. The one she and Eirik had carved together. How? Only a jarl or king should have a dragon on the bow.

Then he jumped off the ship and splashed the rest of the way through the shallow water toward her. The other men also leaped off and pulled the ships farther onto the beach. But Eirik looked only at her.

"I didn't see you here at first," he said. "I thought you'd decided against me."

He was dressed in the finest clothes, a wide gold armband on his bicep. His belt was of the best leather and was encrusted with gold. He looked like a king's son and her heart sped up a bit more. But there was still the matter of her betrothal.

"I was on the ridge above." She crossed her arms. "And how do you know I've chosen to wed you? I might be here just so I can go with all of you and have my revenge on Hakon."

He stepped up to her. "That isn't how it works. I said if you were here, you were mine. You're here."

She raised her head. "You said that, not me. I have a right to seek revenge, the same as any of you."

"No. For if you are not my betrothed, then it is Magnus's right to slay Hakon to see justice done. If you are to be my wife, then it is mine. As it stands, the right is now mine, and so are you."

He took her shoulders and kissed her hard. She tried to pull away, but he circled her with his powerful arms and she couldn't move at all. He plundered her mouth, taking what he wanted, as ruthless as any raider. And yet there was a care to it, as though he held back his strength for her sake. Only when he lifted his head to grin down at her did she hear the cheering of the men around them.

Heat rose into her cheeks as she looked at the crowd of warriors. Among them stood six women, all armed and dressed in thigh-length tunics, much the same as hers. They, too, shouted and laughed. This was the first time she'd seen other shieldmaidens, and they would have to see her like this. The ground could swallow her up right now and she would be happy to just sink away.

She ducked her head into his chest. "I'm going to kill you for this."

"You can try." He dipped his shoulder and tossed her over it. Mortified, she fought him, but he only laughed.

She reared up, trying to find her brothers, but her hair flowed around her and she couldn't see anything. Why weren't they stopping this?

"The first man who comes onto my ship, rows all the way to Hordaland."

With all the men laughing, Eirik splashed back out to the ship and set her over the side onto the deck. Her skin was hot with embarrassment and anger. Before she could scramble away from him and jump off the other side, he was on the ship and had her in his arms. He picked her up and strode toward the back of the ship, where a large length of cloth was tented across the rigging. It made a cabin of sorts, and he carried her into it.

As soon as he set her on her feet, she swung at him. He ducked. "How could you do that to me in front of my brothers and their men? You heard them laughing. I've spent years trying to earn their respect as a warrior and you treat me like some common woman. You wouldn't do this to any of them."

"Gods, I hope not." He chuckled. "Rorik's men may have been applauding for me. But Magnus's men were cheering *for* you. They care about you and were rejoicing that you have finally chosen someone who could make you happy. If you want to look at it this way, you were just bested by a better warrior. It happens to all at one time or another. Accept your defeat. I'll make certain it's very pleasant. For both of us."

"Is that what this is? Defeat?" She shoved her hair out of her face. Was it possible that what Eirik said was true? That the men she'd fought beside all these years were voicing their support of her choice and her future? "I suppose it is defeat since I can hardly fight both you and Magnus, now can I?"

He lowered the front flap of the shelter. "Admit it, Asa. You'd made your mind up to go through with the marriage anyhow, even though I gave you a choice. You're angry because we arranged a marriage without consulting you, but we felt we were doing it for your happiness. I think you're content with it, but it's your stubborn pride that's getting in the way."

He took a step toward her, but she backed away. Months ago, it would have been because she was afraid. Now it was because she was livid.

She paused. She *wasn't* afraid, and that deep, soul-searing rage didn't consume her. Not in the least. The world wasn't turning as red as blood and she didn't fear losing control of herself. Even now, when she was thinking about what Hakon had done to her, she didn't feel any fear at all. Just good, healthy anger at Eirik. It felt wonderful.

"Doing it for my happiness? And what about the alliance? How did that play into it all? Our marriage was to secure the agreement. No more, no less."

"Oh? I told you the alliance would stand regardless. Rorik's warships with hundreds of men on them are anchored among the islands off the mouth of the fjord. They wait for Magnus and his men and ships to join them. Then we'll all sail south together to battle for the freedom of Haardvik, as well as revenge on Hakon. Your family and mine." He walked over to her and she stood her ground, raising her chin and looking him in the eye. "I arranged this without knowing if you'd accept me or not. Even if you don't want me, Asa, the alliance continues. So our marriage has nothing to do with it."

"Oh." Her anger foundered like a ship in a stormy sea. Without oars.

He touched a lock of her hair that cascaded over her breast. Her skin tightened. "Our marriage has everything to do with how I feel about you. How I love you. That's all that matters here, now."

She should stay angry. But if this was defeat, she didn't want to be victorious. He just looked into her soul with his beautiful blue eyes and there was no place she could hide. No way to pretend any longer that she didn't want him.

He brushed her cheek with his fingertips. "One last chance, Asa. You can walk off this ship and I won't stop you."

She gave him a soft smile. "The water is too deep. I might get my clothes wet, and then what would I wear?"

"Nothing." He laughed and took her in his arms. "If I have my way, you'll wear nothing at all." Then he grew grim. "I won't deny that I want you. Now. But I don't want to frighten you. I said we would go slowly and so we will, if it's what you want. Perhaps once Hakon is dead, it will free you from the past."

"You've done that, Eirik. Freed me. With your kindness, your patience, your gentle strength, and your love. There will always be shadows in me, but when I meet Hakon in battle, I won't be that same innocent girl who died within me that day six years ago. She's gone forever. Yet I would not be what I am now without her. If that hadn't happened to me, I wouldn't have the strength I do now, or the ability to fight. And if I die and go to Freya's Folkvang, let it be because I died a valiant death in this battle, and not because I died a virgin."

He gathered her closer to him and kissed her. Reaching up, she curved her hands around the back of his neck and pulled him farther down to her. She was tall, but he was so much taller, and bigger. Everywhere. Already, his body pressed against hers, his desire apparent against her stomach.

"I would see you, Asa. You've already seen me, I know, in the sauna." Grinning, he released her and stepped back.

"I remember something about you seeing me after I fell through the ice." She gave him a mock frown, but her heart raced.

"I don't think that counts," he said. "I was a bit preoccupied with keeping you alive. I don't remember what you looked like. Much."

His smile was wicked, enticing. Her cheeks heated as she swallowed. Facing him here, like this, was far more difficult than facing a dozen warriors in battle. "I don't know if I can."

"Then let me." He stepped back to her and untied the lacing beneath her neck. Running his finger under the cord, he loosened it.

The back of his hand brushed between her breasts and she sucked in a breath. Lightning seemed to strike deep within her body, targeting her between her legs. Something there opened out.

"Lift your arms for me."

She did so and he slipped the tunic over her head. Under it, she wore a linen top for warmth and to protect her skin from the leather.

He untied the lacings and drew it off of her shoulders. Exposed, she shifted so her hair fell forward and covered her nakedness like a gleaming, fiery shawl. No man, not even Hakon, had ever seen her fully unclothed, and her true vulnerability drove into her.

Eirik unfastened the fine leather belt he wore and let it drop to the floor. Then he pulled off his shirt and tunic and cast it aside, his hair pouring, golden, down his chest and back. His body was perfect. The scars on his shoulders and arms only accentuated his male power and his prowess as a warrior. He had fought many battles and emerged victorious, the same as she. The gods had made them for each other, two souls who would soon be one, and desire flared in her to know that closeness with him.

After sliding off her shoes, she untied the drawstring of her leggings, let them fall, and stepped away from them. Her hair still flowed down around her, but she didn't shake it back. Let him discover her, as he wished. Matching her movements, he removed his wet trousers and shoes and faced her. He watched her as she swept him with her gaze, but didn't reach for her.

She'd seen naked men before. Warriors weren't modest, and after battles they'd shed their bloodied clothing and wash in whatever water was at hand. She hadn't thought much of it. Before.

This was very different. *He* was very different. He would lay her down, and she would take him into herself. She let out a trembling breath. How could they do that when he was so large?

"Asa?" He came to her and tilted her head up with a gentle hand beneath her chin.

She tried to smile. "I'm fine."

"You're beautiful, but I would like to see more." Combing his fingers through her hair, he moved it back behind her shoulders so that she stood open to him.

At the heat in his eyes, she crossed her arms over her breasts. He took her wrists and held her arms to her sides, insistent and commanding, but still careful of her.

"There's no need to hide anything from me, ever." His deep voice spiraled straight into her. It held a tone she'd never heard before. It was possessive and very male.

He picked her up and knelt with her onto the piles of furs that lay strewn throughout the enclosure. Positioning himself over her, he kept his movements slow and his weight from her. The muscles on his arms and shoulders bunched as he lowered himself, touching only his mouth to hers. His scent drifted over her, that of leather, the sea, and the winds.

She hadn't been certain how she would react to being beneath a man. Her only experience with it had been filled with fear and horror. But this was Eirik. And this was now, not six years ago.

No matter what happened in the battle, this would be her truest victory over Hakon.

Eirik was so careful of her, watching the look in her eyes, every motion of her body. He understood, and that was why he was perfect for her.

That, and other things. She smiled and ran her hands over his shoulders and down his back. His muscles flowed beneath his skin like iron under silk. His hips were lean and strong, his stomach ridged and flat. Shining and trailing onto her arm, his hair was too soft to be a part of him, and she ran her hand through it as he bent to kiss her again. She returned it full measure.

He relaxed then, and lowered himself to one elbow, putting part of his weight on her shoulder. With that hand, he wrapped a thick lock of her hair around his fist, holding her beside him. With his free hand, he cupped her breast, his thumb caressing the tip. His touch jagged through her and she closed her eyes as a moan broke from deep within her. She set her hand on his, pressing him to her.

His strength mastered her, but he used it for her pleasure. Letting go of her thoughts and questions, she lay open to him, submitting to his power, trusting in his love.

Shifting so she lay beneath him, he let her hair go. He painted her neck and breasts with kisses, and she arched up into them, offering herself, body and soul, to him. He took that offering, as a god would accept a sacrifice. But she gave up nothing. It was he who gave to her as he moved down her body, nipping and kissing her belly, her hips, her thighs.

He lay on her legs so that she couldn't shield herself by bending her knees, his arms cradling her hips. "I'll make certain you're ready for me, Asa. I don't want to frighten or shock you, but I want to be certain I don't hurt you."

Looking down at him, she nodded. He parted her legs and placed his hand between them and she gasped. She rose up on her elbows and stared at him. He only met her eyes as he touched her. When he stroked her, she almost jerked out from beneath him.

"Eirik, what are you—"

"Relax and enjoy this, Asa. Nothing I do will harm you. I swear it. I want your first time to be a memory that will outshine any others you have." As he spoke, he took her hand and kissed her palm. The familiar gesture calmed her and she lay back, taking a deep breath to slow her pounding heart.

He stroked her again, but this time she gave in to the sublime sensation. Her legs grew weak and her body melted as she relaxed into the furs.

The ship, the sounds of the water against the hull, and everything around them faded. There was only his touch. As his fingers delved into her, he nibbled her thighs and the tender skin between her hips. His hair curtained her body, its strands brushing her as he moved.

A pressure built inside of her, like a storm about to break in the mountains. It swirled through her, carrying her along toward a place she'd never been. She spun in its heady force until it burst over her. Crying out as her mind came apart, she clutched at Eirik, needing an anchor in the maelstrom.

He brought himself up to her and held her face in his hands. She looked at him, her body still humming, and he smiled down at her. "Now, I think you're ready for me."

Again? She wouldn't survive it. But he needed to find his satisfaction as well. She did know that much, at least. Nothing, not the talk of the women in the weaving room nor the boasting of the warriors, could have prepared her for this.

Locking her arms around him, she pulled him down for her kiss and let her legs fall apart in invitation. "You've given me pleasure as I've never dreamed of, but I don't know what to do for you. Yet. I'll learn eventually. For now, I hope it's enough that you find your own release."

He chuckled. "And you think that was all for you? It was only to make certain you were ready for me. When I come next, you'll be right there with me and we'll find our pleasure together, as we always will from now on."

"Twice?" She stared at him.

He gathered her hair at the nape of her neck. "The gods smiled upon women when they created them. For men must wait a time between their releases. Women can find enjoyment many times in a row. I'll be quite happy to show you."

She smiled. "I await your instruction."

He groaned and nipped her neck. With her hair held in his hand, he kept her in his control as he positioned himself. "Wrap your legs around me."

Holding him with her arms and legs, she clung to him as he pressed into her. A sharp pain almost made her jump, but she held on and it passed in another moment. He filled her. She buried her head in his chest, love and joy coursing through her. He gave her hair a gentle tug and she lay back, looking up at him.

"I want to see your beautiful eyes when I make love to you." He moved within her and the storm built again.

She speared her hands into his hair and gripped the back of his strong neck as he captured her in his gaze. The power of his body flowed down around her. He'd conquered her and she was now his forever, but she never wanted to be free. Not after this.

She closed her eyes as another storm rose in her soul, but this time, she wasn't alone. Eirik was with her. A bolt of lightning from the tempest struck near them. It exploded into stars that whirled around them. She clung to him, determined never to leave him. But the winds only drove them closer together, wrapping around them as though binding them together. He surrounded her with his strength, his magic, and in the distance, a dragon formed of gold hurtled into the storm above them.

The stars entered her, and the power fractured her mind. Where the stars had been, a burning rune spun in the sky. She tried to reach for it, but she fell and it vanished.

She opened her eyes. Eirik lay on top of her, breathing hard, his skin glowing with sweat in the warm enclosure. When she stirred, he shifted partway off of her, then rolled onto his back beside her.

"By the gods." His voice was just a whisper. "I've never had that happen before."

"What? That you found your release? I find that difficult to believe." She smiled, though it took some effort. She was drained of even the ability to move. If an enemy attacked them right now, she would be doomed.

He gave a soft laugh. "That, I have done. Once or twice."

She wanted to hit him, but she was too weak. He rolled over onto his side so that he faced her, and propped his head on his hand. It was more than she could do at the moment.

Brushing the back of his hand on her cheek, he said, "I had a vision and you were there with me. I saw stars and a great golden dragon that flew toward them. And then he became a rune."

She stilled. "I saw the stars also, and a dragon. And I, too, saw a rune."

"What did the rune look like?" He turned her face toward him, his eyes intense.

"It was the rune that looks like a sideways cross and stands for G."

"Gyfu. It indicates a gift. And that gift is usually love and happiness. Surely it means the gods have blessed us."

He lay back and pulled her over him so her head rested on his shoulder. Outside, voices rose as the men loaded the other ships. They would have to set sail before too long.

"Your cousin has fine ships. I've never seen anything like this one. But why is my dragon on the bow? Did Rorik buy it for this ship? I didn't know you'd taken it with you."

"This isn't Rorik's ship."

"Then whose is it? Don't tell me you have another rich relative with his own fleet."

"Not exactly. The ship is mine. I took the dragon as your dowry."

She sat up and looked down at him. He just folded his hands behind his head and grinned.

"You wanted it, even knowing it's damaged, like I am?"

He took her hand and kissed it. "I desired it because it's beautiful and strong and fierce, like you are, and I want it with me always. I'll have no other."

He wasn't speaking of the dragon, and the truth of his words lay in his eyes. But there was something he wasn't saying. "How can you afford this?" She gave him a hard look. "You said you'd been raiding in the past three years, but still. Even the king would be hard-pressed to have such a ship. And only someone highly ranked can have a dragon on the bow."

"I commissioned Rorik's shipwrights to build it for my father, but, as you know, he died last fall, so it's mine now. I also inherited his title. That of jarl."

Shock spread through her. She grabbed a lock of his hair and gave it a hard tweak. "Jarl? You're a jarl? Why didn't you tell me?"

"I won't accept the title unless I win back Haardvik and retrieve my ancestral sword from the fjord. I won't claim that to which I have no right. And I won't insult you by marrying you before I achieve that."

"But what if you don't win? What happens to us?" She wrapped the lock of his hair tight around her finger.

"If I'm not victorious, then I'll be dead. For that's the only way Hakon will stop me."

She could never live with herself, as well, if she failed, knowing the outcast was still alive and preying on others. "I understand. Another woman might not, but I do. I feel the same way. I will see justice done against Hakon, or die trying."

"Then we'll stand together, as we did in the star storm of our vision." Sitting up, he faced her. "I believe your *fylgjur* is the dragon. That's why you saw him in your mind."

"You saw him as well. It's said our guardian spirits appear to us to warn us of danger, and we do head into battle. But it's also a sign that death is near."

"Death, yes, but not always the death of the one he guards."

She leaned forward and kissed him. "The dragon and the runes. Always they have been intertwined with you and me."

"And they always will be."

As they rose and dressed, she watched him out of the corner of her eye. His movements were so smooth and powerful. He was a warrior in his prime and he had fought throughout the world, vanquishing all he faced. If the Valkyries came for him during this battle, drawn by his prowess and splendor, she would fight them off with her own sword, the gods be damned.

When they were clothed, he took her in his arms again.

"Ready to face them? There will be a fair amount of teasing, I think."

"At least it won't be about my cooking this time."

They walked out onto the deck. The men still loaded the other ships. They brought the cargo alongside the vessels with large-wheeled, high carts they pulled on top of flat rocks that formed a paved area running down into the shallow water.

Asa walked to the front of the ship and put her hand on the neck of the dragon. She looked up at the proud head. "May you guide us, my friend, and lead us to victory. May your fierceness be ours, your strength firm our hands, and your bravery harden our hearts."

And just for a moment, it seemed the paint on the left eye glittered a bit too much for the thin light of the cloudy day.

Outside the village of Haardvik

"I don't understand why we haven't seen any of Hakon's men patrolling beyond the village." Eirik sat back on his heels.

Asa crouched between Rorik and Eirik, peering down into Haardvik. They had arrived late last night, using the cover of darkness to land the ships on a strip of beach in a small tributary far to the west. They'd moved all night, quiet and careful, through the woods. Now they were spread out to the north, west, and east of Haardvik, but they'd encountered no resistance.

"Do you think it's a trap?" Rorik frowned.

Behind them, Magnus said, "With the numbers we've brought, we could challenge the king himself. This won't be difficult."

"Don't forget," Leif said, "Estrid is probably there by now, and they'll be forewarned. Being the cowards that they are, they'll threaten the people of the village to stop us."

"And that's why we're going to attack from different directions," Eirik said. "Rorik and I will take his men from the center right into the village for the main assault. Leif, you'll go to the east with the men you have positioned there now. Magnus will wait to the west with the others. When you hear me go in, you'll move in from the other directions. The only way out will be the fjord cliffs to the south, and believe me, they don't stand much of a chance if they try to escape that way. Estrid and Hjellmar can't know our true strength with Rorik's men. Even if Hakon is ready for us, they'll be overwhelmed. We have to strike hard and fast."

"Is there any other way?" Leif grinned, his eyes gleaming.

"We have to find my mother, sister, and all the other villagers." Eirik took Asa's shoulders. "I don't want to be separated from you. But we should be able to sweep through the outcasts before they know what hit them. If you can, try to get to the longhouse with Rorik's shield-maidens."

On the voyage south, she'd spoken with Kaia, Rorik's sister, who led the shieldmaidens. They were strong, capable warriors in their own right, and Asa would stand with them in any battle.

"We'll protect the people and try to locate your mother and sister," Asa said. At his grim expression, she smiled. "We know what we're about, Eirik. We'll be fine."

"Just remember, Hakon will be out for revenge against you." He took her hand and brought it to his lips. "If you hadn't refused him, he might have had a very different life, and he'll blame you for all of this. Stay clear of him, Asa."

"If I see him—"

"You'll do as Eirik says." Magnus's voice was low but firm. "We'll find him and slay him. Don't forget that he's responsible for Eirik's father's death. He may not have thrown the axe, but he planned it nonetheless. Eirik has more reason for vengeance than any of us. Though if I see him first, that may not matter."

"The same for me," Leif said.

"And me." Rorik crossed his arms. They all looked at him and he shrugged. "What? I haven't killed anyone all winter. My sword hand is itchy."

Shaking their heads, they split up, moving back to where their men waited. Silent as the forest itself, Eirik and Rorik led their men down the mountain. Asa walked between them. It was just first light, and a thin mist hugged the land, hiding them as they approached. Perhaps the gods smiled on them this day.

She touched the thigh sheath where she had hidden a small dagger. Her tunic was slit in the front so she could ride astride and she could reach the hilt without bending. She also carried her seax suspended horizontally below her belt. Her sword was in one hand and her shield on the other arm. It made for a difficult descent, and she slipped a bit on the steep ground. But she didn't want to sheathe her sword or sling her shield across her back in case the outcasts lay in wait for them. The moment it would take to prepare might be the difference between life and death.

When they got to the flat ground at the bottom of the mountain, they stopped and crouched in the underbrush. No women were outside as one would expect at this hour. They should be getting water from the well, gossiping, and going for grain from the granary. Instead, only hard, dirty men stumbled about, as though they were drunk from the night before. All the better for battle, but where were the villagers?

Eirik nudged her and pointed without speaking. The longhouse stood just to the right. She nodded. After the first assault, she would head there with the other shieldmaidens.

She swallowed. Did the hands of the other warriors sweat as hers did? Were their mouths as dry? She gripped her sword, willing strength into her hand so it wouldn't slip. All around her, the others braced for battle, some praying under their breaths, others checking their weapons.

She cleared her mind of everything except determination and confidence. The day's outcome was already fated. All she could do was meet her destiny with honor and a good display for the gods to enjoy.

Eirik looked at her and smiled, and confidence filled her. They would be victorious. He would accept nothing else and neither would she. She returned the smile and gave him a short nod.

"For Haardvik!"

At Eirik's soft cry, they swept out of the cover of the forest and over the village like an avenging wave. The shouts of the warriors of Thorsfjell echoed around them as Leif and Magnus's forces joined them from both sides.

The outcasts unsheathed their swords as more poured from the buildings, yelling. Asa, with Eirik and Rorik at her side, met them head on, clashing in an explosion of steel. They cut through the men like a warship through the waves, leaving death in their wake.

A man brought his sword down on Asa's angled shield and she batted it aside, following through with a thrust to his gut. He fell, screaming. Another came at her, swinging an axe. She went to her knees, her shield over her head, and it glanced off it, jarring her. But she rose, spinning, and sliced his side open. She stabbed the edge of her shield down into his throat and he died.

The sound of wind behind her warned her and she fell to the ground, rolling as a man's sword passed right over her. She used her momentum to come to her feet and he charged her. She took a blow to her shield, her shoulder and arm absorbing the impact. Then she swiped her shield from the outside to the inside, across his front, and trapped his sword arm. She cut his legs and he fell. After ending his pain, she looked for her brothers and Eirik.

Eirik fought only a few steps from her. Several men already lay dead around him, but he never slowed. He kicked the bottom of his opponent's shield upward. The upper edge smashed into the man's throat, and Eirik dispatched him with a short stroke of his sword. He glanced at her.

"Asa, we're fine here. Get to the longhouse."

She didn't hesitate. Shouting to the other shieldmaidens to follow her, she ran for the building, but skidded to a stop. Hakon's men were setting the thatch roof on fire. Some of it had caught already. She had only six women with her. If they tried to kill the men, the people inside might suffocate before they could get them out. If she didn't stop the outcasts, they would spread the fire even more. Either way, the villagers would never have a chance.

Chapter Eighteen

Kaia hefted her sword. "You get the people out. We'll take care of the offal."

Before they could act, a large group of warriors burst onto the street from the woods. Asa raised her shield, muscles braced. Were these more of Hakon's men?

But they cut down the men who were setting the roof on fire. A large, auburn-haired man led them and he slew several of them before he rushed to the doorway. She met him there, and stood before the door, holding the sword to his throat. He didn't challenge her.

"Who are you?" She watched him as two of the shieldmaidens stood at her side, spears trained on him. "What are you doing here?"

He sheathed the sword he carried. "I can ask the same of you, but there's no time. I'm Jarl Eirik's thrall, and I protect his mother and sister. They're in there, along with most of the people, and we need to get them out and the flames doused. Unless you want to stand here and discuss it while the house burns."

She lowered her sword and backed away. They would get answers later. He drove his shoulder into the door, which was locked on the outside, but it didn't give. Then Magnus was there beside her, his shoulder and arm covered in blood. She didn't have time to question him about it. He nodded to Nuallen and they both hit it at once. It burst inward.

Cries met them as they moved into the crowded room. Women and children huddled in the corners as two women came to meet them. One was older, yet still beautiful, with dark, silver-touched hair. She carried a rune staff, an aura of power surrounding her. The other woman was Asa's age. Her hair was white-blond, and her eyes were a silvery blue, like the finest steel.

"Nuallen, you came," the older woman said. "We need to get the others out. And the warriors. They're chained in the weaving room." She looked at Asa and Magnus. "Hakon kept them alive to ensure we cooperated with him. If anyone disobeyed, he'd have one of them tortured or killed."

"I'll see to them, mistress," Nuallen said. "Help the women get the children and the elderly out as fast as you can."

Asa held her hand up and went to the door to make certain it was safe for the people to leave. The men Nuallen had brought were dousing the flames. She stepped aside and leaned her shield against the wall. The villagers poured from the longhouse and took over the firefight, freeing the warriors to join the battle in other parts of Haardvik. She went to the back room where Magnus and Nuallen were. The ceiling was filling with smoke, and even though the fire was under control, they still couldn't take any chances. They had to save the men.

The captive warriors were in terrible condition. They'd been starved and neglected, and looked as if they had been kept in chains the entire winter. Magnus hefted an axe he carried in his belt and brought it down on the main set of chains attached to the wall. They could free them individually later. Right now, they had to get them out of there.

Magnus and Nuallen helped several of them to stand. The young blond woman put her shoulder under another's arm and staggered as she tried to help him walk.

"Here." Magnus set his hand on her arm. "Let me do that."

They looked at each other and both of them stilled. Magnus inclined his head to her.

"If I might help you?" He spoke low and soft.

"Of course." She met his gaze and the corner of her mouth came up in a half smile.

He took the ill man from her. Other men came into the room and, together, they evacuated everyone.

Asa walked out into the street. Villagers dumped water on the roof of the longhouse, and the flames were dying out. The fighting had wound down and the dead lay everywhere. Small groups of men still fought at the outskirts of the village, but the outcasts had been defeated.

Where was Hakon? Had he been found? And where was Eirik? She kept her sword in her hand as she crossed the clearing in front of the longhouse overlooking the fjord. A flash of white-blond hair near a small house caught her eye and she stopped, her blood heating.

Estrid. She'd recognize that hair anyplace, and Estrid would know where Hakon was.

Keeping an eye on where her cousin had gone, she started after her. But someone grabbed her from behind, setting a sword blade against her stomach. He wrapped his other arm around her, holding her arms to her sides.

"I thought she would catch your eye. I only needed you to let down your guard for an instant."

She froze. That harsh voice. That unwashed odor. The feel of his clammy flesh on her skin. The memories roared back and she gasped. Hakon.

"Now, drop your sword, Asa, and you won't get hurt."

Her hand wouldn't work. All around them in the clearing, angry warriors gathered in a semicircle open to the cliff, their weapons in their raised hands. Eirik burst through the line, her brothers and Rorik following.

"No farther, or I cut her now."

They skidded to a stop, their faces dark, murderous.

"If you harm her," Eirik said, "when I kill you, I'll follow you to Hel and slay you every day until Ragnarok takes the gods themselves."

Hakon swallowed hard enough for her to hear him. "I said drop the sword." His voice lacked confidence, but his blade pressed into her. Even though she wore a metal-ringed leather tunic, he could still slice her under it. "Your illustrious brothers must have taught you to defend yourself because of what I did. Without a sword, though, you're just another woman. Nothing."

He was wrong, but she willed her hand to work and the sword fell to the ground.

"Better. Now we can all talk."

"There's nothing to talk about, Hakon." Magnus's eyes blazed. "We have you surrounded. There's no place else to go."

"Yes, there is. You must have a fleet of longships somewhere along the shore, and I think I have enough men left to crew one of them. I intend to take one of them and leave this place. Maybe gain my own fortune where I'm not known."

"You won't get far."

"Oh yes, I will. Because I'll take Asa with me as assurance that you don't follow me. Any sign of you, and she dies. In the meantime, I can enjoy her as I should have long ago."

She couldn't even draw a breath. Eirik surged forward, but Leif grabbed him.

"You said you'd take *me*." Estrid pushed aside the men in the circle and stood in front of them, her face reddened, her fists clenched. "You said we'd always be together, like you did so long ago. But you chose her then, and now you've done it again. And you'll leave again, like they all do." She collapsed onto the ground and wailed.

Nuallen, who stood among the crowd, came forward and helped her to her feet. He held her arm, but she didn't seem to notice. She just stared at nothing, tears streaming down her cheeks.

Hakon tightened his grip. "Bring a small ship to the docks below. And you'll free any of my men you captured. Don't be too long. I haven't time to waste." He leaned close to her ear. "You've grown into quite the beautiful woman, Asa. Once we're alone, you and I will continue right where we left off six years ago."

Asa's blood turned to ice. She couldn't move, couldn't speak. The horror wound through her mind like a poisonous serpent, leaving a trail of darkness behind. Eirik moved and she met his gaze. He gave her a very small smile and a slight nod, as he would to another warrior, confidence in her shining in his eyes.

What had she told Eirik a few days ago when they'd made love? She took a deep breath and reached through the darkness into a moment of brightness and stars. To a place where a golden dragon played, the spirit that guarded her. She'd told Eirik she was no longer a young, defenseless girl. And Hakon had no idea what she was because of him—a shieldmaiden. She was worthy of a dragon *fylgjur*, and it would slay the serpent in her mind.

In that moment of light, when they'd become one, Eirik had told her he loved her. She'd never spoken the words back to him. There was only one way to end this, and if she didn't survive it, she wouldn't leave him without telling him.

"Eirik." She raised her chin in defiance as Hakon shifted the blade to her side as though preparing to slice it into her. She moved so that the bottom of her tunic flared open. Eirik would be able to see the dagger there and be ready. A smile touched his eyes and his hand tightened on the hilt of his sword. She lifted her head. "I love you."

"How touching. But you won't love him for long."

Without moving her upper body, she eased the dagger from its thigh sheath. Shifting her hips to the side, she slammed it into Hakon's leg. His leather trousers were thick, but the dagger penetrated deep enough so that he roared. His arm convulsed and the blade he'd held to her stomach cut into her side. She broke away from him, spun, and brought her small dagger in a reverse strike across the top of his arm.

He came after her, swinging his sword, but Eirik lunged in front of her and met his blow with his shield, blocking it. Magnus ran to her as she clutched her bleeding side and swept her up in his arms. He carried her to where Rorik and Leif stood.

"We need to get you to a healer." He set her down and bent to look at the cut, but she leaned past him to see where Eirik was. He and Hakon circled each other.

"I'm staying. I won't leave Eirik." She sheathed her dagger. Magnus pulled her to him so she could lean against him. Kaia gave her a clean cloth and she held it to the stinging wound as Eirik spoke.

"What do you hope to gain, Hakon? Give up now and you'll have a chance to walk to your execution as a man. The gods watch how we die and take that into account when we meet them."

"The gods have damned me already. And if I take you with me, that bitch who ruined my life will lose you. If that's the only revenge I can have, then so be it." He bent to pick up a shield from the ground, but Eirik rushed at him and he had to dart away.

"You have a shield," Hakon said. "You would fight with such an advantage? Where is the honor in that?"

"You used Asa as a shield, so where is the honor in *that*? But you're right." He tossed his shield away, standing armed with only his sword.

Hakon blanched. He came at Eirik, his sword raised. Eirik hit his sword aside and slashed his arm as he passed. Now he bled from both arms and his leg. Eirik rained a hail of blows on him, never letting up. Hakon blocked, retreating, and the men in the line on that side moved to clear a path. They jeered at him, for he showed no bravery, refusing to stand his ground like a man.

Eirik stopped and backed up into the circle with a grin, motioning him to follow. Angry, Hakon ran after him, picking up a shield from the ground as he came. Eirik thrust his sword into the ground and

Asa almost cried out. What was he doing? She bit down her scream, for it might distract him.

Eirik ducked Hakon's ill-aimed sword stroke and grabbed his shield by the bottom edge. Rising, he brought it with him and smashed the shield into Hakon's nose, breaking it. Blood spurted over Hakon as he dropped the shield. Eirik pulled his sword from the ground and raised it, grinning. They stood only a man's length apart.

Hakon, his face covered in blood, glared at Eirik. "Would you have it said you were a coward who killed a man only when he was weakened from loss of blood?"

Eirik smiled. "You're not weakened yet. But you're right. I shouldn't wait until then."

He moved so fast, Asa almost didn't see the strike. He hit Hakon's sword hand and the weapon spun away from him. He screamed and lunged for it, but Eirik brought his blade down and Hakon's head fell away from his body, his silver hair drenched in his blood. He had died a coward's death, without a sword in his hand.

Eirik was safe, his father's death avenged. Asa sagged in Magnus's arms as her side throbbed with pain and she grew dizzy. Eirik came to her as the men around them cheered, banging their swords on their shields.

"My mother should look at that cut." He picked her up.

"I'm fine. I just need to wash this. There are many others here who are hurt far worse."

"It'll need to be stitched." Magnus nodded to Eirik.

Before he could leave with her, a scream pierced the village. Estrid broke away from Nuallen and ran toward Hakon's body. She threw herself on the bloody ground beside him, keening. Magnus started to go to her, but Leif stopped him.

"She hates you and Asa. Let me take her somewhere safe. She doesn't resent me quite so much."

But as he approached her, she snatched Hakon's sword and rose with it, holding it in front of her. Her eyes were distant, as though she didn't quite see the world around her.

"Father left me." She almost sang the words in a strange, high voice. "Mother left me. Hakon left me twice, and now I have lost Eirik, too." An ugly expression crossed her face as she focused on Asa. "I sent you into the water. I tried to kill the dragon. I stabbed it

246 • *Sabrina Jarema*

and poisoned it, and still it would not die. It took everything from me. Now there is nothing."

Asa looked at Eirik. Estrid had, indeed, damaged her skate and the dragon.

Leif held his hand out. "There's your family, Estrid. All of us. Come back home with us and we'll take care of you."

"No." She backed toward the fjord cliff. Several of the men tried to move into her way, but she darted nearer to the edge and grasped the sword blade in her palm. She drew it across and held up her hand so that the blood flowed onto the ground. "Pretty rubies falling down, sacrificed to the gods."

Leif took a step toward her, but she matched his movements, going closer to the edge. He stopped.

"Wait her out. Where else can she go?" Magnus spoke low and the men moved away from her.

Estrid looked down as part of the cliff behind her crumbled and fell into the fjord. She glanced over the edge and a crack opened up in front of her.

"Estrid, come away from there." Leif's voice shook. "It's not safe."

Pieces of rock fell away and she almost lost her balance. "Nothing left." Then she looked at Eirik and gave him a beautiful smile. "Remember when you read my runes, you said that I must leap into the void? You were right."

He set Asa down on her feet and went toward Estrid. "I meant only that you must try a new life. You have a good future, Estrid. You have to trust us."

Cracks spread out beneath her feet. She shook her head and closed her eyes with a calm smile. "No. I must leap. The void awaits."

Leif and Eirik lunged for her, but the cliff gave way and she plunged down. Asa rushed forward, but Eirik grabbed her and held her back.

"It's too dangerous. There are only rocks below there. You don't need to see her like that."

One of Magnus's men peered over the edge. He backed away, shaking his head. Eirik picked Asa up and said to Magnus, "I'll send someone to get her. I need to take Asa to my mother."

She rested her head on his shoulder as he walked. Her chest was tight and hot tears floated behind her eyes. Estrid and she hadn't been close for many years, but they had played together as children. She would try to remember those times, and not what Estrid had become.

"Why did she hate us so much?" She lifted her head and regarded Eirik. "We all have losses, and people come and go throughout our lives, but it was too much for her."

"I don't know," he said. "Something went wrong inside her mind."

"In spite of all that, perhaps she, alone of all of us, truly saw my dragon spirit. I hope her animal spirit, whatever it is, guides her now to the afterlife. Perhaps she can be at peace there as she never could here."

"I hope so."

He carried her into the longhouse. The fire hadn't had a chance to do much damage, so they had set up a place to tend to the wounded there.

"Mother, please see to this wound." He set Asa on a pile of furs.

The beautiful older woman smiled as she came over to them, embraced Eirik, and knelt beside her. "You're the shieldmaiden who freed us."

"She's also my betrothed. Mother, this is Asa Sigrundsdottir. This is my mother, the rune mistress, Lifa."

Lifa raised her brows. "You must have spent an interesting winter, Eirik. I'll look forward to hearing about it. Welcome, child. I'm so pleased to meet you. Now, let's look at this wound."

Her touch was gentle as she cleaned the cut. "This needs stitches, but it will be fine in a few days. I'll have an ointment brought for it. Silvi?"

The young woman with the white-blond hair came to them. "Please meet my daughter, Silvi," Lifa said. "Silvi, this is Asa, Eirik's betrothed. She was wounded in battle."

"I'll bring the salve and some bandages to use after you stitch her." She turned her silver gaze to Asa. "Great power walks with you. We welcome you here."

"Thank you." She smiled, but glanced at Eirik. He just shook his head.

"I don't need to see anyone. I'm fine." Magnus's deep voice rolled through the longhouse. "All I need to do is soak in the fjord to wash the blood off."

"You're getting your head looked at." Leif shoved him into the room. "That's a bad gash."

Asa sat up. Magnus was hurt? "Leif, what happened?" She tried to stand, but Eirik held her down. "Let me see my brother."

"I don't need anything," Magnus said, his voice rising. "Just get me some water. I can tend to myself."

Eirik grinned at Leif. "Brother and sister. They're more alike than I thought."

"Silvi." Lifa tilted her head toward Magnus. "Please see to him."

"Of course." She lowered her head and walked to the brothers.

Leif was trying to get Magnus to sit down. Silvi put her hand on his arm and he stopped fighting. Magnus looked at her and sank down onto the bench, his eyes wide. She drew back his long dark hair, checking the cut on his scalp. He stayed still, watching her.

Drops of his blood fell onto the floor and Silvi studied them, her color high. Then she parted his hair again.

"Dark as midnight, with a touch of the sun." Her words were as soft as her hands as she washed his wound.

"What did you say?" He reached up and brushed his fingers over her hand.

She took her hand out from under his and rinsed out the cloth. "It is nothing." She dabbed at his wound again. "But it might be everything."

Asa smiled. Magnus might have won the battle, but he was losing his heart. He just didn't know it yet. She lay back, trying not to flinch as Lifa stitched her wound. She had taken her fate into her own hands, with Eirik's love to strengthen her. With one stroke she had freed herself, physically and emotionally, from Hakon and from her past.

Eirik walked among the wounded men, speaking with them, encouraging them. Rorik and Leif joined him beside Magnus and they discussed bringing the ships around to Haardvik. They would need the supplies and food they'd brought. There was so much work to do now to heal the damage to the village and the warriors.

They'd all come together in an alliance, making them stronger, just as she and Eirik would bring the families together. Her breath caught. He said they would marry only if he could find the sword he'd dropped into the fjord and thereby accept his title. It was the only way he felt he would be worthy of her.

If he couldn't retrieve it, and it was lost forever, what would become of their future together?

The wind off the fjord was chilled. He would be far colder soon enough.

Eirik glanced back at Asa where she stood with her brothers and his family. She'd wanted to stand with him at the edge of the cliff, but he wouldn't allow it. The place where Estrid had fallen was some distance away, but it still wasn't safe.

He wore only a thin linen shirt and cloth trousers so he wouldn't be weighed down when they became wet. The current was strong and he would have to dive a bit to one side of where he thought he had lost the sword.

Asa smiled at him, but her mouth trembled and there was fear in her eyes that she would never show to anyone else. She stood, stoic and proud, as any shieldmaiden would. She'd never dishonor him by doubting him.

He returned her smile and faced the water. Many times, before he was grown, he had dived off this cliff on dares. This time, he had to keep swimming downward to find the bottom and the sword. Taking several deep breaths, he raised his arms and pushed off.

The water and the cold hit him like a shield wall, as he plunged down, stroking hard. The current tried to carry him away. He fought it until he found the bottom. He felt along, kicking up silt and sand. Pausing, he looked beyond where he was, away from the disturbed area. A glimmer caught his eye.

He swam toward it and the fog of sand followed him, carried by the current. He couldn't see anything and his lungs were on fire. Reaching through the billowing silt, he swept his hand along the bottom. If he didn't swim for the surface now, he wouldn't have enough air to reach it. His head grew light and his arms stiffened in the frigid waters. He had only another moment to sweep his hands across the bottom.

There. His fingers hit a hard object. He grabbed it and pushed off from the bottom, aiming for the light. Upward he stroked with only his free arm, his lungs screaming for air until he burst into the sun.

Sucking in a large breath, he looked up. A crowd stood on the edge of the cliff, in spite of the danger. Asa, her brothers, Rorik, Lifa, and Silvi all peered down at him, along with many of the warriors.

He swept his arm up, brandishing the sword, and they cheered, laughing and hugging.

The sunlight hit its gold-inlaid cross guard, and though the blade was darkened from its time in the water, it was still magnificent. Lifa had told him last night that his father had used it to fight with instead of his own sword because they'd kept it close to him while he lay dying, before the outcasts attacked. He would be able to grasp it before he breathed his last so he would go to Valhalla. When the battle with Hakon began, he'd left his deathbed to fight. It was the closest sword he'd had at hand.

A longship drew up to him. The men took the sword from him and hauled him over the side, then doused him with bucket after bucket of warm water until he stopped shivering. He wrapped himself in a fur they gave him as they rowed onto the shore and beached the ship.

The weight of the responsibilities the gods gave him as jarl cloaked his shoulders as he grabbed the sword and ran up the path. Everyone met him at the top. His warriors clapped him on the back, his mother hugged him, and even Silvi gave him a quick embrace.

Asa stood with her brothers, watching him. Everything else around him faded. He walked to her and stopped in front of her. She smiled up at him, her eyes no longer filled with fear, but with love.

He touched her face with his fingertips. "When I first saw you, I was so cold and delirious, I thought you were my love. I was right. While I'll never forget Sela and my son, the gods have blessed me with a second chance at love."

Asa put her hand over his. "And they blessed me with a second chance at life. I feared for you. Not that you wouldn't survive, but that you wouldn't find the sword and thereby not feel worthy of me. But you're a *vikingr* warrior, and that is good enough for any woman."

"Before I left here last fall, Silvi told me I would find the sword, but not for the reason I thought. She said I'd give it up within days of regaining it. I couldn't understand that. I wanted to find it so I could claim my title. But it turns out she was right. I did it today for a very different reason."

She frowned. "What other reason could there be?"

He touched her hair. "It is our wedding tradition among the people of the north for the man to give his bride the sword of his fathers to hold in keeping for their oldest son. There have been a lot of graves robbed because of this."

Everyone around them laughed.

"The sword I needed lay in the fjord, not in a grave. The only way I could honor you in this manner was to find it. I didn't seek it for myself or for my title. I sought it for you, so that I could give it to you at our wedding. And now that I have earned the right, I ask you to be my wife. I didn't ask you before, but now I come to you as a jarl, as a warrior, and as the man who loves you. I want you to rule beside me, fight beside me, and be beside me all the rest of our days."

"I would be proud to be your wife." She put her arms around his neck in spite of how wet he was. He kissed her and the men banged their swords on their sheaths. The women cheered, and their families crowded around them, laughing.

Eirik stood amidst the celebration, looking out over his people, his village. A massive fleet of warships lay just offshore, symbolizing the union of their families. He held Star Slayer in his hand and, just as he would never let it go again, so he would never lose what he had won back.

No one would threaten Asa again. Estrid was gone, Hakon was slain, and men who had swept the area looking for any hidden outcasts had found Hjellmar's body in the woods. Hakon and Estrid had cut his throat, as though they had tried to sacrifice him to the gods. Now everyone could live in peace.

Nuallen stood behind Lifa, apart from them but still near to her. Eirik set Asa under his sword arm and motioned the thrall over to them. Nuallen stood before them, his head high, but his eyes on the ground.

"Nuallen, you protected my mother and sister with your life this past winter. You also risked your own life to find and bring back my warriors to join us in freeing Haardvik. You killed any patrols you found so the outcasts thought spirits were taking them. I understand that, because of their fear, many of the men deserted as soon as the weather allowed it, as well. When the ones who remained wouldn't come into the woods any longer, that cleared the way for us to position ourselves around the village and make a strong attack. I thank you for all this."

Nuallen inclined his head. "It was the mistress who told the tales they believed."

"But it was you who implemented her plan. In gratitude, I grant you your freedom. As of this time, you are a free man, equal to any here."

As the people shouted their approval, Nuallen raised his head and looked Eirik in the eye. "I thank you, Jarl Eirik."

"It's our law that I offer you support, advice, and legal protection. I must provide food, clothes, and a place for you to live. It's traditional for a freed slave to be adopted into a family, but I think you're a bit old for that."

Everyone, including Nuallen, laughed.

"This night, as is customary, we'll hold a feast in your honor. You'll serve me for the last time, according to tradition. Though in this case, you will serve my mother. Then, I'll provide you with a way to return to your homeland, if that is what you wish."

He hesitated. "I thank you for your offer, Jarl. One day I do wish to return home, for I must let those I left behind know I'm alive. But, for now, I offer myself in service as one of your warriors. Between the attack last fall and this one, you have lost many good men. I'll stay and help you rebuild Haardvik and fight at your side. I have grown close to those here and they were good to me all this time. I also have other reasons for why I wish to remain." He glanced at Lifa.

She stared at him, her eyes widening, and blushed.

Eirik studied his mother. This was unexpected. But she was a widow and was free to do as she wanted. Was love so common that it should be cast away when it was found?

He looked back at Nuallen. "Then will you swear the oath of fealty to me?"

"I have learned it, just for this time, if it should come."

A servant brought a chair to Eirik and he sat down. He placed Star Slayer on his leg, the hilt on his knee, the tip of the blade between his arm and the side of his body. Placing his forearm along the length of the sword, he grasped the hilt with his right hand. "Speak, then, your oath, Nuallen."

Kneeling, Nuallen placed his hand on the hilt of the sword, lifting his head up as he spoke. "I swear to acknowledge the wealth I receive from you. I swear to always fight for you and to win victory from the men I face. I swear that I will not retreat from battle. And I swear to avenge you if you are killed, or I shall die trying." He rose and stepped back.

Eirik nodded. "I hear your oath, as do the holy Aesir. I gift you with gold and fill you with mead. My sword stands between you and your enemies. May Thor hallow this vow." Smiling, he rose. "Be welcome among us, Nuallen. You'll serve as my mother's personal guard from now on. This night, at your feast, I will give you a silver arm ring to signify your fealty to me."

The warriors came forward and clapped Nuallen on the back. He grinned and moved among them, free and proud. Lifa stood back, her color high. Eirik caught her eye and winked. She dropped her gaze and walked off, Silvi trailing after her.

He wanted to get Asa alone for a time. She had to be tired. Her wound pained her, though she would never admit it. But Rorik came up to them, grinning.

"So I imagine you'll wait until Frigga's day to wed."

"Of course. That's traditional and it's only a few days off. We have many plans to make."

"Then I'll leave after I've drunk your ale and eaten your food at the wedding feast."

Eirik laughed. "You brought most of it."

"So I did. You both are welcome to come with me. Soon, I leave for the west. I have heard that Ragnar Lothbrok plans to raid up the River Umber between Mercia and Northumbria. I hope to join him and see what treasures await us."

Leif joined them. "I may take you up on that offer. If not now, then in the future."

"Leif?" Asa put a hand on his arm. "You would leave Thorsfjell?"

"Only for a season." He shrugged. "After all, I'm a second son, and if things keep progressing as I think they might, Magnus's heir will push me back in the line of succession. Thank the gods."

He nodded to where Magnus watched Silvi as she stood with her mother off to the side. He seemed sword-struck as he stared at her. Silvi glanced at him and ducked her head.

Leif turned back to them, grinning. "And I'd like to see, oh, some of the wonders of the world." He winked at Kaia, who was striding past them. She narrowed her gray-green eyes on him, her hand on her seax, and kept walking. "With scenery like that, it would be an interesting voyage."

Rorik laughed. "If you survive it. The world is treacherous, as are

254 • *Sabrina Jarema*

shieldmaidens. Come with us when you want and be welcome, while I go to find my fortune."

"You already have a fortune, Rorik," Asa said.

He shrugged. "Then I'll find another fortune. Wine, women, and warriors are expensive."

"I have a feeling," Eirik said, "that one day, one of those women will catch you."

"That will never happen. As I said, why choose among them when I have all I want, just for the asking?" He sauntered away.

Eirik shook his head. "When he sinks, he'll go straight to the bottom."

"Oh, and that's your prediction for him, rune caster?" She put her arms around him. "Is that what love is? Sinking to the bottom?"

"Sometimes." He brushed back her beautiful flaming hair. "Sometimes you have to dive very far down to find the treasure." He lifted the sword. "Like this. And like you. In a time of my life when I thought all was lost and could see only the darkness, the gods led me to you and into the light."

"And healed us both."

He kissed her. "And healed us both."

If you enjoyed LORD OF THE RUNES be sure not to miss the next book in Sabrina Jarema's Viking Lords series.

Keep reading for a special sneak peek!

A Lyrical e-book on sale March 2017!

He would stand on the back of a dragon, coming to her in the time of war, with his arrogance and his weapons and his hate. His blood would run into the ground of her homeland. And it would mingle with hers.
—from the vision of Silvi Ivarsdottir

Chapter One

The village of Haardvik
Hardangerfjorden, Hordaland, Norway
851 AD

The sound of steel on steel shattered the calm beauty of the early spring day.

Silvi Ivarsdottir paused, listening to the clash echoing through the trees and the mountains. She didn't need to reach out with her thoughts to know what was happening. The reason for the disruption was obvious. Her brother's weeklong wedding celebrations were still going on in the village, so beer and weapons were inevitable. Anticipated, in fact. It was what men did best.

The sound of combat didn't come from the village. She tilted her head, seeking the source of the disruption. Her breath stilled. They wouldn't dare. It came from the place where the gods walked, the sacred grove. No one brought weapons there, the same as in the great temples. It was sacrilege.

Her stomach twisting, she rushed toward the clearing. She didn't fear facing down warriors. Rather, they should fear *her*. After all, she'd had the gods on her side since birth. She would defend and honor them until she went to Freya's hall in the afterlife.

She burst into the clearing and skidded to a stop. Two men circled each other. They were bare to the waist. Their long, dark hair swirled around their broad shoulders as they came together in an explosion of steel and sparks. They were both massive, men in their prime, fighting with all the skill that made their people so feared throughout the world. They moved with the masculine grace inborn to all the finest warriors as they surged through the clearing like water rushing in a river.

Her cousin, Rorik, laughed aloud as he swung, his black hair sweeping over his shoulders and down his chest. White teeth flashing, he smashed his shield against his opponent's arm, trapping his blade. He thrust, but his blade met with air as the other man stepped to the side and brought his own shield up, deflecting the deadly edge.

He pressed Rorik back several steps with his wicked, fast sword strokes. His hair was so dark it almost looked black, except for the deep golden lights in it. Moving with the skill of a predator, he surged forward, taking his advantage.

Her heart stuttered. *Magnus.* As she watched them, her body heated, her thighs weakening. Maybe it was only because she had just run a fair distance. The sun glanced off his sculpted arms as he swung his sword in a deadly arc. It smashed into the other blade with an explosion of sparks. She held her breath. If she called out, it could distract them. An instant's hesitation might mean death to one of them. Her anger at the sacrilege was not worth the risk. She could do nothing but watch.

Rorik disengaged, then hit Magnus's sword with his own, nearly knocking it out of his hand. He shook his black hair from his face and laughed as he brought his sword around for another blow. Magnus hit the ground, rolled, and came to his knees. He swept his shield horizontally, aiming for Rorik's legs. Rorik leaped over it with a yell and before he landed, Magnus was on his feet. He struck Rorik with his shield and knocked him onto his back.

It wasn't over yet, though. Rorik threw his shield, edge first. Magnus spun out of the way, arching his back as it knifed past him. It gave Rorik time to leap up and charge him. He drove Magnus back until he could grab his own shield and reposition it on his left arm.

They circled each other, grinning. Their bodies glistened with sweat. Rorik's stomach was rippled and flat. Magnus's was the same, save for a wicked, jagged scar crossing his lower abdomen. Both were slim-hipped, broad-shouldered, tall and powerful. But it was Magnus she watched. Rorik laughed and danced as he fought. Magnus stood solid, every move weighted and purposeful. His cuts were clean, direct, with no wasted energy or movement. His strength radiated from him like a storm rolling over the mountains.

She'd seen him in a vision before he'd come with her brother,

Eirik, to set her village free of the marauders who had held them captive all winter. She'd tended his wounds, and while his blood flowed onto the ground, he'd stared at her as one thunderstruck. He'd continued to watch her through the following days. Now Eirik was married to Magnus's sister, Asa, so Magnus was family of sorts. She'd have to see him many times in the future. At least, until she went to live at the great temple at Uppsala. Then she would see no one at all.

She shook herself out of her reverie. This was wrong, that they should bring weapons into a sacred place. They were still feinting, no doubt resting for a final onslaught.

"Rorik." Her raised voice stopped him short and he jumped away from Magnus with a guilty wince. "How dare you fight in the grove, Rorik? Not even you could be that sacrilegious."

Instead of answering her, her cousin clapped Magnus on the shoulder and said, low, "Run. *Now.*" He bounded into the shadow of the trees, leaving Magnus standing alone.

She started after him. "I heard that, Rorik. Get back here."

Magnus lifted his sword in a question. "Rorik, what are you doing?" He turned toward Silvi as she bore down on him. "We were just training a bit, Silvi. How could we know this was your grove?"

"It's the gods' grove, not mine. Rorik knows. He's been here before." She shot him a glare. "As for you . . . Don't you scent the breath of the gods here? Don't you feel their power in the very ground? Or has your dishonor chased them from here?"

"I scarcely think a little swordplay would frighten them from here. Perhaps they're away for the day, seeing to other matters." He sheathed his sword.

She bit the inside of her cheek to keep from cursing. "How can you be so irreverent? The gods will surely smite you for such talk."

He swallowed and looked away from her. "I've seen what comes of too much involvement with the gods. Even as Eirik stayed the winter with us in Thorsfjell, I saw how he was pulled between Odin and Thor, but he balanced them within him. I don't have that knowledge. I know only the steel of my blade and the silver of my coins."

"Thor's Mountain. Even your home bears his name and yet, to you, it is just a name. The gods' power slides past you, never going more than skin deep. Instead of their voices, all you hear is the clink of coins." Her heart sank. Just as he had watched her this past week, so she had been aware of him. And her dreams at night . . . But it could not be. She wasn't meant for the hearth, a husband and children. And even if she were to follow that path, this irreverent warrior was not for her. They walked in two different worlds.

Her soul twisting, she tried to rush past him, but he caught her by the arm. A spark shot between them and she gasped. His eyes widened and he let her go.

"No man may touch me," she said. "I am meant for the gods. They saved me this past winter from the marauders."

"Then they know I pose no such threat to you, Silvi. Just understand that while you dream, enemies could overrun you, as Hakon and his outlaws did last winter."

"The runes will warn me."

"As they did then?"

She firmed her resolve. "The runes showed my mother and me that we'd know great change and loss. It was our own shortcoming preventing us from understanding what the gods tried to tell us. If Hakon had not attacked, Eirik wouldn't have left in the winter to go to Rorik for help. He wouldn't have found your village and spent the cold months with you. He and Asa would not have met, and you'd not have been forewarned of Hakon's plans to attack you in revenge for having him declared an outcast. We could not have come together to defeat him. Now, our families are joined through Eirik and Asa's marriage. It all happened for a reason."

"And yet, for all your efforts, the gods took your father, and so many of your warriors and people."

"My father was dying of the wasting disease. He died in battle with a sword in his hand, as a warrior would want, instead of a shell of a man on his sickbed. In that, the gods blessed him. At the moment of our births, the Norns decree when we will each die. No one, not even the gods themselves, can stop that. It was their time. In all else, the gods will provide."

"The gods favor the strong." His voice was sharp, like the honed edge of his blade. "Don't forget, the blood of warriors guards you. Silver gives you the privilege of food in your belly and a warm house in which to dream your dreams. All the gods do is watch us from Asgard in the same way we watch ants scurrying on the ground."

A shadow came over them as a cloud hid the sun. Were the gods displeased at his words? Silvi shook her head with a sigh at his blindness. If he did not recognize the gods, as he should, how could they bless him? How could they smile on him if he didn't look up to see them? He was lost, like a ship at sea without a sail, and he didn't even know it. She raised her hand toward his arm, then dropped it to her side without touching him. "There's an imbalance in you, Magnus. The answer is not one thing or the other, but a mix of our world and that of the gods."

He gave her a gentle smile and looked into her eyes, something no man except her brother could do. "Then you should heed your own wisdom, Silvi. I know you want to go to Uppsala to become one of the priestesses there. Where's the balance in that? You shun the things of this world, seeking only the starlit realms. Your beauty will be wasted there among the men who dance like women. The strength I've seen in you these past days will thin into insipid chants and rituals." He lifted his hand to her cheek, but didn't touch it. Yet she trembled as though he had. He stepped back and took a deep breath. "Perhaps you're right. I shouldn't be here. Not with the thoughts I have in my mind. Thor's bolt will find me if I remain here any longer." He smiled again and inclined his head to her.

She watched him as he strode out of the grove toward the village. He was strong, beautiful, deep like the roots of his mountain. Crystals sparkled in his blue eyes and his hair was like the night caressing the slopes of his shoulders. The gods had been so pleased when they'd created him that they'd made another who looked like him—his twin brother, Leif. Leif was the breeze swirling up the sides of the mountains in the spring, light and free, to careen off the peaks and be gone, uncatchable.

Magnus bore the weight of that mountain. His people, his trading business, his world. Not hers. He deserved a woman who could be a true wife to him, seeing to his people while he was gone, ruling over the household, warming his bed and bearing him children.

Her body clenched. He was everything any woman could want in a husband. But she was not just any woman. She must keep remembering that.

Sabrina Jarema lives near Ocala, Florida, the Horse Capital of the World. She has a herd of fat, lazy Arabians on forty beautiful acres. She also breeds and shows white German Shepherd dogs and currently has several Grand Victrixes taking over her house. She's joined by a menagerie of tortoises, turtles, birds, fish, and cats. To avoid farm work as much as possible, she loses herself in the worlds she creates through the novels she writes, her art, music, dollhouses, and jewelry. She has worked as a professional fantasy illustrator and has written fantasy romance for many years. Recently, she has branched out into historical romances set in the early Viking era. She is currently writing the Viking Lords series, a family saga set in Norway during the ninth century. She is an active member of the Tampa Area Romance Authors chapter of the Romance Writers of America. Please visit her website at www.sabrinajarema.com to enjoy her art, music, writing, jewelry, and all the other visions the night brings to her.

www.ingramcontent.com/pod-product-compliance
Lightning Source LLC
Chambersburg PA
CBHW020743250626
47155CB00003B/897